I0553767

Jay Hawk:
The Assassin's Lover

By
Sean Eagan

Jay Hawk:
The Assassin's Lover

A Thriller By
Sean Eagan

Published by:
Connecticut Yankee International, Inc.

Praise for the eBook edition of
Jay Hawk: The Assassin's Lover
What Actual Buyers and Readers Are Saying:

★★★★★ "This one hooks you early. A page turner. There are plenty of twists and turns and you never know where the story will lead you."

★★★★★ "...Everything that a suspense/mystery fan likes in a story. Action, adventure and a little romance thrown in for good measure. This was definitely a page turner...as I was reading I kept telling myself I needed to get some sleep."

★★★★★ " Haven't read a book I couldn't put down in a while. Not only the intrigue of espionage and compelling romance but so well researched it feels like something you might read in the NYT or WSJ."

★★★★★ "Action thrillers like this are not my first choice as a genre, but I couldn't put this book down. Despite non-stop action, it was the characters that lifted this book out of the ordinary. The four strong women were fabulous but flawed, nuanced and complex."

★★★★★ "It was hard for me to believe that a male author was able to portray women with such an authentic voice. This novel is going to be my Christmas gift to quite a few friends. Don't miss it!"

★★★★★ "You will be fascinated with these women as you learn their stories and interactions with each other. BJ was especially likeable as a woman who didn't realize how strong she really was until faced with adversity."

★★★★★ "A page turner from the start, *The Assassin's Lover* challenges the reader's knowledge of politics, history, geography, and culture while taking her on a journey of wonder and excitement."

★★★★★ "The story line is "clean" white-collar crime, but there (is) plenty of good old James Bond action and romance scenes in between."

All excerpts are from five-star reviews published on Amazon and Smashwords.

Sean Eagan

Story Description

Britt Jaeger, a thirty-something, self-described "little Midwestern farm girl," flees an abusive marriage, only to suffer a terrifying assault on her bus ride to New York.

Physically and emotionally bruised and scarred, with one suitcase and money for only two months, she lands an entry-level Wall Street job. Working late one night, she is befriended by CEO Mackenzie Collingwood and introduced to "all the right people."

All the right people become all the wrong people when the women are caught in a cauldron of lies, violence, intrigue and sex. Mistaken for the firm's most important client, Colonel Rebekah Chayat, a former Mossad assassin, Britt is kidnapped when in a conspiracy that could change the world's balance of power.

The action and conflict in this romantic, espionage thriller are unnervingly interconnected as the story moves from New York to London, Tel Aviv, Tehran and Athens, even a private Caribbean island owned by seven of the richest women in the world.

Framed against real world geopolitical threats—including Al Quds commandoes, the first Iranian warships to transit the Suez Canal into the Mediterranean; the Stuxnet computer virus that destroyed thousands of Iran's uranium centrifuges and the assassination of Iranian physicists—*Jay Hawk* is an extensively researched story of agonizing personal choices, individual responsibility and unintended consequences.

To view more of Sean's work, visit:
http://www.seaneaganthrillers.com

CHAPTER 1

Sandusky, Ohio
16 November

The Greyhound bus rolled through the night when, eight rows behind her nearest fellow passengers, Britt Jaeger awoke with a knife in her ribs and a hand pawing her breast.

"Make a sound and you're a dead woman," hissed her attacker as he shoved the point another millimeter deeper into the soft tissue between her sixth and seventh ribs. Her head snapped to her right to see the mugger who, had slipped into the aisle seat next to her, cutting off any possible escape. He jabbed once again and snarled, "Close your eyes or look out the window."

Snow, sleet and rain from an unseasonably early fall Nor'easter pelted the windows. It was pitch black outside and, except for a few pilot lights along the floor, nearly as dark inside.

In the moment before she looked away, two features registered—the mocking grin of a Cleveland Indians logo on his dark stocking cap and the unmistakable smell of Skoal Bandit. She recognized that smell immediately. Dippin' snuff was a rite of passage for boys from the Kansas farm country where she grew up.

Go ahead; dip another pinch, she thought. *Get lip cancer and die, you animal.*

A dozen rows ahead, the driver, struggling to stay on the road and on schedule, was oblivious to everything but the pounding November storm. The dozen or so other passengers near the front of the bus slept or tried to.

She guessed her attacker had slithered into the seat when she fell asleep sometime after the New York-bound bus pulled out of South Bend. The weak glow of distant city lights flickered like a kaleidoscope through the sleet-splattered windows. She glanced to her right once more. He dragged the sharp point up her ribs, drawing a thin line of blood, and stabbed it slightly into her right breast, which he had pulled free by lifting her bra and pushing it up higher on her chest. "I wouldn't think twice about shoving this straight through both of them, like a skewer through a shish-ka-bob. That would make a shish-ka-boob, wouldn't it?" He laughed at his sick little joke, and a trickle of brown juice dribbled from the corner of his mouth. He withdrew his groping hand and spit into his cupped palm three times, maybe more. She didn't keep count, but she would never forget the puddle of diarrhea-colored liquid in his hand as he reached back into her blouse.

"Let's lube these babies up a little."

I hope you die a long, painful death, pig! she almost said it out loud.

The groping, squeezing and jabbing continued for unbearably long minutes, even when the bus wheeled off the interstate, down the cloverleaf ramp, toward the city. Through the rain she saw a flashing three-legged Greyhound on the side of the Cleveland bus terminal—the lights behind one leg burned out. Only then did she begin to hope he might not kill her.

As the bus pulled into its bay, she looked straight at him, and opened her mouth to scream. He reacted so quickly, she realized he had been waiting for that moment all along. From out of nowhere, he shoved a latex glove deep into her throat. A finger of the glove lodged in her trachea, gagging her, strangling her. While she struggled to withdraw the glove, her assailant casually sauntered up the length of the bus and, bidding the driver good morning, stepped off into the irregular shadows cast by the other buses and the overhead mercury-vapor lights. The engine noise, plus the other buses idling nearby, drowned out Britt's coughing and gasping. Her belated scream, mixed with uncontrollable sobs, was inaudible to the groggy passengers well forward of her twelfth-row seat.

By the time the police arrived, her attacker was long gone. They searched the bus and found a second latex glove near the front door. The only "weapon" found was a silver ballpoint pen with a sewing needle taped to it—the point projecting three or four millimeters beyond the tip. It could not seriously injure anyone, much less kill. The realization that she had allowed herself to be abused without ever being in real danger made her ordeal all the more humiliating.

Hours later, after two male detectives had grilled her, more like a suspect than a victim, a uniformed female cop escorted her, ahead of the other passengers, into the front right seat of the eight a.m. bus to New York. In that seat, she would be in the driver's peripheral vision. The cop knelt beside Britt and patted her knee. "Forget New York, sweetie, it's not for you. Turn around. Go back to Kansas or wherever."

"You don't know what I went through there. I can't go back to Abilene. I just can't."

"If you won't listen to me, take this," said the cop, pressing something slightly bigger than a spice rack canister of cinnamon into Britt's hand and closing her fist around it. "This is law enforcement strength, not the crap you get in a drugstore."

Britt uncurled her fingers and looked in her hand. She held a black, knurled cylinder with a red squeeze handle that ran down one side.

"This is the real deal. Don't be afraid to use it and ask questions later," said the cop, giving Britt a farewell pat on the shoulder. Britt smiled and tossed the small pepper spray canister into the air, then grabbed it before it fell into her lap and dropped it into her purse.

"Good luck, sweetie. You're going to need it."

CHAPTER 2

Herzliya, Israel
16 November

There is a seven-hour time difference between New York and Tel Aviv so at almost the exact time that Britt's bus pulled out of the Cleveland depot, Dani Abramowitz walked into his cubicle to start his three to eleven shift. A month before he'd started his job as a computer security specialist at the Institute for International Operations Service, the official name of Israel's legendary spy agency, the Mossad. He'd long dreamt of being a Mossad agent, but he settled for an entry-level technical job, turning down several more lucrative civilian offers.

All day he analyzed computer traffic into and out of the global intelligence assessment and communications center, looking for any attempt by hackers to penetrate the system. He studied printouts, searched a desktop monitor array and scanned a real-time 50-inch LED monitor that monopolized his cubicle wall. The job had turned out to be anything but the exciting, glamorous world of international intrigue he envisioned. The days were already becoming monotonous.

This afternoon was more of the same. Three hours into his shift, just as he was about to wander out for coffee and a brief escape from the tedium, he looked at his screen and froze in his tracks. He dove back into his chair and grabbed his joystick controller so fast that he knocked over the picture on his desk. It was his favorite picture of his father, General Yonaton "Yoni" Abramowitz, one of Israel's most highly decorated soldiers—missing in action since the first pullout from Lebanon back in 2006.

He pushed the joystick to his right, reversing the graphic display of computer traffic on the large monitor. Something had caught his eye in that narrow band of "useless" hash or static surrounding the computer and satellite communications spectrum called white noise. The Mossad found white noise very useful. The secret decryption keys needed to decode the most sensitive top-secret dispatches were buried in the white noise spectrum. Later, each key would be matched up with the appropriate message and its content decoded. Twenty-four hours a day, those hidden encryption keys spiraled through the white noise, theoretically invisible to an enemy hacker attempting to penetrate the system security.

"Concealing critical message pieces in the white noise is like hiding in plain sight," his manager had explained. He equated the Mossad global intelligence assessment center to a bank. Every day agents from around the world deposited messages in this bank's vault. "Our enemies are very good at cracking safes," he said, "and just in case they succeed, we don't put everything into the same vault." Some of the most critical pieces were diverted into the white noise, which he likened to a newsstand on the sidewalk outside the bank. "Who is going to steal the petty cash from a newsstand when there's a bank next door?"

Dani had seen something strange lurking in that "newsstand." Something had penetrated the white noise. He could not identify it, read it or remove it, but the same static that masked the encryption keys was masking the hacker. But with nothing to show, who could he tell?

Staying beyond his scheduled shift, Dani searched for the intrusion, whatever it was. By two in the morning, he could no longer focus on what he'd seen or not seen. He gave up and headed toward the car park and his beat-up old Fiat.

Two major north-south expressways slice, in parallel, through the Tel Aviv suburb of Herzliya. In between highways 2 and 20 lies an archipelago of unremarkable warehouse-looking structures. If the airspace above that area was not restricted, six hexagonal-shaped buildings could be seen clustered together like an organic chemistry molecule—the headquarters of the Mossad. A concrete fortress, created by those highways and their cloverleaf on-off ramps, guards this castle of the clandestine service. Within that bulwark, and the two-mile radius surrounding it, lies the densest concentration of high-tech companies outside of Silicon Valley—almost all of them founded or run by Mossad alumni.

Dani pulled out of the car park and headed north, up the unmarked road that leads from the fabled spy agency to the Highway 20 entry. He took the southbound entrance on to the highway leading toward his small Tel Aviv apartment, about 25 minutes away. As he waited for the light to change, he leaned back against the headrest and closed his eyes. Just then a limousine-sized Mercedes S-600 jolted his vehicle from behind, jarring him back into the survival of the fittest mentality needed to drive in Israeli traffic.

Before any information was exchanged, the Mercedes driver announced he had diplomatic immunity and could not be held responsible for the accident, but he offered to pay for any damage, on the spot, in cash. There was very little damage—so little, in fact, that if the accident had occurred in a car park, it might have gone unnoticed. The driver offered an obscenely generous cash settlement. Dani quickly accepted the cash but not without memorizing the diplomatic plate number.

He had driven only a few blocks when he noticed a manila envelope lying on his passenger seat. It must have been put there while he was outside his car talking to the Mercedes driver. Without slowing down, he opened the envelope and glanced inside. As he saw its contents, his whole body began shaking uncontrollably. He nearly lost control of the car before hitting his brakes and guiding the car to a stop at the side of the road.

His tremors were so violent he had to brace his hands on the steering wheel to hold the eight-by-ten photo of his father. He looked much older than in the picture on his desk. The folder also contained a two-day-old front page of the *Iran Daily* the English-language newspaper, published in Tehran by the official Islamic Republic News Agency (IRNA). Scrawled across the newspaper was his father's signature—no note, just a signature. A business card with a 971-4 country code phone number was clipped to the paper. There was no name on the card but Dani recognized it was a Dubai exchange. Someone had printed above the number in English: *Call with a prepaid phone card from a public pay phone.* Below the number was a handwritten note: *Do as you are asked and your father can be freed. Tell anyone about this and he dies, not pleasantly.*

Dani sat trembling in the car for untold minutes, trying to regain control of his emotions. He alternated between staring at the picture, the signature on the newspaper, and the note. He flipped the card over a dozen or more times, hoping something might appear on the blank side. Then he returned to study the picture, the card, then the whole process once again.

Eventually he calmed down enough to drive. He slipped the battered old Fiat into gear and eased back into the light late-night traffic and headed for home. He'd gone about two blocks when he slammed on the brakes and made an abrupt, tire-squealing U-turn in the middle of the road and raced back to Mossad headquarters. He bypassed his department and went directly to the Political Action and Liaison Desk. The "Political Desk" is a major department of more than a hundred staffers—only six on the graveyard shift—keeping track of nearly every diplomatic posting around the world, especially of intelligence agents working in embassies, under diplomatic, cover, usually as some type of attaché—cultural, commercial or political officer. Once identified as an intelligence officer, that agent would be tracked for life wherever he is assigned, whatever his title. Once a spy, always a spy.

The actual desk, where the officer of the day sits, is buried in a back corner of the large room, right outside the executive office suite of the Deputy Director Political Liaison. Dani zigzagged his way through the maze of empty desks to find the duty officer to ask if he could look up a Mercedes with diplomatic plate CC 22 08 016

The duty officer yawned, then asked for Dani's ID and why he needed to know. A half-true explanation about a hit-and-run fender-bender with the car seemed to satisfy him. "Oh, where did he hit you?" he asked as he typed the license number into a computer terminal.

"In the boot," Dani replied.

"No, I mean what address or intersection."

Dani told him the intersection and the night duty officer typed that in too. Then a paper was spit out of a printer.

"Hmmmm," the officer groaned as he studied the printout. "If he has diplomatic immunity, you're probably screwed. You can't force him to pay. Even if the police find him, they can't even give him a ticket." He tapped a few more strokes into the computer. "Yep. You're screwed. It *is* a diplomatic car registered to the Egyptian Consulate and usually driven by—hel-lo. Isn't that interesting? That car was reported stolen six hours ago."

Combined with the information in the manila folder, that sounded very ominous.

"You're right. I'm screwed. I am totally screwed."

As Dani turned and left, the duty officer noted their conversation under "exceptions" in the daily log of the world's most storied spy agency, wondering, *Am I now just a traffic cop writing up fender benders?*

CHAPTER 3

Tel Aviv, Israel
15 December

For the next month Dani was a near zombie. He didn't eat. He barely slept. He walked around with a blank stare. He no longer cared about blips in the white noise. The handwritten note made it clear he could not talk to anyone about the "accident," so he stopped talking to everyone—everyone except the IDC study buddy he had unexpectedly met several days earlier in the Mossad canteen. The Interdisciplinary Center is an internationally known university, excelling in business, computer science and especially government diplomacy and strategy. It is often referred to as a wholly-owned subsidiary of the Mossad and the private recruiting preserve of Israel's foreign intelligence service.

"Dani," she'd yelled, waving a hand high above her head. She smiled warmly as he approached her table. Her shoulder-length, layered black hair cascaded over the collar of her red leather jacket. Her black leather skirt barely covered the top of her over-the-knee Italian leather boots. "You work here, too?"

"I'm a computer systems security analyst," said Dani. "You know, keeping out the real bad guys and those pesky hackers showing off how smart they are." He slid into a chair on her right and eyed the photo ID badge hanging around her neck: *Seiderman, Hélène* and beneath her picture in red letters, *All Areas No Escort Required.* She was way too young to be a senior bureaucrat with an All Areas credential. With her bangs pulled loosely to one side, nearly hiding one of her sparkling green eyes, she looked like a Hollywood spy, not an intentionally nondescript agent.

Dani's supervisor had pointed out other young people with the same kind of pass and whispered, "Baby spy—waiting for first field assignment." He warned Dani that baby spies—even those just out of training—outranked civilian technologists. "Be careful around them."

She has to be a rookie field officer, thought Dani, a *Katsa*—a spy runner—but he couldn't imagine having anything to fear from her. He'd helped her pass a basic computer science course. And she'd helped him with Middle Eastern history. "What are *you* doing here?" he asked.

"You know, just snooping around," she said with a just a hint of a twinkle that could have cost her a demerit in training. Hélène's face and eyes were so expressive, the very antithesis of a poker-faced agent, that on her own she went for Botox shots on her first free weekend in training. Otherwise, she would likely have washed out. "You?"

"Like I said, I'm a computer security specialist but I hope to be a katsa, like you," he said.

The twinkle vanished instantly. "Dani," she glared at him and picked up her sunglasses beside her coffee cup, "don't ever say that again. I am *not* a katsa," she lied, "but never, ever say that, about anyone, especially outside this building, unless you want to get them and maybe yourself killed. Bad for your career."

Now I know for sure you're a katsa, he thought. He had been ready to tell her about the computer incursion and even about the accident and the photo. He had no doubt now what she would advise: immediately report everything to Mossad security. She might even turn him in, even though his father's life was at stake.

"How's your friend," asked Dani, trying to change to an innocuous subject, "that woman you used to meet for dinner all the time?"

"I wouldn't say Rebekah and I were friends." She put on the sunglasses that she'd been holding since Dani's faux pas. "We don't keep up." She stood to leave. "Rebekah started a very successful business intelligence software company. She's a gajillionaire and spends most of her time in America or Europe. She told me to apply for a job here and insisted I could use her as a reference, but we haven't spoken since I went into training. She said to call her when I got my first assignment." Then she leaned over and kissed Dani on the cheek. "Remember what I told you. People could die," she said, then flashed the same radiant smile she showed when she first saw him.

His hope for a friend and confidant faded away with the click of her heels as she disappeared into the hall. He was in this all alone.

After that, he avoided her and everyone else. He would get in his car at the end of his shift and drive North on Highway 20, away from his apartment, toward Tel Aviv's Azrieli Centre.

The sprawling Azrieli mall is the perfect place to get lost in a crowd. Nestled among three towering skyscrapers, the multi-level shopping mall is one of the largest in the Middle East. At least three nights of each week that month, Dani would survey the menus of a dozen or more of the thirty restaurants and pace back and forth past the bank of pay phones on the first floor. Then he'd ride the glass elevators to the third floor and repeat the exercise in front of those pay phones—all the time fingering the card in his pocket.

He looked at his watch. 2035. In twenty-five minutes, the mall would close. He bought a prepaid phone card from a kiosk, walked to the bank of phones and picked up the one farthest away from the flow of shoppers.

CHAPTER 4

New York City
15 December

A thunderous pounding snapped Britt's chin up from its resting place on her knees. She was scrunched into a small rust-stained bathtub, her long legs forcing her knees high up out of the water. She had landed an interview in Midtown at four-thirty, and she still needed to wash her hair, get dressed, get uptown to the library to print some more resumes and then to the interview. "Who is it?"

"Is landlord. I vill make talk to you," shouted the burly Russian through the apartment door, less than six feet away.

"Can't you come back later, Dimitri?" She never could remember the landlord's last name, never mind trying to pronounce it. "I'm in the tub."

Britt hated the old claw foot tub, with chipped porcelain and separate faucets for hot and cold. It sat smack in the middle of the tiny, one-room, fifth-floor walk-up. When she was not scrunched into the tub, a board laid across the top served as her kitchen table and TV stand. Washing her hair bordered on torture. With the separate faucets she had a choice of scalding or freezing. Eventually she settled for filling a sauce pan and dumping that over her head time and again. The pounding resumed.

"Nyet. Ve make talk now." Comrade Charmski, as she called him behind his back, sounded like he was standing right next to the tub. "Open door. I give to you something of very much important."

She wrapped herself in a towel and dripped her way three short steps to the door, opening it only as far as the safety chain would allow. A plain white number ten envelope partially obscured the eyes that leered through the crack. Dmitri had a coarse, craggy face, like Leonid Brezhnev—minus the charisma. He shoved the envelope toward her.

"Read. This to inform you, you have ten days to make proof you have job—real job, not coffee shop waitress job—and can pay rent."

"But I'm not behind. I paid my first and last months' rent."

"I not vait for you fall behind. Ten days or out. You vant stay vith no job, I give to you job. You make plenty money. And no move."

"You can't do this to me. It's illegal!"

"You vant sue me?" he said, walking toward the stairs at the end of the roach-infested hallway. "Trial take three years, maybe more. You could be dead by then."

Britt slammed the door shut and threw the letter as hard as she could. "I haa-aate New York!" she howled as it fluttered to the ground about eighteen inches from her wet feet.

"You make good squeal," Dmitri yelled through the door. "Some customers vant that. You make good earner. Da!"

Avenue D and Seventh Street was a far flung outpost of Alphabet City, an area named for its avenues identified by letters instead of names or numbers. Somehow this corner of the neighborhood remained insulated from the incursions of gentrification. Steel pickets in front of the Roaring 20s-era tenements guarded rows of garbage cans and crumbling concrete steps leading down to windowless subterranean units.

It just like *Cheers,* she thought, except instead of Frazier, Cliff and Norm, the only patron is the Count of Monte Cristo, chained up to the dungeon wall. She never saw anyone going down those steps but occasionally she'd see a rough looking man or two emerging from what struck her as black holes never intended for human habitation.

* * * *

Manny Klein was one of those unfortunate souls who could put on a tuxedo fresh out of the dry cleaner's bag and ten minutes later look like a rumpled penguin in an unmade bed. Manny ran the backroom operations at Collingwood & Company, an elite, if little known, international investment-banking boutique.

"You can start today. Isn't that nice?" he said in a singsong ridicule. "Nobody strolls in here at a quarter to five and starts today. Hell, today's over." He alternated looking at the woman sitting across from him and his own help-wanted ad from the *Times* that Britt had paper-clipped to her resume. He was not subtle about letting his gaze follow the line down her long neck and stop abruptly at the V of her white blouse. BJ didn't intentionally show a lot of cleavage, but it didn't take much to get Manny Klein's undivided attention. Manny was a shining example of a man without polish.

"Thirty-one. You're kinda old to be starting out." The wholesome farm girl from the flatlands and Manny from Flatbush could not have less in common. "Oh, I guess that's not properly PC of me. I'm supposed to say you're highly overqualified, what with your valuable experience in a silo somewhere, and I see a double major in English and Agricultural Business. I have only a humble clerk job to offer."

The ridicule was not lost on Britt. "I'll get back to you if we're interested," said Manny, getting up to usher her out of his office—a see-through cube, in the center of a sea of desks with women busily typing at computer workstations.

Britt did not get up. As Manny approached her chair, she lifted her chin and swallowed hard. She could see the reflection of almost everything in the room in the transparent ceiling.

"It was more than a silo." She spoke with quiet resolute determination. "We bought, sold and stored thousands of bushels of wheat, corn and soybeans every day. And we hedged just as many futures contracts on those same commodities. You never knew what you bought in September, and stored all winter, will sell for in April. Think of that silo as a really tall, giant derivative."

From his vantage point, standing right in front of her chair, Manny had an even better opportunity to look down her blouse. *What a great pair of silos!* "I hear ya," he said, focusing on her breasts. "But we got a rule here. We never touch anything with roots or hooves. That commodity stuff ain't all that useful to us."

"So, do I have a chance?" she asked, rolling her eyes toward the ceiling. "Or is that glass ceiling up there my answer?"

Manny looked up and frowned. "Honey, that glass ceiling doesn't stop just women here, it holds down anyone who's not a rainmaker. So technically, yeah, you got a chance, I think, because you're a woman there's some law against me saying you got no shot."

"One shot, that's all I need, but I really need it, now."

As Britt walked to the elevators, Manny Klein stood in the doorway of his glass office watching her brown ponytail swing from side to side. The click of her high heels echoed as she walked across the raised floor covering hundreds of miles of computer and fiber optic cables. As she entered the elevator, she squatted slightly to get even with the panel buttons to make sure she was pressing the right button for the lobby. She exuded an easy grace and elegance. Manny just saw a nice ass and a damn nice rack.

Manny would never admit he was a sucker for someone who needed a chance—but he never forgot that someone had once given him a chance, and that had changed his life.

He went back to his desk, picked up his phone and dialed the receptionist at the lobby security desk. "That girl you sent to see me—don't let her leave. Put her on the phone."

Through the receiver a minute later, Britt heard the raspy Brooklyn accent say, "You can start Monday, but you're on probation. We open at nine. You better come in at eight-thirty. You got a lot to learn, kid. Lesson one, don't ever tell anyone you can start today. You just blew away any bargaining power you had. At least try to make me think you're in demand, sweet cheeks, even if you're not."

CHAPTER 5

Tehran, Iran
18 December

Slivers of the early morning sun seeped through the tiny cracks of the heavy blackout curtains in the Department 36 conference room of Iran's Internal Security Intelligence division. It is the most secret, most autonomous, most feared secret police and spy agency in Iran. Officially, it reports to the clerics running the Council of Guardians of the Islamic Revolution.

"This is a black day." The voice at the head of the conference table belonged to Muhammad Ali-Albadi, the chairman of Department 36. Three decades ago, he had been one of the "students" who overran the U.S. Embassy and held fifty-three Americans hostage for 444 days. As a hero of the revolution, Ali-Albadi was accountable to no one except his uncle—the Supreme Leader.

The most sensitive operations of Department 36, such as the assassination of dissidents living outside Iran, were entrusted only to the secretive, extremely effective *Al Quds* intelligence and special operations commandos. Ali-Albadi had the power to order the death of almost anyone, even a mullah. He wielded it ruthlessly. Only the Supreme Leader could overrule him.

"Our revolution is under attack from within. Overnight, six senior Revolutionary Guard commanders were assassinated, including the head of all ground forces, helping our brothers on the Pakistan border. Our president will blame the Americans, but the perpetrators were our own people. The Guardians fear counter-revolutionary forces may once again take over our country and lead us away from the path of Allah while our enemies grow stronger." Ali-Albadi stopped and looked each man in the eye before continuing. "We eliminated the son of the would-be president, but still he does not get the message to stop questioning the outcome of the election. Nor do the people. Then some stupid paramilitary sniper shot that girl through the heart in the middle of the street. Neda Agha-Soltan is now a household name all over the world. Our own paramilitary *Basiji* made her a martyr for anti-Islamic, anti-government forces. Her death has become the most widely viewed death in the world."

Ali-Albadi threw up his hands in frustration. "What progress do you have to report?" he demanded of the agent standing at the other end of the conference table.

"We have successfully made an initial contact, Excellency, with a potential asset within the Mossad."

"You reported that contact a month ago. I re-ask my question. What progress do you have to report?"

"Our agents maintain daily surveillance. The target shows no signs of having reported our contact to Mossad internal security, Excellency."

Ali-Albadi's impatience was clearly signaled whenever he began tapping the table with the huge gold ring on his left hand. The centerpiece of the ring was a large diamond scimitar with rubies that looked like blood dripping from the crescent-shaped sword. The scimitar seemed to slice through two columns. Upon closer inspection, those two columns were the twin towers of the World Trade Center.

"May I remind you, the fate of the Islamic revolution and our achieving the destruction of the Zionist parasite state are at stake. Both depend on learning the Israeli plans for a preemptory strike on our nuclear facilities. They have already inflicted a near fatal blow by destroying thousands of uranium centrifuges with a computer worm. Zionist assassins on motorcycles murder our top nuclear scientists in the street. Failure is not an option."

"Be it Allah's will, we will have a response soon, Excellency," said his senior agent. "We have presented the target with a highly motivating dilemma." He went on to explain how the picture and note had been delivered to Dani.

With his temple and neck veins bulging, Ali-Albadi slammed his hand on the table. "Why do I know I am about to hear a report of failure when you invoke the will of Allah? You have nothing to report. You have wasted my time. Get out!"

Ali-Albadi picked up his phone, dialed a number and resumed tapping the ring on his desk as he waited.

"Uncle," said Ali-Albadi, "I pray that you and the Prophet, all peace and blessings be upon him, will be merciful. I have failed to recruit the asset I told you about. Weeks have passed and we have heard nothing."

"The bird that is not pushed from the nest will never fly," rasped the Supreme Leader. "Your failing is in not forcing the issue. Make him fly to us, nephew."

"Insh'Allah," said Ali-Albadi. Be it God's will, indeed.

CHAPTER 6

New York City
23 December

It was going to be the loneliest Christmas that Britt could remember. Before the end of her first week on the job, she began staying late, telling herself she was figuring out a better way to complete her tasks. Actually, she was just avoiding going back to her Lower East Side roach motel where she didn't even have a real bathroom, only a water closet—literally, a toilet in a closet that had once been part of the adjoining apartment. Her "closet" was a three-foot bar and wire shelf all secured with giant lag bolts that went clear through her wall and came out on the hallway side. Her entire job-hunting and work wardrobe hung there: two black skirts, black pants, two white and two black blouses and two black sweaters—a summer-weight boat-neck pullover and a cable knit turtleneck. A couple pairs of jeans, some shorts, tees and sweatshirts all fit in two drawers, along with all her lingerie: three bras—one black, two white— and enough cotton underpants for a clean pair every day, if she got to the Laundromat on the weekend.

By nine, she usually surrendered to the reality that she had nowhere else to go, nothing to do and no money to do it with. Leaving Collingwood & Company's Third Avenue office, she'd walk to Grand Central, catch the number Four subway to Union Square, change to the L train to Fourteenth Street and First Avenue, then a fifteen-minute walk, cutting diagonally through Tompkins Square park, to Avenue B and Seventh street. The last block to Avenue D was always the scariest. After dark, she had visions of someone jumping out of one of those basement doors and dragging her down the steps to one of the dungeons. That's when she'd dig in her purse for the pepper spray the Cleveland cop had given her and carry it in her hand until she locked her roach motel door.

Last night, she'd broken her routine and walked four blocks across town to see the Saks Fifth Avenue windows and the lights of Rockefeller Center, the skating rink and the big tree. A few days earlier, she'd treated herself to an eighteen-inch tree with blinking lights and tiny decorations included. Two days after giving it a place of honor on her combination TV-stand, kitchen table and tub cover, the lights blinked off for the last time, dead.

Merry Christmas, Charlie Brown, she thought. This would indeed be the saddest, loneliest Christmas ever.

Tonight, if she was lucky, she would have enough hot water for a bath and maybe even enough to wash her hair. Usually she had to choose one or the other. Either way, she would then go to bed and another lonely night would pass.

Tomorrow would be Christmas Eve. Anything was better than going back to her apartment tonight. Pacing the corridors to further delay her departure, she followed the lights to Mahogany Row, the richly paneled hall of executive suites. Through an open door she saw another woman working late. She did not look at the name or title on the office door.

Mackenzie Collingwood, the CEO of Collingwood & Company sensed the presence of another soul but did not look up. Instead, she reached under her desk, pulled out the wastebasket and held it out with one arm, never taking her eyes off her work. "Just empty this. You can do the rest of the office later."

"Oh, okay. I don't know where it goes, ma'am, but I'll figure it out."

Mackenzie Collingwood was startled to hear a voice without a Spanish or Haitian accent and even more surprised to see a professional-looking woman reach for her wastebasket, using only her thumbs and index fingers, as if it was full of dirty diapers.

Britt carried it toward the corridor, wondering where to empty it. Before leaving, she asked if she could do anything else to help.

"No, thank you," said Mackenzie. "Now if you don't mind, I'm trying to revise my presentation for a breakfast meeting tomorrow. Why I ever agreed to give this thing on Christmas Eve is beyond me. Damned interest rates and energy costs."

"Isn't that what hedging's for?" asked Britt.

"What did you say?" Mackenzie blinked and tilted her head quizzically. "Get back in here and put down that silly wastebasket. Who are you? What do you know about hedging?"

"I'm sorry. I didn't mean to intrude." She stuck out her hand to shake, not knowing which question to answer first. "Britt. Britt Jaeger," she said, pronouncing her name phonetically, *Yay-ger*. "It's spelled with a J. I'm new here."

Mackenzie shook her hand, perfunctorily, but did not introduce herself. She didn't need to. Everyone in the firm knew she was the boss. "My secretary went home sick. Do you know anything about PowerPoint?"

"I get by," replied Britt.

As the night edged toward morning, Britt grew more energized and excited than any time in recent memory. She was, for the moment, half of a team, working side by side on something important. She gloried in trading notes and above all, escaping from the roach motel.

They worked until nearly two a.m. "I cannot thank you enough," said Mackenzie at last, closing her laptop. "You were a Godsend. My car will be downstairs in a minute. I'll drop you at home."

Just the thought of her boss seeing the roach motel made her stomach knot.

"Oh, that's not necessary. I'll take the subway."

"Not at this hour you won't."

"Then I'll grab a cab," she replied hurriedly, knowing she could ill afford a twenty-dollar cab ride. "You said you had to be up at the crack of dawn for your presentation. If I take a taxi, you can get home and get a little more sleep. Besides, I'm in no hurry to go back to my apartment."

"See here, miss uh, ah..."

"Jaeger. Britt Jaeger."

"Let's do this! My driver will take me home first, then he'll drop you off."

Mackenzie poured two glasses of white wine from the tiny fridge in the back of her limo and handed one to Britt. "Merry Christmas. If you're like me, you're too keyed up to sleep when you've worked this late."

Britt put up her hand. "No, thank you. I really shouldn't."

"Come on!" insisted Mackenzie, looking at her watch. "It's already Christmas Eve. You earned it and I insist." Mackenzie took a sip. "So how long have you been with our company, and what do you do for us?"

"About a month. I just moved here from Kansas. I'm a clerk in Mr. Klein's department."

"Manny! My God! Manny is an institution here. I call him our human fire insurance policy. He knows absolutely everything that goes on in this place and has a record of it— probably two or three—squirreled safely away somewhere."

What kind of institution? To Britt he was just a Danny DeVito twin who never missed a chance to look down her blouse, but he had given her a job when she really needed it. On her second day he nicknamed her "Silo." When she asked why, he laughed. "'Cuz I can't spell derivative." *He was actually listening to me during that interview,* she thought.

"He started in the mailroom," continued Mackenzie, "when I was a little girl and my father was taking over from my grandfather. Grandpa kind of adopted Manny, practically forced him to go to night school at NYU. Eventually he graduated and my dad made him Vice President of Operations, not right away but eventually. A bit of advice for you, never underestimate the importance of the Manny Kleins of the world." She took a long sip. "Well, I think we've talked enough business for tonight. Tell me about you. You're from Kansas, I believe."

"Abilene, population six thousand and falling."

"Sounds like the middle of nowhere," said Mackenzie.

"I wouldn't say the *middle* of nowhere." Britt cracked a slight smile. "But it's walking distance from there. Folks say, when your dog runs away in Abilene, you can still see him for three days."

"Sounds utterly charming." Mackenzie smiled indulgently. "You must tell me more, but not tonight, dear." Mackenzie looked out the window, hiding her grin, as the limousine slowed. "Well, this is my place. Where again is Charles taking you?"

"Alphabet City," said Britt.

"Good part or bad part?" asked Mackenzie. "Charles," she continued without waiting for an answer, "you will please take Ms. Jaeger home and see her *all* the way to her door? Please, make *sure* she's safely tucked into her apartment, understood?" Mackenzie had a habit of asking questions that were not questions. They were directives. Despite the 'please,' her tone left no doubt she was issuing an order, not asking a favor.

"Of course, ma'am," replied the driver

"That's really not necessary," protested Britt.

"See here, Bitsy, Betsy, what was it again, Brenda?"

"Britt."

"Whatever."

"Maybe BJ would be easier to remember."

"When you've known me longer and better—" Mackenzie's eyebrows shot up like she'd discovered a pearl in her Oysters Rockefeller. "BJ? I like that! BJ it is. Where was I? Oh, your apartment. You might as well learn from the beginning that I am very protective of the assets of this firm." Mackenzie patted Britt's knee making her shiver at the unexpected touch. Touching had become frightening to Britt since her husband started the rough stuff just before the end of their first year.

As Charles guided the car into the no parking zone in front of Mackenzie's Sutton Place condo, Jimmy the doorman was already at the curb reaching for the door handle.

"I think you just might prove to be one of them," Mackenzie continued, swinging her legs to get out of the car, unaware of the turmoil she had caused. "You should know, Charles, here," she leaned forward, reaching through the open divider between driver and passengers to pat his shoulder, "is not some glorified cab driver. He was a Navy Seal—fully trained in anti-terrorist, anti-kidnapping evasive driving. He is licensed to carry a weapon and he does. This car is mostly bulletproof. That is an unfortunate necessity these days because having my name on the building makes me kidnap bait. So when I say Charles will accompany you, he will do exactly that and you will let him. Do I make myself clear, young lady?" It was another question for which she did not want an answer. "Oh, and Merry Christmas."

CHAPTER 7

Mossad Headquarters
Herzliya 25 December

Nine-twenty on Christmas morning at Mossad headquarters was simply the start of another Wednesday morning. Dani sat in his cubicle staring at his father's picture. Three times he had partially dialed the Dubai number from the phones in the mall but could not bring himself to complete the call.

Long ago he had accepted the official declaration: missing and presumed killed in action. It was far better to think he was dead than to imagine him languishing in some Syrian or Iranian prison. He picked up the picture and looked into his father's eyes. "What do I do, Abba?" he asked aloud, using the Hebrew word for Papa.

He could almost hear his father's voice from when he was a child. "Just do your duty, son, and everything else will take care of itself."

If not for his father, the Mossad would never have considered hiring Dani. Military service—distinguished military service—was an unwritten prerequisite, and Dani had served only the minimum reserve requirement, but his bloodline counted. Dani was hired straight out of the School of Computer Science at the Interdisciplinary Center. Western intelligence agencies called the IDC "Head Start for Spies." Its International Policy Institute Research Center, where Hélène had studied, was headed by Shabtai Shavit, chief of the Mossad for most of the 1990s. Dani and Hélène Seiderman were both recruited at the IDC, but neither knew about the other.

He picked up his phone to call her. Yet after staring at the phone and his father's picture, he put the receiver back in its cradle.

"I won't let you die, Abba, I swear. I won't."

With a tear running down his cheek, he listlessly pushed the joystick to his right reversing the graphic display of that narrow band of "useless" hash called white noise.

Nothing.

"How do you find 'irregularity' in white noise?" he asked his father's picture. "White noise is nothing but irregularity in its purest form. How do you find a random grain of wheat in a sea of chaff?"

Then it hit him—a technical epiphany—a classic, forehead-slapping eureka moment! The answer was so simple, so obvious that he felt stupid for not thinking of it sooner. "Stop looking for a needle in a haystack," he told himself, "look for a bit of hay in a stack of needles." Look for blips of order—short logical sequences—no matter how short—floating in the white noise. Look for unscheduled message parts among the top-secret decryption keys buried in the white noise. Reassemble enough of those sequences and they could form an unauthorized entry into the system. He leaned back in his chair and smiled. "You would be proud, Abba."

His personal cell phone rang. He looked at the Caller ID and blanched. It was the same number he'd been carrying in his pocket for weeks.

"Shalom." He was shocked to hear the Hebrew greeting. "It has taken you a very long time to call. We must discuss the package you recently received."

"What do you want from me?" asked Dani.

"Do nothing. Say nothing. Go to your home after your regular shift. You will be contacted."

"*How* do you know where I live?"

"We know," said the voice. "Ask no more questions. You know what is at stake."

Dani left work early to avoid traffic. It took less than thirty minutes to drive to his small apartment. When he arrived a newspaper lay before his apartment door. He did not subscribe to a paper. Picking it up, he found the second section was folded open to the movie listings. Circled in red was a French movie he'd never heard of, in black and white with subtitles, playing at a small art house. A circle within a circle noted the 22:30 late show.

* * * *

A handful of students, a few older couples, plus a half dozen singles were scattered throughout the cinema when Dani walked in. One younger couple in the back row seemed far more passionately interested in each other than in the scratchy black and white movie with Hebrew subtitles on top of English subtitles. Dani took a seat in the same row but on the other side of the theater. Anyone watching him instead of the movie would have to turn around and look away from the screen. Fifteen minutes passed before one of the singles, a casually dressed dark-haired man in a light windbreaker, got up and walked out toward the lobby. Five minutes later, the man returned to his seat, dropping a note in Dani's lap as he passed by. *Wait thirty minutes. Then use the toilet. If you are not being followed, go to Le Jambe de Grenouille. Sit in the last booth on the left, by the kitchen.*

A half hour later, as he left the men's room, the woman from the back row came out of the ladies' room, shaking her wet hands to dry them in the air. *No towels in there, either*, thought Dani as he walked toward the outer lobby. He never looked at her face, only at her flapping hands, exactly as she had planned. She watched him leave the theater, then reached in her purse and pulled out her cell phone.

* * * *

The Frog's Leg was a small out-of-the-way bistro run by a French-Lebanese chef who'd never heard of nouvelle cuisine. Dani knew of it but had never eaten there. At this hour, the chef was also the maitre d´, waiter and busboy. "I expect out-of-town friends to join me," Dani said, using the exact words written on the other side of the note.

No sooner had he been seated in the back booth than two well-tailored men stepped out of the kitchen. One slid into the seat next to him, effectively pinning him against the wall. He immediately recognized the second man, who sat down facing him on the opposite side of the booth. He was the Mercedes driver.

"You're Iranians," Dani said before either man spoke. "What do you want?"

"We want you to help save thousands, perhaps millions, of innocent lives. Your people and ours," said the Mercedes driver.

Dani was no fool. "By betraying my country?" he shot back.

"We don't want you to reveal any military secrets. We know your country is targeting what it thinks are nuclear weapon sites."

"I certainly hope so," said Dani.

"We do not have any nuclear weapon sites. We do have some commercial, power-generating stations. We want to insure that you have not mis-targeted innocent civilian towns under the mistaken impression that nuclear facilities are hidden there," said the man sitting next to Dani.

"What about my father?"

"Give us just a little help to protect innocent lives, and it may be discovered that he has been mistakenly held all these years. These tragic errors do happen," said the driver.

"You will actually be helping your country and your father," added the second man.

"You saw how world public opinion turned against your country when you invaded Gaza. If Israel used nuclear weapons on the wrong Iranian city, it would force a full-fledged nuclear response and destroy any international support for your country. Preventing that would make you an unsung patriot."

A classic recruitment line, thought Dani. *Tell the target he's a hero, not a traitor.*

"Those decisions are made far above me. I have absolutely no access to any targeting information."

"Pray that it is Allah's will," said the driver, "that some of that information flows through you and that you know how to recognize it."

"You want access to our intelligence systems?"

"We are merely trying to save innocent lives—your people and ours."

"Release my father and I will try to find out what I can. I really will."

"No, you help us first," said the Mercedes driver, "and if the information proves useful, your father can be released. Otherwise—you don't have martyrs in your religion, do you?"

"You've got to give me time."

"There is not much time to give. Prisons are not pleasant places and they can always become more unpleasant."

And if the hero pitch doesn't work, thought Dani, *go to step two, threaten his family.*

The man sitting next to Dani slid out of the booth and shrugged his shoulders indicating Dani should get out too. "Say nothing about this to anyone." Then he nodded toward the door.

As he walked out into the night, Dani knew exactly what he had to do.

He took no notice of the couple kissing in the Mazda 3 parked across the street. The moment he opened the door of his old Fiat, they broke their embrace. As the man behind the wheel started the car, Hélène Seiderman flipped open her cell phone to speed dial Mossad headquarters.

CHAPTER 8

New York City
12 January

After that first late night working on Mackenzie's presentation, Britt never left without walking past Mackenzie's office, hoping she would be needed again. At least one night a week, Mackenzie asked for her help. They never worked until two a.m. again, but often until eight or nine o'clock, even midnight. Afterward, Mackenzie insisted on taking her for a late night dinner and "a glass of wine—or three." Those nights always made Britt feel special. The first time in her life she ever felt that way.

In time, Mackenzie began showing up in Manny Klein's office just to chat—even bringing visitors to Manny's department as part of an office tour. The tour route always passed Britt's desk. The first time Mackenzie "accidentally" touched her shoulder, Britt jumped, like the first night in the car. On subsequent tours Mackenzie never failed to touch her hair, pat her shoulder or just rest a hand on her chair, followed by an "Oh, excuse me, Britt," while looking at the nameplate on her desk, as if they barely knew each other. The nameplate read "Ms. Jaeger." Gradually, BJ stopped jumping.

Though she enjoyed their time together, Britt knew almost nothing about the CEO beyond outward appearances. She was obviously rich, very intelligent and very driven. No matter how late they worked, Mackenzie was always back in the office before nine, often by seven-thirty.

She dressed elegantly, but simply, with exquisite makeup. Her shimmering deep brunette, almost black hair, with just a few strategically placed platinum highlights, was always perfectly coiffed in an asymmetrical cut, like Meryl Streep in *The Devil Wears Prada*. A platinum swath, precisely one-half inch wide, slashed across her brow from her part to her temple. Britt had never seen a six-hundred-dollar, two-step "do" and she was impressed. Stunning was not an inappropriate adjective—certainly for Mackenzie's age—whatever that was. Britt guessed she was about ten years older, roughly forty, but it could be more. Hard to tell. Diamonds adorned her left index finger and both ring fingers, but she never revealed her marital status, even indirectly.

After several weeks of working together, Britt's knowledge of her had increased by only two tidbits of information.

One: She traveled frequently—especially weekends and holidays—to some warm-weather destination. She tried to avoid travel during the week. People came to her.

Two: She definitely had a social life outside of work. She would often talk about "chatting with friends over cocktails," "at a dinner party over the weekend," "while having drinks after the theater," or "sitting through another boring fund-raiser."

Other than those casual references, she remained a mystery. Britt, on the other hand, had revealed her most private thoughts. Over those late dinners, Mackenzie probed the deepest recesses of her budding protégé's personal life with an off-handed ease. Mackenzie soon knew where BJ went to grade school and high school; how boys on the middle school bus had teased her mercilessly about her early budding figure with the singsong chant, "BJ's got big jugs." She knew how her father died in a farm accident; and that her mother leased out the acreage, took a job in town and a second mortgage to try to save the farm, before she died of a massive coronary. A male doctor had misdiagnosed her heart disease as chronic indigestion. That put him near the top of BJ's list of reasons why men were not good for her, just behind her husband and the creep on the bus.

Mackenzie was so easy to talk to, little by little, Britt even revealed where, when, how and to whom she had lost her virginity and every unfortunate detail of her four-year, abusive marriage to Jack, the hulking ex-jock who never outgrew his high school football hero days.

Mackenzie knew about her disillusionment with the men she'd dated after her divorce when she realized they were often more immature than her ex. They didn't care about her. All they cared about was "a notch on their gun" so they could brag around town about banging the "captain's girl."

Of all the things she'd revealed, the hardest by far was recounting her bus ride to New York. Mackenzie elicited that story after one of those dinners while reassuringly holding BJ's hand in the back of the limo. Britt was sobbing as the car stopped to drop off Mackenzie first, as always.

Extracting a tissue from the passenger convenience console that disguised the little fridge, Mackenzie dabbed Britt's tears and softly kissed each cheek. Then she brushed a gentle kiss across her young protégé's lips—the first truly tender kiss Britt had felt in three years. It was a chaste kiss but a tiny current of sexual energy rippled through it.

"You are a very special young woman, BJ," she said as Jimmy, the doorman, opened her door.

Britt would barely remember how her body had initially stiffened during that intensely intimate moment. Although confused by what had just happened, she also felt special and deeply cared for, feelings she'd not had all the time she was married.

Inevitably, Mackenzie knew everything about Britt. And she was clearly pleased with all that she'd learned about the firm's newest asset.

The first time Britt met Rebekah Chayat, she had finished her work for the day and taken the elevator to the penthouse floor for her regular trip down Mahogany Row, past Mackenzie's office, hoping for a task.

"BJ, come in. I'd like you to meet Colonel Rebekah Chayat, spelled C-H-A-Y-A-T, but pronounced Hyatt, like the hotel," said Mackenzie.

"Rebekah is a very good friend. She and her company are a very important part of the success of this firm. She started a business intelligence software company in Israel and we took her public in this country. It is one of the great success stories of Collingwood and Company."

The woman was slightly shorter than BJ, at least in the mid-heel pumps she wore. She was athletically built, in a body-hugging khaki pants suit that showed no fat. Her short-sleeve jacket revealed Michelle Obama-like sculpted arms. Britt extended her hand. "It's a pleasure, Colonel."

Instead of shaking hands, the woman reached for Britt's shoulders and air kissed her on both cheeks, European style. "Please, 'Colonel' is completely unnecessary," she said in an accent BJ had never heard.

"Is that what they call data mining?" asked Britt.

"I'm impressed," said the colonel with a nod, "but from what Mackenzie tells me, you have far more interesting stories, like how you got to New York."

"I'd really rather not relive that."

"I understand." said Rebekah, "Mackenzie does have a way of sharing a little too much information. Still, I understand you were very brave."

Mackenzie swooped in to take Rebekah's elbow and steer her toward the door." She and I are late for a dinner meeting about a women's shelter we're helping."

The colonel paused on her way out and put her hand on Britt's shoulder. "I know a little about self-defense. It helps keep me in shape. Perhaps I could teach you a thing or two. You'd never have to worry about another bus ride again. If you're interested, that is. And if it's OK with Mackenzie, of course?"

Britt was left standing in the middle of Mackenzie's office. As the two women headed down the hall, she heard the accented voice say, "Three words, Mackenzie: need to know. That young woman does not need to know."

* * * *

Dozens of feet below street level, the L train rattled out of the Third Avenue station toward First Avenue, its last stop in Manhattan, before plunging into the tunnel under the East River toward Brooklyn. At First Avenue, Britt climbed the stairs to Fourteenth Street and began the thirteen-minute "walk in the park" toward the roach motel. It used to take her 20 minutes but she now walked at a New Yorker's pace.

It was cold, dark and snow fell as she took the serpentine path past the lighted street hockey rink in Tomkins Square park. Kids, but mostly young adults—males and females on the same teams, sported every manner of hockey equipment from nothing but hockey gloves to full goalie outfits. Skates were the only missing equipment. Players ran around in sneakers slapping at a street hockey ball. *Only in New York*, she thought, as she looked down at her own sneakers. She'd learned to leave a pair of heals under her desk and wear sneakers to and from the office. She was glad she'd worn her turtle neck today. She pulled it up to cover her nose and mouth.

Beyond the rink, the path was dimly lit and the lights cast shadows that could easily camouflage a mugger. As she emerged from the park, she shoved her hand into her purse to feel for the pepper spray. Between Avenue B and Avenue C, with its trendy cafes and watering holes, she felt fine—safe. It was the last block between Avenue C and Avenue D and her Seventh Street walk-up that she felt the threat-level changed dramatically. As usual, at night, she walked down the center of Seventh Street, staying far away from whatever lurked in those basement entrances. She knew the steps led to nothing like *Cheers* and no one gave a damn about your name. Just then, a dark Lincoln Town car—matching any of the twenty-thousand or so sedans in the New York car service/gypsy cab fleet—turned the corner and slid to a stop at the snow-covered curb in front of BJ's building. The driver quickly doused the headlights, jumped out, opened the backdoor. Another burly man, like she sometimes saw during daytime, climbed out and began dragging a screaming woman out of the backseat toward one of the gates leading to the sub-level basements.

This was not a happy drunk who needed to be taken home. This woman, wearing only a tank top, a mini skirt and totally out of season white, "Fuck me" platform pumps, was terrified. *That's not a tank top,* she realized, *it's her bra! They've ripped her blouse off.* She was kicking, biting and screaming. The only word BJ recognized was "Nyet!"

BJ tightened the grip on her pepper spray canister and veered to the far side of the street quickly retreating toward the Yuppie safety of Avenue C. Then something snapped, literally, snapped and she stopped. She was sure she'd heard an actual snap and wasn't conscious of popping the protective cap off the canister but she spun back toward the black sedan. "No! Not here, not tonight, you bastards," she hissed, "not at my house!"

She ran down the far side of the street to come around the back of the car. The driver had returned to his seat, preparing for a fast getaway. She ran behind the car, coming up behind the abductor and sprayed his face at point blank range. He screamed and released his captive. The driver jumped quickly out of the car only to meet the same fate.

BJ threw her coat over the woman's shoulders and grabbed her by the hand and tried to lead her up the stairs to the safety of her apartment, which only made the woman scream and resist her even more frantically. She let go of the poor woman who immediately ran, disappearing around the corner of Avenue D, wrapped in Britt's only winter coat. She looked at the two groaning men by the car. She was sure they could not identify her with the turtle neck still pulled up over her nose and mouth. But now it dawned on her how stupid it would have been to let them see where she lived by going directly to her own apartment. She returned to the car and emptied the remaining pepper spray in their faces, just to be sure. Then she followed the same path as her escapee around the corner, down Avenue D, to catch a cab on Houston Street. "Fifty-third and Third Avenue, across the street from the Lipstick building," she told the driver, who breathed a sigh of relief at not having to go to Brooklyn."

She slept on the couch in Mackenzie's office and told the night guard to wake her at six so she could go home, bathe and change clothes.

It was five to nine as BJ draped her only other coat, a faded, purple puffy jacket, over her office chair when Mackenzie called.

"Good morning. How was your evening? Rebekah and I had to sit through the most boring fundraiser."

Mackenzie never calls to ask about my night. Why this morning? "I didn't get much sleep."

"I hope you have enough energy for a little lunch time shopping. We'll go to Daffy's, it's a fabulous discount store and they have some fantastic winter coats on sale. Then maybe I'll treat you to a manicure."

Britt said nothing but stared her broken nails and the scratches covering her hands made by the woman trying to get away. *How could she know? I'm imagining things.*

"BJ?" said Mackenzie. "Are you there? Meet me out front at twelve-thirty, OK?"

"I really can't afford a shopping spree right now."

"My treat," said the CEO, "a little thank you for all the help you've given me. OK?"

"OK. Fine," answered Britt, in a puzzled monotone. "Twelve-thirty." *She can't possibly know, can she?*

CHAPTER 9

Mossad Headquarters
Herzliya 14 January

After a sleepless night, Dani walked into the outer office of the Director of Technology, Natan Levi. "I must speak to the director," he told the secretary.

"And you are?" she asked.

"Abramowitz, Dani. I am a system security specialist and I must speak with the director. I have been recruited to become an Iranian spy."

The color instantly drained from the secretary's face. Without saying a word, she slipped her hand under her desk and pressed a button, then stood and disappeared into the director's office. Moments later, when she re-emerged to motion Dani in, two internal security agents were already walking down the hall.

"Stand right there," said the director, as the agents arrived and began frisking Dani. When they finished, the director ordered them to stand by in his outer office, then took out a tape recorder, pressed the record button and placed it on his desk. "Sit down."

Twenty minutes later, the director called for the agents and said, "You will escort us to the office of the Deputy Director General."

* * * *

Yaakov "Jock" Ayalon glared across his desk as he assessed the young computer specialist. The two armed agents stood on each side of Dani's chair, scowling down at him.

"Dani," said Jock, "your father saved my life in the Golan. I came home. He didn't. If you had not come in, you would be on your way to jail by this time tomorrow."

"I don't understand, sir. I didn't do—"

"Stop!" ordered the number two intelligence officer in the country, pressing a button to lower a projection screen from the ceiling. "Don't say another word."

Jock Ayalon broke the mold when he was plucked directly from the field to become the Deputy Director General of the Mossad, bypassing several older headquarters bureaucrats.

He was the son of a career foreign service officer who had risen from Israel's Deputy Consul General in the Windy City of Chicago, through numerous diplomatic positions, including London, Washington, Paris and New York, before retiring as Israel's Ambassador to the United Nations. To his American schoolmates, Yaakov had quickly become "Jock." The nickname stuck even after returning to Israel to complete his military service and grad school. When he joined the Mossad, he signed his papers and reports "Jock."

He followed the time-honored path from uniformed military intelligence into the spy agency, distinguishing himself as a spy-runner in the clandestine service, a *katsa*, then a station chief running several katsas.

He pressed a second button from the TV-like remote on his desk, and an LCD projector flashed to life showing a security camera tape of Dani's "accident" of a few weeks ago.

"After you asked the Diplomatic Desk to look up the license plate that night, the duty officer ordered a search of the security cameras that look at everything within a three mile radius of this building. The first thing we saw was that it was not a hit and run as you reported. Naturally, suspicions were aroused."

"Sir, if I could just—"

"Not another word," repeated the DDG, cutting him off. "We saw everything, even things you did not see. We saw the passenger from the Mercedes drop the manila envelope into your car while you talked to the driver. When the tape was blown up and enhanced, it showed that both driver and passenger were known Iranian agents who had entered the country on false Jordanian passports.

"The tape," he continued, "showed you accepting a cash payment from avowed enemies of the state of Israel. Since then, our own internal security agents and Shin Bet domestic intelligence agents have followed your every move, monitored every call, looked at every email and searched your apartment and car, and your girlfriend's apartment."

Reaching into his desk, Jock Ayalon withdrew a manila envelope and handed it to Dani. "Here are stills of you entering and leaving the cinema and the restaurant last night. You will be interested to know that your dining partners were most recently advisors to Hamas, in Gaza, and before that Hezbollah in Lebanon. We also have video with a reasonably complete transcript of your meeting, thanks to laser eavesdropping systems that can read voices by measuring the vibrations of the window in the room. We have not yet found the agent who contacted you in the theater, so they still have at least one active unidentified asset in the country."

"Oh, my God! They'll kill my fath—"

Ayalon silenced him again. "No, they won't, not if they don't have him. I know they told you he was alive. I'm sure he's not, but there is that very slight chance they told the truth, out of character as that would be. That is why we did not arrest them on the spot." He placed his hands flat on the desktop. "Yoni saved my life, Dani. I owe him. If we can't find him, maybe I can save you."

Dani did not reply, and Jock went on. "Since you came forward and never compromised any information, instead of charging you with criminal failure to report contact with agents of a hostile foreign power, or worse, I will attempt to limit this to an administrative action. You *are* guilty of a reporting delay. As such you are immediately suspended without pay for a period to be determined."

As the enormity of the situation washed over him, Dani seemed overwhelmed. A practiced interrogator, Ayalon stared back in silence. Finally, in almost a whisper, Dani said, "I'm dead, aren't I? I will never be back in this building, will I? What about my father?"

"I am sure he's gone, but we will launch an operation to find out."

Addressing the agents, he said, "Collect Mr. Abramowitz's passport, ID, any building passkeys he has and escort him from the building. He is *not* under arrest, for now."

As the agents led Dani from the building, each holding an elbow, Hélène Seiderman walked toward them down the same corridor. "Dani, how are—" She stopped in mid-sentence, as cordiality turned to apprehension. "I'm sorry. I hope it turns out all right."

"We need to be going," said one of the security agents as they both pushed Dani more firmly toward the bulletproof airlock that led to the building exit.

"I'll call you," said Hélène, forming her thumb and little finger into an imaginary phone

"That would not be wise," said the trailing agent.

* * * *

Jerusalem's King David Hotel is one of the finest hotels in the world. Its palatial two-story Presidential and Royal suites have housed nearly every world leader who ever visited the Holy Land. King George V, Presidents Carter, Clinton, and Bush chose to lay their heads there. British Prime Ministers Winston Churchill to Tony Blair stood on the same balconies as Jordan's King Hussein and Egyptian presidents Anwar Sadat and Hosni Mubarak to marvel at the views of the Old City of Jerusalem.

Nearly every word those dignitaries spoke was recorded by Israeli intelligence with ever more sophisticated eavesdropping gadgets located in ceilings, walls, light fixtures, television sets, room service carts, salt shakers, even toilet paper holders. Their personal security entourages invariably found and disabled many of those, but never all of them, especially the laser devices aimed at windows from blocks away. The King David may be the most thoroughly bugged hotel outside China, Russia or North Korea. Government electronic eavesdropping equipment was permanently installed in strategically selected rooms and suites, especially on the fourth floor. Directly above those listening posts are the two-level Presidential and Royal suites, each with rooms on the fifth and sixth floors.

Rafi Herzog was responsible for all that equipment. He assigned the technicians who manned those eavesdropping stations round the clock, whenever "special visitors" were in residence. He knew those suites would be vacant on this night because no political dignitaries were in the hotel.

Herzog took his own car from Mossad headquarters to the King David. He went directly to room 413, the small suite directly beneath the Royal Suite, and used his personal room key. He removed his jacket, splashed some water on his face and took the elevator to the business centre and again used the room key he kept permanently in his possession. The business center was empty. Sitting at the computer least visible to any other visitors, he signed in to a Yahoo account as "hiker787878" and wrote a short email note about a troublesome shipping clerk and a temporary delay of shipments, but stated the problem was under control. He didn't try to address or send the email. He simply saved it as a draft, signed off, and powered down the computer.

He returned to the suite and ordered dinner for two with a bottle of champagne from room service. At seven-twenty, the room phone rang. Herzog picked up the phone but did not say anything. "I'm in the lobby," said the voice on other end.

"It's OK, come up."

Four minutes later, following a discreet knock, he looked through the peephole and opened the door. "I'm glad you could get here," he said before taking his visitor in his arms and kissing her. "Dinner will be here momentarily. Do you want to take a shower and slip into something more comfortable? Like this?" Rafi handed her a small velvet covered box, obviously jewelry.

"It's stunning," she said, extracting a hefty sixteen-inch yellow and white gold chain. With a gram weight of fifty grams, it contained about two thousand dollars worth of gold, and that was before the craftsman turned it in into a beautiful piece of jewelry.

"I thought with yellow and white gold you could wear it with anything," said Rafi, mentally patting himself on the back for his clever practicality.

"I could also wear it with nothing," she said, fastening the clasp under her chin, then spinning it a half turn to rest behind her neck. "Did I tell you my father is a diamond cutter? As a child, I had flawed diamonds for markers on board games. So I know you spent way too much on this." A laugh passed between them before she added, "but if you really want to prey on my weakness, my passion is clothes, Paris and Milan designers."

At seven-forty, room service knocked on the door. The waiter was not surprised when he was paid in cash. Almost everyone who stayed in this suite paid cash for anything ordered. Invariably they were lousy tippers. A technology firm permanently rented the suite for meetings and visiting clients. But rumor among the staff was that the company was a Mossad front.

At seven-fifty, Hélène Seiderman stepped out of the shower, wrapped herself in the lush white terry cloth robe and walked into the living/dining room, just as Rafi Herzog popped the champagne cork. "Thank God you didn't do that while I was still in the bathroom. I would have been sure someone was trying to—"

"And they would have succeeded. You left your purse out here with your weapon in it." He was dead serious when he added, "a mistake that could get you killed."

"I didn't expect my lover would try to kill me."

"Duty may require you to take a lover that would happily kill you, if he knew who you really were." Still holding the champagne in one hand, Rafi Herzog stepped closer and pulled free the terry cloth belt. "Or you might have to kill him. Are you ready for that?" He slid his hand into the open robe.

"If you are, I've been ordered to start researching potentially needed documents and a legend for a mission that is the kind that can make a career. It is extremely dangerous. You could be killed. Should I recommend you? Don't worry, I'll have your back." He grinned as he slid his hand up to her breast. "...and your front."

CHAPTER 10

The next morning, Hélène sat in Jock Ayalon's office as he thumbed through her file, muttering half aloud, half to himself:

"Hélène Al-Farad Seiderman. Grew up on the edge of the Arab quarter of Old Jerusalem. Your father is a former air force officer and now a successful diamond cutter. Mother—oh, this is interesting—Palestinian Christian from Bethlehem. Now, Professor of Forensic Anthropology and Archeology at the University of Jerusalem.

"Languages—accent-free Levantine dialect Arabic. So you could pass for a Palestinian or Israeli Arab, a Jordanian, even a Lebanese. Passable French. Any Farsi?"

"Before the Intifada, I grew up playing with Palestinian kids. My mother studied at the Sorbonne and I had a couple of semesters of Farsi," she said. "I'd never pass for a Persian, but I would have a basic idea of what people are saying. They use the Arabic alphabet, so I can read a little more."

"That's good enough for now," he replied. "This says your Queen's English is nearly accent free. Show me."

"Well, guv, you know, the rine in Spine falls minely on the pline." It was her best Eliza Doolittle Cockney. Then switching effortlessly to an upper-class Etonian accent, she added, "Mumsy, you know, is Oxford ed-u-cated." She separated the three syllables with exacting precision, then smiled. "You said, show me."

Jock's professional stone face brightened with a slight smile. "You're right. I have no one to blame but myself. Now," he said, reclaiming his expressionless face and checking the file again. "This says you were born in Jerusalem, so you're a Sabra, but not a Jew. Interesting."

"Technically you're right, under Talmudic law," she said, "but we did observe the high holy days in our house, even though my mother didn't convert until after I was born."

"But you practiced," he said, shrugging. "We never practiced at all in my house. So you may be a better Jew than me. This also says you're ethnically ambiguous," waving her file in a fanning motion. "What does that mean?"

It means, she thought, *you're not sure I can be trusted?*

"It's hard to tell if I'm an Arab or a European, just by looking." Hélène squared her shoulders and stared straight at her boss until he looked up from her file. She waited until their eye contact was locked in. "Does it matter if one of us is a good Jew or bad Jew? I'm a loyal Israeli and proud of it. If you have any doubts about that, I'll leave now."

Little shows of petulant bravado did not impress Jock. "I have no doubt about your loyalty, young woman. Rebekah Chayat recruited you and vouched for you, that's as good as any lie detector test I know of."

He resumed scanning her file. After one year at the University of Jerusalem, she began her compulsory military service at eighteen. When basic training commanders became aware of her linguistic ability and stunning physical attributes, she was assigned to military intelligence. The background that made her so attractive to the intelligence brass also scared them, resulting in an extremely rigorous security clearance vetting.

"How well do you know her?"

Hélène smiled for the first time. "I guess you'd say she mentored me. She recommended me for military intelligence. I have her personal cell phone number and I feel like I could call her if I had a serious problem, but I never have."

Jock laid down the personnel folder and pushed his chair back slightly from his desk. "How did you wind up at the IDC, if you started at the University of Jerusalem, and your mother was on the faculty there?"

"Rebekah insisted I go to the IDC."

Jock arched an eyebrow. "Rebekah?"

"Colonel Chayat, except she was no longer in the army, made it sound like I had no choice. She'd already spoken to people there and she promised me a scholarship. She said, 'They want you.'"

"Did you know she meant the Mossad wanted you?" asked Jock. "At least she wanted you for the Mossad?

"Not at the time.

"You know Dani Abramowitz, right?"

Hélène nonchalantly crossed one leg over the other. At least she hoped it appeared nonchalant. She didn't know why she had been part of the detail following him as he came out of the restaurant, but she knew being tailed wasn't good for him. *Our association can't be good for me either.* "We were at the IDC at the same time. But neither of us knew the other would be working here until we met in the canteen."

"Do you know who his father is?"

"He told me the story. It's tragic."

"Did he tell you he might still be alive, in an Iranian prison?"

"No. Is that true?" She uncrossed her legs and straightened in her chair.

Ayalon answered her question with one of his own. "Have you ever been to Tehran?"

Hélène laughed. "Every year, high holidays with the Grand Ayatollah. Wouldn't miss it for the world."

He offered not even a hint of a smile. "Sarcasm won't get you out of Iran if somebody you once knew recognizes you on the street and says, 'Hélène, what's a nice Israeli girl like you doing in Iran?' Casual recognition is an agent's worst nightmare."

"Yes, sir. I understand. Sorry."

"There's a slight chance General Abramowitz is still alive. I doubt it, but I want you to find out."

"Me? Why me, sir? I'm just out of training."

"You're what the Brits call a 'new skin.' The only record that exists anywhere in the world of you as an intelligence officer is right here." He picked up the manila folder with both hands and bent it into horseshoe shape, partially hiding his face. "So you're not on anyone's radar." *You're so new, if the worst happens, you don't know anything that could take down any other operations.* This was the cold calculus of espionage. *I don't lose an experienced agent. You are expendable.* He tossed the folder back on his desk and looked up at Hélène. "Right now, even a little Farsi makes you my only available choice."

"When do I leave?" She tried to sound confident.

"We need to create your legend. You will be well trained with a working knowledge of your cover. The technology department will hack into the computers of the relevant issuing agencies and insert fake records—birth certificate, drivers license, marriage license, fake parents, siblings, transcripts, a job history, even fake newspaper articles about you. But once you're in-country, it will be a very low-tech op. You will be on your own, no backup, and obviously no diplomatic immunity."

She could feel a wave of adrenaline twisting her stomach into a knot as she tried to control the classic fight or flight emotion. She wasn't sure which she wanted to do.

"Are you up to it?

Hélène Seiderman glanced quickly at her hands. *Are they shaking?* Then she looked Jock straight in the eyes. "Yes, sir."

"Effective immediately, you may not discuss this conversation or any part of this operation with anyone except me or the senior case officer I assign, and above all, not a word to Dani Abramowitz. Am I clear?"

"Yes, sir. How soon do I go?"

"Sooner than I'd like."

CHAPTER 11

New York City
15 July

"You were a pretty depressed young woman when you came here. It's been what, BJ, a little over a half year now? Have your horizons gotten any brighter?" asked Mackenzie, lifting her stem of Val de Loire Chenin Blanc while waiting for dinner to be served.

"Well, I've seen a lot of museums and a bunch of art galleries."

Mackenzie probed a little deeper. "But no boyfriends? No dates?"

"Not really."

"Not even a cat?"

Mackenzie Collingwood's constant questioning, usually over a late night meal, knew no bounds. Britt craved the companionship of those late night dinners and the escape from her apartment. This was one of the good nights.

"So back in Kansas—I've been dying to ask you this—did you ever actually go for a 'roll in the hay'? I mean, really in the hay?"

Britt could feel the blush rise like thermometer mercury from her neck to her hairline. She looked down at her glass to hide a smile. "Well, almost."

"You *have* to tell me."

"Well, it was after the high school homecoming game, my junior year. Jack and I found this hay stack in a farmer's barn and we were just about to—you know—but my hay fever kicked in. I started sneezing and I couldn't stop. I sneezed like I'd been snorting pepper."

Britt's giggles started slowly, but grew to an infectious laugh. "I sneezed so hard and so loud I woke up the farmer's dog. The damn mutt started barking like mad. The farmer came out with his shotgun and we went running bare-assed naked back to the car with clothes flying like flags on the Fourth of July."

Mackenzie Collingwood—usually the very essence of female dignity—laughed so hard she sprayed a mouthful of wine through her nose. No one made Mackenzie laugh like BJ. Certainly no one had ever made her spray wine through her nose in public. Mackenzie dabbed her napkin over her wine-speckled dress and wiped the tears from her eyes.

"Believe it or not," she said, regaining a modicum of composure, "I had some business I wanted to discuss with you away from the office, but I can't do it with wine dripping through my sinuses."

Oh my God! I'm fired? was all that ran through BJ's mind.

"Can you meet me in my office at seven-thirty?"

"This is going to be something bad, isn't it."

"No, darling. It's something good. Just be there."

"Yes, ma'am! You're not going to fire me, are you?"

"BJ, please. Drop the 'ma'am'. Call me 'Mackenzie' or I *will* have to fire you."

"Yes, ma'am."

"You are so fired, my friend." Mackenzie laughed and raised her glass to clink Britt's.

* * * *

At twenty after seven the next morning, Britt walked into Mackenzie's office carrying coffee and croissants from the deli down the block. Five minutes later, the CEO walked in, not at all surprised to find her young protégé already there—"and with coffee!"

"You're a Godsend," she said, pouring the contents of both paper cups into a sterling silver pot, then into a pair of Lenox china cups. "Thank you."

"You're welcome. I hope you like croissants."

"Love 'em," said Mackenzie. She sat down on her couch and placed the cup and saucer on her coffee table. "So where was I last night?"

"Laughing about my misadventure in the hay?"

"Exactly, and speaking of late night activities, young lady," she continued with mock gravitas, "your assistance to me, after hours and on your own time, has been immensely helpful. You've learned a lot about our company, our business and the way I work."

"Thank you, but I really haven't done all that much." Britt followed Mackenzie's lead and sat on the other end of the sofa.

"I'll be the judge of that." Mackenzie broke off a ladylike pastry bite. "I sensed that first long night that you had 'legs' and could climb the ladder in this company, if that's what you want to do. I actually wanted to promote you sooner, but Manny told me you were in the midst of a major project, something about electronically archiving our files."

Britt licked the tip of her index finger and stabbed at a stubborn croissant crumb on her skirt. "We were running out of space, and archiving electronic—" She stopped in mid-word and her eyes snapped open. "You're *promoting* me?"

"Don't look so surprised," said Mackenzie. "You're moving up to this floor. You'll report directly to me. I've found space for you. Right now it's a glorified broom closet, but building services promises it will be a presentable office by the end of the week. Technically, you're on Mahogany Row—more or less across from me—but you'll be on the inside of the hall. Sorry, I don't have a window for you yet, but I'll have it furnished very nicely."

"I really don't need an office," BJ protested. "I can work from the desk I have."

"You *need* an office. You'll be handling some confidential information. What I don't have for you is a proper title. I was going to make you 'Special Assistant to the CEO,' but that makes you a glorified secretary, and the one I have would be very unhappy. So, for lack of something better, you are Collingwood & Company's first 'Corporate Programs Executive.' I have no idea what that means, but it sounds like it qualifies you for an office near mine on the Row."

Britt wondered if Mackenzie heard the rattle of her cup and saucer as she lifted them from the coffee table to her lap. *I should have kept the paper cup with the lid on,* she thought, watching the coffee slosh over the edge of her cup. "I don't know what to say, except, thank you. Thank you."

"You might ask about the money. Effective Monday, your salary is one hundred, fifty-six thousand dollars—three thousand a week, plus bonus. Your bonus is guaranteed to be at least forty-four thousand dollars. So, you will make at least two-hundred thousand a year."

Britt was stunned. "Two-hundred thousand a year! They'd never believe this back at the grain elevator."

"Two hundred is not that much on Wall Street, but together we can enhance that bonus, so you're not in Kansas anymore, Toto."

Britt smiled at Mackenzie's shop-worn joke.

"Your days of toiling in blissful anonymity in Manny's little sheltered workshop are over. I need to warn you, as a female, you'll be under the microscope of everyone in the company now. This business barely tolerates women. It destroys pussies."

CHAPTER 12

Mossad Headquarters
Herzliya 28 July

Dark, puffy circles under the woman's eyes were mute testimony to the rigors of compressing three years of medical school into six months of ten-hour days, while learning about the global public health projects of *Les Medecins San Frontieres*.

"You've done well, Dr. LeDeoux," said Jock Ayalon in fractured French.

"Merci," said Hélène Seiderman.

"The day after tomorrow, you fly to Dublin on your personal passport. A British passport will be delivered to you at your hotel. The next day, you fly to London, then take the Eurostar train through the Chunnel to Paris, where Dr. Adrienne LeDeoux gets a French passport. From Paris you fly to Ankara, Turkey, as Dr. LeDeoux, of Doctors Without Borders. Hélène Seiderman will now have effectively dropped off the face of the earth, but Dr. LeDeoux is going to eastern Turkey, where Doctors Without Borders has been working with victims of last year's earthquake. In Ankara, you'll buy a bus ticket to Rayat in Eastern Turkey. A smuggler, who's been reliable in the past, will take you across the Iranian border, near Tabriz, with a truckload of medical supplies. Route 3 is the major truck route from Turkey south to Tehran. It can be a four-day trip, but the point of entry up there lacks the sophisticated technology at Imam Khomeini airport in Tehran. Dr. LeDeoux's French passport will have a ten-day tourist visa for Iran. That's the easy part."

Ayalon picked up a sealed manila envelope from his desk and stared at his agent, so young and fresh six short months ago. "Here is your list of contacts and the location for your first dead-drop. You must memorize everything in here, then burn it before you leave Israel. We arranged a meeting for you with Dr. Arash Hamdi, Dean of Public Health at Tehran University of Medical Science. We hope you can get him to give you a broad view of government health programs including prisoners. That may give us a clue where they're holding the general."

She nodded seriously. She looked five years older but seemed excited, not frightened.

"You've been rehearsing your legend," he said. "I'm told you're very convincing."

"I hope so, sir."

"I've seen the travel documents created for you. They're very well done. The deputy director of technology will go over each piece with you, one by one. His name is Rafi Herzog."

"I've heard the name," she said, averting her gaze. "Not sure if we've met."

"No matter. He will find you. He set up the interview by sending a bogus email from the deputy minister of health telling the good doctor Hamdi to cooperate with you fully. He's really quite good. He'll send everything by diplomatic pouch to Paris. We can't risk having them found on you in case you get selected for a random search somewhere along the way. Are you scared, Seiderman?"

"A little, sir."

Jock looked at her for signs of fear. Darting eyes. Beads of sweat. Trembling. "Only a little?"

"A lot." Hélène took a deep breath. "Terrified, actually."

"Good. Stay that way. Only a fool would not be. If you weren't, I would cancel the mission and fire you for stupidity. If you get caught, there's no way we can help you. You realize, if caught, you will be tortured for information, raped as an article of faith, then executed?"

"As an article of faith?" she said, cocking her head to one side.

"The Shia, at least the Shia who run that country, say an executed virgin goes straight to heaven as a martyr. They want the women they execute to go to hell."

"I'm not a—"

"They will make sure of that." Ayalon looked for a reaction, seeing none he moved on to the next topic. "You know your objective, but do you know the definition of success?"

"Successfully completing my mission, sir."

"Wrong. Most operations fail. What's a passing grade these days in college?"

"Depends," she said. "Probably seventy-five."

"If we ever get even seventy percent of the intelligence we're after, that officer is getting a medal. Success is getting in and getting out alive, so we can fail again. Fail enough times and we'll get a few successes. Do you understand me?"

"But—"

"One more thing," he said, ignoring her. "There is still a substantial Jewish community in the north end of Tehran, even a synagogue practically in the shadow of Evin Prison, the most likely spot for him to be held. We have legacy contacts in that community. An old source there gave us the name of Dr. Arash Hamdi."

"An Iranian Jew with the name Arash Hamdi?" Hélène rolled her eyes. "He sounds Persian through and through."

"He is. He is also the chief of medicine for the nine exclusive hospitals operated by and for the Revolutionary Guard. If Yoni, excuse me, General Abramowitz, has been treated in one of them, he will know. He is expecting Dr. LeDeoux."

"If he's willing to see me," asked Hélène, "why not just have whoever set up the meeting ask the question?"

"He's willing to meet Dr. LeDeoux and hoping Dr. LeDeoux can arrange an invitation for him to speak at a medical conference in Paris, or anywhere outside Iran."

"Can I promise that?"

"Of course you can. You can promise him anything you think will work." Jock patted the manila envelope lying on his desk. "It's all in here."

"Some of those legacy contacts have or had mid-level government jobs but we have to assume they have been co-opted. I wouldn't even trust the rabbi. If you're at all suspicious, he may report you just to stay out of prison himself." He handed her the sealed manila envelope.

"If you think you're in trouble, somehow get to the South African Embassy. Your code phrase is 'DeBeers diamonds are flawed.' That should get you inside. Then we can try to figure a way to get you out. I don't think I need to repeat what will happen if you are caught."

The young woman looked across the desk, straight into Jock Ayalon's eyes. "Sir, may I ask a question? Do you give every new agent this same pep talk before she leaves?"

Slowly the spymaster's mouth curled upward. "I'm beginning to see why we recruited you. Rebekah Chayat saw a lot of herself in you."

* * * *

Later that evening, Hélène picked up the house phone in the lobby of the King David Hotel, once again, and called Room 413. Five minutes later, she knocked on the door. "Dr. Adrienne LeDeoux, I presume," said Herzog before taking her in his arms and kissing her.

"I've missed you," she said.

"Me too, but I have a lot to show you." He gestured toward the dining table nearly covered with documents from passports and used airline boarding passes to restaurant matches and laundry receipts. "This will all be delivered to you along the line. There's a lot to go over if we're going to have any time for us."

She fingered a few prominent items—a French passport and drivers license, medical notes from an actual severe malnutrition program run by Doctors Without Borders, and copy of an article from the society page of *Le Monde*, the major French newspaper. "What's this?"

"I'll go over everything after dinner. Before it's delivered, why don't you take a shower and slip into something more comfortable?"

"Will you take one with me?"

"I'd better be here for the waiter."

He listened to her humming in the shower and smiled.

Dinner was waiting under keep-warm covers on the room service cart as she emerged from the bathroom wrapped in a large towel. "I'm especially proud of this." He handed her what appeared to be a three-month-old clipping from LeMonde, France's largest newspaper. It featured a picture of Hélène, identified as Dr. LeDeoux, at a Paris fundraiser for *Medecins Sans Frontieres*. She was pictured between the former French president and his supermodel wife, who had in fact attended the actual event, honoring a real doctor for her heroic work.

Hélène's evening dress featured a plunging neckline so daringly revealing that even the supermodel first lady appeared taken aback, despite the fact that her own nude photos were readily available on the Internet.

"I don't even own an evening dress," said Hélène, "nor would I be seen in one like that if I did."

On second thought, that's exactly what I would wear if I didn't want some Iranian security agent studying my face. And if he did look at this picture, my face is not where he'd be looking.

"If anyone Googles you, this will be one of the first items they find. We embedded it in the *Le Monde* site. Of course, if they happen to have an old copy of the actual paper, you won't be in the picture with the president."

She could not hide her amazement that he could be so clever.

"Then again, you never attended the Sorbonne or McGill University Medical School, either, but their computers now spit out complete transcripts for you, for a twenty-five dollar fee. By the way, you struggled with chemistry but," he extended his hand and slowly undid the towel where it was tucked together above her breasts, "in anatomy you were A-plus."

"I still am," she said, wrapping her arms around his neck as the towel slipped to the floor.

CHAPTER 13

New York City
06 August

The newly minted junior executive threw herself into her job with a missionary's zeal, often working directly with, or on projects specifically for, Mackenzie. She occasionally worked with some of the other investment bankers. Her favorite assignment was sitting in on the in-house reviews of deal pitches that were about to be presented to prospective clients.

She didn't make many friends during the first weeks in her new role. She usually sat behind Mackenzie in the row of chairs along the wall, in the huge conference room, listening to rehearsals of client presentations. In her smiling, unassuming manner she would decimate a business pitch and excoriate the banker making it with her simple, self-effacing "down home" questions that sliced through boilerplate fluff like a cutting torch. "I'm just a farm girl from Kansas," often prefaced her question, "so would you simplify that for me just a little so I could explain it to the boys back at the grain elevator?" She didn't say those grain elevator "boys" lived or died every day hedging the corn, soybean and wheat crops in their silos against orders in hand and what they expected to come in with the next harvest.

Her agricultural business degree, that Manny Klein so charmingly discredited, included required courses in Commodity Markets and Hedging Commodity Futures. She never had any money to risk trading futures but she absorbed more than a passing knowledge about futures and derivatives.

"We're not just trading paper," her boss at the grain elevator used to say. "Those little pieces of paper flying around the New York and Chicago Mercantile Exchanges are food—bread or hamburger on somebody's table. If the price of that winter wheat future contract is too high, someone in a third world country will go hungry; too low, and the farmer can't afford to grow the stuff, then we all go hungry."

"So we're trading real food, real bullets," she'd asked.

"Of course, flying paper is merely a metaphor. The trades are all electronic."

Although Mackenzie Collingwood's name was on the building and the letterhead, she had the sense and sensitivity never to humiliate the rainmakers who made her and her firm so much money—especially when BJ did such an excellent job of it. Mackenzie hid her smile as she watched her protégé make some of the firm's most powerful, pompous windbag bankers fumble and "fummph" like sputtering old tractors.

Britt's aw shucks, homespun questions were no laughing matter to several senior partners. Whenever Britt would start a question with "I'm just a farm girl...", everyone knew what was coming. "Could you explain to a little old Midwestern farm girl those subprime-mortgage credit-default swap things we're selling our clients?" she asked one whose grandiose title was longer than his name or the company's name combined: Senior Executive Vice President, Derivative Strategies.

"I really don't think you would understand," he said, dismissively turning his back on her.

"If you can't explain it, maybe you don't understand it either," she shot back. "And that worries me. That should worry all of us."

Brad O'Malley, one of the "baby rainmakers" as Mackenzie called them, leaned his chair back against the wall and looked at Britt with an impish grin, then hid his face behind a leather-bound portfolio to keep from laughing outright. He was a standout in the junior corps of young, hotshot MBAs who sat along the walls of the conference room behind the senior dealmakers. Britt had to look away before his conspiratorial smile and dancing eyes would make her look like she was enjoying her job too much.

The senior partners complained to Mackenzie, "You've made that country bumpkin a one-woman profit-prevention department," but Britt was beginning to understand the pillars of power: authority, influence and access. She had none of the first; a little of the second; but plenty of the third, especially during her late night dinners where no one could rebut her. Her unique after-hours access to the CEO meant she could talk to Mackenzie like no one else.

Following one of those dinners, Mackenzie walked into the office the next morning and ordered that the firm divest all subprime holdings and credit default swaps and stay clear of them. Partners raised fierce objections. They knew only BJ could talk Mackenzie into such a radical decision, but the order was carried out—just in time.

As iconic names like Lehman Brothers and Bear Stearns disappeared from Wall Street, Collingwood & Company emerged as a small but profitable luminary in the financial industry. Mackenzie became an internationally sought-after star. Britt never claimed credit for what she'd done and few acknowledged her role, but Mackenzie knew.

So did Brad O'Malley. He was also the first of the young guns to begin showing up in Britt's little office, when none of the older bankers would notice, to preview his pitch in private before the formal in-house review. Her questions were just as piercing when asked in private, but then the young presenter could make revisions. Sometimes he needed a couple of trips to "Britt's woodshed," as some called it, but at the formal review even "the boys back at the grain elevator" would approve of the crux of the deal.

Britt liked Brad. He was brawny, on the stocky side, like a hockey goalie, but he always wore a Brooks Brothers or Paul Stewart suit. If he took off his jacket, his French-cuff shirts were sleekly tailored with no excess cloth flapping around the middle. His ties hung exactly to his belt buckle, not an inch below nor an inch above; his shoes, Bruno Maglis, always perfectly shined.

They were often the last two people left in the conference room. So as Britt gathered up her papers, she was not surprised Brad was only now closing his laptop.

"You always make a very good case for going after a company or not," Britt told him after everyone else had left. "You always seem to have the best handle on a target company's strengths and weaknesses, its competition, its management team, the whole nine yards—even if you do get a little highfalutin sometimes." She winked.

"I can't take all the credit for that," he said, "but thank you. I learned being thorough pays off. A few years ago, I latched onto a piece of very sophisticated, extremely expensive business intelligence software. It's a spinoff of the intelligence software used by the Mossad.

"The who?"

"Israel's CIA," he said. "Have you ever read any of Daniel Silva's books? They're stay up all nighters. Anyway, I talked the firm into buying the program—a million-plus a copy back then—when nobody had ever heard of it or the company that made it. Then we took the company public and it shot into the stratosphere."

"And that would be, don't tell me, Google."

Brad waved away the idea. "In a way, it's more than Google and it's less. It's the commercialized cousin of the stuff the CIA, the FBI, the Mossad and several other intelligence organizations use to track all kinds of things."

Britt sat back down. "And you know this how?" Her voice edged toward her explain-this-to-the-boys-back-at-the-grain-elevator timbre.

"I had friends in a previous life who follow this stuff pretty closely. Before I stuck my neck out and said we absolutely had to buy it, I asked them if they thought any software in commercial business intelligence could do everything this thing was rumored to do. They laughed at me, but they said they'd take a look."

"What did you see?" *Who are they?* she wondered.

"They were shocked that it was ever allowed to come to market. They found the root kernel, the master architecture, is almost identical to the data mining software of our own national intelligence agencies."

"I'm sorry. What did you used to do in that 'previous life'?"

"I worked for the government."

That would fit with that high and tight military haircut. His blond crew cut was more truck driver than trader, but she was OK with that. *With a decent haircut, he would be flat-out handsome.* She could ignore the hair, or lack thereof, and focus on the blue eyes and that slightly conspiratorial smile. Those were hard to turn away from. "So you did data mining for the FBI or something?"

"I worked for the GOVernment." That would be all the explanation needed if Britt had grown up inside the Beltway instead of in the Corn Belt. "If I told you, I'd have to kill you." He winked as he sat down cater-corner from her at the big conference table.

"You're so melodramatic." *Even if you said that with a straight face, I still wouldn't believe you.* "I just asked what you did."

"And I just told you, I can't tell you. So ask me another question."

She nudged her papers into a slightly neater pile. *Maybe he's not kidding.* "OK. What does your magical, expensive software tell you that Google can't?"

"Actually, it tells you less. Google can drown you in information. Raw data, we call it. Business intelligence software breaks down that information, then stacks it back up in neat piles comparing apples to apples."

"It separates the wheat from the chaff, as we say in Kansas?"

"I thought they said that in the Bible."

Did I just get slammed? Then she saw that impish grin. *Maybe not.*

"OK, the Bible said it first, but we say it more often in Kansas. It's what we do there. You know, nation's breadbasket and all."

"Speaking of breadbaskets, you look like a girl who could use some lunch. I'll buy."

In more than six months she'd rarely eaten lunch away from her desk. In her new job, she had even less time. *Did I just get invited out to lunch?* "Could the girl share her sandwich with you at her desk and have you explain more about this stuff to me.

"What kind of sandwich? I hate baloney."

"This girl would never try to feed you any baloney."

"If you promise no baloney," he said, picking up his laptop, "I'll be back at your office at twelve-thirty and I'll bring Starbucks."

Thirty minutes later Brad tapped on the woodwork framing Britt's open door, carrying a cardboard tray holding two Frappuccinos and a deli sandwich in a white paper bag .

"My sandwich not good enough for you?"

"I just didn't want you to starve on half a sandwich," said Brad

"Whadja git?" she asked, exaggerating her Midwestern accent. "I'll go hav-zies."

He cocked his head and wrinkled his nose, enjoying a playful side of her never seen in the conference room.

"You wouldn't like mine."

"Come on. Whadja git?"

He took the two cold drinks out the cardboard tray and put one in front of her. "Baloney."

Surprised, Britt giggled, followed by a Bronx cheer. She stuck out her tongue, then smiled warmly as Brad pulled up a chair right opposite her.

He took a bite out of half of his bologna sandwich and pushed the white deli paper with the remaining half across the desk. She studied his hands; clean as a surgeon's, nails manicured, buffed, not polished. *That would never go over in Abilene,* but she liked it. Everything about him was squeaky clean, pressed, starched, creased and crisp. *I'll bet you could eat off his kitchen floor.*

"So what do Google or business intelligence do differently from national security software?"

"They both do data mining," Brad said. "Google can give you mountains of geo-political trivia piled so high you can't see over it, around it or through it."

His face showed his exasperation with conventional searches. "Commercial business intelligence software sifts those mountains into little foothills of interesting, informative stuff with a few nuggets of really insightful information sprinkled on top. We hope."

He put down his half-eaten sandwich at the same time she reached for hers. Their hands grazed, setting off a pleasant tingle up her arm.

He pretended not to notice, but something unexpected had flared within him. "National security intelligence software grabs those nuggets," he said, glancing away, "then burrows inside those foothills. Techies say 'drill down,' until it sees specks of information invisible to the human eye, or commercial data bases, and connects those specks into a mosaic picture that's fuzzier than a color-blindness test. It refines that mosaic into a wispy, impressionist watercolor. Then the analysts step in and paint sharper lines through it."

BJ nodded and took a sip of her drink. He responded with a bemused look. *He's such a perfect gentleman on the outside,* she thought, *almost too perfect.* "Then we dispatch Jack Bauer or James Bond. Defuse a few bombs, bed a few pretty women and presto, problem solved. Right?" She was playing with him.

"Not exactly. In a perfect world, the analysts paint the picture as actionable intelligence to the section and division chiefs and hope they take action. Which, of course, they may not because they've all been in headquarters too long and are too wrapped up in office politics to make a decision. And if they do, the lawyers may overrule them anyway."

"Politics," said BJ. Her inflection said, "What else is new?"

"Of course, if any of the bad guys could tap into that, their analysts can decipher a mosaic pretty well themselves. Then they know what we know, and more importantly, they know what we *don't* know. So now they're smarter than we are."

What bothered her was how he knew all this stuff and what he did—or still does with it? "How do you know the software we've got is Israeli national intelligence software?"

"That's the interesting part. We funded the start-up and did the IPO for the company that developed it. Actually, it was really just one woman who's responsible for it, Colonel Rebekah Chayat, a former Israeli intelligence officer."

A chill ran up Britt's spine as she thought of the snippet of conversation she'd heard down the hall. "I've met her!" she said. "Mackenzie introduced us in her office one day."

"Then you know all about her."

"Not really. Mackenzie called her a great friend, a very important client and said she used to be a spy, only she spelled 's-p-y.' Then the two of them left for some meeting. Rebekah was infuriated, told Mackenzie she talked too much." Britt was still shocked by that. "You don't tell Mackenzie she talks too much."

Brad chuckled. "You can if you're our most successful IPO client. We saw to it that her company is incorporated in the U.S., even though her propeller heads write all the software code in Israel." Brad took a sip of his Frappuccino and began stuffing his sandwich wrapper back in the deli bag. "Then we did the public offering."

"That still doesn't mean she sells, or we have, national security intelligence software."

"People that have access to the real thing say her commercial version, Intellitekk, is almost the exact same software used by the Israeli intelligence services. Releasing that software commercially should have been illegal, and it would have been if the CIA, the NSA, the FBI, the Mossad and who knows what other agencies were on their toes."

"What went wrong there?" She took the paper bag from him and put it in the wastebasket under her desk. "Were you involved in that?"

"Someone—a lot of people—dropped the ball." He scoffed at the idea that he personally could have been to blame. "I was already here. Somehow, the colonel got her commercial version patented and the product to market before her government or ours realized what it was. Now it's out, legally, and it's so damn good all they can do is embargo it for sale to non-NATO countries like Russia, China and all the Yucky-stans."

"So you're telling me, we use CIA software to decide if we underwrite merging a pair of grocery store chains." She rolled her eyes skyward as she stuck the drink straw between her lips. "Yeah, right."

Brad leaned back in his chair and rocked one hand left, then right. "There's really not much difference in spying on a company or on a country. The skills are very transferable. Luckily, in business intelligence, a lot fewer people want to shoot at you."

"There's a perk, if I ever heard one," she said with faux enthusiasm. She couldn't imagine people wanting to shoot at her. "Two weeks' vacation and fewer people want to shoot at you. Apply within."

"Mackenzie and the colonel probably shared other perks," Brad remarked dryly. "They became good friends—very, *very* good friends—if you know what I mean. So Mackenzie rolled the dice on her, big time."

"What's wrong with that?" asked BJ. She knew Mackenzie could be stubborn but she wasn't reckless. *How much money was he talking about?*

"It wasn't all Mackenzie's money. Many of the partners complain privately it was way too big a roll of the dice, but she never asked them. She just did it. In the end, it paid off big time for everyone. The deal made a ton of money for Mackenzie and for the firm. If the colonel isn't a billionaire yet, she's halfway there. That's a lot better than her Army pension."

"Ya think?" said Britt.

Brad's smile showed his appreciation for her. "A real life GI Jane—the first female reconnaissance-intelligence officer in the *Sayeret Mak'tal.* She was a recruiting poster girl for the Israel Defense Forces."

"What's the *say-it-again-Sam* or whatever you called it?"

Brad repeated the name, adding, "That was the outfit that rescued a hundred hostages in Uganda, in 1976, from a hijacked Air France flight."

"Oh, come on, she's way too young for that."

"She wasn't there, but that unit is *the* elite intelligence-commando unit in the Israel Defense Forces, the IDF, and a stepping stone into the Mossad or Shin Bet. One day her recruiting posters came down, and she was never publicly seen or heard from again. But her reputation grew larger than life—a computer whiz, a master of disguise, and a trained assassin. She was called the 'Tip of the Spear.'"

"So she multi-tasks, like every other woman." *Score one for our side,* she thought with the hint of a smirk. "She's got to have some sort of public face. She's a billionaire CEO of a publicly traded company."

"She keeps a very low profile—so low, in fact, that her lack of visibility really hurt our syndicating her IPO. That's one reason Mackenzie stepped up at the last minute and took such a huge risk for the firm."

"What was the other?"

"I know she's your friend," he said, shifting uneasily in his chair, "but a lot of people believe there was more than a straight business relationship between the two, if you know what I mean."

Britt bristled. "Are you suggesting Rebekah seduced Mackenzie into underwriting her IPO?"

"Only two people on the planet know that for sure, but the rumor has been repeated so many times it has taken on the imprimatur of common knowledge."

"More like common gossip—or slander!" Britt was not about to see her beloved benefactor trashed. "This whole story is a crock, isn't it?"

"Look," said Brad, pushing back from the desk and raising his hands in innocence, "some of her exploits may never have happened, but they've achieved urban legend status in the intelligence community."

"Yeah, like seducing Mackenzie. I know Mackenzie. That is so not happening."

Brad wondered if he'd pushed too hard. "I didn't say who seduced whom. Besides, you did it."

Britt dropped her sandwich. Her head snapped up as she shot a withering glance across her desk.

"You have Mackenzie eating out of your hand," Brad pointed out. "You know they call you 'Water Walker' behind your back because as far as Mackenzie is concerned, you can do no wrong."

"You...you..." She stopped herself before saying something she would regret to the only person, except Mackenzie, who had shown any interest in her as a human being. She gathered up her dignity and her best Kansas twang. "You know, back at the grain elevator, Brad, we have a saying about the difference between work boots and wingtips."

"And that would be?"

"With work boots the bullshit is on the outside."

CHAPTER 14

Mossad Headquarters
Herzliya 09 August

Jock Ayalon threw the inch-thick report on his desk for anyone to pick up. "If everyone has read this and we're all in agreement, I'll have him sent in." He studied the faces of Natan Levi, the Director of Science and Technology; his deputy, Rafi Herzog; and the director of internal security. "Herzog, you don't look happy. Do you object?"

"Not specifically, sir, I just don't see an upside. My other specialists have found no evidence of improper entry or intrusion. I've been checking myself and find no reason to believe it ever happened. At worst it may have been a benign hacker who wanted bragging rights in the underground community."

Jock looked around the room. Rafi's boss, Natan Levi, was noncommittal.

Making a give-me-more hand gesture, Jock motioned for Rafi to continue.

"Schedule-wise, I'm covering everything, so I could reallocate his salary for other things. Specifically a bigger travel budget for conferences, because there are a lot of things happening out there."

This time the Director of Technology, a political appointee with his eye always on the budget, nodded slightly. "So you vote no, Levi?" asked Jock.

"Well, not exactly no, sir. I was just saying it's always good to have a little more budget flexibility."

Jock shook his head and exhaled audibly. *Gutless political hack,* he thought. *You guys are all alike.* Jock had promised Dani a fair shot at returning, and he didn't break promises unless it was operationally necessary. "Since no one will lodge a specific objection," he turned to the Director of Internal Security, "I think you're free to go. Would you please send in young Abramowitz on your way out?"

After cursory pleasantries, Ayalon said, "Dani, a twenty-eight-week investigation and ongoing surveillance has cleared you of everything but naïveté, slash, stupidity. We know you're not stupid, and we actually need you, so your application for reinstatement will be accepted."

Dani was not contrite. "Sir, I would like it understood that I do not need a job. I have a very good job. I work for a business intelligence—"

Jock cut off Dani in mid-sentence. "We know where you work and what you do and how much money you make," he said. "I know your friend Hélène Seiderman contacted Colonel Chayat, with my permission, to get you a job at Intellitekk." He leaned forward and growled, "Now, I want you back. If necessary, I can see to it that you *will* need a job."

As he said Seiderman's name, Ayalon's thoughts flashed to his newest katsa. She should have crossed the border by now. The Turkish smuggling ring they'd used had not reported any trouble. The smuggler might not even be back in Turkey yet. But Ayalon was concerned that he'd not heard anything via the dead-drop.

"Colonel Rebekah Chayat is a legend here," said Jock. "She also knew your father. That is why you were hired, at both places."

"Sir—," began Dani.

"We monitored your progress there," said Natan Levi. "You have moved beyond the entry-level system security specialist position. You will be reassigned when you start. That will also help Rafi's budget issues."

Dani's face constricted into squared-jawed determination. "With all due respect, sir, I'd like to go back to my old job. I have some unfinished business there. Before I left, I think I discovered an intrusion."

"An intrusion?" Herzog's voice rose. "That's ridiculous. This is the most secure system in the world. I know."

"Sir," said Dani, ignoring his former supervisor and looking directly at Jock, "I guarantee you that the collective knowledge base needed to penetrate our system exists just two miles down the road at Intellitekk. It could also exist elsewhere."

"That's all I need to hear," said Jock, his mind made up. "You will return to your previous position. Reinstatement effective immediately."

Less than a week after returning to his old cubicle, Dani Abramowitz was back in the office of Jock Ayalon, flanked once again by Rafi Herzog and Natan Levi. It was Saturday afternoon, the Sabbath. Ayalon looked up from the last paper he was signing. "This better be important to drag me in here on a Saturday."

"I was supposed to be in Geneva for a conference," said Herzog, quickly adding, "at my own expense. Since I'm carrying an extra body on my payroll that I don't really need, you know my travel budget is limited."

"Herzog, quit whining," said Jock. Dani did not look up from the stack of index cards he was studying.

"Sir," began Levi, "as you will remember, Abramowitz here wanted to return to his former security specialist position because he thought he detected a system intruder before he left. I think I'll have him pick it up from there."

Dani looked up from his index cards and took a deep breath. "Where to begin..."

"In the middle would be nice," interjected Ayalon, "I don't have much time."

"Index cards?" sneered Rafi. "Surely you could upgrade to a couple of PowerPoint slides."

"Index cards don't live forever on a server somewhere," said Dani. "Index cards can't be copied with a keystroke and emailed around the world. There is no backup copy on a mirror site somewhere that you don't even know about. When I destroy them, they're gone."

"Point taken," said Jock with a nod, understanding about half of the techno-babble.

"As you know," Dani looked at his two bosses, "every encrypted incoming message from every station chief, every embassy, every intelligence agency with whom Israel shares information is logged by time, date and file size. Each is stamped with a message number." Levi and Herzog nodded. Ayalon steepled his fingers and rested them on his chin.

"Every message has its own decryption key that is sent separately in the white noise. Somewhere else, above my pay grade, those messages are matched up against their decryption keys."

"Are we near the middle yet?" asked Jock.

"Sir, I think I've found additional code sequences in the white noise that don't match up with anything. In other words, more entries than we have messages."

"What are you saying?" demanded Jock. "What does that mean?"

"It could mean an intruder is able to enter our system and come and go at will. The problem is, once they get in, they disappear. They leave no tracks, no file alterations, not even a record of a file being accessed."

"That's impossible," said Jock, glancing from one face to the next. "That *is* impossible, isn't it?"

"Well—" Rafi Herzog looked down at his watch and leaned to one side in his chair, creating as much physical space as possible between him and Dani. "Young Abramowitz here has a theory about that."

Said in the highest tradition of a take-no-responsibility bureaucrat, thought Jock. "And that is?" he demanded.

"If you'll remember, sir, when you reinstated me, I said—"

Exasperated, Jock threw down a pen on his desk. "Do I look senile?" The pen bounced off the desk and skittered across the carpet. "You people start every sentence with 'If you remember...' I don't forget conversations less than a week old! Get on with it or I'm leaving."

"Why not just take up our entire weekend?" echoed Rafi. "I'm sure no one has anything else to do."

"Sir," said Dani. "I think I've detected another intrusion."

"Intrusion? From where?" asked Rafi.

Dani looked around the room. *Just five days back and I'm about to commit career suicide. And there's no safety net this time.* "I don't know. But I do know if the people at the colonel's company put their heads together, they'd know all the pieces to our system."

"That would require a massive conspiracy," said Jock. "Not likely."

"Not necessarily. If—and I emphasize if—an original developer had written a backdoor into the program kernel, he or she could use that backdoor to re-enter the system."

"And?" asked Jock, now visibly uneasy.

"And come and go as he pleased. If the original code was written with that in mind from the very beginning, the intruder could enter the system and disappear." Trying to boil down a very complicated explanation to its simplest terms, Dani gave the example of a word processor and how it notes the last time a document was accessed. "But in this case," he explained, "the original programmer wrote the code so that whenever she entered the system through the back door, any file she—or he— looked at would re-record the same date, time stamp and user as the last time it was legitimately accessed. In other words no foot prints."

Jock looked at his two technocrats. "Who was the original developer?" Levi was taking notes. Herzog was looking at Dani and nodding slightly.

"Sir, I believe it was Colonel Rebekah Chayat."

"That was not directed at you, Dani, I was talking to the people who were here at the time. Director Levi?"

"Colonel Chayat is generally given credit for leading the project that gathers and sifts information and can make it instantly available to military intelligence, Aman; domestic intelligence, Shin Bet; and friendly powers with whom we share intelligence."

"Sir," said Dani, "did you know that Colonel Chayat's business intelligence software is amazingly similar to our own?"

"Are you saying she stole the system she designed for us for her own commercial purposes or that she's just spying on our system?" asked Jock.

"Sir, either one is possible. But she might just be keeping track of any improvements or enhancements we make so that her commercial software will stay ahead of her competition."

"Herzog was on the job during that time," Levi noted. "He certainly deserves some of the credit, sir, for what was done."

"I was just a cog in the wheel," answered Herzog, looking down at his papers, "keeping schedules and work flow charts, budgets. I never did any real hands-on design or code writing."

"Well," said Jock, "you're going to get your hands on it now, because I want you to get inside this thing and figure it out."

"Yes, sir, there's nothing to worry about. I'll take care of it."

"And," added Jock, "I want you to work with Abramowitz here. Keep me updated."

Five minutes later, Dani was smiling as he ripped up his index cards on his way to the parking lot. He threw them on the passenger seat of his battle-scarred Fiat and headed for home.

In his office, Jock switched his cell phone out of secure-scramble, Caller ID restricted mode, dialed a number and waited as the signal hop scotched from Tel Aviv to Europe, under the Channel to Goonhilly, England, the world's largest earth station, and across the Atlantic. He was about to hang up when he heard the ring tone. Too late to hang up. His number would show up as an incoming call. He might as well leave a message.

"Jock here. You still owe me a favor from Beirut. I'm sorry, but I'm calling it in. Call me."

Just as he disconnected, his phone rang. His deputy chief of operations was on the line. "We've had an asset go dark, two actually."

"Where?" asked Jock.

"Tehran."

CHAPTER 15

New York City
09 August

As her calendar grew tighter, the new Corporate Programs Executive found less and less time for her treasured one-on-one, after-hours work sessions with the boss. Those were still the highlight of her job—and her lonely life in the big city. Her favorite thing was when those late work sessions ended with "a glass of wine or three," as Mackenzie liked to say—over a late night supper, often at Le Brasserie. Big, bright and loud, it may be the most upscale late night restaurant in New York and you can almost always get a table far from anyone else.

Tonight would be different. Mackenzie had called her in the middle of the afternoon.

"I'm on my way out to a meeting, but I'd like you to meet me out front at six. I want your opinion on something. Charles will drive us. After that we can get a bite."

Later, Britt spun through the building's revolving door and wove her way between bustling homebound pedestrians just as the limousine pulled into the no parking zone in front of Collingwood & Company. Charles opened the back door for her and she slid into the seat. Mackenzie was waiting. She leaned over and kissed her protégé on the cheek. "I want to show you something, darling. I've been looking at a new apartment."

"You're moving?"

"No, no. It's an investment. With real estate the way it is, it seemed like a steal. I can rent it out, then eventually, when things go back up, sell it. I'd like your opinion on it."

Britt did not feel one bit qualified to judge Manhattan real estate, but she agreed to look.

"Eighty-fifth and Lex, Charles."

A few minutes later, the limo pulled to a halt in front of a gleaming new East Side building. A uniformed doorman held open one of the double glass doors. "Good evening, Ms. Collingwood."

"We're just going up to look at 38-B again. I have a key," she said, waving it.

"I've been advised." The doorman led the way to the express elevator and pressed 38 for them. He withdrew his hand just as the doors closed.

As they reached the penthouse floor, Mackenzie dangled the key tantalizingly in front of Britt's nose, then handed it to her.

"Go ahead. Open it."

Britt unlocked the door.

"I hope you like it or I've made a big mistake."

Britt stepped inside. "It's beautiful! I love it!"

"Let me show you around," said Mackenzie, putting her hand on the small of BJ's back and gently pressing her forward. One entire wall was glass, giving an unobstructed view toward Park Avenue and Central Park. There was a large living-dining combination and full-size kitchen with a small pantry. Then she took BJ's hand and led her toward the bedroom. Another glass wall looked south toward the Fifty-ninth Street Bridge and midtown. She could see the jets turning toward LaGuardia airport. The bedroom alone was bigger than BJ's apartment, a lot bigger. Mackenzie opened the bathroom door. It was huge— walk-in steam cabinet shower, Jacuzzi tub, even a bidet.

"Oh, my God! What does this cost?"

"Two," said Britt. "Two-hundred thousand! That's a steal."

"No, two million," Mackenzie corrected her, "but it's still a steal. I've offered one-point-eight and it should double in value in five years. Now how about dinner and a drink?"

"Take us to *Daniel*, please." said Mackenzie from the back of the limo. "It's just down at Sixty-fifth and Park."

Britt was about to learn that, in the foodie world, the two proprietors, legendary chef Francois Bruel and Daniel Boulud were beyond aristocracy, they were deities. Mackenzie ordered the signature black sea bass with Syrah sauce for three and had one sent to Charles in the car. Both men stopped by Mackenzie's table to ensure that she was happy. When introduced, they greeted Britt with effusive friendliness. "Any friend of Madam Collingwood is a friend of ours," insisted Daniel.

Is he speaking for the two of them, the restaurant, or is he so important he speaks in the papal "we"? wondered BJ.

As they walked to the car after dinner, Mackenzie's phone rang. "Yes!" she screamed, grabbing BJ in a bear hug and kissing her. "They've accepted the offer." She high-fived Charles as he opened the limo door for them. "We got it!"

Britt and Charles looked at each other, both wondering who "we" was.

"Your house, Ms. Collingwood?" asked the driver. "Then I'll take Ms. Jaeger home?"

"No, Charles. Ms. Jaeger is buying me a nightcap to celebrate. We'll go to her place first."

A small bomb exploded in Britt's stomach. She was sure she was going to throw up. *This woman just bought a two-million dollar glass palace without batting an eye! Now she wants to go to my roach motel. Is she just trying to humiliate me?* Sick at the prospect, she tried to think of a way, any way, to derail this fast-approaching train wreck.

In what seemed like no time, the limo stopped at her walk-up building in Alphabet City. Charles opened the door, saying he'd escort them up to Ms. Jaeger's apartment.

"I'm sure we'll be fine, Charles. Just wait in the hallway till we're in."

"Excellent, ma'am."

As they reached her fifth-floor door, Britt fumbled for her keys, then burst into tears. Turning to her boss, she sobbed, "Please, please. Don't make me show you this place. It's too embarrassing. I plan to find a new one. There just hasn't been time."

Mackenzie pulled BJ's head onto her shoulder and gently took the keys from her hand. She caressed the younger woman's brown hair for a few strokes. "With the right stylist we could do so much with this," she commented. As she opened the door, Britt could barely pull her eyes from the sanctuary of the shoulder.

"It's really no worse than I expected," assured Mackenzie, brushing the hair off her protégé's face and wiping the tears from her cheeks.

"Remember, I asked Charles to check it out after your comment that first night about not wanting to go back to your apartment. It's OK," she soothed.

"You're not shocked? Disgusted?"

"This is New York, Love. I once had a place much like this."

"You did?"

"I did, but, that was back in my rebellious, 'I'm-not-playing-the-corporate-game-with-daddy's-money era.'"

"Really?"

"Really, but thank God I outgrew that period, just as you have outgrown this charming place. Now, are you going to offer me that nightcap?"

Britt went to her cupboard and removed a box of four wineglasses she'd bought at Crate 'n' Barrel. Three were still wrapped in tissue paper. She unwrapped two and set the box and tissue paper aside, not noticing that she'd covered her blinking answering machine. She poured two glasses from a re-corked bottle of Kendall Jackson chardonnay in the refrigerator. After a couple of sips, Mackenzie asked, "Would I be terribly wrong to assume that you don't have to supervise the remodeling crew this weekend?"

"I gave them the weekend off—with pay."

Carrying her wineglass, Mackenzie took a few steps around to inspect the apartment and stopped behind Britt and wrapped her arms around her waist. "Fire them," she whispered into her ear, before lightly kissing her neck.

Britt stiffened with the kiss, but found it warm and reassuring. Though definitely not what she called "one of those touchy-feely people," BJ accepted, perhaps welcomed the tenderness of Mackenzie's affection. There was a certain comfort that came with having her hand held in the back of the limo, the caress of her hair in the office, even the goodnight kiss on the cheek or occasionally the lips. *But kissing me on the neck, like that!* She tried to step away but Mackenzie held her tight.

"You're moving to Eighty-Fifth street. I have movers coming this week."

"I'm what?"

Mackenzie spun Britt around so they were face to face. "There may be a lot of people in New York, but it can be a very small town, my dear. People figure out your address and this is not a good one." Her tone was firm, businesslike. "It's not safe. And it's not good for our image—yours, mine or the firm's. I will not have you living down here any longer."

She raised one hand to caress Britt's hair and brushed a kiss across her lips, whispering, "I care about you way too much."

CHAPTER 16

Tehran, Iran
14 August

Steamy narrow corridors and dark alleyways weave for more than six miles through Tehran's Grand Bazaar. The first Bazaaris opened their tent stalls around 4,000 B.C. In the next sixty centuries, it grew into the world's largest bazaar. But the immense oil wealth generated under the Shah, in the second half of the twentieth century, never trickled down to the merchants. Rapid industrial modernization put them on the path to extinction. In self-preservation the Bazaaris became the strongest supporters of Ayatollah Khomeini's revolution, to reclaim the sixteenth century. Today the Grand Bazaar is a bastion of support for the iron-fisted ruling mullahs. For a female Israeli intelligence officer, this was the belly of the beast—the least logical place Muhammad Ali-Albadi's Revolutionary Guard agents would look. That was exactly why Hélène Seiderman's dead-drop location was in the Grand Bazaar.

She melded in with hundreds of other younger women wearing a loose-fitting, figure-hiding coat to the knees with pants covering her ankles and the mandatory hijab headscarf. Most women her age did not cover their faces but she pulled the hijab down almost over her eyebrows and added thick black-framed uncorrected glasses. She wished for dark glasses, but in the dimly lit alleyways of the bazaar they would draw attention. She walked down the jewelers corridor, stopping to look at rings and necklaces in several stalls. *What was it like here when the Shah was in power and Iran was rich?* she wondered. *Because this stuff is mostly junk.*

At the junction of the jewelry, cookware, fabric and rug corridors, a uniformed security guard watched passersby. *He's staring at me.* She was sure, but he turned away and strolled toward another corridor.

In the August heat, rivulets of sweat dripped from her underarms, down her ribcage. Someone jostled her from behind. She turned quickly to look back over her shoulder. Then she was bumped from the left side. Her head snapped that direction. It was not an accident. A man in an open-collared shirt was walking the same direction and leaning into her. She sidestepped to her right but another man cut off her escape route. She tried to stop suddenly, but the original jostler pressed his groin into her rear, pushing her forward. Then a fourth man stepped in front of her, obscuring her vision and hiding her from the surrounding crowd. She felt hands on her hips from the man behind. He controlled her speed and direction, steering her through the crowd.

Two more men appeared and took up positions at ten o'clock and two o'clock, effectively blocking any view of her by other shoppers. Then she felt a hand slide from her hip around her front and into her coat, cupping her mons.

"Non! Monsieur, s'il vous plait," she said in a loud whisper, as his other hand moved to her bottom. From behind, another hand invaded her coat to maul her breasts. The fondling and groping grew more aggressive as the men realized she was protected by at least three layers of fabric—her shirt and the layered cups of her slightly padded bra.

"Ceci a tort, monsieurs, s'il vous plait." This is wrong, please. But the assault continued as they pushed her down the corridor, all in plain sight but invisible to any passerby. They ignored her pleas, speaking in Farsi about Iranian soccer.

I could do real damage to a couple of them but I can't take them all out. I'm trapped. I can't yell for help or even make a scene. She tried to memorize her attackers' faces, their clothes. They were near carbon copies of each other—mustaches or swarthy close-cropped beards, open-collared, button-front, earth-toned sport shirts. A thousand men within the bazaar fit that description. *They never said anything about dealing with this in training.* Then just as quickly as they'd appeared out of the ether to surround her, they dispersed, still talking loudly about the goal scored the previous night by Emad Muhammad Ridha, the striker for the league-leading Sepahan soccer team, his twenty-sixth of the season.

Shaken but relieved that she'd not been exposed as an Israeli spy, she hurried toward the cookware alley. She wove her way past stalls filled with pots, pans, plates and bake ware made of brass, copper, iron and earthen pottery, and watched another cluster of men materialize out of nowhere, like a school of piranha, surrounding and pinning their prey, then grabbing and fondling their victim. Then the cluster dispersed only to reform around another target. None of these unfortunate women wore the chador. Each was trendily dressed—by Tehran standards—even allowing a wisp of highlighted bangs to show beneath their headscarves. They could have been friends or classmates of the dead girl, Neda Agha-Soltan.

Then the light bulb went on for Hélène. These were *Basijis,* the plainclothes paramilitary forces controlled by local clergy, less disciplined and regulated than national security officers, which only made them more dangerous. Their mission was to intimidate women who did not wear the chador or cover their faces.

They might even be the people who shot her dead in the street. But if they recognized me, why not just arrest me?

Near the end of cookware alley, where it wound back toward the fabric corridor, she found a stall manned by a woman selling knitting needles and yarn. She bought two of the longest, sharpest knitting needles she'd ever seen and a stout but sharp crochet hook. It could rip a man's eyeball out by the optic nerve.

She made her way to a small outdoor sitting area with a bubbling fountain. For the third time in two days she sat down on the bench she'd been told about. As promised, a bolt was missing from the third slat of the bench seat. The hole was the perfect size and place to surreptitiously drop a coded message. The system was clean, simple, effective and totally low tech, as Jock had said—ingenious, actually, and almost totally risk free. As instructed, Hélène had made her drop the first morning she was in town. The code: a green M&M meant she had arrived safely. The next afternoon there should be a reply—a yellow M&M, to proceed with mission, or a red one to abort. Her green M&M was gone but nothing had replaced it. The messenger didn't even need to know what the code meant or who it was from. All he had to do was leave that green M&M at a second dead-drop, where he would retrieve a yellow or red to drop back at the bazaar. Even if caught in the act, losing one of your M&Ms is not reason for arrest. But now, twenty-four hours later, there was still no message.

Absent a direct order to abort, she was determined to complete her first mission. She found a stall selling full-body covering chadors, bought one, slipped into a woman's WC and put it on. She resolved to return to the hotel and prepare to initiate contact, as planned. Tomorrow morning she would meet Dr. Arash Hamdi, who would cooperate fully with her, thanks to Rafi's bogus email from the deputy minister of health.

Now dressed identically to millions of conservative, subservient, covered women, Hélène actually relaxed during an incident-free, two-hour surveillance-detection route back to her hotel. As the elevator doors opened on her floor, she was envisioning a leisurely warm bath when, she stepped into the hallway and froze. Uniformed police stood at the open door to her room. She spun around to get back on the elevator but two machinegun-armed cops blocked her way as the doors closed.

CHAPTER 17

Genève Aéroport
Cointrin, France 14 August

Lufthansa flight 3664 touched down at Geneva International Airport, just five kilometers northwest of the Swiss city, inside the French border at Cointrin. One of the best-designed passenger facilities in the world, its designers planned a walking distance from plane to train that is no more than two hundred meters. Passengers can clear entry formalities and be in the city center less than forty-five minutes after touchdown. The French-speaking city was one of Mr. Hu's favorite stops. He loved the sparkling lake from which the city took its name and the temples of neoclassical architecture, and most of all, he loved that he had never had to do any wet work in Geneva.

A fifteen-minute ride on city bus #10 dropped him in the center of town on the hectic Place Bel-Air on the Rive Gauche. A short walk up Rue du Commerce toward the river brought him to the prestigious business addresses of the Rue du Rhône.

Hu Wang-Chien, conservatively attired—in dark suit, white shirt, circular horn-rimmed glasses and a grey fedora covering his stylishly cut hair—frequently took this route to visit a different temple at Rue du Rhône 8.

Mr. Hu was the favorite courier of China's Ministry of State Security, Second Bureau—foreign intelligence. There were three reasons why this young man, born in a Chinese prison, was the *Guóanbù's* most valued agent: he had proven himself to be totally reliable; no nation's counterintelligence service had identified him as a Chinese agent; and traveling under one of several false passports—this day, Canadian citizen Hubert Wayne Church—he could shuttle between the great cities of the West without a single passport control agent ever seeing anything but a successful Caucasian businessman.

To all outward appearances, Mr. Hu was a *Gweilo*—Chinese for "foreign devil." His mother, a French journalist, died during childbirth in Beijing's Tiantanghe Women's Prison. She went to China in 1970, unaware of her pregnancy, to report on the atrocities of ten million deaths and imprisonments at the height of the Cultural Revolution. Accused by radical Red Guards of spying, she was tried in a twelve-minute kangaroo court and sentenced to ten years in prison.

The birth of her male child six months after she entered prison was recorded, her death during childbirth was not.

By chance, First Lieutenant Hu Ning of the People's Liberation Army, Second Bureau—foreign intelligence, was visiting the prison the day of the birth. He was shown the Caucasian infant that was about to be disposed of with the trash. Something about his round hazel eyes mesmerized the fast-rising young officer. Plus, after two years of marriage, his wife had not conceived. He said he would "take responsibility" for the child.

His wife named the child Hu Wang-Chien. His adoptive father, now Major Hu Ning, used his connections and position to see that his son, taller and stronger than others his age, was selected for one of the special school/training camps run by the Ministry of Sport for potential elite athletes.

Ostracized as a *Gweilo* by his fellow athletes, he had only one friend, but that friend's father was a senior officer in the Ministry of State Security. He recognized that young Hu had to be tougher, better, smarter and faster at everything he did just to survive in the school—and he had to do it alone, without help and without friends. The exact qualities demanded by the *Guóanbù*.

Since his tenth birthday, Mr. Hu had been groomed to be the perfect, undetectable Chinese spy.

Carrying a black duffel bag and a soft leather briefcase, he walked into a branch of the global Swiss banking giant UBS. On this beautiful Geneva day, Mr. Hu presented a key to UBS lockbox FFN321, and the box was delivered from the vault to him in a small private room. He opened his briefcase and transferred its contents—$200,000 U.S., the usual amount—into the safety deposit box. He never withdrew any money but, if he found a CD or flash drive nestled among the banded bundles of well-circulated bills, he took that and the trip was another success. When finished, he watched the box be returned to the vault and locked in place with his key and the bank's key. With his key safely back in his pocket, he always visited the well-appointed men's room adjoining the private banking section.

No one saw the man identified as Hubert Wayne Church leave the big bank at Rue du Rhône 8. If paying attention, one might have noticed a thirty-something, American-looking backpacker with fashionably long hair but no glasses—wearing expensive hiking boots, a bicycle team shirt and Manchester United cap—leave the bank and stroll next door to 14 Rue du Rhône, the Regus Office Centre.

The young man, with the full knapsack slung casually over one shoulder, looked vaguely familiar to the building receptionist as "one of those techie guys" who worked in the small computer company office on the seventh floor. "Bonjour," he chimed over his shoulder as he passed her desk heading toward the elevators

Mr. Hu opened the door to Suite 706 and turned on the lights. The six-room suite was unoccupied. It was an instant enterprise, just add people and it looked like a flourishing start up.

He went to the small office that was his whenever he needed it, took out his laptop, and smiled as he logged into his email. His address featured the two luckiest numbers in Chinese numerology, repeated three times. He never bothered to look in the inbox. The auto-generated *Welcome to Yahoo* confirmation was still the only incoming message ever received. Instead he clicked on the saved drafts box. The only entry had a blank subject line. The note mentioned a troublesome shipping clerk whose return could endanger future scheduled shipments. But the situation could be contained if packages continued to arrive in Geneva as planned. He sighed. *Beijing would have to be informed. They will not be happy.*

He deleted the note, shut down his computer and looked out the window at the boat traffic on the river Rhône. *Maybe today was not so lucky, after all.*

CHAPTER 18

New York City
16 August

Britt was examining a set of sheets and pillow cases, late Thursday afternoon, in the living room of the thirty-eighth floor apartment. The labels read *1600-thread count Egyptian cotton* but they felt more like silk.

"Do we love it?" shouted Mackenzie from the front door after letting herself in with her own key. She carried a chilled magnum of '95 Dom Perignon Oenotheque Brut.

"I said it's magnificent," Britt replied matter-of-factly, without looking up, "but I told you I can't stay here. I can't possibly afford it."

"And I said we're not discussing that right now. We can work out the money another time," said Mackenzie.

Britt wore flip-flops, shorts and a faded t-shirt pulled tightly across her chest.

J. Alfred Prufrock's
Libations & Sustenance
Abilene, Kansas.

Did J. Alfred actually intend, wondered Mackenzie, *to lewdly nickname a woman's breasts 'Libation & Sustenance?'"*

"Does J. Alfred serve barbeque?" asked Mackenzie.

"Ye-ah," said BJ, "the best."

"Good," snapped Mackenzie, "FedEx that outfit back to J. Alfred with instructions to throw it in the barbeque pit and burn it to ashes. May I never see you in it again."

"If you don't like it, just say so," was the monotone reply.

On Monday, three days before, a battle royale had raged behind closed doors in Mackenzie's office. Britt swore that she would move out of the roach motel within the month but into something she felt she could afford on her own. Mackenzie had insisted that the money would be worked out but she wanted BJ uptown where it was safer, closer to the office and nearer her own Sutton Place condo.

There'd been more than a little swearing on both sides—a rarity for either woman. Finally, Mackenzie had looked at her watch and said, "Well, I think you've vented enough for now. The point is moot. It's five-thirty. I'm sure the movers have removed everything worth taking from downtown and should just about have all your clothes hung in the closet on Eighty-fifth Street."

"I see you found the linen closet," said Mackenzie, pointing in that direction with the champagne bottle. "There should be plenty of towels, sheets, pillow cases, bedspreads, anything you need. There are nighties and whatnot in the bedroom dresser. Did you find the dishes in the cupboard?"

"Just like you said," replied BJ, flatly. "Everything is always just like you say."

"Oh, come on. Put on your big-girl panties and stop pouting. This is not exactly Siberia. Charles's contacts tell him your old building is a human trafficking transit station—a sexual slavery depot, where girls are held before being trucked around the city for their assignments." Mackenzie unwrapped the foil around the cork as she walked to the kitchen. "When I heard that, I wanted you out of there, now. God only knows what happens to women in the basement of that place."

"I have a pretty good idea. Why not tell the police, now that I'm out of there?"

"The police *have* been told. Nothing happens. That's why I had you moved." Mackenzie opened and slammed cabinet doors like a woman on a mission. "There should be an a electric corkscrew here someplace. Greatest invention since the wheel."

A few minutes later, mission complete, with each woman carrying a champagne flute, Mackenzie led Britt arm-in-arm to the balcony railing. "Look at that sunset!" She raised her glass to Britt, "To us and a new life for us, together."

"To us," answered BJ, clinking glasses, "friends forever."

The expression on Mackenzie's face made it instantly clear that was not the response she was looking for.

Bzzrrr. "What's that?" said Britt, looking in every direction back inside the apartment. "This is the doorman, Ms. Jaeger," came the voice over the intercom. "Your Chinese food is here. Should I send him up?"

"I didn't order Chinese food," she called toward the disembodied voice.

"I did," said Mackenzie. "It's not as fancy as the Dom Perignon but I didn't think you'd want to cook. Now tell the nice man yes."

Britt walked over to the intercom and pressed the button. "Yes."

After dinner, Mackenzie dribbled the last drops of the champagne equally into each flute. "You know, I think your living room view may even be better than mine."

"Are you jealous?" giggled Britt. The surliness in her voice had disappeared somewhere between the second course of moo-shoo chicken and the fourth glass of champagne.

"What's the bedroom view like at night?" asked Mackenzie.

"I don't know. Let's go look," said Britt, rising unsteadily from the glass-topped dining room table. "I'm new here myself, you know." Another giggle.

"You *do* have a better view than mine," said Mackenzie, as they looked at the flickering lights of the city beneath them.

She pulled Britt closer and kissed her on the lips. It was a passionate, sensual kiss. At first, Britt giggled again. Then as Mackenzie's tongue began to probe, she realized this wasn't a joke. The pit of her stomach churned into a vicious swirl. She tried to push away but Mackenzie was holding her tight with one hand while running the other up under J. Alfred Prufrock's t-shirt. "No, Mackenzie. No, I'm not ready for this."

Mackenzie's kiss was relentless. Her hand was already under BJ's bra tweaking and teasing her erect nipple.

"Mackenzie, we're drunk!" said BJ, her head spinning with alcohol. "We will both be sorry about this."

Mackenzie stepped back and laughed. "You're right. We're drunk. That's not the way I want our first time to be."

"Good," said BJ, assuming that overly dignified posture that tips-off cops to get out the breathalyzer.

"Don't worry. We'll have many nights to enjoy this view," said Mackenzie, "together."

Britt said nothing and concentrated on readjusting her bra and t-shirt.

"Tomorrow morning early," continued Mackenzie, seemingly not fazed by Britt's rebuff, "we're flying to an international women's conference on a private island. You're coming with me."

"What? Where? I'm not—I can't..."

"You're babbling. There's nothing to discuss," said Mackenzie, making her way to the front door. "You're coming with Rebekah and me. Charles will pick you up at six-ten in the morning, me at six-fifteen. We'll be at LaGuardia by ten to seven and wheels up by seven-fifteen. There are women, important women, expecting to meet you." Mackenzie kissed her own palm and blew the kiss to Britt.

"What is this conference about?"

"It's about you, darling, all about you," she said, opening the door. "I'll let myself out."

CHAPTER 19

New York City
17 August

As soon as Mackenzie closed the door, Britt locked it and grabbed her cell phone. Both hands were shaking. It took three tries before she dialed all the numbers correctly.

"Brad, it's BJ. I know it's late, but I need your help—at least your advice. Mackenzie just tried to seduce me." She was panting, almost breathless.

"Just?" said Brad. "It took her until now? Everyone in the office assumed that happened a long time ago."

"Brad! I'm serious. I made her go home but I don't know what to do."

"Whatever feels good is my advice."

"Damn it, Brad, this is not funny! She wants me to go with her and Rebekah to some international women's conference in the morning."

"You're traveling with Rebekah?" He sounded urgent. "When?"

"Tomorrow morning, early. What's that got to do with—"

He interrupted, "Beej, I must see you before then. This is extremely urgent. It can't be done over the phone. I absolutely must see you tonight."

* * * *

Britt wished she'd never called Brad because now everything had changed. Here she was in his apartment at one in the morning and her perfect gentleman wasn't so perfect anymore. He'd asked her to violate her most basic tenets of honesty and trust. Worse, she was close to agreeing.

She was on the mend but not quite totally sober when she had met Brad a little after eleven at L'Express, an all-night hidden jewel in the Flatiron district. She didn't recognize him at first, reading his Blackberry in the far corner of the little bistro. He was a different person without his suit and tie.

He wore an expensive black linen pullover, light khaki cargo shorts and Italian slip-ons with no socks. She'd never seen him in short sleeves. No tattoos. He looked good casual, really good. *Don't even think about it,* she told herself. *You know you and men don't mix.*

She ordered coffee, an omelet and toast. *Maybe that will soak up the last of the champagne.* Brad ordered a club soda. That should have been a tip off. The omelet came quickly. They made small talk, while BJ downed the omelet just as quickly, and Brad asked for a check.

"That was very good, thank you, but what is so important that I had to meet you here right now and then all you do is make small talk."

Brad laid a few bills on the table, enough to cover the check and a generous tip. "I can't discuss it here but if I said 'come up to my place,' I was afraid you'd get the wrong idea."

"Go to your place now? It's midnight. I'm being picked up in six hours."

"This is extremely important and extremely confidential."

Reluctantly she climbed into a taxi. Brad gave the driver his address. His leg brushed her thigh and she jumped, her instinctive response was to move away, but he reached over and took her hand. "I need to repay a very big favor and I need your help."

The mere touch of his hand sent a warning shiver through her, his gentleness throwing her off balance. *Don't be stupid,* she lectured herself. "What can I do?"

They both noticed the cabbie's eyes studying them in the rearview mirror.

"Not now." She had to lip read Brad's words. "When we get to my place." He squeezed her hand. She looked at him quickly, questioningly. Only then did she realize she'd been squeezing his. *Don't be stupid,* she repeated to herself and pulled her hand free.

Her eyes recorded everything about his apartment, as he poured freshly made coffee into mugs and placed a bottle of French vanilla flavored "plastic cream" on the coffee table. His place looked like a page out of an interior design magazine. Everything was in its place and as spotlessly clean as she had imagined.

"Beej, I hate doing this. It's one of the reasons I got out, or at least one of the things that made the decision to get out easier."

"Got out of what?" Britt sniffed the creamer and crinkled her nose, then poured some in her cup. "You keep talking about old friends in the government and now this mysterious favor. What does your repaying that have to do with me?"

"When I was in Beirut," he continued, "an op went bad. There was an explosion and—"

"I thought they had explosions in Beirut all the time." She glanced around the table until she saw a spoon then stirred the chemical cream in her cup.

"There used to be. We were usually the targets. This time it wasn't their bomb. It was ours. The mission was technically a success, but there was collateral damage."

"I watch the news." Her voice was flat, sullen. "There's always collateral damage."

"A kid was delivering something to the target house. He was still fifty yards away on his bike, but the concussion knocked him unconscious. He was bleeding from the ears and his nose. I went to help him. Next thing I knew, the target's backup security people were on top of me. I was a prisoner. They beat the crap out of me for a while. Then they turned me over to Hezbollah."

"I'm sorry." Her tone was less cold. "I'm glad you're OK. I really am but what does this have to do with me?"

"We had no agents, no contacts inside Hezbollah." Brad silently clapped his hands together then steepled his fingers under his chin. "The Mossad did have an agent inside, but to find me, they'd have to blow his cover and that would probably get him killed. The station chief, a guy named Jock, burned his agent and saved my life. Amazingly, they got the guy out of Beirut alive and gave him a new identity. But Hezbollah killed his parents, his brother, his sister, even his dog. So I owe Jock and that agent a big favor. There's no way I can repay the agent but I still owe it to both him and Jock to come through now."

I knew there was a bad chapter you weren't telling about. "Why are you telling me this?"

"Colonel Rebekah Chayat may be a spy," he said bluntly. "She may be running a backdoor through her software into Mossad computers, then tunneling back to their intelligence partners like the CIA, NSA, Britain's MI-5 and MI-6."

"You can't be serious. You told me yourself she was a legend." Britt put her face in her hands and shook her head. "I don't believe it."

"That guy Jock I told you about, he's now the number two guy in the Mossad. He needs to find out if there's any truth to that allegation and I need your help."

"So you want *me* to spy on her? Spy on our company's most important client for the Mossad?" Britt folded her arms tightly across her chest, classic body language for *I don't want anything to do with this.*

"Beej—"

"Please," she interrupted, "call me Britt. Beej is something for a few really close friends and right now I'm not sure you fit in that category. I can't believe you're asking me to do this—to spy on client for another country."

"Not for the Mossad, and not for me," he clarified, "but critical to both countries. If she's using her software to infiltrate the Mossad, the damage potential is incalculable for every Western nation that shares intel with the Israelis. That's basically all of us."

"Why would she do that?" She looked for a hint of that impish grin, some sign, a clue, anything to indicate this was all a bad joke. Nothing.

"People change. They get manipulated, get greedy, blackmailed, you name it. It happens, believe me."

She took a sip of her coffee and stared into the mug for a moment, then set it back on the table. "What do you want from me?"

Brad opened a drawer under the coffee table and pulled out miniature, hotel-sized bottles of Dove shampoo and conditioner and set them on the table.

"Do I look that bad?" asked Britt.

"You look fantastic but they're not for your hair. Open one." Without waiting for her, he picked up the conditioner bottle and twisted off the cap, revealing a small silver plug—a USB connector.

"These are specially programmed flash drives, obviously disguised to look like shampoo and conditioner. We need you to stick them both in Rebekah's laptop with the power off. If she's got two USB ports, you can put them both in at the same time. If only one USB port, insert the shampoo first, then hit the power switch."

Britt picked up the shampoo bottle and twisted off the cap, exposing an identical USB connector. She sniffed the bottle.

Wow! Talk about Mars-Venus, thought Brad. *A guy would never think to smell that to see if it was ever a real bottle.*

She crinkled her nose and sniffed again, then screwed the cap back on, hiding the silver connector, and set it back on the table.

"That one," said Brad, pointing at the shampoo, "overrides the laptop's operating system—Windows, Snow Leopard, and some other more exotic systems. It will boot up the computer. It will also install the hard drive cloning software program."

Brad wiggled the fake conditioner bottle in his hand, then put the cap back on. "This is the target drive. The entire hard drive will be cloned onto it, up to eight hundred gigabytes. If she only has one USB port, shampoo," he picked the shampoo off the coffee table, "then conditioner. Just like real life. But the two-drive method will be much quicker."

"You're joking."

"I could not be more serious. You don't have to worry about passwords or anything else. Just make sure the laptop's turned off. Insert these then hit the on button. They'll crack the password when they're downloaded." He slid the bottles across the coffee table, closer to her.

Britt looked at them, then at Brad. "Who will crack the password?" She shook her head slightly and leaned forward to stand up. "Never mind. I don't want to know."

Brad pushed them toward her again. "It may take up to an hour. Then yank out both drives and come home." He nudged the bottles once more, making them teeter on the edge of the table. "If you don't do it, there's no telling how many innocent kids, like that one in Beirut, will die."

"He died?" She was ready to leave.

"Yeah. The guys who got me didn't lift a finger to help him."

Britt stepped toward the door, stopped, then turned around and picked up the bottles. She stared at them in the palm of her hand then dropped both into her purse. She watched Brad unclasp the safety chain on the door. "I'll think about it."

As she reached for the door knob, his arms encircled her, one hand in the small of her back, pulling her close. Her soft curves molded to the contours of his gym-sculpted body. He brushed a gentle kiss across her forehead. "Girl, 'you're amazing,' like the Bruno Mars song, "just the way you are." He kissed the tip of her nose. "Just the way you are."

"I, I have to go," she insisted, confused by her unexpected response to his kiss.

"No, you don't," he said, kissing her softly on the lips. "Stay." His kiss was slow, thoughtful, his lips more persuasive than she cared to admit. She knew, intellectually, she should step away, but she had no desire to back out of his embrace. He picked up a lock of her hair and caressed it gently, then pulled it to his lips and kissed it. "Please stay."

That's one of the sexiest things any man has ever done, she thought, his touch almost indescribable in its tenderness. She inhaled sharply.

He whispered, again, his breath hot against her ear, "stay." Her instinctive response was to back away, as his hands explored the soft lines of her waist, her back, her hips. Her nipples firmed as he pulled her to him, her breasts pressed against his hard chest. As he moved his mouth over hers, she savored the softness of his lips.

"Beej, am I allowed to call you Beej?" between each word, he made tiny nibbles up her neck to her earlobe.

She nodded, her eyes closed, "Um-huh," and for a moment she felt weightless, as if she were floating. Her consciousness seemed to ebb, then flame into an unwelcome surge of excitement.

Step away, she chided herself. *You and men don't mix.*

His lips touched hers, feather-light, but with tantalizing persuasion. "Stay."

With a low, breathy sigh, she snuggled closer, her lightheaded nod almost imperceptible. Then she felt it. Her eyes popped open. Her entire body stiffened visibly. Through the cargo shorts she felt the growing firmness of his erection.

"Beep, beep, beep," she said in her soprano squeal, pushing him back. "That's the sound of me backing away before I get burned again." She heard a faint thread of hysteria in her own voice. "This will only end badly."

"What if we don't want it to end at all?" He tried to hold her, to be reassuring but not threatening. Her body language spoke an adamant "no." He let go, as she reached for the door knob.

"It will still end badly," she said, stepping into the hall. "It always has."

"Where is it written that it has to end?" He stood in the doorway and watched her push the elevator button. *Where?*

CHAPTER 20

Tehran
17 August

"We need a war," said Ali-Albadi, "a nice, little manageable war we can win politically and at least a military stalemate."

The Chairman of Department 36, of Iran's secret intelligence apparatus, had called an emergency meeting, just hours before Friday prayers. "The presidential elections have proven to be a total disaster. Western sanctions are pushing the economy into failure. The people are turning against the Revolution. If the Zionists, in concert with the Americans, had destroyed those centrifuges with bombs it would have been an act of war. But you can't see their Stuxnet worm that sent our centrifuges spinning out of control. The Supreme Leader wants a provocation to attack.

"The American drone we captured was unarmed—not an excuse for a war. American aircraft carrier battle groups sail within meters of our territorial waters. We could call that a hostile intrusion and block the Straits of Hormuz but every Gulf-state OPEC nation would turn against us. .

"We need a provocation that our Muslim brothers will see as a justifiable reason for us to unleash our nuclear capability before the Israelis completely destroy it. Another bungled raid like Jimmy Carter's helicopter fiasco in the desert in 1980 would be a perfect excuse to attack."

An Al Quds agent stood behind an LCD projector. "To provoke the limited incident you desire, Excellency, we need to understand the Zionist trigger points—what will cause them to launch a small attack for which we can retaliate."

Muhammad Ali-Albadi tapped his big gold ring impatiently on his desk and scanned the faces of his subordinates seated around the conference table.

"Excellency, we were nearly successful in recruiting a young Mossad IT worker who could have unlocked doors for us—doors that lead to the heart of Israeli and Western intelligence systems," said the man seated to his right.

"You were 'nearly successful'? You failed miserably! He reported himself to the Mossad. They now know every detail of that operation. Two agents were compromised and you dare say you nearly succeeded?"

"But we persevered, Excellency," said the agent manning the LCD projector. "For more than six months, we kept the target under surveillance even after he returned to work at the

Mossad. We stole his mail, opened it and redelivered it the next day without a trace. We have copies of his official suspension and reinstatement by the Mossad. We have copies of an employment agreement with a company while he was suspended. We sifted though his garbage We even have copies of his payroll stubs."

"And what did this colossal waste of time and money provide?"

"Until a few days ago, nothing, but Allah blessed our perseverance. We have now learned more than we ever expected." The agent turned on the LCD projector and motioned for the overhead lights to be dimmed. Some ripped pieces of paper appeared on the screen.

"How did we come into possession of these images?" asked Ali-Albadi.

"We found the discarded remains of several index cards in his garbage only a few days ago. I apologize for the condition of these images, Excellency," said the Al Quds agent. "The cards had been ripped apart and we had to piece them back together. Not all the pieces were found. On card three," he said as the red dot of his laser pointer drew a circle around bullet points written in Hebrew down the right side of the card, "the writer outlines his evidence, or hypothesis, indicating the Mossad intelligence computer system has been or could be hacked."

"So who could have penetrated the Mossad computers?" Ali-Albadi folded his hands, intertwining his fingers, in front of his face. As the LCD projector light reflected off the screen illuminating the huge gold ring on his left hand, he answered his own question. "Only the Americans, I suppose."

"That is precisely what we thought. It had to be the Americans." The briefer's laser pointer circled the next card. "On card five, he makes a point of staggering importance. He says an intruder has entered the system without leaving any computer tracks or signature. In other words, it is impossible to tell if the system has actually been hacked."

"That has to be the Americans," said the Chairman.

"Once again, Excellency, we thought exactly the same thing. However, on card seven," he said, enlarging the image of the card to take up most of the screen, "he suggests there is a backdoor. In other words, the original code writers designed and created a secret entrance so they could re-enter the system—not unlike the Egyptian tomb builders who left themselves a way to get back inside the pyramids to steal the wealth buried with the Pharaohs."

Another card, with a jagged edge across the top, filled the screen. Written on it was a single name, "Colonel Rebekah Chayat," but the portion above her name had been torn away.

"We do know the young man worked for her software company for the time he was suspended by the Mossad, but we don't know what this card means. We think this means she designed the system or she can lead us to the designer. In either case, if we captured her we could force her to reveal the code that opens the back door or lead us to one who can. Need I say more?"

A murmur of excitement raced around the conference table. Finally the Chairman spoke once again. "Let me save you some trouble," he said, still leaning away from the reflected glow of the screen. "Colonel Chayat is probably the top female intelligence agent of the infidel Jews. She is *Kidon*, a member of their assassination squad. She personally killed at least seven freedom fighters, including my own nephew." His anger grew as he spoke. "This heathen whore lured my very own devout, pious nephew into her bed of fornication, then murdered and mutilated his martyred body. She would be the perfect target. The Zionists would definitely initiate and operation to get her back.

"For her capture and delivery to Tehran, I will personally pay a reward of one million Euros. If she has information to be extracted, Allah will have blessed us with an additional bonus. I need a plan. It is a matter of my family honor." For emphasis, he rapped the table with his gold ring, indicating he wanted the plan placed right in front of him.

"We have a plan, Excellency, that with the Prophet's blessing, we will bring the murdering Zionist whore to Tehran."

"How soon can it be implemented?"

"It is already in progress. We have an intermediary target who will lead Colonel Chayat to us. That target has already agreed to meet us in London."

"Once in Tehran," Ali-Albadi was nearly gleeful at the thought, "I can easily force information from her and manipulate the Zionists into a rescue attempt. Then we have our little war—and I have my family honor restored."

* * * *

Not far from Ali-Albadi's office, Hélène stood in her hotel hallway. Her stomach churned wildly. Her face glistened with perspiration. Her armpits were soaking. She could smell a distinct odor. It wasn't the smell that came when she ran or went to the gym. This was the smell of rank fear.

"Dr. Ledoux?" asked the officer in charge.

"*Oui.*"

His voice and mannerisms were polite, even deferential as he questioned her in Farsi.

"*Je ne comprends pas,*" she answered, looking toward her room. It had been completely trashed.

He nodded, pulled out his two-way radio, and told his headquarters he would need a French-speaking interrogator. She shuddered at the word "interrogator."

She was not allowed in her room for twenty minutes when a man in a brown suit jacket and a tan open-collared shirt appeared and showed her an official-looking ID card. She glanced at it but brushed it aside. If she tried to read it, she would reveal that she could at least read Farsi.

"*Bon soir,* Doctor LeDeoux. May I see your passport?" She nodded and fished in her purse. "As you can see, we have a problem," he continued in French, as he looked at the fraudulent document. "You entered through the Turkish border, I see," he said, thumbing through the passport. You know you have to leave the same way, but I guess you're going back to Turkey anyway."

She barely heard what he said. *What could they have found in my room?* "What happened?" she asked. What she wanted to know was, *Who turned me in? Was I spotted making the dead-drop?*

"The maids discovered this," he said. "We will need you to provide an inventory of all your personal possessions and everything you bought since entering Iran," said the detective. *Maybe this really is only a civil matter.* "We are very sorry that this should happen to such a distinguished visitor."

Nothing is as it seems. There are no coincidences, she told herself. *You're being setup.* "What happened, inspector?"

"We have thoroughly interrogated the maids," said the detective. "We do not think they had a hand in this."

I'm sure they had a pleasant experience. "Well, I didn't have very much with me, just a few things I'd bought yesterday in the bazaar, and a few more little things today."

"You like the bazaar a lot, I take it."

She surveyed the room while she tried to think of an answer. "It's very exotic." The room had been thoroughly tossed. Pillows, seat cushions, even the mattress had been cut open. Everything was gone except what she had in her purse. "They must have been looking for jewelry," she said, changing the subject rather than answer the question.

"You were traveling with a lot of jewelry?"

"I bought a little necklace in the Grand Bazaar. I tried on some more expensive pieces. Someone must have thought I bought them, then followed me back here." *Had they intercepted the two green M&Ms she'd left in the dead-drop?*

"You still have money and credit cards in your purse?" asked the detective, still in French, as he slapped her passport in his hand.

"*Oui, monsieur.*"

"*C'est bon.* The hotel will give you a new room and its insurance will take care of your losses. I need you to complete that inventory, in your own handwriting, Doctor. When we find the culprits, we need to identify your goods. Since you're a distinguished foreign visitor, you need to bring that to the Interior Ministry, Department 36. It's just a formality, but they will want to know you were treated satisfactorily and that you're fully compensated for your loss. Of course, they won't want you saying bad things about Iran when you leave. You understand."

I understand what you want is evidence in my own handwriting to use against me.

"I will be there to introduce you to the right people," the detective droned on. "Your passport will be returned then and then you'll be on your way." He handed her a card with the Interior Ministry address. "I'll see you there at eleven-hundred."

In other words, surrender in thirteen hours. They know there is no way I can get back to the Turkish border in that time. They just expect me to come in and give myself up during regular business hours. How convenient for them.

"Eleven o'clock. I will see you then, *monsieur*."

South African embassy. DeBeers diamonds are flawed, was all she could think. *In thirteen hours, I'm dead.*

CHAPTER 21

Queens, New York
17 August

In six hours, thousands of screaming fans would fill Citi Field, just across Astoria Boulevard from LaGuardia Airport, as their beloved Mets would face the Evil Empire—the hated Yankees—in a makeup game rained out in June. But at seven-twenty in the morning it was deserted as the sleek private jet banked sharply overhead to the southeast.

There were only three passengers on the twelve-passenger luxury rent-a-jet. An exhausted Britt was strapped in to the single easy-chair seat. Directly across the aisle, Mackenzie Collingwood and Colonel Rebekah Chayat faced each other over a table. She'd not slept a wink. The colonel held a cup of black coffee. Mackenzie sipped a mimosa. She raised her glass toward her protégé, "hair of the dog?" Britt did not hear or see the toast. She was looking out the window as the jet banked over the thirty-three courts of the Billie Jean King National Tennis Center below.

"Were we naughty last night?" Rebekah asked playfully.

"Bad question," said Mackenzie.

The pilot then reduced power suddenly, in a required noise-abatement procedure, and pushed the nose slightly down. Britt cupped the far side of the glass but the tropical umbrella drink of strawberries, banana and rum, sloshed into her lap, forming a small red puddle in the hollow of her skirt. *Why am I even drinking this at seven o'clock in the morning?* she thought. *It's certainly not settling my nerves.*

"You look so tense, dear," Mackenzie remarked. "I promise we won't run out of those little umbrellas before we land." Britt smiled. Until last night, Mackenzie had a gift for making her feel at ease in the worst situations.

"We should have told you these little jets take off at a much steeper angle than a commercial airliner," said the colonel.

Britt found herself staring at the woman. Outwardly she looked the same as when they'd first met, but after her midnight meeting, she would never regard her the same way. The same went for Brad.

Now the colonel seemed to be studying her in return. *I'm just imagining that,* she told herself, looking back toward the window. *Damn you, Brad,* she was thinking. *If this window opened I'd throw your Goddamned shampoo bottles out.*

"Ms. Jaeger," said the colonel, "tell me how you managed to get back on that bus after that terrible attack?"

"What? I'm sorry. Were you talking to me, Colonel?"

"It's Rebekah," she corrected. "I would really like to hear the whole story from you."

"Well, as you know..." Britt released a long, exasperated sigh. By the time she had retold the story, the colonel was out of her seat, squatting in the aisle next to her.

"Let me get this straight," said Rebekah. "You were going to scream even though some maniac had a knife in your ribs and had already threatened to skewer both breasts."

"But it wasn't a knife," protested BJ. "It was nothing more than a sewing needle taped to a ninety-nine-cent ballpoint pen."

"It was a knife as far as you knew." The colonel rested one hand on Britt's forearm. "So in the face of what you perceived as mortal danger, you took strong defensive action and screamed. Did I hear that right?"

"I never got to scream. He shoved that rubber glove halfway down my throat."

"Doesn't matter," insisted the colonel. "Facing grave danger, you risked your life to stop the assault. In my world, that is the definition of bravery."

Britt had never considered herself brave but the colonel made her feel less humiliated.

"You could have dissolved into a whimpering shell of a woman," added the colonel, "but you continued on the bus to New York. That tells me a lot. If I was still in the military, I'd want you in my foxhole."

BJ felt a flicker of pride in the way she'd handled the attack. "Maybe I just didn't have the courage to go back and tell people I couldn't even make it to New York."

The colonel stood up and patted Britt's shoulder, with an athletic, job-well-done thump. "You don't lack courage," said the Israeli, "you lack self-defense skills. When we get back to New York, I will teach you some hand-to-hand combat techniques." She then turned back to Mackenzie. "She will have no trouble getting the votes."

"Votes?" asked BJ, shaking her head warily. "What is this conference about?"

The colonel now turned toward Mackenzie with a frown. "You *have* explained what's going to happen, haven't you?"

"As I said last night," replied Mackenzie. "It's about you. We're going to Seven Sisters Island. Technically, it's a country," she explained. "We own it."

"We?" BJ inched forward in her seat. "Who are 'we?' You and the colonel?"

"Partly. About fifty years ago, immediately after Britain granted Grenada complete independence, the island was purchased by seven very wealthy women,. The name came from a nickname for the seven international oil companies that used to control the world's oil. They were called the 'Seven Sisters.' Those women had a goal, a vision, and they saw great irony in equating themselves, and their club and their island, with the seven biggest, most powerful, most female-phobic companies in the world."

"The Seven Sisters. Who are they?"

"That, my love, is a closely guarded secret. Our founders believed that women were the world's greatest undeveloped resource. If that resource could be mined and refined, nurtured and supported, then just as oil is refined and distributed, women could be pumped into the leadership pipeline of the world. They believed that would make the world a better place for everyone. We, of course, agree."

Britt was clearly intrigued by the concept. "You mean they intended to 'pump women,' as you say, into all the positions of power around the world?"

"Absolutely not," said Rebekah. "The world can ill afford to lose any brilliant, capable leaders—men or women—but if they could just prime the pump and get the best women into the right positions, let the cream rise to the top and the chips fall where they may."

"That's very commendable. Why is it such a secret?"

"Not everyone finds it so commendable, especially some men," corrected Mackenzie.

"Many men," interjected the colonel. "You've heard of the Belizean Grove. It was founded with similar intentions. Their website describes the group as *"A global constellation of influential women, who build long term mutually beneficial relationships in order to both take charge of their own destinies and help others to do the same."*

"Your Supreme Court justice, Sonia Sotomayor, had been a member but she had to resign because certain senators on the judicial committee thought wanting to help women 'take charge of their own destinies' was a good reason block her confirmation. A half century ago, it was worse. Some of our founders risked their lives to start this little club."

Mackenzie swelled with pride telling how one of the founders was "a sitting queen, married to an Arab monarch. Another was a European princess married to the heir to her country's throne.

Two others were married to high-ranking U.S. officials. The other three were heirs to fortunes from companies founded by their fathers or grandfathers but at a time when women were not considered leaders capable of running a business.

"Those seven women got together and decided to use their positions and money to quietly push other promising women into the leadership pipeline, even if it was too late for them. Of course, the very act of founding their own country could have been considered disloyal at best and treasonous at worst. They risked their citizenship, their positions, even their lives for the crazy idea that women had something to offer the world."

"Has it worked?"

"The club began in the mid-sixties. Less than six years after its founding, things began to happen. From 1974, until now, there have been at least fifty elected female heads of state—presidents or prime ministers. As you know, our congress elected the first-ever female Speaker of the House and a year later, a woman could have been elected president or vice president."

"They all came through the Seven Sisters' pipeline?"

"Hardly," replied Mackenzie. "Most did it on their own, but we helped wherever we could. Most who we helped had no idea what we'd done on their behalf, and that's the way we want it. Now the pump is primed and you are seeing many more female heads of state, governors, judges and CEOs. Although voters seem to be far ahead of corporations in recognizing the talent women bring to the table."

"Why bring me?" asked Britt. "I'm not a judge or politician and I certainly don't have the money to join your club."

"You are coming so the sisters can meet you," said the colonel. "We've broadened our horizons beyond politicians. When Mackenzie told me about your bus ride, I said, 'she has a warrior's heart. That's another kind of woman we want to help.'"

"You knew all about the bus ride and still made me retell the story?"

"Of course, but I wanted to hear it from you, in your words. Now, I know I'm right," said Rebekah, giving BJ another pat on the shoulder, this time softer and friendlier. "So relax. Enjoy the flight. You've got a long day and night ahead of you."

BJ had dozed off before the tires of Mackenzie's plane squealed loudly as it touched down and taxied to a remote corner of Pearls Airport—the small airport where American planes and helicopters had landed during the U.S. invasion of Grenada. Pearls was rarely used now, replaced by the big Port

Salines International Airport at the other end of the spice island near the capital, St. George.

Once the jet stopped, its door opened and stairs folded down toward the tarmac. As the women stepped into the sunlight, a uniformed man greeted them. He was movie-star handsome but so stunningly black that the dramatic contrast of his skin against his crisp, immaculately-white uniform made it difficult to distinguish his features.

"Chief Constable Chauncey MacTavish at your service, Ms. Collingwood," announced the officer with a crisp, heel-clicking, palm-forward salute and an unexpected accent that sounded exactly like Sean Connery.

"Hello to you, Chief Constable. It's so good to see you again," replied Mackenzie Collingwood. "I hope you've been well."

"Never finer, Madam Collingwood. And Colonel Chayat, it's been a while. Retirement seems to agree with you. Do you miss the old days?"

"Quite the contrary, Chief MacTavish. I am anything but retired, but these days I'm simply Rebekah Chayat, a humble software designer and peddler. And that's just fine because a lot fewer people want to shoot at me."

The chief constable smiled, nodding his understanding, as he turned to Britt. "And you must be Ms. Jaeger. Madam Collingwood was kind enough to fax the passenger manifest."

Britt nodded silently at the officer. *"Fewer people want to shoot at you,"* that was Brad's phrase at lunch and how could she forget his other nugget, *"more than just a straight business relationship."* Then she thought back to last night. First Mackenzie had unsettled her world, then Brad shook its seismic foundations, in more ways than one. *What have I gotten myself into?*

"Now, if you ladies will make yourselves comfortable in my Jeep," said MacTavish, "I'll just whisk you over to the motor launch dock and have you on your way. My lads will collect your luggage and cargo for a quick inspection and all that will be sent over later."

BJ looked toward the baggage door of the plane. If the colonel had a laptop with her, it had to be in there because she wasn't carrying one. *Now I won't even see the bags.*

They boarded an ancient but exquisitely maintained motor launch, and soon they were chugging through the calm sea, covering the fourteen miles from the Greenville beach to the island in just over an hour. Forty-two feet of gleaming teak decks and polished brass reminded BJ of a luxury version of the

African Queen, one of her favorite Netflix movies. *All this needs is Katharine Hepburn and Bogie to complete the picture.*

As the launch approached the island pier, Mackenzie told BJ, "Don't be surprised when everyone knows your name. Don't worry, no one will expect you to know theirs. For now, Simone and Jai will take you to the guest cottage." She winked. "They will tend to all your needs and then some. I've already given instructions. Just do as they say and I promise you'll be glad you did. Rebekah and I shall go to the Sisters Villa."

By any standard, the two islanders were very pretty, and very put together. Jai appeared to be Eurasian with just enough black heritage to give her Asian complexion a warm café au lait glow and wavy, shimmering black hair. Her eyes were a rich, warm brown, but they had a unique clarity.

Simone was a mulatto, blessed with beautiful features of both races. She was small boned with cocoa brown skin and fine, almost aquiline features, framed by gorgeous, shiny curls. Her eyes were an unforgettable blue—as deep and clear as the Caribbean itself.

The guest cottage reminded Britt of an Italian villa, with a red tiled roof and arched doorways leading to individual verandas.

Each of the twenty rooms in the U-shaped building was a suite. Everyone had a view of the ocean, a private veranda and most had indoor and outdoor spa pools. Britt's suite was elegantly appointed and accented by signed, numbered prints of Georgia O'Keefe's famous floral paintings.

"We understand you had a very short night and very little warning of this trip, Ms. Jaeger," said Simone, "followed by a hard day's travel."

"Madam Collingwood faxed ahead last night that you are to be given a bath, a massage and nap before dinner. And we'll be organizing all that," said Jai, sounding more British than Caribbean. "Now if you'll just go with Simone, she'll tend to your bath and I'll get things ready for tonight."

* * * *

The sun was setting as Britt sat before a theatrical-style makeup mirror framed by clear light bulbs. Working with a comb, brush, curling iron, blow dryer and lots of spray, Simone was swirling, twirling and twisting Britt's hair into a very formal, elegant up-do that accentuated her height and long neck. Jai, working in feather-light strokes, applied a second layer of makeup. Britt used very little normally. It took time and never came out looking as good as she hoped, certainly not as flawless as the face she now saw in the mirror.

"You're going to be absolutely beautiful for your presentation. Exactly what I wanted."

"Mackenzie!" exclaimed Britt as she spun around. "Good evening, Madam Collingwood," the other two women said in deferential unison.

"Good evening," she answered, "I see you are taking very good care of my special guest." She leaned forward and kissed Britt on both cheeks. "You've enjoyed your day, so far, I presume?"

"You have the gown I selected, and you'll have her ready promptly at seven-thirty for presentation in the Sisters' private dining lounge?" With Mackenzie a question was not necessarily a question.

"Absolutely." "Definitely," assured Jai and Simone.

"What kind of presentation is this, Mackenzie?" BJ asked, as Mackenzie turned toward the door. "You still haven't really told me what's going on."

"Think of it as cocktails and dinner with some very important women," she answered, disappearing through the door, "women who've come a long way to meet you."

A second later she stuck her head back in the room. "Oh! I almost forgot, " she said, handing Jai a long, thin, narrow velvet covered box. "You know what this is for." With that she was gone and the women energetically resumed their work.

Forty-five minutes later, every hair was perfectly coifed, her face flawless—made up so exquisitely that except for lip gloss, she appeared to wear no makeup at all. Thanks to body makeup, something she had never worn, every epidermal square inch also appeared flawless—skin tone and color were identical from nose to toes whether in an area regularly exposed to the sun or never exposed. Britt felt more beautiful and special than she could ever remember.

Simone and Jai then slowly draped a two-piece, ankle-length, toga-like chiffon gown over her shoulders. The scoop neck décolletage revealed more cleavage than she had ever displayed, then cascaded into a three-layer drape that flowed gracefully into the floor-length straight skirt. The back was cut the same way but plunged to the top of her hips before the drape began. A gold sash secured the two pieces at the waist with a faux knot that looked like a small obi knot on a geisha's sash. Gold-strapped, medium-heeled sandals completed the look.

"Just one final touch," said Jai, opening the velvet box and removing a one-inch wide diamond choker. She stepped behind Britt to fasten the Tiffany necklace in place. It was just snug enough to stay high on her neck. "Madam Collingwood wants you to have this."

"I get to wear this?"

"Her exact words were 'I want her to have this,'" said Simone.

* * * *

Jai and Simone opened a pair of French doors and ceremoniously led Britt into a large formal sitting room. Highlighting the walls were original acrylic canvases by Judy Chicago and originals of the signed and numbered Georgia O'Keefe prints that hung in the guest cottage. Every picture was a celebration of feminine sexuality from Chicago's series of breathtaking central-core imagery to O'Keefe's abstract floral tributes to female genitalia.

Six women, plus Mackenzie and Rebekah, clustered in two conversational groups, each holding a champagne flute or wineglass. Each was dressed almost identically to Britt, except the color of their gowns seemed to be specially selected to highlight and compliment their skin tones and hair color.

The moment she made eye contact with Mackenzie, they both broke into broad smiles. Then Mackenzie announced, "Sisters, I am pleased to present my special guest, Britt Jaeger. BJ, welcome to the island nation of The Seven Sisters."

The women offered polite applause and quickly surrounded Britt. All the women appeared middle-aged—forty to fifty—Britt guessed. Rebekah looked like the youngest. "What can we get you to drink?" someone asked.

"She'll have a chardonnay," Mackenzie answered for her.

Besides Rebekah and Mackenzie, the other women looked slightly familiar, not movie star familiar, but maybe women she'd seen on the news or in the paper. *That's it!* She *had* seen these women in the news. She could not put names with faces, but she recognized some as officials in the U.S. or foreign governments; others were major executives. One was a TV talk show host, but her show aired at three in the afternoon, while BJ was at work, so she was never able to watch it.

Rebekah handed BJ a glass of wine and stepped forward to whisper in her ear, "I knew from the moment I heard your story—even before I read your dossier—that you were perfect for the program and the program is perfect for you. Just be yourself and don't be intimidated by the questions."

Then the questions started from all sides.

"Did you enjoy our little island stress reduction ritual, relaxing isn't it?"

"You're from a pretty conservative state, Ms. Jaeger, what do you think of Roe v Wade?"

"Did you enjoy your afternoon?"

"Do you think women are too empathetic and sympathetic to be strong commanders-in-chief?" another voice asked.

"How do you feel about American women serving in combat?"

Britt's mind was spinning. The questions were coming so fast and from so many directions, it was impossible to answer one before another was asked. "It was an unbelievable day. I don't like abortion but it's a woman's right to choose. I've never enjoyed anything more. I think a woman president would do whatever is needed to protect our country, but she won't go to war because of a testosterone surge. Did I miss anything?"

"I told you she could think on her feet," said Rebekah from somewhere behind her, as the women once again applauded politely.

"She's not just smart, she's brave," said a woman who stood out from the others. "At least that's what Rebekah tells us." She was tall, slender, with stunning silver hair done in a striking asymmetrical cut, perfect facial features and skin that looked like it would never see a wrinkle. The others treated her with deference. "Beautiful" barely did her justice because she was more than simply physically attractive. She exuded a presence—an aura. "I am Danielle. Thank you for coming."

"I'm Britt Jaeger." She extended her hand. "I'm pleased to meet you."

"Rebekah, you were absolutely right about her and her performance thus far confirms everything in her dossier.

"Before I continue," said Danielle, "Mackenzie has something to say."

Mackenzie stepped directly in front of her protégé and put her hands on her shoulders. Looking directly into her eyes, she said, "I love you. That is why you are here, because I love you and want you to find happiness, I hope as my partner, in business and in life." Then she kissed her—a warm, tender kiss on the lips.

If BJ's mind was spinning before, it was now a swirling centrifuge. She unquestionably loved her mentor and benefactor, but she thought of it as the love for her best friend— her only friend. *Mackenzie loves me? Like I-love-you love you? Last night was not just the champagne talking?* With her mind swimming, all Britt could manage to reply was, "And I love you, too. I really do, but not like—we need to talk, alone."

"We will talk, back in New York. As your sponsor, I'm obviously biased and not really allowed to take part in these proceedings, besides I'm leaving first thing in the morning for JFK, then the four o'clock to Gatwick. A major business opportunity has come up very suddenly and I have a ten a.m. meeting, Sunday, in London," said Mackenzie. "They're offering a million dollar fee for a two-hour meeting."

"I'll fly back to New York with you." To BJ that was a simple statement of fact. "We can talk on the plane."

"No. You're staying here. These women have come from all over the world to meet you. They will have many more questions and will be very disappointed if you do not stay." Mackenzie lifted her glass in a salute to the group and walked toward the door. "Ladies, I leave you my friend, protégé and future partner, Britt Jaeger. Someday, I expect her to be one of us." Applause filled the room.

CHAPTER 22

Tehran
18 August

Hélène Seiderman's time was running out as she went from hunter to hunted. Immediately after moving into her new hotel room, she darted across the hall and down a utility staircase to the laundry area where visiting Filipina guest workers were folding sheets and towels, then out through the loading dock and into the alley behind the hotel. She half-walked, half-ran to the nearby Metro station. She ignored the usual surveillance evasion procedures. Either they had her made and would grab her immediately, or they weren't on to her yet. She exited the Metro in Tajris and took a taxi to 5 Yekta Street. She told the driver to let her out across the street from the gate of the South African embassy. At this late hour, it was faster to dodge a little traffic than drive on looking for a spot to negotiate a U-turn. She was just stepping onto the median strip when a car squealed to stop where the taxi had dropped her. Two men in plain clothes jumped out and began jogging toward her. Now it was a foot race to slip inside the gates before they reached her.

"DeBeers diamonds are flawed!" she yelled, running toward the embassy gate. "DeBeers diamonds are flawed!" A guard stepped from his shack and the men broke into a sprint, shouting "Halt! Halt!" They were halfway across the street and gaining on her. She could hear their footsteps as the guard looked at her and the men charging behind her. "DeBeers diamonds are flawed!" she yelled again. "DeBeers diamonds are flawed!" she screamed, but the guard turned his back and stepped back into the shack. *He heard me! That bastard!*

She spun to face her pursuers and backed toward the iron gate to prevent anyone from getting behind her. She dropped into her martial arts stance. *Dr. LeDeoux is not going down without a fight,* but she did. Before the men reached her, she was on her back struggling to get up. The guard had re-emerged from his shack, after pushing the button to open the gate, and was pulling her backward into the embassy compound. A second guard charged out of his shack on the far side of the gate, his assault rifle locked and loaded. He snapped to port arms, his weapon diagonally across his chest, barring entry through the closing gap in the gate. Less than a foot separated the guard's nose and the first man, as the electric gates clanked together. The armed guard stared through the gate at the two Iranian agents, then smiled. He made a sharp, heel-clicking left face and marched back to his shack, while the first guard helped Hélène to her feet and escorted her inside the chancery.

In less than an hour portable floodlights, the kind used for overnight highway repairs, and armored personnel carriers had formed a gauntlet leading to the embassy gate. Any car or person entering or leaving, day or night, had to slowly zigzag through the maze of military vehicles while security officers shined spotlights into and under every car. Only one car at a time could run the gauntlet. Ironically, weaving through the APCs was quicker than getting through ordinary rush hour traffic in Tehran.

That night, a caravan of four black Toyota SUVs pulled out of the embassy compound at ten p.m. The first and last vehicles each carried four armed embassy security guards. One guard and an armed driver rode in the second car with two consular officials, Greta Van der Voort and Philippa Jacobus, returning to Cape Town, via the one fifty-five a.m. KLM flight to Amsterdam. Both were dressed in western attire, as a diplomatic and cultural courtesy, their hair was covered by hijab scarves. The third car carried the Charge´ d´Affairs, Right Honorable Hendrik Coetzee and cultural affairs attaché, Madam Agnetha Mkeba, dressed in traditional South African tribal attire. She wore a *Mbako*, a colorful floor-length, circular, wrap around skirt; two *Ibhayi*, ornately braided shawls decorated with beads and mother-of-pearl buttons; and an equally colorful *Iqhayi*, the voluminous, towering headdress, over which she also draped one of the shawls. She was dressed for the *Mgidi*, the traditional homecoming ceremony of the *Makwetha* tribe.

As the lead SUV stopped under the bright lights at the perimeter security checkpoint guarding the entrance to Imam Khomeini International airport, heavily armed Revolutionary Guards leapt from parked armored personnel carriers. They encircled each car, taking travel documents and identification from everyone. The security detail was quickly disarmed and separated from the diplomats. Ten soldiers began herding the four diplomats into one APC.

The South African guards were divided among three others. The three Caucasians were led in first. As the tall black woman stepped over the armored tailgate, a man in civilian clothes came forward and barked an order at the Revolutionary Guard commander. His soldiers, not waiting for an answer, yanked the woman's arm pulling her out of the APC and back onto the pavement. A heated discussion incurred. Eventually, the Revolutionary Guard commander motioned for the Charge´ d´

Affairs to be removed from the APC before it pulled away. He and Madam Mkeba were placed in a military SUV.

To their surprise, they were driven to the passenger terminal. After checking in, clearing customs and security, both were escorted to KLM's VIP lounge for the flight to Schiphol airport.

At the last minute, just before entering the jetway, Coetzee demanded his luggage be removed from the plane, insisting he had to stay to ensure the safety of his fellow diplomats.

He launched into a full-fledged temper tantrum, repeatedly slamming his briefcase on the gate agent's countertop, and demanding to be taken to Van der Voort and Jacobus. Soon airport security men were fully occupied trying to calm his outburst. The tall black woman boarded the flight alone.

Over the next six hours, Charge´ d´Affairs Coetzee had grown hoarse demanding to be taken to where his two female diplomats were being held. He knew their diplomatic passports ensured their eventual release, but it was important to keep up the charade. They'd all been through this before. Almost every non-Islamic envoy, from deputy attachés all the way up to ambassadors extraordinaire and plenipotentiary, had been through this Kabuki dance with Iranian authorities at least once. The two diplomats were finally released, along with the embassy guard detail and the four SUVs, just as KLM flight 240 touched down in Amsterdam.

Forty minutes after landing, Agnetha Mkeba cleared customs and passport control and had boarded the Eurostar train that runs through Schiphol airport. Thirty minutes later, she was in a taxi in The Hague. "Buitenhof 47," she told the driver in English.

At the gate to the Israeli embassy, Madam Mkeba presented her South African diplomatic passport to the senior security agent and said she urgently needed to see the Mossad agent in charge. Assured there were no Mossad agents connected with the embassy, she agreed to meet with the political liaison officer. "He'll do," she told the guard.

Once inside the chancery, an armed guard escorted her to the outer office of the political officer. There she began removing the African headdress and shawl. "It's good to be home," she told the receptionist in Hebrew. "Please tell the chief of station that *Katsa* Seiderman is here. She needs a secure line to Herzliya, a nap and lots of cold cream to get this makeup off."

CHAPTER 23

Seven Sisters Island
20 August

A girl could get to like this, thought Britt as Jai and Simone repeated the whole process of hair, makeup, nails and wardrobe from the night before.

"Madam Chayat has asked to have dinner with you," said Simone.

BJ's stomach jumped into her throat. *The flash drives!* She drew a deep breath, trying to appear blasé. "I'm pretty much stuck here until everyone leaves tomorrow, so I don't have much choice, do I?"

"You can say no," said Jai, as she produced a black-trimmed, sun-gold linen pencil skirt, cut just above the knee. "I'm sure one of the other women would love to have dinner with you." The color was striking, but it was the trim that made the effect sensational. A black stripe, about two inches wide, ran from the black waist band straight down each side of the skirt to the hem, making her hips and waist appear two inches smaller. One black stripe, she noticed, was slit to the hip. Jai helped her slip on a snug-fitting black see-through sleeveless top, clearly intended to be worn braless. Even the little Midwestern farm girl could not imagine ruining the look with the white cotton bra she'd worn on the plane. Simone put on the diamond choker. The same strappy gold, medium-heeled sandals from the first night completed the outfit. The entire effect was spectacular. Tossing her hair, she squared her shoulders and picked up her purse. The trio stopped to look at the full-length mirror on the suite door. *This would sure turn heads at the Tastee-Freez back in Abilene,* she thought. *They'd be talking about this outfit for months.*

The colonel had reserved the small, elegant dining room at the back of the villa. This was a smaller more intimate room than last night's dinner, where the Sisters' questions had continued but in a much friendlier, more conversational way than the rapid-fire interrogation that hit her as she walked in the door.

"Shalom. You look smashing," said the colonel. She embraced Britt and kissed her warmly on each cheek. Before they completely separated, Marianne, the club manager, appeared at their table to offer wine selections.

Tonight's place settings were identical to last night: a shining array of sterling silverware flanked gold-rimmed service plates—three forks, two knives, four spoons, and a butter knife. There were three different styles of gold-rimmed crystal stemware for water, white and red wines.

"Ms. Jaeger will have chardonnay, if I remember correctly, and I will have a pinot grigio," said the colonel.

"Thank you, colonel, you have an excellent memory."

"Please, we've been through that. Call me Rebekah, not Colonel."

"And I'm Britt or BJ, if you prefer."

"L'Chayim, BJ, to life." Rebekah lifted her glass in a toast. "Have you enjoyed your time here, so far?"

Britt drummed her fingers on her wine stem, and looked nervously down at the purse near her feet, before answering the toast. "To an experience unlike anything before," she said, raising her glass.

"You've done well. You've opened some eyes even among the skeptics."

"The skeptics? You make me sound like some sort of reclamation project."

"Not at all," said the colonel, pausing to take a sip. "As I said on the plane, I think you're a very brave woman and you never even mentioned the woman you saved being dragged out of the car."

Britt's eyes nearly bulged out of her head. "How do you know about that?"

"Mackenzie told me."

"Mackenzie? How did Mackenzie know?"

"After Charles took you home the first time and reported to Mackenzie where you lived, she had her security firm watch your building whenever she wasn't having Charles take you home."

"She had me followed?" Britt's eyes rolled toward the ceiling. *What else don't I know?*

"She would say 'watched over' and your watcher saw what happened and called the cops, but you and the woman had already escaped by the time they got there. You did the right thing by not going into your building. By the way, it's owned by a Russian mafia boss from Brighton Beach."

"Why didn't she say anything?" Britt's mouth was tight and grim. "If you knew, why didn't you say anything?"

"I did. I said she'd better get you into a safer place. I also said we had to bring you here. You could be a stand out among the women the Sisters have helped."

"That's why she moved me without even asking?"

"That's one reason."

"She could have said something instead of treating me like a piece of furniture."

"That's Mackenzie. She likes to be in control."

"So what happens next? Am I a puppet on invisible strings?" She flopped her arms and shoulders marionette-like, "Will the Sisters just dance me to the front of the—what do you all call it—the pipeline?"

"You go on with your life. No one is quite sure because every other woman we've helped had some public presence and an agenda—a politician, a college dean who could be a university president, a surgeon who could be chief of surgery at another hospital. We'll wait to see what your agenda is. If it's good for women or good for the world, we'll do whatever we can. Money. Influence. A good word to the right person at the right dinner can do wonders."

Britt studied the colonel's face. *Is this an offer or a tease?*

"You are a special person, if not, you wouldn't be here today," said Rebekah, "but I still wonder why you didn't get on that bus back to," she paused, "Kansas, I believe?"

"My mistake was going back to Abilene the first time after graduation. I didn't want to make the same mistake twice." True to form, Britt recapped her small town life story almost devoid of adjectives. "My life was a verse right out of *Jack and Diane,* the John Mellencamp song. You know, chili dog at the Tastee-Freez, boyfriend got his hand between my knees, then we run off behind a shade tree, and I married him."

"I know that song. I like it." She extended her hand and drew a perfectly manicured finger nail slowly down Britt's forearm. "And you were 'the two American kids from the heartland?'"

"There are millions of kids like us. That song's just a slice of small town life."

"Not just in your country." Rebekah found her fascinating—not what she'd been but what she'd become. "The same thing happens in mine, though we don't have a Tastee-Freez."

Dinner was simple but elegant. Conch consommé; pan seared grouper with fresh mango and pineapple salsa; asparagus with a dollop of no-fat yogurt, seasoned to taste just like Hollandaise sauce, but without the eggs or butter. Salad was served in the European style as the penultimate course.

"In many ways, we are very much alike. You're a farm girl from the middle of America. I'm a farm girl from the middle of Israel, a kibbutz near a town called Har Megiddo."

"Har what?"

"Har Megiddo. You know its Anglicized name—Armageddon."

"Armageddon? You're not really from Armageddon?" Britt put down her fork. It was her turn to be fascinated. "Isn't that a Bible story place about the final battle between good and evil?"

Rebekah's was a face that showed pain but now her eyes twinkled. "That's what my parents accused my brother and me of waging everyday when we were kids."

"Who was good and who was ev—" *The evil spy?*

Before Britt finished her question, the colonel continued, "I was one of those sun-drenched blondes, a tomboy, running up and down the hills in hiking boots and khaki short shorts that you see in the travelogues."

"I was called a tomboy," said Britt, "but we didn't have many hills where I come from." She felt a tear forming as she recalled her childhood before *the* accident. *I wish my dad were still around to take me hunting with him, but not fishing. That was boring.*

Rebekah smiled. "If you promise not to tell," she said, "I gave the sun a little help in the blonde department, but I could outrun and outwrestle most of the boys—even my brother sometimes, though I think he let me win now and then. I went into the army at eighteen, because that's what you do in Israel. For years, a lot of boys from our kibbutz went into the same army unit. I was the first girl to go into the Sayeret Mak'tal."

"Where I come from," said BJ, picking up her fork and pushing the food around her plate, "not too many girls go into the military, but when a boy graduates from high school, he gets behind a plow or he gets behind a gun. And—" Alarms were dinging loudly in her brain. The Sayeret Mak'tal was the elite commando-intelligence unit Brad had mentioned a few weeks ago. *He's been right about everything so far.*

"And?" prodded the colonel.

"And? Oh, yeah, and four years later, you come home, and if you're all in one piece, then you get behind a plow, and like the song says, life goes on." *Long after the thrill of living is gone.* She wondered if Brad had also been right about Mackenzie's relationship with Rebekah. "I know you've had a much more exciting life than you let on."

"Excitement is not always good." The colonel laid her hand lightly on top of Britt's. "The world can show you things you prayed to God you would never see."

Marianne wheeled in a dessert cart with selections consisting entirely of fresh fruit. Each offering could have been a subject model for Georgia O'Keefe, like the peach half with a small raspberry half placed at the top of the peach pit hollow.

"Colonel," said Britt, "may I ask you a question?"

"No, you may not. My name is Rebekah. There is no colonel at this table."

"How well do you know Mackenzie?"

"She discovered me and my company when I was struggling with a lot of things. She mentored me and helped me with start-up money." She lifted her glass but did not drink. "Mackenzie incorporated my company as an American enterprise, then she took it public. She and her firm remain the largest shareholders." Following a dramatic pause, she took a very slow sip. "Or perhaps you were asking about the other rumors about us?"

Britt gulped, covered her mouth with a napkin and looked away as if excising a fishbone. "Other rumors?"

"You're much too smart to pretend you never heard the rumors that we were lovers."

As if recounting what she'd had for breakfast, the colonel then looked her in the eye and said, "We were."

Britt did not expect such unbridled candor. Looking to change the subject she finally said, "I have a friend who knows a little something about national security software. He says we use your program very profitably."

The colonel tilted her head slightly, giving BJ a quizzical look.

"My friend actually talked Mackenzie into buying your software. Apparently Mackenzie didn't really appreciate its value except as a stock offering."

"Then I owe your friend a great debt. Have I met him?"

"I don't think so, but he is enamored of you, or at least the legend of Colonel Chayat."

Rebekah picked up her wineglass. "I would surely disappoint him. I'm anything but legendary."

"He says you were the youngest female full colonel in that famous commando outfit. You were highly decorated in the 'Play it again, Sam' brigade, or whatever it's called and you became an Israel Defense Force recruiting poster."

Rebekah laughed. "I thought I'd invited you to a friendly, casual dinner. I see someone's been doing a lot of homework. To answer your question, the IDF shoots random pictures of thousands of its soldiers every year. You never know you're on a poster until you see yourself on the side of a bus or in front of the post office. That doesn't make me a legend."

"He says you dropped out of sight for several years, then emerged as a senior Mossad agent responsible for tying together all your intelligence agencies so you could all share information with the West."

"Who *is* this boyfriend?" Rebekah's voice now had an edge.

"He is *not* my boyfriend," BJ said uncomfortably. She picked up her wineglass and without taking a sip, added, "I'm not going down that road again."

"Did he tell you I dropped out of sight because my husband and daughter were blown to bits by a Hamas bomber, right in front of my eyes?"

Britt's face turned ashen. She needed two hands to put down her wineglass without spilling. "I am so sorry."

"I've never told a private citizen what I'm about to tell you. So I don't think he told you how I let the scum of the earth dump their seed in my body, for four years, until one by one, they led me to the men who destroyed my life? Did he tell you I happily sent each one to Allah's reward, unequipped to deflower any heavenly virgins?"

"I'm sorry sounds so inadequate, but I have no idea what to say," Britt said with tears in her eyes.

Rebekah reached across the table and laid her hand on top of BJ's. "Thank you. There is nothing anyone can say."

"How long ago was it?"

"Nine years ago, almost ten. We were both in the Army at the time. We were in an outdoor pizzeria. Zach and I had had a stupid little fight. I don't even remember what it was about, but I walked across the street to a shopping center to cool off. I wasn't gone five minutes. I was coming back to kiss and make-up. The bomber was a nice-looking Palestinian kid, not even sixteen. He targeted them because Zach was wearing his uniform. The kid walked right up to the table where Zach was sitting with our daughter, Marni." Her voice turned hollow. "I saw the kid smile at them and reach inside his jacket. I screamed but I was too late. Everything that mattered in my life vaporized right in front of me. I couldn't find a recognizable body part to say 'I'm sorry' or 'I love you' or even 'goodbye.'"

"Why? If you never told anyone else, why are you telling me now?"

"Maybe, because I think you're harmless. After ten years, maybe I needed someone to feel something, just a little, not analyze incident reports." Rebekah looked down at her lap and whisked away some imaginary crumbs with her napkin. "Maybe it was a mistake."

"No one has ever revealed anything so painful—so intimate—to me. It makes me feel, I don't know—" Britt ran her finger around the rim of her wine glass, studying its contents. "How did you go on living? I couldn't have."

"Mackenzie. Mackenzie came along and helped disguise the pain. She was like a drug—a painkiller—and I was addicted. I needed her. She gave me a reason to live—the business, our business."

Tears were streaming down Britt's face. She'd never met anyone who'd suffered such horrific tragedy. But it was the colonel who tried to comfort her, reaching across the table with her napkin to dab at Britt's tears. "I need to talk about something else. You understand?"

"I opened up terrible wounds," said Britt. "I'm sorry. You were talking about Mackenzie."

Rebekah now dabbed at her own tears. "Mackenzie can be very insensitive. Last night was one of the worst things I've ever seen," said Rebekah. "Perhaps we could continue this over a nightcap in my suite."

Britt wondered where this conversation was headed but she had another reason for her nervousness. *What do I say, 'I'm sorry you lost your husband and child Now can I have an hour alone with your laptop?'* Britt looked at her purse a few feet away. *Even if she has her laptop, how would I get those things in and out without her seeing me?* "What?" said BJ. "I'm sorry. My mind wandered."

"I said we could continue this conversation over a nightcap in my suite."

BJ was wary. "You're Collingwood & Company's most important client and Mackenzie's close friend." *Whatever 'close' means and you're inviting me up to your suite.* "I'd feel very uncomfortable going to your room to discuss my boss."

"Well, I don't and you shouldn't. Last night was one of the most insensitive tricks I've ever seen Mackenzie Collingwood play and I've seen several. She ambushed you. You were completely blindsided and totally unprepared. Unless she knows you *do* love her. Do you?"

"How could I not? I was lonely and depressed. She rescued me from that, promoted me, mentored me, befriended me, but most of all, she spent time with me. She changed my life. Of course, I love her. I'm just not *in* love with her."

"No, you changed your own life." Rebekah emphasized her statement by tapping her fingernail on the back of BJ's hand in cadence with her words. "I know Mackenzie's pattern. You are loyal and you feel indebted to her. I've been there and I know Mackenzie. She will expect to control your life. She needs to be in complete control."

"Will she fire me if I don't let her?"

Rebekah slid her chair back from the table. "Probably not, she's much too devious and sophisticated for that." She swirled her wineglass, drained the remains in one swallow, then stood up, bent over and kissed BJ on the cheek. "Remember what I said. She will try to control everything about you, but, who knows, you may like that. I didn't."

CHAPTER 24

London
21 August

Mackenzie's flight landed at Gatwick fifteen minutes early, four hours and forty-five minutes before her Sunday meeting. A chauffeur-driven Bentley limousine was waiting as she cleared Customs and Immigration. At that early hour on a Sunday morning, she arrived at the InterContinental Hotel in less than an hour, where a livery-clad doorman opened the rear door of the limousine. The concierge, a young woman in a blue suit with crossed keys embroidered on the jacket pocket, escorted her directly to her suite while assuring her that all check-in formalities and payment arrangements had been "sorted out by your hosts."

After a two-hour nap and a shower, Mackenzie was wide-awake and energized when her breakfast was delivered along with the morning papers. They arrived just after she'd towel-dried her hair and put on the thick terry cloth robe with the InterContinental logo on the breast pocket.

She ate a leisurely breakfast while skimming through *The Times,* the *Guardian* and *The Independent.* By eight forty-five she was back at the bathroom mirror blow drying her hair and finishing her makeup.

At nine-thirty she sat down at the desk, fully dressed. Sipping a third cup of coffee, she reviewed the one-page briefing memo explaining whom she was meeting and who they represented.

At nine-forty-nine she walked back to the bedroom, dipped into her overnight bag and withdrew a thin silk-wrapped envelope package about eight inches square, then walked into the bathroom. She opened the silk envelope. After consulting the directions and illustrations for use, she carefully wrapped the *Hijab*—the women's Muslim scarf—around her head with one end going around her neck, concealing all but a wisp of her bangs.

At exactly nine fifty-eight, she knocked on the double doors of the second-floor conference room where her ten o'clock meeting was scheduled.

"Good morning, Madam Collingwood. I am Prince Abdul al Aziz bin Faisal," said the dark-complexioned man in a hand-tailored suit by Gieves & Hawkes, 1 Savile Row, tailor of choice to the Prince of Wales. He pulled open both doors and stepped back to allow Mackenzie to enter. "We are honored that you would come so far."

"It is I who am honored to be here," said Mackenzie, attempting the flowery formality of Middle Eastern discourse, "Prince bin Faisal."

"Please, call me Prince Abdul. There are hundreds of bin Faisals in the royal family, so many I have trouble keeping track myself."

She wasn't expecting anyone quite so charming or good looking.

"Now, before I introduce my associates," continued the Prince, handing her a European, formal-sized envelope, "please indulge us by accepting this token of our respect for your wisdom and your time. As discussed, it is the check drawn on the Bank of Dubai for one million U.S. dollars." As he handed her the check, she focused not on the envelope but rather on the curious gold ring with a diamond and ruby scimitar in the center. She stared at the ring as she took the envelope.

"As I said," he was already speaking before she looked up from the ring, "it is a small token of our respect for you and your firm and a demonstration of our sincerity in wanting to do business with you. The payee was left intentionally blank. You may make it out to your firm, your foundation or yourself, at your discretion. There are absolutely no strings attached."

There is no such thing as a million-dollar check with no strings attached, she thought. "Shakran," she said, folding the envelope in half and sliding it into her thin leather-bound portfolio.

The highly polished conference table clearly reflected the faces of the other four men in the room, and their faces clearly reflected discomfort at hearing the Arabic "thank you."

"You speak Arabic, Madam Collingwood," said Prince Abdul, "what a convenient surprise."

"Not a word. Well, one word and you just heard it."

"Pity," said the prince. "Permit me to introduce my associates." Two younger men, sitting closest to the empty chair at the head of the table, were as impeccably dressed as the man who greeted her. Both had the same black mustaches and dark wavy hair as Prince Abdul—but without his flecks of gray. "This is Sheikh Ibn Al Rashid."

From her standing position, Mackenzie bowed slightly, looking for a signal, no matter how subtle, to extend her hand. None was forthcoming, but the sheikh thanked her for coming.

"Thank you for asking me."

"His cousin," said the host, nodding toward the other man in a suit, "is Sheikh Jabar bin al Saud."

The Prince then turned back toward the men at the table. "This is Prince Bin Zayed." Both men wore the flowing white robes and kalifah headdress of Middle Eastern aristocrats from the Arabian Peninsula. The younger of the two robed men rose and bowed slightly to Mackenzie. "I hope my notoriety will not dissuade you from working with us."

Should I know your name? "Your notoriety?"

"Should I say infamy? You perhaps remember when your country chose not to fire a Tomahawk missile to kill Osama Bin Laden because he was hunting with an Arab prince."

"I am aware of that story," replied Mackenzie.

"I am that prince."

Mackenzie tried unsuccessfully to hide her surprise.

"I see I've troubled you," said the Prince.

"Actually, I was just thinking how lucky you were," said Mackenzie, "that you were hunting with Bin Laden and not our former vice president. He might have shot you in the face." She expected at least a chuckle, but no one seemed to get the joke.

"Even luckier I was not with him in Abbottabad. Your political leaders seem to make a practice of shooting people in the face."

"Touché," said Mackenzie.

"And sitting at the head of the table," interjected Prince Abdul, his tone and body language clearly aimed at changing the subject, "is Crown Prince Muhammad."

The Crown Prince nodded slightly without standing. He spoke to Prince Abdul in their language. Another nod made it clear he was talking about Mackenzie.

Prince Abdul waited a moment before translating. "The Crown Prince is appreciative of your wearing the hijab and the respect you show for our customs. He says that confirms our respect for you is well-placed."

"Again, I am the one who is honored," said Mackenzie, making a slightly deeper bow toward the Crown Prince, who nodded silently and gestured for her to sit.

Clearing his throat, the host began, "Our consulate and banking connections in New York studied many firms for this project. We selected Collingwood & Company for an initial discussion because your firm has a reputation for expertise and discretion. Your small size allows a degree of maneuverability and the ability to fly beneath the market's radar, so to speak. That is essential to us."

"Size does matter," she said with a straight face.

"Our dollar-denominated holdings—especially major investments in your country—have been severely impacted by your weak currency and the crash of real estate property values and securities. It further diminishes our current real income from petroleum sales both in volume and dollars. Complicating matters further, we are very large shareholders in British Petroleum. I don't have to tell you what the Gulf oil spill has done to our stock value and dividend income."

She remained silent, but was thinking they were unlucky investors, indeed.

"Contrary to conventional wisdom, the Crown believes somewhat higher oil prices will actually spur yours and the rest of the Western economies. You have seen a deflationary spiral where no one will buy anything—a house, a stock, a car—because, if they buy it today, it may well be worth less tomorrow. Higher oil prices will affect so many things, the Crown believes, that people will begin to buy in anticipation of prices going up. Perversely, this will actually help get your economy moving. It will increase the share value of your biggest oil companies, which are Dow components. A rising stock market will help restore confidence, eventually strengthening your dollar and economy and thus restoring the value of our petrodollar holdings and income."

"And you're quite sure it will have that effect," said Mackenzie, "assuming you can raise prices."

"Need I remind you that in 2008, we successfully ran the price of oil up to 147 dollars a barrel. We know how to manage petroleum prices. While there is no intention to return prices to that level, our petroleum minister will soon announce a production decrease of as much as thirty per cent. This will force higher crude prices around the world. Our target is eighty to one-hundred dollars a barrel. That will help restore the value of our holdings. In the short term, however, decreased production will dramatically reduce the personal and family incomes for every man here."

The investment banker nodded. "And you wish to hedge against that loss of income, correct?"

"Precisely, but it is critically important that no one, absolutely no one, in our country, your country or anywhere else knows about this."

"I understand."

"I'm not sure you do. The Crown has decreed that all members of the royal family—no matter how distant—will share the hardship of lower petroleum production equally. It would be a fatal error, if you understand my meaning, for any of us to be discovered trying to subvert the royal decree."

"And you picked my firm because we are small enough that our activities do not attract attention."

"And because you are an American firm," continued the host, "your intra-company transactions are exempt from many of your Homeland Security regulations that would have to be reported if you were transferring money to and from an enterprise in the Gulf states."

"Let me be sure I understand. You want to buy call options at the current price so you make money on higher prices per barrel while your sales volume goes down due to production cuts, right?"

"Exactly."

"And what size position are you considering?" Mackenzie reached for the pitcher of ice water.

"Approximately two billion dollars," said bid Laden's hunting partner in excellent—but accented—English, "but we could double or triple that."

Mackenzie had to steady herself against the table so she could set down the water pitcher without spilling. "Two billion dollars is by far the largest single transaction Collingwood & Company has ever made. That will *not* fly under the radar. That will scream on The Street."

The prince smiled to show he had already considered that problem. "Perhaps, but a series of intra-company transfers among an array of American-owned hedge funds, with offices in London and New York, would go unnoticed. Two billion dollars could be invested over ten business days with forty transactions per day of only five million dollars. That is, as you say, 'a drop in the ocean' of the nearly four trillion dollars in daily international wire transfers. Four billion dollars would simply require another ten days. Naturally, the standard full-service commission will apply to all transactions executed on our behalf."

Mackenzie withdrew the envelope with the check from her portfolio and laid it on the table. "Gentlemen, Collingwood and Company is not in the business of subverting or circumventing SEC regulations or our Homeland Security laws."

"And we would never ask such a thing," replied the man wearing the ring. "We fully expect that those laws will be followed to the letter. If we are misinformed about your reporting requirements, we can adjust the size and frequency of the trades to conform. Our priority is not circumventing your laws but protecting the privacy of our trades."

"With that understanding," said Mackenzie, "we can proceed. I will need time to establish the hedge funds and open a London office for them." She rose to her feet. "If you will excuse me, I would like to make a couple of calls—in private."

When Mackenzie returned to the room, she informed her audience that first indications were it would take at least three weeks, perhaps more, to open a London trading office, and set up the hedge funds in New York. Prince Abdul handed her a card and said, "Call me when you are ready to execute trades. We will wire fifteen million dollars via a London bank for each fund within twenty-four hours of your call. Then you may transfer the money from one American company to another American company for each tranche of oil future options."

Mackenzie picked up the envelop off the table and slipped it back into her leather binder. "Your Highnesses," she said, extending her hand to Prince Abdul, "Collingwood & Company is pleased to be of service. Thank you." He took her hand, then clasped his left hand on top.

They all rose, except the Crown Prince. He simply nodded toward Mackenzie. The host escorted her to the door.

Prince Abdul closed and locked the door behind her. He watched through the peep-hole as Mackenzie Collingwood disappeared down the hall. Muhammad Ali-Albadi, Chairman of Department 36, then dropped his Arab prince persona and turned to the men at the table. "Once we control her firm, we control her," he said in Farsi. "He who controls Collingwood, controls the Zionist and her company," he told his elite corps of agents assembled around the table. "The trap has been baited, my brothers."

CHAPTER 25

Greenland
22 August

The American flight #101 departed Heathrow on time at 10:00 British Summer Time and was arcing over southern Greenland en route to JFK to avoid a cloud of volcanic ash that was disrupting transatlantic flights. The pilot announced he still expected an on-time landing at "thirteen-forty local or, for our stateside passengers, one-forty p.m." Mackenzie took out her Blackberry to text Brad O'Malley that she wished to see him late today. "Please wait."

* * * *

Charles was waiting in the limo outside Customs at JFK to take Mackenzie past LaGuardia where Britt's flight was to arrive within the hour. "Madam Collingwood, Ms. Jaeger's flight is delayed. They had a mechanical and they're waiting for a part from Miami. But there's major storm in the Gulf, stretching across all of South Florida, so the flight carrying the part can't take-off either."

"Very well," she sighed, "straight to the office, then."

Forty minutes later, as Mackenzie's car approached the Midtown Tunnel, she looked out her window, across the East River and south toward Wall Street. *Eat me, boys! Your old boys club sneered when I inherited this company because I was Daddy's girl. Now you'll see, Daddy's girl is no pussy.*

Once back in the headquarters of the company that her father and grandfather had built, she spun from office to office, smiling, patting backs, shaking hands, showering A-frame hugs and air kisses on everyone in sight, thanking them for their hard work in her absence, and sprinkling her pixie dust on one and all.

Mackenzie strode unannounced into Brad O'Malley's office and plopped down in the visitor's chair. Before he could stand to greet her, she was telling him how she needed his help to set up the new hedge funds. "It's a trifle complicated because we need American-owned funds in London to trade with partner funds we'll set up here. And we need to do it fast."

Brad was not thrilled at what he was hearing. "We can't do these things overnight. There are regulatory issues on both sides of the Atlantic. Why does this have to be done in such a hurry?"

Her answer would warm the heart of any self-respecting Wall Street barracuda. "Because you want to be rich, and be a partner. Do you need two more reasons?"

* * * *

Britt's flight didn't touch down in New York until after midnight. Rebekah and several other Sisters had waited with her for the same charter to Miami, so she was never alone and never had a chance to call Brad and tell him about the flash drives. She would have told him also he was completely wrong about Rebekah. She'd mentally rehearsed that part. *She is an unbelievable woman, with an incredibly painful past. She may have been a spy but there's no way she would ever spy on her own country.*

When the charter finally landed at MIA, and the group cleared the long lines at customs and immigration, they all scattered for other flights to different destinations. Rebekah was flying to Israel for a two-day trip. Britt had to run for her domestic connection, the last flight out of Miami that night. Calling Brad would have to wait until she landed at LaGuardia, but Charles greeted her in the gate area to escort her to the limo. "Charles, I expected to see you in baggage claim," a flustered Britt said, "Is everything all right?"

"Everything's fine. I have an LGA airport ID," he said, using the three-letter airport abbreviation. "I do some special security moonlighting." They walked the rest of the way to the car in silence, where he opened the rear door where Mackenzie was waiting inside.

"Miss me?" asked Mackenzie.

Somewhat shocked, Britt climbed into the car. "I didn't have time to miss you." Mackenzie shot her a withering glance.

Oh, shit! Wrong thing to say. "I'm sorry. I just meant—" She slid across the seat and kissed Mackenzie on the cheek.

"That's better," said Mackenzie, giving her a hug. "I knew you missed me."

"I thought of you in more ways than you can imagine," said Britt, returning the hug.

"That's what I wanted to hear," said Mackenzie as she took BJ's hand. "And I thought about you constantly, especially our late night dinners. I especially treasure that night I had wine spraying out of my nose. I think that's when I realized I was in love with you. I want to re-kindle that magic before you move in with me.

So now that's a done deal? What if I don't want to? What then, do you fire me? "That's very kind. I can never thank you enough for taking me under your wing. I've cared so much about you."

"Cared? Is that past tense?" interrupted Mackenzie.

"No, not at all." *Now I've put my foot in it.* "I meant I cared so much while I was on the island without you. You've been up for what, thirty hours? It's close to twenty for me. I'm done in," said BJ, "maybe we don't come in until nine-thirty tomorrow. Whadya say?"

"You won't be coming in."

Britt gulped like a hand had grabbed her throat and squeezed.

"Until we've done some shopping," Mackenzie continued. "You need new clothes before you can come in." In the dark of the limo she did not see the chilling fright she'd just sent through Britt.

"I've got clothes." *What I need is to get into the office to give Brad his damn flash drives.*

"I've hired a personal stylist," said Mackenzie. "She's gone through your closets and basically emptied out everything."

"You what?"

"You're not a clerk anymore. It's time you stopped looking like one."

Britt was shaking her head in disbelief. "What did you do with them?"

"Do with what? Oh, the clothes," said Mackenzie, as if they meant nothing. "Goodwill. Salvation Army. I didn't ask her. It doesn't matter. She'll be at the apartment at ten to get your sizes, measurements and color palette. I'll be there at eleven to pick you both up downstairs, OK?" It was not a question. "We'll work from the foundation up, starting at La Perla."

"What's La Perla?"

"It's Victoria's Secret on a champagne budget—actually, a Dom Perignon budget—a '59 or '73 Dom Perignon. Here's the list of where we'll go. We'll go every day until done. Probably Friday."

*Allesandro Dell, Acqua, Anne Klein, Prada, Balenciaga, Bendel's,
Bergdorf's, Blanc de Chine, Celine, Chanel, Jimmy Choo, Dolce &
Gabbana, Donna Karan, Feragamo Gucci, La Perla, Manolo, Marc
Jacobs, Valentino, Versace*

"Unfortunately, phone and cable won't be installed until next Monday when you're back to work," said Mackenzie, handing Britt another list, "and then your schedule looks like this. "Mondays and Wednesdays at six, you have a standing appointment at Vertical Club Elite. Your trainer's name is Derrick. They will give you your membership card the first day. Tuesdays and/or Thursdays, depending on Rebekah's schedule, you will meet her for that self-defense training she is so hell bent on giving you. I've explained to her that you won't be riding Greyhound all that often. She'll be back Thursday so that's also at six. You will meet me for dinner, most nights, at eight. That will give you an hour to shower, dress and meet me, wherever. "

"Let's see." Britt licked an imaginary pen to check off imaginary boxes in her empty palm. "I see a space between lather, rinse, repeat. Surely," she said, barely keeping her sarcasm in check, "you can schedule me for something."

"Of course," said Mackenzie, "I nearly forgot hair! Sally Hershberger will give you some style and color." She ran her fingers through BJ's hair with an air of disdain, "And these split ends must go. I'll make an appointment for you. Who knows, you may even meet Sandra Bullock or Madonna there. Sally does their hair."

As the limo pulled up in front of the 85th street building, Rebekah's words rang in BJ's ears. *She needs to be in complete control. Even hair color?*

"Goodnight kiss," insisted Mackenzie, leaning toward her.

Britt pecked her perfunctorily on the cheek and hurried inside. She was glad there was an elevator with an open door waiting in the lobby. She raced upstairs, let herself in, secured the safety chain, then turned around and leaned her back against the door exhausted. After a deep breath, she checked her purse to make sure the flash drives were still there, and planned what she'd tell Brad. That's when she discovered her cell phone was missing and there was no phone in the apartment.

It was after three Tuesday afternoon when Britt was finally had a moment alone to call Brad from a pay phone on the street. "I'm sorry, BJ," said the secretary, "I know he'll want to talk to you, but he's in a meeting outside the building and left strict orders not to be disturbed. He flies to Europe tonight for the rest of the week, but I'll have him call you. Give me a number. I'll text him."

"I can't."

CHAPTER 26

Mossad Headquarters
Herzliya 27 August

"Sir, I may have been wrong about Colonel Chayat."

"What?" The last thing Jock Ayalon expected to hear was the voice of Dani Abramowitz. It was Friday night, ten p.m., four hours after the start of Shabbat—the Sabbath. Mossad headquarters was closed, except for "essential personnel." That didn't matter. Jock was still there, walking toward the underground garage where his driver would be waiting. His day had been filled with one crisis after another. Now all he wanted was to go home for what was sure to be a cold dinner.

"Sir, it may be worse than what I first thought," said Dani, catching up to the country's chief spook. "There may be an accomplice, an insider, who is still active."

"How did you figure this out? Give me a headline."

"Wine cellar, sir, one obscure paper memo," continued Dani, "with both sender and addressee names obliterated. That's what I found."

The "wine cellar," ironically located on the third floor, housed The Archives, detailed records of every Mossad agent, asset, operation, success or failure, ever.

"Does Herzog agree with this?"

"He's out of town, sir."

"Dani, I'm tired and I want to go home, but if someone wanted to purge his or her name, why would they leave the memo?"

"Because no one can remove anything from the Wine Cellar, sir, but they could slice little pieces from a hard copy document with a razor blade."

"And how would they walk out with a handful of confetti?"

"Did you ever make a spitball when you were a kid, sir?"

"My office, now," said Ayalon, flipping open his cell phone and speed dialing internal security. "Ayalon, here. Find my Director of Technology, Natan Levi, and get him in my office immediately."

"You know it's Shabbat, sir?" asked the duty agent answering the phone.

"Did I ask what day or night it was. Find him!" Jock flipped closed his phone then reopened it and began to dial. Dani saw only the country code, one, before Jock waved him away. "Go home, Dani."

* * * *

Paris wakes up late, especially in August when the town empties out for its month-long vacation. In the pre-dawn hour, the Champs-Elysees was nearly deserted. The entire length of the famous avenue is just over a mile long from the Arc de Triomphe to the Jardin de Tuilleries. This morning, no more than a half dozen cars—mostly taxis—were going in either direction, when the telephone broke the silence in the Georges V Four Seasons Hotel guest room.

Finely sculpted and lacquered nails snaked from beneath the covers reaching to silence the insistent ringing. Before she could answer, a hand clamped over her mouth.

"I'm not here," whispered her bedmate. Then he nodded for her to answer.

"Shalom," she yawned into the mouthpiece.

"Please hold for the Deputy Director General," said a female voice.

With that greeting Hélène Seiderman was instantly wide awake, sitting up and covering her nudity by tucking the sheet under each arm.

"When I said take some time off, I didn't mean at the Georges V," said Jock Ayalon. "This better not show up on your expense report."

She cast her bedmate a dirty look. "No sir, it won't."

"I've read the transcript of your debriefing in The Hague. Here's the part you didn't know. The smuggler never made it back across the border. Your cover was probably blown before you even changed your socks in Tehran."

And were you going to simply let me twist in the wind? "You could have sent word."

"We tried to abort but could not. The courier who covered your dead-drop was in an auto accident and was unconscious for three days. When we did not receive confirmation that he'd dropped the red M&Ms, we warned our South African friends that you might be stopping by unannounced."

"They were brilliant, sir."

"The two female diplomats were manhandled a bit during questioning, but they weren't injured. A little slap and grab but a love fest compared to what would have happened to you."

"I'm sorry about that, sir. And I'm sorry about Dani's father." *I failed. I know it. I nearly got caught on my first operation.*

"We're not giving up on General Abramowitz, Seiderman."

"Sir, can I talk to Dani now and tell him we tried?"

"No. I'll tell him what we can, when we can. You did well for a first operation, where everything that could go wrong did. But one lucky escape does not make a career."

"I never got to Dr. Hamdi."

"And you never will," he said dryly. "He's been executed."

A barely audible gasp escaped her lips. For a long moment, all she heard was the slight hissing sound of the descrambling circuitry waiting to encode and decode the next words.

"Oh, Seiderman, one more question. How well do you know Rafi Herzog?"

She glanced across the bed, pointed to herself then to Rafi. "He prepared all my documents and pocket litter and briefed me on how to use it all. Very thorough."

"Thorough, huh? That's an interesting word. OK. Next week you're back here, packed and ready for another assignment."

"Where, sir?"

"I haven't decided, but you won't need to pack a chador. Shalom."

As she hung up the phone, Rafi leaned over to kiss her, but she pulled away.

"What's wrong?" he asked.

"He asked about us, then ordered me back to Herzliya and told me to pack for another assignment. Do you think he knows about us?"

Rafi leaned back against the headboard and cupped his hands behind his head. "A new assignment? That's good news. I'm lobbying to get you a real plum," he said. "If I do, you could be in Europe and we can meet often in Paris. Besides, how could he know about us?" He extended his arms, inviting her to snuggle into his embrace.

"Rafi, don't be stupid." She pulled the sheet loose from the bed, stood up and wrapped it around her shoulders. "He gave me time off to come here. I am a *katsa*. Regulations require me to tell where I'm going if I leave my assigned base, which for the moment was Tehran and Amsterdam. If they ever compare your travel schedule and my days on leave, they will connect the dots pretty quickly."

His face was smug as he put his hands back behind his head. "Another six months, Hélène, and it won't matter. I will retire and you can quit. We'll live wherever you want: New York, London, Paris, Vancouver, Barcelona. Money will not be an issue."

He'd made allusions like this before and she was puzzled. "And where will all this money come from? Not a Mossad pension."

"I have a little technology consulting business in Geneva and my clients have provided me with a Swiss retirement account."

"You have a Swiss bank account?" She bent over to pick up her bra and panties from beside the bed. "Who exactly do you consult for?"

"The Americans."

Hélène walked toward the bathroom holding the sheet with one hand and carrying her underwear in the other "Which Americans?"

"An American software company. Look, everybody who leaves the Mossad becomes a consultant to someone. I'm just starting a few months early."

She stopped at the bathroom door then turned around. "I like you very much, Rafi, but this doesn't sound good."

"The Americans pay well. How do you think I'm paying for this weekend and your little shopping excursions? Remind me, again, where are we shopping today?"

"Dior, eleven-thirty," she said, turning on the shower and closing the bathroom door.

"Ah, D-Day. How could I forget D-Day?"

CHAPTER 27

New York City
29 August

The following Monday morning, at eight-fifteen, after six days out of the office, an exquisitely dressed, coiffed, and slightly tanned Britt walked through the double glass doors of Collingwood & Company. At nine forty-five a messenger delivered a box of two dozen long-stemmed roses. She searched for a card. There was none. Thinking it must have fallen amongst the stems, she lifted the flowers and broke into a beaming smile as she unwrapped the deli sandwich half she found hidden beneath the thorns. Written on the wrapper was, *12:30? Your office or mine?*

"Let's eat in the park," said Brad. Britt looked up from her desk, surprised that it was already lunchtime. The morning had flown by. She picked up her purse and asked, "How was London?"

"Hectic, crazy hectic. The only good thing was a late night hamburger at Joe Allen's in the theater district, almost as good as the original over on Forty-sixth street."

"Never been there." The two walked wordlessly to the elevator.

"Did I tell you, you look fabulous?" he said before anyone else got on.

You didn't just say 'fabulous,' she thought. *This is no time to go all metro on me.*

He reached out and caressed her hair. "Your hair is amazing."

At his touch, Britt clutched the railing in the elevator for just a second. *Did my knees just wobble?* she wondered, as she remembered the way he kissed her hair in his apartment.

"Thank you, I think," she shot back, almost contemptuously flipping her dark, Belgian-chocolate hair, now streaked with the honey blonde highlights on chestnut low lights. "A mere eight-hundred dollars at Sally Somebody-Famous, down on Fourteenth street. I never thought I could even afford to walk by the place. If I'd contributed that to Save the Children, not that I ever had eight-hundred bucks to contribute to anything, it might have kept a kid in clean water and clothes and maybe even paid for grade school for God-knows-how-long."

"You spent 800 dollars on a hair-do?"

"Mackenzie paid. It's the cut and color just way she wanted. It wasn't my idea."

"Brad," she said as soon as they were out of the building, "I tried but I never got near her laptop. I'm not even sure she had one with her. We had dinner and she even asked me up to her suite. Even if I'd gone with her, I would have had to spend the night and hope I could put them in while she was sleeping. Tell me you were not expecting me to do that."

"No worries. You did great. No matter how this turns out, I will always think you're awesome.

"So you won't be upset when I give these back to you," she said, as she fished in her purse for the shampoo and conditioner bottles, "and pretend all this never happened."

"Oh, here. I brought this for you." He handed her a wrapped deli sandwich and a Styrofoam drink cup. It was a deliberate distraction. He knew she couldn't hold her purse, the sandwich and the drink, and fish for the flash drives at the same time. "Would you like to have dinner tonight?"

"I would, but my schedule is impossible." Now she was juggling purse, drink and sandwich. "If it's Monday or Wednesday, it must be Derrick, the personal trainer, then dinner with Mackenzie. Tuesdays and Thursdays, it's Rebekah and 'Mr. Predator,' and dinner with Mackenzie."

"Mr. Predator?"

"The rubber dummy she makes me beat up on. Hold this, will you?"

Brad relieved her of the drink with one hand and put the other on her wrist that was diving into the purse.

Slowly he lifted it out of the bag. "Beej," he said, "hold on to them. We have to try again."

"I can't. I won't."

His face hardened slightly. The impish grin she liked so much was gone. "You have to."

First thing the next morning, BJ emailed Brad. "On Thursday, Rebekah and I are going to dinner at a Chinese restaurant. Can you join us?"

Ten minutes after she sent the note, her phone rang. "You're asking me to dinner with Colonel Chayat? I thought Mackenzie had you booked solid every night of the week."

"She's going back to London on Wednesday and coming home Friday." When he did not reply, she continued. "I know you'll like Rebekah. She's a fascinating woman and not at all what you think."

"Are you asking me out or fixing me up?" Brad quipped.

Men! thought BJ. "I'm asking you to dinner because *you're* the one that has to meet her to understand what she is really like. OK?"

"I'm never sure who comes first in these introductions," said Britt, "but Brad O'Malley, Rebekah Chayat. Rebekah meet Brad; Brad meet Rebekah. I think I covered every option."

"Colonel Chayat, a pleasure," said Brad, extending his hand.

"Thank you," said Rebekah, shaking his hand coldly.

Tension, dripped from Rebekah's every word. Britt was baffled by the instant show of hostility.

"So, you're teaching BJ karate," said Brad.

"Wrong," replied Rebekah, pointedly looking at BJ, not Brad. "You're learning Krav Maga, dear. Karate is a sport with rules like bowing and shaking hands, plus points for coming in second. Krav Maga is lethal close-combat warfare. There are *no* rules, except to kill or permanently disable your opponent."

"Sounds pretty hardcore," said Brad, looking away from the colonel toward BJ.

"You never told me all that stuff," said Britt. "I thought I was beating up Mr. Predator so I could fight off a subway groper or that guy back on the bus."

"Not fight him off," Rebekah clarified, "kill him."

"Training to be an assassin," said Brad with that impish grin. "How do you feel about that, Beej?

Beneath the table, she clenched and unclenched her fists. Brad didn't sound like himself tonight. He and Rebekah reminded her of a quarrelling couple who would not speak to each other except by funneling their remarks through a third person in the room.

"What gives with you two, anyway? You guys seem ready to kill each other right here at the table." Britt forced a smile, trying to lighten the moment. "And I'll get stuck with the bill."

"He called me 'Colonel' and you did not introduce me that way. So alarm bells go off."

"I've called you 'Colonel,'" said BJ. "You don't treat me like this."

"I'm sorry," interjected Brad. "It was meant as a sign of respect."

Understanding finally dawned in Rebekah's eyes. "Is this the man, you told me about that got Mackenzie to buy my software package?"

"Guilty as charged," said Brad, before BJ could answer.

"I apologize," said Rebekah, extending her hand once again. "I may have over reacted." Then she smiled and raised her glass. "To a fresh start and new friends."

"May we beat the odds and live long enough to be old friends," added Brad. Britt watched them closely. Beneath their polished exteriors, they both exuded a distinct air of mutual skepticism.

"You know, people say your software program is really way ahead of anything else in business intelligence. How did you develop it?"

"Did I miss some silver-tongued segue?" asked Britt, putting down her wineglass. "In one sip, we went from hating each other to a love fest to how'd you develop your software."

"A good vintage will do that," said Rebekah casually.

'I really am interested," insisted Brad. "You know, people say—"

"What people?" demanded Rebekah, showing her claws. "If you know of any 'people' probing into it, they're violating my patents and copyrights, and the laws of this country and Israel. So I would certainly like to know who they are. In fact, I'll pay a reward for that."

BJ was sure Brad would be offended, but he threw back his head and laughed. "Now I know why you have such an excellent reputation, Colonel." *She's every bit as good as Jock said, maybe better.*

CHAPTER 28

New York
8 October

Britt's workload was heavier than ever. Her favorite assignment remained critiquing previews and rehearsals of upcoming client presentations. There seemed to be more of those than ever.

Dinners with Mackenzie were quiet, comfortable. She was caring, charming and considerate—the old Mackenzie. Britt actually looked forward to them. She felt valued and important, a confidant to her boss, let in on the latest gossip from "The Street" about deals that may take place and whether the firm had a chance to be involved. Strangely, she never heard details about Mackenzie's many trips to London.

Mackenzie listened intently to Britt's take on the economy, office life and pumped her for office gossip, but got few nuggets in return. "I just don't gossip," said BJ.

"You need to start," said Mackenzie. "I expect to know what's going on in my shop."

Unless scheduled to attend a lunch meeting, she rarely went out. She grabbed a sandwich with Brad almost every day. Sometimes they talked about business, sometimes about life, even about religion and politics—without arguing. She imagined his prep school and college classmates, would have laughed aloud at the likelihood of their fellow Ivy Leaguer hooking up with a farmer's daughter called BJ. Yet he seemed genuinely interested in her former small town life and how she was adjusting to the big city. He was definitely interested, of that she was sure.

At dinner on Tuesday, Mackenzie said she had been elected the first female president of an investment industry lobbying organization. "This is something I've wanted for a long time. It meets on Thursdays to strategize on legislative matters, so you'll have to fend for yourself for dinner those nights."

Thursdays became a standing three-way dinner date with Brad and Rebekah. Britt had an uncomfortable premonition that she was somehow going to be asked to choose between the two.

It was raining when the three finished dinner together for the third time. Brad braved the elements to hail a cab to take everyone home. Britt was sitting in the middle of the back seat when the taxi pulled to a stop in front of Rebekah's townhouse.

She opened the door, then fumbled in her purse for her share of the fare. "I've got this one," said Brad, "you get the next one."

"Thank you," she said, leaning toward Britt. Without warning, Rebekah threw her free hand around BJ's shoulder and kissed her passionately. Britt froze in stunned silence as Rebekah bolted from the cab, slammed the door and yelled over her shoulder, "Night, night. See you Tuesday, love."

The cab pulled away from the curb, heading uptown to Britt's address. "What was that address, again?" asked the driver, craning his neck to look at BJ in his rearview mirror.

"Eighty-fifth and Lex," was the monotone answer.

When they arrived, Brad bolted from the cab and ran inside to get an umbrella from the doorman, then escorted Britt into her lobby.

"What was that all about?" he asked quietly.

"I don't know," she said, entering the elevator.

"Can I come up and we'll talk about it?"

"Not tonight," she answered. "You need to get home and get out of those wet clothes."

"OK," he said, "but could I get one of those kisses, too?"

He leaned forward to give her a good night kiss. She offered her cheek as she pressed the button for the thirty-eighth floor and the doors slid together.

The elevator had barely moved when she kicked the door, almost as hard as she was learning to kick "Mr. Predator."

"God damn you, Brad O'Malley!" she barked. *The least you could do was get in the elevator and try to talk your way up.*

When the doors opened on thirty-eight, she was still fuming. *You could just grab me and kiss me like Rebekah! Why do you have to be such a Goddamned perfect gentleman all the time?*

Once inside her apartment, she went to the sliding glass doors and looked down on the rain-soaked city, glistening below. Traffic on Lexington Avenue was light, but it surged and stopped in rhythm with the traffic lights. She picked up her replacement phone and called Brad. "Come back. I'll put your clothes in my dryer."

He sounded distant and preoccupied. "I'm almost home and it's late. Not tonight. Rain check?"

"Rain check. Very funny. It's not easy for me to invite a man to my apartment. It's just not me."

"I didn't mean I don't want to come back. I just—"

"Brad, if this flash drive business is really important to you, I will get those damn things in Rebekah's computer one way or another. Then we'll all see that you and your friend Jock are wrong about her—none of this God and country business."

* * * *

On Monday another box of long stemmed roses appeared on her desk. This time the card read: "Sorry. I should have come back." Grinning, she put the card in her desk drawer and dialed the phone. "Is he in? It's Britt."

"He stepped out with Manny and some other men. He didn't say when he'd be back."

Brad is meeting with my old boss? "Manny Klein?" asked BJ.

"Yeah," said the secretary. "Go figure. I'll put you through to his voice mail."

"I *do* want to talk," she began after the beep. "I *do* want to see you. Would lunch be soon enough?"

Twenty minutes later her phone rang. "I can't do lunch," said Brad. "I will be out of the building."

"What's going on? Why are you so hard to reach all of a sudden? I want to talk to you about what happened in the cab with Rebekah."

"That's between you and her," said Brad, "and I can't go into the other thing, especially on the office phone."

"Brad!"

"There are some things you're better off not knowing."

Britt was halfway out of her office door when her phone rang. Its in-house caller ID showed Mackenzie's extension calling. *Shit! She can't be back from London already. She only left yesterday.* It was supposed to be another two-day trip that had become a weekly occurrence. Britt stormed out of her office anyway.

As her taxi threaded its way toward the Upper East Side, she called Rebekah on her cell. "I need to see you."

"You sound like there's something wrong."

"There is, but I don't know what and Brad won't tell me."

"Umm, Jade Panda?" asked Rebekah. "Better yet, just come to my place."

"No, Museum of Natural History, by the big dinosaur skeleton. Twenty minutes."

* * * *

In the vest-pocket park, a block from Collingwood headquarters, the youngest of three brown baggers finished his sandwich and sipped on his straw. "Manny, why are you doing this?"

"Because some things are just not right," growled Manny. "Her father and grandfather would never let the name Collingwood be attached to what I think is going on."

"You have records of all this?" asked the man in the off-the-rack suit, bought on sale, mail order white shirt and tie.

"He has the records," said Brad. "That's not the issue. Will you act on them?"

"You can't fuck this up like you did when you were warned about Bernie Madoff," said Manny Klein, wiping a drop of mustard off his tie.

A phone beeped in the younger man's pocket. He opened it and read a text message. "I have to go, but I promise you this. The terrorist money-laundering potential here makes this bigger than any SEC investigation. This is going straight to the FBI, Treasury, Homeland Security and the CIA. That's what this text was about. I'll send a note to that Gmail account we set up about our next meeting, and you do the same if something comes up." He stood up, shook hands with his lunch partners and turned to leave. "Manny, you know, in the end, whistle blowers always get screwed," said the young man, putting the phone back in his pocket.

"He knows," said Brad, "sometimes killed."

"We'll try to protect you," said the younger man, "but we've tried and failed before."

Manny Klein watched the young man walk away. "Who was that?"

"That," snorted Brad, "is a messenger boy with a badge. He can make you a promise and then get transferred, or get a new boss, and you're screwed. I'm warning you, you're swimming with sharks."

CHAPTER 29

Leeds, England
10 October

The tall, fit-looking woman adjusted her hijab outside the entrance to the women's prayer balcony of the Leeds Grand Mosque. She walked in just before Friday prayers were to begin, carrying her own expensive *sajada*, the Muslim prayer rug. Hers displayed an image of Jerusalem's Al-Aqsa Mosque, intricately woven, in to the Arabesque design.

She paid very close attention to every word of the *Khutbah*—the sermon of the week—a fiery diatribe against Israel, America, England and the rest of infidel Western society delivered by the radical imam, Sheikh Jabril Abu Rahim. She wanted to take notes, but that would draw attention. Scotland Yard Special Branch and MI-5 knew that several of the London Underground bombers attended his services.

As the faithful filed out, chants of "Death to Israel" and "Death to America," faded quickly as they passed through the doors onto the street.

She exchanged polite greetings in Arabic with the women nearest to her while nodding politely to the Pakistanis speaking Urdu. She drifted away toward the rear of the mosque, down Hyde Park Road, across and up Alexandria Road where she sat down on a bench, took off her shoes and massaged her feet. When she was sure that no one had followed her, she slowly slipped her shoes back on and headed into Kings Road, then down the last block to the busy Burley Lodge Road. Checking once again for any sign of a tail, she removed her hijab, folded it into her purse and hailed a taxi to Leeds City Station, the busiest rail station outside London. Every day, fifty thousand passengers came and went on nine hundred trains. She walked straight from the cab to the ticket booth, where she bought a one-way ticket to Manchester—a ticket that would never be used. She strolled through the station, stopping at a refreshment stand for an orange squash, then headed back outside for a cigarette, even though she did not smoke. Finally, she took a circuitous route to the W.H. Smith newsstand with its circular bookracks and kiosks of newspapers from across Europe.

A bearded young man wearing a knitted Muslim skullcap stood near her, browsing through books on the far end of the shelf. She thumbed through a book on Islamic history, surreptitiously sliding five £100 notes between the pages. She put the book back in the rack and stepped down a few feet to examine the jacket notes on some historical novels. Moments later, the young man stepped around to her side of the shelf and picked up the Islamic history book. After a studious-looking perusal of several pages, he replaced it on the shelf, minus the £500.

"Well done, Hassan." she whispered in flawless Levantine-dialect Arabic. "I heard his *Khutbah,* but there was nothing specific to act on. It was all standard rhetoric. You need to get into his inner circle—the group that meets with him in private. Let him know you're ready to die to free the faithful from the infidel oppressors."

"I'm trying."

"I know you are. That's why there's an extra £300 in your reading material, but you must get inside. There will be much larger bonuses when you do, *Inshallah,* but until then I can't pay you £200 a week to report on sermons that I can watch on the Internet. Contact me when you are in his inner circle."

The woman then went to another rack, selected a tawdry bodice-ripper, paid for it, and headed toward the main concourse. She checked the electronic signs. The next departure to Manchester was train 1845 on track 11B. She took her time, walking nearly the length of the platform, while surveying her fellow travelers, before boarding the train. She looked at her watch and began a mental countdown. Thirty seconds before the scheduled departure, an electronic voice warned passengers to stand clear of the closing doors. She counted twenty-five more seconds, then bolted off the train. No one followed her and no one was left on the platform. Breathing easier, she strolled to track 9C and her two hour and thirty minute ride back to London's King's Cross station on the Great North Eastern Rail train.

As first assistant attaché for Educational and Cultural Affairs, Hélène Seiderman approved applications for students wishing to study in Israel or Palestine—from high school up to post-graduate level. Every application required a background check. She ran very few backgrounds herself. That was left to lower-level consular staff, but her title provided diplomatic cover for the newly-assigned Mossad case officer to keep tabs on radical Islamist clerics throughout Great Britain, infiltrate their small cells of Muslims who might become suicide bombers, and identify "clean skins"—potential terrorists heretofore unknown to authorities.

Agent Seiderman was young, especially for such a sensitive position. Whispers throughout the Mossad questioned why only six months out of training and with only one assignment under her belt, she was given a premier job in Collection—the overseas espionage detail, where the actual spying takes place. It was widely believed that someone high in the Mossad food chain had engineered her promotion. Some passed-over agents said privately, and not so privately, "She fucked her way into the job."

Next week she would be sitting demurely at her desk, stamping and signing visa applications. In between, she would go to Paris for a weekend get-away and some shopping. She had a weakness for designer clothes. Only two days before, the station chief had approved her travel request.

CHAPTER 30

New York
12 October

Britt darted from her cab and hurried alongside the column of school buses parked on Central Park West in front of the Museum of Natural History. *Did every suburban school district in the area decide that today was the only day to schedule a field trip to see the dinosaurs?* Inside, hundreds of the screaming little darlings were joyously entertaining the stoic T-Rex skeleton.

Bet he's glad when this place quiets down for the night. She smiled, thinking of the Ben Stiller movie about the museum guard. Just then, she saw Rebekah enter the room, stunning as usual in a designer skirt suit. She wore a long red and silver metallic scarf looped around her neck. A large, thin rectangular over-the-shoulder bag that nearly matched the scarf completed the outfit. *Oh my God! That's no bag.* Britt realized *that's her laptop! I never thought she'd bring it with her.*

Her highest hope had been to find a time and place where, maybe, she just might get a chance to plant the damn flash drives for Brad. She never dreamed now would be the moment.

She stood on tiptoes and waved to Rebekah across the undulating sea of prepubescent school urchins. *Shouldn't they be getting back on their buses and going home by now?*

"Thank you for coming." She extended her hand, which Rebekah ignored, instead leaning forward and offering a cheek, expecting an exchange of air kisses, at the very least.

Britt looked down her nose, to the left then right, at the noisy critters encircling her. She sniffed, "I never thought about all these little ears. Can I buy you a drink, somewhere else that's a bit more conducive to chat?"

Rebekah looked around the room. "It's too noisy anyway. My townhouse is a five minute walk."

After opening her deadbolt double locks and turning off the burglar alarm, Rebekah set the laptop case in the leg space of her desk, leaning it upright against the panel on one side. She turned back to Britt. "Now, what's so urgent and inappropriate that we can't share it with a fifth-form field trip? I'm all ears."

Britt's eyes tracked from the laptop up to Rebekah's face. *Make this good,* she told herself. *Make it believable.*

"I need to talk to you about Mackenzie and you and me, and what was the meaning of that kiss in the taxi?"

"Well, said Rebekah flashing a smile and a wink, I see we're going to be here a while. Excuse me, I need to use the bathroom. There's a powder room down that hall, if you'd like." She pointed away from the desk. "I'll go upstairs. Then pour us a glass of wine, maybe some cheese and we'll talk."

Britt was about to turn down the powder room offer but then she realized that declining it could destroy her chance. Rebekah might decide to stay downstairs.

"Sounds like a plan," said BJ. "Back that way?" She pointed with her eyes and a nod of her head.

"First door on your right," answered Rebekah, turning away. She had one foot on the carpeted stairway when she turned back and called to Britt with a grin. "If you're planning on tackling world hunger or world peace tonight, I'd better order more wine."

Britt closed the powder room door without laughing. *Go upstairs. Just go upstairs.* She waited thirty seconds with her ear pressed to the door then flushed. Her hand shook as she reached for the faucet to run water as if she was washing her hands. Then she rumpled a monogrammed guest towel.

Fifteen seconds later she knelt beside the desk, unzipping the laptop case. The shampoo and conditioner bottles lay on the floor beside it. She could see the top black plastic edge, so smooth and shiny it actually reflected specks of room light. She cracked open the computer just enough to slide her hand between the screen and keyboard searching for the USB ports. Her fingers traveled over every key, pressing every button she could feel. *Where the hell is the Goddamned power button? It has to be here somewhere.* A spasmodic trembling rumbled up from her stomach into her chest.

She lifted the laptop slightly out of the bag to feel along the bottom edge. *You're hyperventilating,* she told herself. *Get in control. Inhale. Deep breaths. One, two, three...* She heard the upstairs toilet flush. *Too late.*

Put it back and get out. She moved her hands back around to the side so she could ease the computer back down into its bag without dropping it. As it slid between her fingers, she felt a tiny indentation at the very front left corner. She pried at it with her index finger nail. It moved. The entire edge was a dust guard protecting the array of ports and receptacles for the power cord; earphones, microphone, Ethernet connection but she could not identify any of them by Braille.

She heard water running. *She's washing her hands. She'll be down any second.*

Britt pressed along the opened side. Pressing the open slots as if they were buttons. Trying to calm herself, she exhaled another long sigh and with her other hand she grabbed both bottles, then reminded herself of Brad's instructions. *Be sure it's powered down then stick each drive in a USB port. If only one USB port, Shampoo first, hit the on button, then replace it with Conditioner. They will do everything after that.*

She was hyperventilating again as she ran a finger along the slots on the side panel feeling for a USB port. In the dark of the carrying case it was hard to feel the difference of one slot from another. She saw her chest rising and falling in short panting breaths. *Inhale. One, two, three...* With her hand shaking she stopped feeling for the correct opening with her finger. She started trying to insert the shampoo bottle flash drive tip into each slot. It didn't fit in any of them.

She heard a click behind her. *Too late,* she thought, *I'm dead meat.* She clenched one fist so tight her nails stabbed into her palm. Her breath seemed to solidify in her throat like an icy knot. Beads of sweat formed on the back of her neck, like when she ate really hot Mexican food. She slowly turned her head to look over her shoulder, expecting to see Rebekah inches away, but no one was there.

Could this flash drive somehow be a different size? Her legs shook beneath her. She'd squatted too long in the same position. *Maybe it's upside down.* She flipped the flash drive over in her hand. On the third pass down the row of slots, it finally snapped into a USB port near the power cord adapter plug. *Thank God!*

Now just turn the Goddamned thing on. The floor creaked. Sounds, real or imagined, came from the hallway. She shot a glance over her shoulder toward the stairs. No one. *Inhale. One, two, three...*

She continued pressing the smooth edge where the ports stopped. She felt a long, thin slit—the CD/DVD drive. Then the side was smooth again, no slots, no holes, no buttons. She slid her fingers over the other three smooth sides feeling for a sliding on-off switch.

She eased open the laptop again, sliding her hand between the screen and the keyboard. She pushed every key and indentation, fumbling for the power button. Nothing. Britt rarely swore. Her mother had taught her to be a lady, but she knew all the words. At times she could think a blue streak that would make a stevedore blush. This was one of those times. *Come on you little motherfu—*Something gave, just a little, but it did give.

She'd found the little depression she'd felt earlier. Now she pressed hard. *Come on, God damn it! Boot up!*

Just as she was about to give up a chime pealed. *That has to be the loudest Goddamned chime in history!* The screen flickered to life displaying a little rectangular notice, "Installing," with a sliding color bar showing "Percent Complete."

Britt heard Rebekah humming in the kitchen. She grabbed the flash drive in the fake conditioner bottle and started jamming the connector into any port near the shampoo bottle. Nothing. She rolled it over and started again, just as she'd done with the first drive. *God damn it!* she thought, as she finally clicked the drive into a port next to the shampoo bottle. *What fucking idiot designed these with the labels facing down?*

She stood up quickly and immediately felt dizzy. She knew she'd squatted too long when her knees cracked as loud as the chime and she had to steady herself on the edge of the desk. *Breathe. breathe,* she told herself, tossing her hair and shrugging her shoulders to relax.

She tugged at her skirt to straighten any wrinkles and wagged her knees; from bowlegged to knock kneed, to restart the circulation. *How the hell did she get to the kitchen without seeing me?* She forced herself to inhale another long, slow deep breath. *One, two, made it, three, four, Thank God!*

She had barely stepped away from the desk and was pretending to study a photograph on the wall when she looked back at the desk and could plainly see the light of the laptop screen radiating from the open case. She quickly bent down and zipped the carrying case closed. She stood up and turned around just as Rebekah came around the corner carrying two glasses of white wine. *How do I ever get the damn things out without getting caught?*

Rebekah had changed out of her suit and was wearing a pair of designer jeans and a baggy mohair sweater. *That's what took her so long! If she hadn't changed I'd be dead meat.*

"I'm out of chardonnay. Can you live with a pinot grigio or should I send out?"

Rebekah should definitely be a model. Britt imagined her in a magazine ad, petting an Irish wolfhound by the fireplace—a perfect showcase for the wine, the jeans, or the sweater. *No wonder she was the IDF's recruiting poster girl. If I was a guy, I'd sign up. Hell, I'm a girl and I'd sign up just to be that glamorous and alluring.*

"Actually, Mackenzie's teaching me there's more than one white wine."

Rebekah's face darkened. "What else is she teaching you? Mackenzie *is* what you want to talk about, right?"

Britt frowned. "Sort of."

"Where should we start then?" asked Rebekah.

"The kiss. Why did you kiss me that way in the cab?"

"Why does anyone kiss any—"

Britt didn't hear the forced nonchalance in Rebekah's voice. She didn't hear anything after that.

Her heart was racing and her head hurt as she sat at Rebekah's breakfast table in one of her robes. It was still dark outside and she was roped onto a kitchen chair with both her ankles secured to the chair legs and her left hand clothes lined to the slatted back. She was naked under the loosely tied robe.

"If it was anybody but you," said Rebekah, "they'd be dead."

Britt said nothing. She had a dreadful hangover. Whenever she tried to pick up the coffee cup Rebekah had placed in front of her, it rattled loudly with the saucer. She remembered agreeing to go back to Rebekah's townhouse because there were too many children and teachers crowded around the dinosaur exhibit.

"I can't believe you would do this to me," said the colonel, whirling toward her. "So are you satisfied?"

"With what?"

Rebekah set a bottle of pills on the kitchen table with a distinctive click. "Take one. It will steady your nerves."

"What's this?" asked BJ, picking up the small amber plastic container and rolling it between her fingers to read the label.

"It's just a Valium. You'll feel better. It won't hurt you. I'll take one, too," said Rebekah. Britt picked up the small amber cylinder and shook out two white pills, each with a V punched out of its middle. She took a pill and washed it down with a sip of coffee.

"You violated me and you drugged me, not once but twice. I think that's enough for me to take to the police." She slid the other pill across the table toward Rebekah, who dropped it back into the prescription container.

"Well, before you go to the police, I hope you'll do something about your hair. You really could use a good shampoo." Rebekah tossed the shampoo bottle flash drive in the air, caught it with the same hand, and slammed it down on the kitchen table.

Shit! The flash drive. The night was beginning to come back to Britt.

"These are really pretty ingenious," said Rebekah, setting the conditioner bottle down next to the shampoo bottle. "Something new at CVS?"

BJ looked silently at the two bottles with the silver USB connectors protruding out of their tops.

"You're not going to the police, now, or ever. Your fingerprints are all over my prescription medication and it will show up in a urinalysis." She pointed at the prescription container on the table. "And Valium is a Schedule Four controlled substance. So unless you have your own Valium prescription, you're not going to the police until it's out of your system, at which time the Rohypnol will be completely out of your system, so what are you going to tell them?"

Why did I ever get involved in this? "Where are my clothes? What did you do to me?"

"You don't remember, do you? Of course not," she added without pausing.

"I remember coming back here."

"And I said, I had to go to the bathroom, then I'd pour us a glass of wine. When I came out of the kitchen, I saw you stick that," she pointed to the flash drive on the table, "into my laptop. You're either a spy or a plain ordinary thief. Which is it? FBI? CIA? Or is it strictly commercial? IBM? Oracle?"

"I'm none of those things. Why didn't you say something then?"

"Say something? I thought about shooting you on the spot." Rebekah's eyes were piercingly cold; I had my weapon cocked and ready.

The click! thought BJ. *I really could have been dead.*

"Instead I went back to the kitchen and spiked your wineglass with a ruffie. That's why you don't remember."

Britt shook her head in disbelief and looked down at the robe. "And that's why I have no clothes?"

"I had to find out," said the colonel.

Finally she looked up at Rebekah. "Well, how was I? Was it good for you because I don't remember it being all that great for me?"

"I guess that will be our little secret." Rebekah permitted herself a wry smile.

"You're not going to tell me?"

Another six to eight hours and you should remember." The colonel refilled her own coffee cup but didn't offer any more to Britt. "Besides, I am the one who was violated."

"How long are you going to keep me tied up?"

"Until I decide if I'm calling the police or just going to shoot you."

You can't be serious. "I'm not a threat. You've got the flash drives. If there's anything incriminating on them, you've had time to destroy it. Besides, anything you do to me just puts you right in the spotlight."

"What if I just untie you, give you your clothes and these?" Rebekah picked up the flash drives and tossed them into Britt's lap. "And tell you to get out?"

"I'll go straight to the police, tell them you drugged me and raped me."

"That would not be smart," Rebekah said sharply. "My security-cam system clearly shows you inserting those custom-disguised flash drives into my laptop. That's first-degree grand theft, not to mention the Homeland Security and terrorist laws you might be violating. Would you like to see the video?"

Britt shook her head. "Does it show what you did to me?"

"I knew I wouldn't be especially proud of that, so I'd turned the cameras off.

Anger was boiling inside Britt, but she was cornered. "You're a spy, aren't you?

"Am I a spy? What a stupid question." Rebekah shook her head in contempt. "But then, I guess that fits with your naïve little farm girl legend. I have to say, you worked it brilliantly. You had me completely fooled." She knelt behind the chair and untied Britt's legs. "You know my answer has to be no." She stood up and reached for her wrist. "I'm going to free your arm now. Don't try to swing at me. Your reactions are still impaired and I wouldn't think twice about breaking it."

"I won't. Why did you have to—" The flash drives fell to the floor as Britt tried to stand up.

"Pick those up," Rebekah said, coldly. "I'm sure you're supposed to give them to someone. They're probably waiting."

"Please believe me," said Britt, steadying herself on the chair as she bent over to pick up the two bottles. "I did not want any part of this."

"Why would I believe anything you say? Your clothes are hung in the closet. Your underwear is in on the bathroom floor, in shreds. I'm sorry, we'll have to look around for your shoes."

Sorry? thought Britt, *sorry for what you've done to me or sorry to have to look for my shoes?* "And my purse?"

"Over there by my laptop, just where you left it. You'll have to refill it. I dumped everything out if it.

Not a word was spoken as Britt dressed. The Valium had kicked in. Her headache was almost gone—anger, agitation and fear were now mellowing into a comfortable lassitude.

Rebekah unlocked the front door to let her out, and the two women stared at each other for a long moment of silence. She opened the door and said, "You're not going to the police." She stated it as an indisputable fact—the world is round; two plus two is four. "Nor am I. We are just going to pretend this never happened." She dangled Britt's watch in front of her nose, like a dead mouse hung by its tail. "Now, get out before I change my mind."

Britt grabbed the watch. It read 3:27 a.m. The museum closed at five forty-five p.m., almost ten hours ago. *Where do I go now,* she wondered, *to the police or the hospital?*

CHAPTER 31

Bandar e-Abbas, Iran
14 October

The Iranian submarine *Yunes*, IS-903, regularly patrolled the four hundred mile length of the Persian Gulf down to the Straits of Hormuz—the most vital shipping lane in the world. Everyday, nearly forty percent of the world's crude oil shipments pass through the bottleneck at the south end of the Persian Gulf. After its regular twenty-one-day patrols, the *Yunes* would return to Iran Naval Headquarters at Bandar e-Abbas. Normal routine called for six days of loading supplies and making repairs to the quarter-century old Russian-built Kilo-class diesel sub.

American military satellites and U.S. Air Force reconnaissance planes, flying out of Prince Bin Sultan Air Force Base in Saudi Arabia, noted a break in that pattern. After its most recent patrol, IS-903 laid up in port for twelve days, taking on unusually large stores of supplies and fuel.

As the sun came up over Bandar e-Abbas on Sunday morning, reconnaissance satellites reported that IS-903 was no longer in its berth—presumed to have departed under cover of darkness.

Fifty meters below the surface, IS-903 cruised southeast toward the Straits and the Arabian Sea. When Captain Mahoud Escandari opened his sealed orders, he could barely believe his eyes. This was the first time any Iranian sub had been ordered anywhere beyond the Arabian Sea and the Gulf of Oman. That explained why he carried more fuel and supplies than ever before. It did not explain the ten Iranian Revolutionary Guard elite *Al Quds* commandoes he was transporting.

* * * *

At that same hour, Jock Ayalon was pacing his office, his scrambled cell phone pressed to his ear. In his other hand he held the flash drive disguised as conditioner. "It's blank. Zero. Nothing." He threw the flash drive across the room in the general direction of a wastebasket, but came nowhere close. "All that proves is Colonel Chayat is smart enough to catch an untrained amateur and erase the damn thing. As far as I'm concerned, she's still a possible mole and you still owe me a favor."

Jock listened to the voice on the other end of the conversation. "I hear you," he shot back, "but I'm not talking about some Ukrainian college kid swiping a few credit card numbers. She has access to the crown jewels—the mother lode! We're talking about putting every active agent and their families at risk—even fallen and retired agents and their families—and you know exactly who and what I'm talking about. You still owe me that favor and I need it more than ever. This time tell her to stay awake when she sleeps with her."

The phone crackled in his ear, the yelling from the other end so loud the voice was distorted to the point of indecipherability, but the message was clear as a bell. Two words were unmistakable, "you cocksucker!"

"I'm sorry," said Jock. "Calm down. I didn't mean that about either one of them. I'm just frustrated. I need answers and I'm only getting questions on this end."

He closed his phone and pressed the intercom to his secretary. "Get me Rafi Herzog and tell him to wear his asbestos underwear."

CHAPTER 32

New York
26 October

Britt walked down the office corridor to Brad O'Malley's office. His door was closed. She reached for the handle, but before she turned it his secretary warned, "I wouldn't do that. He's not taking any calls and he said he was not to be interrupted."

"Is he OK?"

"He's not really himself but he won't say what's bothering him."

"Would you just ask him to call me when he gets a chance?" said Britt.

When she returned to her office, she was surprised to see Rebekah coming down the hall. "Good afternoon. May I help you, Colonel?" She emphasized colonel, still seething over Rebekah's behavior. "Excuse me, I meant Ms. Chayat.

She was furious that Rebekah had been right, again. She could not go to the police. She was powerless to retaliate, but Rebekah was true to her word. She'd not gone to the police, nor spoken a word about what had happened to anyone, including Mackenzie, and that could have gotten her fired for a variety of reasons. Rebekah was and is "our most important client," as Mackenzie had often said.

"I have a meeting with Mackenzie. She's on the board of my company, you know. She's actually chairman."

You're a woman. Ever hear of a chairperson? thought Britt. "She has somebody from London in her office. You can wait in my office across the hall. May I get you something? Water, coffee, tea?" Her tone was, what is referred to in diplomatic communiqués as, "correct." In other words, icy as the bottle of water she offered. *Arsenic, strychnine, hemlock?*

Britt returned with two bottles of water.

"So, Mackenzie tells me you're moving in with her."

"She what?" said Britt. *Why do you know this before me?* "When?

"You sound thrilled. Surely you knew that was her plan all along?"

"What if I tell her no?" *I can't believe I'm asking you for advice.*

"Well, you could always—"

"Oh! I hear her," interrupted BJ, getting up to lead Rebekah across the hall where Mackenzie was just shaking hands with a handsome man in a Gieves & Hawkes Savile Row suit.

"Rebekah! Britt!" said Mackenzie upon seeing the two women. "I'd like you to meet Sheikh Abdul al Aziz bin Faisal. Prince Abdul, this is Rebekah Chayat, one of Collingwood & Company's proudest successes. She is the CEO and creator of Intellitekk software—a company and stock I can highly recommend—and this is Ms. Jaeger, my associate, friend and soon to be p— p—"

"Program executive, Britt Jaeger." BJ extended her hand.

"It is a pleasure," said Ali-Albadi. Then, quickly turning toward Rebekah and extending his hand, he said, "And Colonel Chayat. It is an honor. I am familiar with your company. I only wish Madam Collingwood had advised me earlier about your stock offering."

"Prince Abdul," Mackenzie was quick to assure the prince of his favored client status, "I didn't even know you then or I most certainly would have."

Rebekah shook hands without speaking. She stared at Ali-Albadi's ring as he turned and walked down the hall. Mackenzie took Rebekah by the elbow and escorted her past Britt into the office. "If you will excuse us."

* * * *

Ali-Albadi had barely reached the street when he took out his cell phone but then put it back in his suit pocket and walked two blocks to the entrance of a vest-pocket park—a public space with two or three benches a play area for kids—nestled between buildings. On a far bench, Manny Klein, in his baggy white shirt, tie and no coat, was brown-bagging his lunch, once again alongside a younger man in a suit coat. They were well out of earshot. Ali-Albadi stood near the entrance to the little park and pressed a speed dial number on his cell. "Our assessments were accurate," he said in Farsi. "The adulterous infidel murderer Chayat was in Collingwood's office. I could have killed her on the spot, Imam. I wish I had."

"And that would accomplish what?" answered the other voice in Farsi. "You would be arrested, tried and maybe executed. You said yourself we need her alive. She alone has the knowledge we need of Zionist computer systems. I know our family's honor requires her death. That will come later after you have extracted the information we need. *Inshallah*."

"I understand, Uncle," said Ali-Albadi. "I think it may be time to spring the trap."

"May the wisdom of the Prophet, Allah's mercy and blessings be upon him, guide you in these details. I counsel you to get out of the arms of the Great Satan and come home before you do anything. And one more thing, nephew, when this business is concluded, see that you leave no tracks—no blasphemous witnesses—leading back to our Islamic Republic. Are we clear? Allah akbar."

"God is great," said Ali-Albadi, snapping his phone closed.

* * * *

That evening Mackenzie greeted Britt wearing a thick floor-length terrycloth robe and holding two chilled goblets of white wine, as Britt stepped out of the elevator and directly into Mackenzie's palatial condo entryway. It was nearly seven o'clock.

She gave her a wineglass and a quick peck on the lips. "Just put your things down and follow me. I have a little surprise for you."

Dutifully, Britt set her purse on the entryway table and followed Mackenzie past a spacious formal living room and dining room with a table for twelve but set for two. Down a long hall and off the master bedroom, they entered a luxurious marble spa. The tub, surrounded by flickering candles, bubbled effervescently. Without saying a word, Mackenzie threw off her robe, tossed it onto a dressing bench nearby, and slowly descended the three steps into the warm water.

Britt tried to politely look away but could not. She'd never seen a body so meticulously nipped and tucked. *Pencils will be antique relics in the Smithsonian before she fails the pencil test,* she thought.

"There's nothing like a warm Jacuzzi and a cold glass of wine at the end of the day. It makes dinner so much more relaxing." Mackenzie raised her glass. "Well, don't just stand there. Get in."

"I wish you'd told me beforehand we'd be doing this. I would have brought a bathing suit or at least a big old t-shirt or something."

"Just get out of those clothes and get in." Mackenzie covered her eyes and mockingly turned her head. "I promise not to look."

Britt turned her back to undress. The expensive lingerie Mackenzie had bought her was practically transparent even when dry but she left it on and with a sigh of resignation she slipped into the tub. "No peaking." The bubbles tickled her nose as she slid up to her neck in the water.

Each woman held a shatter-proof goblet of chilled Enate 234 Chardonnay, at one-hundred-eighty dollars per bottle, it was Mackenzie's favorite du jour. "I'm having dinner brought in from *Daniel*," said Mackenzie. "I thought you'd like that. You remember eating at *Daniel*?"

The weirdest twenty-four hours of my life started at Daniel. You think I'd forget?

As BJ took a sip of her wine, Mackenzie turned around to pick up a small velvet ring box that BJ had not noticed sitting beside the rim of the tub.

"I have a little present for you, sweetheart."

"What's that?" asked Britt, sure that she heard her own voice quaver. *How stupid did that sound?*

Mackenzie handed the box to Britt. "Open it."

"Right now?" BJ stalled. Reluctantly she reached for the box with two fingers. "Shouldn't I save it for when we're having dinner?"

"I wasn't planning on you eating it."

The situation wasn't funny but a little snicker escaped Britt.

"Just open it." Mackenzie leaned back against the side of the tub and took a satisfied sip from her wineglass.

I'm trapped. Mackenzie was actually following through on her proposal on the island. With her hands shaking, BJ opened the box and gasped.

"Well?" said Mackenzie. "It's yours. What do you think?"

Britt stared at the bright, shiny object nestled in the velvet crevice of the ring box.

"It's a key. It fits the lobby entrance and should you come home when Jimmy's not working, it operates the penthouse elevator right to this floor.

"Mackenzie, I don't know what to say." *I know I'm not a Goddamned piece of furniture that you can just move from one apartment to another without even asking me.* This was another of those times when she might make stevedores blush if she spoke her mind, but the words that came out were not nearly so blunt. "I heard you were planning this."

"Oh, my, my. Rebekah can be talkative, can't she? This was supposed to be a surprise. Surely it's no surprise I want you here with me."

"You've changed my life, Mackenzie, in every good way imaginable. But what if I'm not ready for—"

A discreet rap on the door interrupted her question. "Si, Hortensia?" said Mackenzie.

"Dee-nair ees on the table, Senora Collingwood."

"Gracias, Hortensia. Is everything ready as I instructed?"

"Si, Senorita."

"Would you mind to bring Ms. Jaeger a robe and put her things in the dryer on low heat, delicate."

The two women dined wearing large, fluffy terrycloth robes. Britt said little, just picking at her black sea bass. Then she decided her best course was to frame the conversation with a non-stop litany of questions about the fish, the wine, the two restaurateurs, all the while planning how she was going to broach the subject of becoming roommates—more to the point, not becoming roommates—certainly not bedmates.

Two more bottles of wine were consumed. Midway into the second bottle Mackenzie looked across the table to make sure she had Britt's undivided attention. "You know, our relationship has progressed beyond employer—employee and simple friendship. So I'm sure you can see where I'm going with this."

I wish I didn't. Britt had a huge knot in her stomach. *Will you fire me? Kick me out of Eighty-fifth street?*

"I expect you to be a partner and that brings certain duties and pleasures."

"Partner?" *So you've decided we're already a permanent couple?*

"Of course, 'partner.' That's why you'll be starting Series Seven classes, just as soon as you've finished with that Jerusalem jujitsu foolishness with Rebekah. Without your Series Seven, you can't be a partner."

"A partner in the firm?" Britt breathed a sigh of relief. "I thought you meant—"

"That goes without saying. Otherwise, why would I give you a key?" Mackenzie opened a third bottle of wine, the fourth counting the one shared in the hot tub, and started to refill the crystal stems. Britt put her hand over her glass. "I should be going. Seven a.m. will be here before we know it and I'll be late to work."

"You're in no condition to leave," said Mackenzie. "You're staying here with me. Don't worry. I won't force you into anything."

Britt stood up to go. "I really can't stay—" She grabbed the table to steady herself and realized Mackenzie was right. She was in no condition to leave. "I can sleep on the couch."

Mackenzie took Britt's elbow. "This way, sweetheart. Mackenzie's got you," She led Britt down the hall. In the bedroom, Mackenzie handed her a nightie. "You can put this on in the bathroom."

As BJ closed the door, Mackenzie scurried to turn off their Blackberries, the bedside phones and the lights. She did not want any ill-timed disturbances. She lit a row of candles on the dresser.

The room suddenly brightened again as Britt opened the door from the master bath. "I don't think I can drink with you anymore, Mackenzie." Britt stood backlit in the doorway. The light behind her silhouetted every detail of her figure in the translucent chemise that Mackenzie had given her. It reached to mid-thigh. "At least not like tonight. If I was sober, I'd be home now."

"But you're not," said Mackenzie, peeling back the covers and holding them up. "Get in." Mackenzie drew the covers up to Britt's neck and kissed her on the forehead. Then she walked across the room to turn off the bathroom light. She stood in the darkened doorway looking at the motionless figure in her bed, illuminated only by the flickering candlelight.

"Are you still awake?"

BJ mumbled something akin to yes.

"Good. In the morning," said Mackenzie, "we're not leaving here until we've talked about *us* and our future together—or lack thereof."

There was no reply.

"You *did* hear me, didn't you?"

Again there was no reply. Mackenzie walked around to the other side of the bed and got in.

CHAPTER 33

New York City
26 October

Both women were sound asleep at six a.m., New York time. The exact hour when Iran, Venezuela and the rest of OPEC jointly announced a coordinated move to dramatically boost oil production. European markets imploded. Crude oil futures dropped off a cliff. Spot market prices fell to record lows.

All of the positions Mackenzie had taken for the Arab princes, herself and her firm, anticipating a production cut and price jump, became worthless as they slept. She and Collingwood & Company were technically bankrupt, but no one could get through to alert Mackenzie to the market meltdown.

The clock read 7:10 when Britt awoke to hear the shower in Mackenzie's bathroom. She made her way to the kitchen and began making coffee. She switched on the TV, which was always tuned to CNBC, but the financial network was in a commercial break, so she switched over to *The Today Show*. The news and weather were over. They were interviewing a pair of actors plugging their latest movie. It would be seven twenty-five before the next news insert.

Mackenzie was standing in front of the mirror, in her La Perla bra and panties, drying her hair and looking very self-satisfied. She had kept her word and done nothing more than hug Britt as she slept but she had succeeded in making her spend the night and that was a very successful first step.

Now BJ was in the kitchen pouring a cup of coffee to take to Mackenzie when the news finally came on. "Oh my God! Mackenzie!" she screamed, spilling the coffee. She tossed the cup and saucer into the sink and ran to the bathroom. "Mackenzie!" she yelled over the dryer. "Europe is crashing. The Iranians and everyone else are boosting oil production. The price of oil has imploded."

Mackenzie's look of delight over the previous night turned to horror. "That's not possible! The Saudis are going to announce a *decrease* in production, driving prices up! This can't be happening! The firm's holding nearly a billion in *calls* for our own account plus our clients' accounts, all on margin."

She ran to the bedroom, switched on CNBC and her Blackberry. Margin calls for options that had gone "underwater" as they slept were already popping up on her Blackberry screen. "God damn it! Charles was taking the car in for service this morning. Call Jimmy the doorman and get me a cab! I'll see you at the office later," she said, "if there is an office." She wriggled quickly into a simple dress and a pair of slip-on heels. "Zip me up."

In moments, she was out the door and headed for the elevator without makeup, towel drying her hair on the way. Her cell phone rang in the taxi. "Madam Collingwood, this is extremely embarrassing," said Prince Abdul. "I can assure you, this was not what we expected. I hope this has not, how should I phrase this, inconvenienced you or your firm?"

"Do you call personal and corporate bankruptcy inconvenient?"

"I am so sorry."

"'Sorry' doesn't cover margin calls."

"I know, but we have the resources to do that. Money to cover our margins should be flowing into your accounts as we speak. Of course, trading for your personal and corporate accounts is your responsibility."

"Thank you. I'm quite aware of that."

"As a show of our good faith," said the prince, "we would like to help ameliorate the rest of your margin calls. We have just one little favor we would like to ask."

"And that would be?"

"May I come by to discuss it?"

* * * *

"Madam Collingwood," explained the prince, "we have a small interest in a company in Greece. That company would like to become a much larger company and a client of your friend, Colonel Chayat."

"You needed to come here, today, to tell me that? I'll give you her number."

"It is not quite that simple. Technically, our small stake in Argos-Dimitrios, an otherwise perfectly acceptable European Union enterprise, means the business intelligence software she sells is embargoed for sale to it."

Her eyes narrowed. "I don't know what I can do about that."

"I believe you are on her board of directors."

"I am."

"So you are not without influence. We would like you to prevail upon her and her company to sell the software to Argos-Dimitrios. I've taken the liberty of bringing an annual report, in English. You will see that it is a very profitable shipping and trading company, and with our backing, Argos is prepared to make several acquisitions around the world. That software would be an important resource. Except for the annoying technicality of our very minor position, I think you will find that Argos is a highly qualified customer."

"If it's only a technicality, I don't see a huge problem."

"Your firm would naturally be the investment banking advisors on any merger and acquisition activity Argos might undertake. All we ask is that you prevail upon her to make a sales trip to Athens, one that Argos will completely fund. It is prepared to enter a major contract for the software plus consulting services to manage it.

"How major?"

"When one is spending fifty billion Euros to buy an enterprise, ten percent of that over five years—two percent a year—to avoid a terrible mistake, is a small price to pay. So we are thinking something in the neighborhood of five billion Euros over five years. I know we would not be her biggest client, but we would be an excellent success story for her."

Mackenzie was weighing her odds. "And if I cannot do that?"

"We would find it considerably more difficult to cover your margin calls. If you were to convince her, those positions might recoup some value—perhaps even a small profit?"

"Rebekah, you must go!" said Mackenzie, tossing the glossy full-color report across her desk. "This is a major shipping and trading company. It could be a huge sale. I just received their annual report. Look, this could be a seven billion dollar deal!"

"I will not go to Athens." Rebekah walked across Mackenzie's office and looked out her window. "Security there is notoriously bad anytime. Now there is rioting in the streets. Greek society is breaking down and there are still people out there trying to get their hands on me, and Athens would be an ideal place."

"As a member of the board, my obligation to shareholders, including me, is to enhance shareholder value," Mackenzie warned her. "Failure to pursue an opportunity like this demonstrates an egregious display of contempt for shareholder value. I would be obligated to ask the board to find a CEO who is prepared to accept the responsibility that goes with that title."

"You wouldn't dare," Rebekah fired back.

"I would have no choice, but I'm sure it will never come to that. Collingwood & Company uses your software and we use it quite successfully. BJ can attest to that. I will send her with you to give an in-person customer testimonial. She can also be your bodyguard."

Rebekah was incredulous. "BJ, my bodyguard? You must be kidding."

"Actually, I was thinking she could be a valuable customer reference. We use your software, you know, rather effectively."

Rebekah thought about her ruptured friendship with BJ. "I don't think she'll travel with me."

"Nonsense. She'll go," said Mackenzie, "because I'll tell her to." Then changing to a soft pleading tone, she added, "I need you to go. Come on, Rebekah, they held the Olympics there and nothing happened. It's the right thing for your company and for you, if you want your stock to go up, again. You have no idea how important this is."

Rebekah remained cautious. "And you have no idea how risky this trip could be."

"I trust you haven't forgotten the huge risk I took for you. If it wasn't for me and Collingwood & Company, you would not have companies clamoring to give you a five billion Euro contract. In fact, you wouldn't have much at all. Come on, Rebekah, it's Athens, not Afghanistan. And it's seven billion dollars!"

CHAPTER 34

Paris
27 October

Hélène Siederman rode down the escalator from the Chunnel train to the main level of Paris's EuroStar train station. As she reached the main passenger level, a beep in her purse signaled a text message on her phone. "n-11-e-7-p-9-c." It was a simple code. Subtract four from every digit, add four to every letter: r-7-i-3-t-5-z. She smiled as she mentally separated the numbers from the letters.

Twenty minutes and one Metro transfer is all it would take to reach her destination; purple line to Les Halles; change to the yellow to the Tuileries; then a short four-block walk to Place Vendome. But she would take four trains and two taxis, making sure she was not followed to the home of Chanel, Givenchy, Christian LeCroix, Balmain, Van Cleef & Arpels, Louis Vuitton and Cartier.

She asked the Ritz concierge for a message for room 735. *Such a simple code,* she thought, *why bother?* She took the envelope surprised that there was no key. Inside was an address written on a card clearly intended for a taxi driver and a separate note to her. *If you're not being followed take a taxi to this address.*

Her phone rang as the taxi turned onto the Quai de Seine. A blue light indicated a scrambled call on her secure line. "Sha—" she stopped mid-word to avoid revealing her nationality. "Oui."

The London chief of station spoke in Hebrew. "You have a friend in Leeds who shares your taste in literature?"

"Oui."

"He was found beheaded in the basement of a low-income estate, not far from the bookstore where you last met. Five new £100 notes were pinned to his jacket. You may not have been followed there but it appears he was. We must assume they have a picture of you, even without a name."

She gasped. The implied threat to her own safety was obvious.

. *"Oui. Je retournerai tout de suite."*

"Not necessary. You're probably better off there, for now," he said. "MI-5 and Special Branch will share what they have with us, but they want a debrief when you return."

If she was going to turn around and go back, now was the time. She reread the card Rafi had sent with the Cartier blue Safire bracelet. The man knew how to get her attention. She mentally sang the Joan Jett song, *I hate myself for loving you. I can't break free from the things that you do.*

As the light changed, she yelled at the driver, *"L'arrêt!"* and he slammed on the brakes. Horns began honking behind them. She looked out the back window. *"Non, continuez."* The driver's head snapped around to look at her, *"Lequel l'est?"* Which is it? She glanced once more at the card and the bracelet. The song played on in her head. *I want to walk but I run back to you.*

"Continuez, s'il vous plait," she told the driver.

She stepped out of the cab on a seedy-looking waterfront quay. The driver pointed to a narrow passage, then sped away. Houseboats, called barges on the Seine, were tied up three deep, like the Hong Kong boat people she'd seen in post cards. *I'm getting a very bad feeling.* Thick mold-encrusted hawsers, some not moved in years, wrapped around mooring pylons. *This is not Rafi's kind of neighborhood.* She made her way down the passageway between boats. *At any moment one of these doors will open and I'll be dragged inside never to be seen again.* She reached into her bag and pulled out her pepper spray.

Just as she was about to turn around, she stepped onto the deck of the outermost barge. There was Rafi, in a beige linen sports coat and black Pierre Cardin pullover, champagne flute in hand, with a magnum in the ice bucket, and votive light candles flickering on the umbrella-shaded table. This was no Hong Kong junk. It was an opulent floating apartment with tour boats gliding up and down the Seine, passing so close they could almost hear the cameras clicking. He poured and handed her a stem.

"Like it?" he asked, with a sweeping gesture to show off the boat. "I found you could rent one of these for less than a suite at the Ritz, and this is so much more romantic."

Hélène took a sip. She'd been warned that spying was a lonely business but she was not prepared for the isolation of a single girl with a double life. She met lots of men but couldn't allow herself to get close to any of them. *Except Rafi, he is such a romantic and so good in bed. And I can open up to him.*

She threw her arms around his neck and pulled him into a kiss, "I've missed you." She continued the kiss and began pushing his sport coat off his shoulders. "I want you."

He returned the kiss and set down his glass. Devouring her lips, he began unbuttoning her blouse, then unhooked her bra. His hands roamed over her smooth breasts. In no time, she was bare from the waist up. His lips brushed her nipples. She convulsed in a surge of pleasure.

She grabbed at the pullover, yanking it out of his pants and trying to raise it over his head. "Where's the bedroom? It's been a terrible two weeks." He pointed with a tilt of his head and unzipped her skirt

She stepped out of it and backed him toward the bedroom, pushing him onto the bed. He kicked off his trousers as she wriggled out of her panties. She climbed on top, straddling him.

Whenever he tried to speak, she put a finger on his lips. She didn't want to hear what he had done for her career or talk about work. "Don't talk. Don't spoil it." She knew what she wanted and right now she needed to be on top.

A long, low moan built higher and louder as her insides began the gentle cycle of contract and release that preceded that glorious spasming. Then she plunged over the edge, burying her face in his neck. "You have no idea how much I needed that. Next time it will be about you, I promise."

Later she sat on the bed, naked under the sheet, a towel wrapped around her freshly washed hair, sipping a glass of champagne. Today it was Perrier Joulet. Rafi was in the shower. *He always has champagne on ice. I like that. Every other man I meet, the conversation starts with me lying about what I do and ends with me breaking a string of dates with no plausible explanation. Rafi understands my life is not my life.*

The Blackberry vibrating on the bedside table interrupted her thoughts. She picked it up in case it was a call from Mossad HQ. She discovered that it wasn't a call at all, but a short text message, so short she could read it in the preview pane.

She walked into the bathroom, still naked, as he stepped out of the shower. She put her arms around his neck, hiding the phone in one hand, and ground her pelvis against his. "Rafi," she cooed as she reached down to fondle his testicles. The coo turned to a hiss as she squeezed so hard he yelped. "However much that hurt, and I don't really care, it doesn't hurt nearly as much as this." She stepped back and slammed the phone into his hand. "Read that! Read it out loud so I'm sure I didn't miss anything."

He looked at the phone and sputtered.

"Read it! I said."

"Your—your..." he stammered. "'Your love is precious. A million kisses for you.' I can explain—"

"I was falling in love with you, really. Then this; what is her name?"

Rafi shook his head rapidly. "I swear there is no she. It's all business."

"What business would that be?"

"I told you, I have a little technology consulting business on the side."

"Consulting for whom?"

"The Americans. The kisses refer to my fee, one million dollars."

"A million dollars! Who exactly is this client and what do you do for them?"

"It's an American software company that wants to develop a business intelligence program to compete with Rebekah Chayat's Intellitekk." He paused before explaining himself. "Since I did most of the work on that, there's no reason I shouldn't get rich from it, just like she did. I swear there is no one else. If it wasn't for the consulting, how do you think I could afford these little weekend shopping trips?" He seized her hand and kissed it Parisian style. "When I retire, and that will be soon, I want you to marry me. We'll live wherever you want. Beverly Hills. Paris. London. San Francisco."

He looked good, fresh out the shower, now holding a towel protectively in front of him.

"I know you are not the first Mossad executive to have an affair with a young agent," she said. "And I'm not the first new agent to be charmed by a handsome senior officer." She took his hand and led him back to the windows. The City of Lights splashed its colors against the pale pink sky of the setting sun. Sheer curtains masked their nakedness from the passing tour boats behind a gauzy surrealistic mist. As he reached for his champagne flute. She wrapped her arms around his neck and kissed him.

Without warning the glass exploded in his hand. The window disintegrated into a thousand shards. *I was followed!* "Get down."

They dove away from the glass on the floor and crawled behind the bed. "Do you have a weapon?" she asked.

"No."

"I left mine at the office," she said. "I'm on leave. I didn't want to bother filling out French and British forms."

Rafi raised his head above the bed, expecting another shot. He was shaking.

Hélène had her bra and panties on and was crawling toward her skirt. "Stay down!" she said. "They could still be out there." The tour boat was a hundred yards upriver.

"Who?"

"I lost an asset today," she explained, lying on her back to put on her skirt. "He was beheaded. You know what that means. I thought I was clean but maybe not. We've got to report this to headquarters. They'll say if we should call the police."

"No!" Rafi's reply was nearly a shout.

"No? Are you crazy? Someone has just shot at two intelligence officers on private leave in a supposedly friendly capital." She was buttoning her blouse but stopped and stared at Rafi in disbelief. "We don't even know which one of us was the target and you don't want to report it?"

Rafi shook his head. "I'm not here on leave. I'm on official business, attending a conference."

Hélène put her face in her hands and tried to rub away her exasperation.

"Give me your phone. I want to see what other text messages you have and who's in your speed dial. Now!" she barked. "Or I walk off this boat, turn us both in and never speak to you again." She took the phone and began scrolling through it.

"When will I see you again?" he asked, sheepishly.

"Soon," she said. "In headquarters."

CHAPTER 35

New York City
30 October

British Airways 0178 had barely lifted off runway 31-L at JFK when it began a steep bank to the left, crossing Jamaica Bay, over the densely populated ocean front strip known as the Rockaways, toward the Atlantic Ocean. It crossed over the rows of high-rise apartments along Rockaway Beach. Even on a fall day, the cluster of buildings was reflecting the sun's heat skyward. The updraft gave the plane a slight lift, but then it crossed into rougher air where the cooler air off the water mixed with the warm updrafts radiating from the concrete canyons below. The plane gave a shudder, then dropped nearly thirty feet. It rocked right, then left, before catching another updraft that catapulted it higher into the sky.

Britt gulped and grabbed Rebekah's hand resting on the divider between the two first-class seats. Rebekah gave her white knuckles a reassuring squeeze.

"It's OK," said Rebekah as the plane leveled off, "just a little clear air turbulence."

Rebekah smiled at Britt and patted her hand. "Feel better now?"

"A little," said Britt, releasing her iron grip.

Rebekah wiggled her fingers and flapped her hand. "I'm surprised you came with me, and pleased. Thank you."

"At first I wasn't going to but when I thought about it," answered Britt, "it wasn't that hard a decision." She raised and lowered her upturned hands, alternating them like an invisible scale weighing one option versus another. "Come with you? Have Mackenzie's movers totally move me in with her this weekend?"

"You really don't ever want to do that, do you?"

An oddly primitive warning sounded in Britt's brain. *Should I even be having this conversation with the firm's most important client? But she seems to know everything before I do.*

"I didn't say that, exactly. I wish I loved her like she says she loves me." She rolled her eye skyward. "Until now, I'd never thought about sex with a woman, never considered it a possibility. Well," she paused, "there I said it. It's out on the table now."

Rebekah turned slightly in her seat so she could study Britt's face. "Never? That would make you a statistical abnormality. So is it sex with a woman or sex with Mackenzie you don't want to think about?"

"All of the above. None of the above." Britt turned and looked out the window while she thought about her answer. "God knows men have not been good for me, but an intimate relationship with my mentor, my boss, my landlord? What could possibly go wrong with that?"

"What about your boyfriend, Brad?"

Britt's consternation softened at the mention of Brad's name, if only for a moment, before she put up her guard again.

"He's not my boyfriend. We've never even been on a real date. You've been with us whenever we've had dinner."

"So you could have refused to come on this trip and had dinner with him all alone. Why didn't you?"

"Like I said, it was you or Mackenzie. You have an expiration date—next Saturday we fly home." Britt made the weighing motion one more time. "And the last three days are vacation in the Greek Isles."

"Is there any expiration date on your anger over what happened at my town house?"

Britt looked at Rebekah dead-on, anger and hurt showing in her eyes. "You tied me up, drugged me, threatened to shoot me and I still don't know what else you did to me while I was out. Those things have a long shelf life."

"I never thought you would fail to have complete recall by now. I did give you two milligrams of Rohypnol, the date rape drug, because I thought it was safer than physical combat. You've already learned enough to be lethal," said Rebekah. "How did I know you wouldn't come at me with lethal force?"

"I couldn't do that." To Britt the idea was preposterous. "Besides, I would never do that."

"You're much better than you think, but then, isn't that the story of your life, BJ?"

Britt quickly opened her mouth to deny that oversimplification, but no sound came out. *You just summed up my whole existence in one sentence, and I don't know if it was a compliment or an insult.*

"That is the story of your life, isn't it?"

"My life is my business. *You* had sex with me while I was unconscious." That came out much louder than Britt expected and she was sure everyone onboard must have heard but no one seemed to have noticed. They were listening to their iPods, watching the movie, engrossed in their own conversations, or asleep.

"Sex!" hissed Rebekah. "That's ridiculous."

"Shhhh," said Britt, "not everyone has to hear."

Rebekah continued unimpeded. "If that's what you hoped would happen, I'm sorry to disappoint you. If you'd just caught me stealing proprietary information worth millions of dollars out of your computer, would your first inclination be to have sex with the thief?"

"Then why undress me?"

"I undressed you because I had to find out if you were armed or wearing a wire."

"And that required taking off my underwear?"

"For female agents, they make bras with dozens, maybe hundreds, of nanochips woven right into the fabric so you don't even need a wire. The microphone can be hidden in the little floweret where the cups come together. Conversations are recorded right in the bra fabric where the chips are. It's the same technology as a musical birthday card but hundreds of times smaller. I was also looking for an ID, if you had one. Other than that, I didn't touch you except to put my robe on you and tie you in the chair."

"My underpants? Why were they off?"

"Marks, scars and tattoos can be more informative and permanent than an ID card."

"You should have told me all this at the time. If nothing happened, you had an obligation to tell me, not let me think I'd been raped."

"I had no obligation to you at all," said Rebekah flatly. "I was the violated party. But now it's over. You didn't go to the police and neither did I. You gave the flash drive to whoever but I guaranteed that there was nothing on it." Her tone changed abruptly, becoming more of a warning. "But now we both have to be very careful."

"About what?"

"No matter what Mackenzie told you, Athens is not safe, especially given their economic turmoil. The budget crisis has forced lay-offs of huge numbers of senior national police and National Intelligence Service officers. They were replaced with younger, cheaper, inexperienced people. What do you call them in the States?"

"Rookies?"

"Exactly, rookies—people with no experience. Not to mention all the teachers, garbage men and you name it who got fired."

"You should have brought Brad instead." The passing thought was out of her mouth before she realized it.

"I'm sorry if you hate being with me," Rebekah said politely, like apologizing for bumping into someone on the street.

BJ sighed, then tried to explain. "I don't hate you, now, and I can try to put what happened behind us." *I hate myself for agreeing to try planting Brad's flash drives again.* "It's just that Brad would be much better at this." *And a lot better at that.* "He could better explain what we do and how we do it and how it makes money for the firm. All I can say is Collingwood and Company uses your software and it's very effective."

"You'll do just fine. And you're so much more attractive than Brad," Rebekah added with a conspiratorial grin. "Those men will be so busy drooling over you, they probably won't hear a word you say."

"Should I be flattered by that? Now I'm just fluff—a piece of cotton candy?"

"That's not what I meant and you know it," said Rebekah. "But it is a fact of life that attractive people are the most successful sales people. Maybe not fair, but that's life."

"Never mind. I'm here now and I'll do what I can to help make this sale."

"Excuse me," interrupted the flight attendant, launching the opening salvo of the transatlantic eat-athon that is still found in first class.

* * * *

The surveillance officer aboard the JSTARS reconnaissance flight pressed the talk button for his encrypted radio channel. "Cowboy up, NASSIG. This is Golf-Romeo-Eight-Bravo-Sierra. Ya'll got work to do." The Joint Surveillance Target Attack Radar plane, flying out of the US Air Force 4404th Air Wing, was on mission from Prince Sultan Air Base, Saudi Arabia, over the eastern Mediterranean.

Naval Air Station at Sigonella, Sicily, NASSIG, is home to the Navy's Mediterranean fleet of P-3 Orion Anti-Submarine aircraft. "This is Golf-Romeo-Eight-Bravo-Sierra confirming we have visual on submersible Igloo-Sierra Niner-Zero-Three. I say again: We have visual on Igloo-Sierra-Niner-Zero-Three."

IS-903, Iran's Russian-built Kilo-Class submarine was militarily antique, except for one vital asset. Rigged for silent running, it was the quietest diesel sub ever built—nearly undetectable. This was the first time it, or any of the three submarines Iran bought from Russia, had been tracked beyond the Arabian Sea and the Gulf of Oman. It had just exited the north end of the Suez Canal, at Port Said, Egypt, and was approaching open water in the Mediterranean.

"Target is heading north-by-northwest approximate bearing three-three-zero and is preparing to dive. Ya'll best saddle up. We will lose visual soon. I say again, submarine Igloo Sierra

Niner Zero-Three heading course three-three-zero from Port Said. At current course and speed, I estimate she will be looking through her periscope at the Acropolis in approximately forty-two hours,."

"Copy that. We'll take it from here."

"Ya'll have a nice day, now, ya'hear. Golf-Romeo-Eight-Bravo-Sierra returning to base."

The reconnaissance flight had banked steeply to the east, returning to its Saudi Arabian home base, as Britt bolted upright from her nap and shook her traveling companion.

"Rebekah, I got it!"

"I'm so glad," yawned the colonel. "Got what?"

"What I'm going to talk about!"

"Just talk through your part of the presentation deck," said Rebekah, turning her back toward BJ and pulling her blanket up around her shoulders. "You'll do fine."

"No. I'm not going to talk about Collingwood at all."

That made the software executive sit up. "You have to. That's why you're here."

"But I can talk about something much more impressive—something those guys will really listen to."

"And that would be?" asked Rebekah, raising an eyebrow.

"I'll talk about *them!*" Britt was almost yelling with excitement. "I'll tell them stuff about themselves they won't believe we could know."

"Go on."

"As soon as we land, I'll call Brad and ask him to run your program to get a complete hostile-takeover profile on Argos-Dimitrios—and all their officers. Then I will just read them a list of who's who in the company, where they went to school, who married who, how many kids they have, what other companies or boards they're involved with. Who knows? Maybe how many outstanding parking tickets they have."

"You're brilliant," said Rebekah. "Do it."

I'll show 'em cotton candy. Britt smiled.

BA0178 touched down at Heathrow half an hour early at 2100. With only carry-on bags and nothing to declare, the women cleared Customs and Passport Control relatively quickly, exiting into the Arrivals Hall at about 2140, London time—4:40 p.m. in New York. They would spend the night at the Heathrow Sheraton before flying on to Athens in the morning.

As soon as they exited the customs and immigration quarantine area, Britt took out her phone and dialed. "Brad, can you do us a huge favor with your business intelligence magic and run that company we're going to see, Argos-Dimitrios?"

"I'll try but don't count on it," he said tersely

"I know you're busy," said Britt, "and I'm sorry to ask such a huge favor. I just think—"

"Beej," Brad interrupted, "busy is not the problem. Look, you need to know, I won't be here when you come back. Neither will Manny Klein. We're both leaving the firm. Manny may be going into witness protection."

"You're what? I don't believe you!" Britt didn't think she was yelling but she noticed everyone nearby looking at her. "Manny is old man Collingwood's 'other son.' He'd never leave. And you're going to be a partner!"

"That's exactly why I'm leaving. For my own sake, I can't take a chance on becoming a partner."

Britt silently mouthed, "Brad is leaving Collingwood," with exaggerated precision for Rebekah to lip read.

"Beej," said Brad, "I will try to run that company for you, I really will, but I don't want to talk anymore on this line. Leave your cell phone number on my home machine and I'll try to call you tomorrow with what I find. Bye for now."

"Brad?" shouted Britt. "Brad?" but he was gone.

The next morning, British Airways 0680 to Athens lifted off the runway.

"I didn't sleep well, last night. I'm taking a nap," said Rebekah. Then she reached into the seatback pocket and pulled out her laptop. "Here, there's a folder on the desktop named 'Athens.' In it is a PowerPoint presentation. You need to know your part, in case Brad doesn't come through. Then there's the itinerary Argos-Dimitrios prepared from when we land at 1355 this afternoon to when we leave on Wednesday for Santorini."

"You're giving me your laptop after what happened?" Britt's stomach was spinning like an Olympic platform diver doing a three and a half. Yet she was thinking, *My purse is in the overhead! Shit!*

"I *can* trust you, can't I?"

"Of course," said Britt, forcing a smile. "I wouldn't want you to tie me up and undress me again, especially on the plane." Yet she was thinking, *The stewardess can get my bag after you fall asleep.*

As Britt read the itinerary, Rebekah yawned and asked, "Did you get to the part about the new building?"

"First item, meet Argos-Dimitrios limo driver outside Customs and Immigration. Drive past Argos' new headquarters en route to hotel."

"I really don't care about it, but the Argos people seem extremely proud of it. So just practice a little ooo-ing and ahh-ing." Then she tipped her seat to the fully reclined position, and pulled a blanket over her head. "G'night."

Britt continued to scroll through the itinerary.

*1600 Arrive Athens Imperial hotel from Athens International. Free to rest, sightsee and eat dinner.

*1030 Monday, limo at your disposal for sightseeing, shopping, etc.

*1000 Tuesday pick-up by Argos-Dimitrios limo. Drive to current Argos headquarters for presentation. Lunch will be served.

*1915 Tuesday evening, guests of the company president at a private reception.

*Wednesday morning, Argos-Dimitrios limo for return trip to Athens International for commuter flight to Santorini. Wednesday, Thursday., Friday suite booked at Heliotopos Hotel (exclusive ten room boutique), Santorini.

*Saturday morning, island commuter flight back to Athens International; connect to Olympic Airways non-stop flight to New York. Arrive JFK 1940. Sunday.

As she finished studying the itinerary, Britt rested a hand on Rebekah's back.

"Mmm-mm," came the sound from under blanket.

When Rebekah's breathing slid into the slow rhythmic pattern that signaled sleep, Britt pressed the flight attendant call button.

"How may I..." Britt looked up at the flight attendant, quickly putting one finger to her lips and nodding toward Rebekah. "Sorry," whispered the woman in uniform, "How may I help you?"

Britt pointed toward the overhead bin and mouthed, "My purse, the black one, please." The cabin attendant opened the bin and handed the bag to Britt, then slammed the hatch shut. Rebekah sat bolt upright.

"It's OK." Britt patted her back reassuringly. "It's nothing. I just wanted something out of my bag. Go back to sleep."

"I wasn't really asleep," said the colonel, pulling the blanket up over her head again. Britt resumed patting her back. From beneath the blanket came another "Mmmm."

Right, you were all kinds of wide awake, thought Britt as she dug in her purse with one hand for the flash drives. *Airport security never looked twice at them,* she recalled. *So reassuring.*

"Nice hair," mocked Britt when the flight attendant awoke Rebekah to insure her "seatback was in the full upright and locked position for landing."

"It looks like you styled it with a Cuisinart," she said, handing Rebekah the pink Yankees hat she'd also taken from her purse. "Put this on so you don't scare all the little children."

CHAPTER 36

Athens, Greece
1 November

A uniformed limo driver waited for Madam Chayat outside customs at Eleftherios Venizelos—Athens International Airport. He was a large, beefy man with huge hands that seemed to miniaturize the six-inch by twelve-inch sign he held with the Argos-Dimitrios name and logo printed on top, "Chayat" hand printed with Magic Marker below. Britt spotted the sign first and waved at the driver, who immediately headed in her direction. "We'll be right with you," said BJ, "as soon as my friend gets back."

With one gigantic hand, the limo driver wadded the cardboard sign into a ball as if it were a sheet of notepaper. "You are not alone, madam?"

"No, there are two of us. Is that a problem?" asked Brit.

"Not at all. I was not informed there would be two passengers," he said as Rebekah walked up from behind him, wearing the pink cap with the universally recognized interlocking NY symbol.

"OK, then. We're on our way," said BJ, sounding very much in charge.

As soon as the limo pulled out of the terminal area onto the Attiki Odios Expressway—the airport highway—the driver speed-dialed a number on his cell phone. He looked at the women in the rearview mirror and told them, "I am reporting your safe arrival."

He continued speaking softly into the phone. Rebekah didn't know Greek, but what little she could hear did not sound like the movie *Zorba.*

Six miles and fifteen minutes up the airport highway toward downtown Athens, the driver pointed out a huge skyscraper under construction. A giant banner hung about a quarter of the way up the building's super structure, where passing cars were sure to see it. "Argos-Dimitrios Future Global Headquarters" it proclaimed in English. Below that it said something in Greek—presumably the same thing. At ground level, a large billboard showed an architect's rendering of the completed building and the same inscription that was painted on the banner. The finished building would be truly impressive.

Moments after the limo passed, four black-clad men tight roped across the steel girders to where the banner hung, cut it down, folded it up and began to work their way back down to the ground floor. Then, out of sight of the guard shack at the main construction site entrance they scaled up the back of the billboard and cut down that banner.

Traffic was light on Sunday afternoon, and the limo reached the hotel on Karaiskaki Square in less than forty minutes. The driver quickly removed both suitcases and motioned for the doorman. Rebekah stepped between her bag and the porter, indicating that she needed no help. Britt had come to know that Rebekah never surrendered possession of her pull-along. She took that as her cue to wave off the doorman and drag her own wheelie to the front desk.

The clerk disappeared to the back office behind the counter while the two women scribbled on their registration cards. He returned shortly with their passports. "I'm sorry. there's been a mix-up, but the manager would like to offer a two-bedroom deluxe suite, instead of two single rooms. All charges have, of course, been prepaid." He took Rebekah's registration card and an imprint of her American Express card, explaining that it was only for incidentals, "but I believe those have been taken care of also."

The suite reminded Britt of the guest cottage suite on the island—except that instead of a veranda there was a second bedroom and bath off the living room. Rebekah picked up one of the phones in the living room and asked the concierge to make dinner reservations. "I want a great restaurant with a spectacular view." After showers and a change of clothes, the two women climbed into a taxi. The doorman told the driver, "Karamikos, 81 Piraeus Street."

They were on their second glass of wine at Varoulko—a world-renowned seafood restaurant with a spectacular view of the Acropolis—when BJ said, "Yesterday, you asked what I'd do if I caught you downloading my computer. Well, I would not have threatened to shoot you."

"What if the software I was trying to download from your laptop could open up computers at intelligence agencies all over the world, what would you have done?"

I've got to get those flash drives back to Brad. "I probably would have done what you did."

"Well, some people think my business intelligence software can do that. And I have to admit, I gladly let them think that. That's one of the reasons it sells so well, at such a high price. IBM, Oracle and others make stuff that's almost as good, but it doesn't have the Mossad mystique of mine. Theirs sell for about half of what I charge. For the money, they might even offer a better deal, so I'm not about to deny those rumors. It's all about that Mossad cache."

Totally plausible, thought Britt. "Have you ever considered, that the wrong people might believe those rumors? Like the Mossad might think you're back snooping around inside their computers?"

"Impossible." Rebekah reached for her glass and lifted it quickly to eye level, as though she'd seen some foreign object in it. It was a well-practiced move to disguise her surprise. "The chief of operations is a friend of mine. He'd just call me and ask."

"Or he might..." Britt stopped and took a sip of wine then set down her glass, "call someone else."

"And that someone used you to get into my computer. Is that what you're saying?"

BJ tried to imagine how Brad would jauntily deflect that question. "I'm saying it's time we ordered dinner before we're both totally hammered."

CHAPTER 37

Athens, Greece
1 November

A phone rang faintly somewhere down the long hall of the Athens Imperial as the two slightly giggly women got off the elevator. "That was a really good dinner," said Britt. "I think that waiter really liked us."

"That waiter was really hitting on us," Rebekah corrected. "I don't know about you but I'm going to need another shower." She grabbed a lock of her hair and pulled it to her nose. "At least it doesn't smell like flaming goat cheese. I was sure it would be set on fire by one of those saganaki plates the waiters kept carrying right past my chair."

"They would have doused the flames with one of those trays full of ouzo shots. But we sure drank our share."

Rebekah agreed with a resounding "ooh-pah!"

"Ooh-pah!" they roared together, each thrusting a celebratory hand in the air and whirling around in little circles mimicking a Greek folk dance.

As the two women giggled and twirled and ooh-pah-ed their way down the hall, the ring grew louder and closer. Simultaneously they realized it was coming from their suite and they race-walked down the corridor, fumbling in their purses for their magnetic-striped key cards. They reached the door together, but Rebekah found her card first, opened the door and let Britt dash in.

"Yes!"

"BJ, is that you?" asked the voice on the other end with a sense of urgency, bordering on alarm, that she had never before heard from Brad. Even when he asked her to spy on Rebekah, he was Mr. Measured, calm and deliberate.

"Brad, are you OK?" Britt's tone changed immediately. "You sound like something's wrong."

"Something is wrong, *terribly* wrong."

Without responding Britt motioned frantically for Rebekah to pick up another extension. "What are you talking about?"

Rebekah ripped another phone off its cradle so roughly you could hear the click all the way to New York.

"What was that?" demanded Brad.

"Rebekah just picked up. What's wrong?"

"Good. Listen, both of you," he insisted. "There is no such company as Argos-Dimitrios. They are not a subsidiary of anything. They are not traded on any exchange—anywhere.

They are supposedly a shipping and trading company, but they have no import or export licenses, no ships, no planes registered in their name, not even a pickup truck. They're not even in the phone book. It's all a sham—a fraud."

"Brad—" BJ attempted to get in a question but he never slowed down.

"You must get out of there right away. You are in grave danger!"

"From whom?" asked BJ.

"Rebekah, you know you are a high-value target. You are most certainly being watched, probably tailed," he continued.

"Why?" demanded Britt.

"I don't know, BJ. We're working on it."

"We? Who are 'we,' Brad?"

Her question went unanswered.

"From now on, only call me from a pay phone bank. They've been tapping cell phones in Greece since before the 2004 Olympics. Get some prepaid phone cards and only call my cell or my home phone from a bank of pay phones in a public place, like a bus or train station. and never the same phone twice." Then his tone changed, showing a hint of deference, "Beej, don't worry. Just stay with Rebekah. She's a pro."

"Brad—" BJ tried one more time.

"We've talked enough for right now."

Britt looked at the now silent receiver, then dropped it back in its cradle. "Don't worry? What the hell's going on, Rebekah?"

"If I knew, I would tell you."

"And what did Brad mean by 'you're a pro?'"

"Just a confidence booster, I'm sure."

"He meant you *are* a spy, didn't he? You never stopped being one, did you?"

The colonel ignored the question, just as Brad had. "Whoever they are, if they were going to move against us tonight, they would have done it. We were very easy targets. So," she announced, making a decision, "we do nothing to make them speed up their timetable."

The mystery and intrigue surrounding Rebekah was not so alluring right now. Britt managed forced a weak smile. "I guess that means sightseeing is off for tomorrow."

"Your bedroom is accessible from the hall. Would you like to sleep in my room? Mine has no outside access. It's safer and it has two double beds," reassured Rebekah.

Britt didn't hesitate. "I'll take the bed by the window."

"And I'll take first shower," said Rebekah. "We better get some sleep. We'll be leaving early. Will you please turn off our phones, like Brad said, but put them on charge, just in case?"

Britt was wearing a gray, athletic t-shirt and boxers as Rebekah emerged from the shower. A scrappy cartoon hawk, the Kansas mascot, adorned each cheek on the baggy shorts. Rebekah was drying her hair with one towel. A second fluffy bath sheet, tucked under her arms, protected her modesty to mid-thigh. Her olive skin glistened with vanilla-scented moisturizer and droplets of water falling from her hair; her legs sleek but powerful, like a ballerina. Sinewy calves tapered gracefully to well-formed, almost delicate ankles. "Next," she said, her face hidden beneath the terrycloth.

Britt walked toward the bathroom focused on her toiletries kit and muttering to herself. *Where is my damn toothbrush cord? I know I packed it.*

Neither woman was looking when they collided, knocking BJ's nylon bag out of her hand. Each made a futile effort to catch the falling assortment of beauty products scattering across the carpet. Rebekah stretched for the bag. Her towel fell to the ground.

"I'm sorry," they said in unison as both knelt to pick up the cosmetics strewn across the floor.

"I wasn't looking."

"My bad," countered Britt as they crouched nose to nose. She found herself staring into Rebekah's eyes.

Straight out of the shower, not a speck of makeup, hair wet, uncombed—the Colonel was a singularly beautiful woman— smelling of body wash, Pantene and vanilla, fresh and clean.

"No harm, no foul, Rebek—" BJ stopped mid-word, her eyes locking on an ugly, plum-colored scar on Rebekah's left breast only inches away. "What happened?" She pointed to the three-dimensional mutilation. "Is that a biopsy scar? A lumpectomy?"

Rebekah took Britt's hand and pressed it against the fifty-cent-piece sized disfigurement. It looked as if a short semi-circle of thick, purple yarn had been stitched beneath the skin to dam-up the underside of the scar. Above it, an unnaturally white puddle of scar tissue bubbled with pimple-sized Keloids, threatening to crest the dam and flow down the side of her breast toward her ribcage.

"Stab wound," explained Rebekah.

Britt's fingertips slid over the hard, raised edge, then traced the entire jagged-edge scar. She pictured an assailant, his knife held high in his right hand, plunging from two o'clock to seven o'clock toward Rebekah's heart.

"Does it hurt?"

"Sometimes. The sternum deflected the knife and he missed my heart by millimeters," recalled Rebekah, "but he twisted the blade, then he yanked it out like coring an apple." Rebekah guided Britt's hand from the scar to beneath her breast.

Cradling it like a precious jewel, BJ asked, "Who did this?"

"It doesn't matter. He won't do it again. He can't do anything again, but now you know why I find your courage on that bus so admirable."

The combination of seeing the scar, having her own bravery reinforced, and their conversation on the plane, evaporated the last of Britt's anger. She looked into Rebekah's eyes and was drawn by the same mix of power and pain she'd seen in the candlelight on the island. She couldn't explain why, but she knew she cared deeply for this woman. "Whoever it was, I hate him. I hate him worse than the guy on the bus. I—"

Her words were cut off by Rebekah's kiss—soft, sensuous, seductive, erotic—causing a nearly mystical warmth to course through BJ's body. "Rebekah, please, I'm not a—" She was shocked at her own response to the touch of Rebekah's lips. Blood pounded in her brain, her stomach swirled wildly and her heart thundered. "Please—"

"Please, what?" interrupted Rebekah, using one hand to keep Britt's hand pressed firmly against her disfigured breast. Sliding her other hand into the small of Britt's back she urged her up to a standing position.

Why me? Britt asked, not sure if she'd spoken aloud. In the blinding flare of that first kiss, her mind flashed back to their dinner on the island when the colonel dragged a fingernail down the underside of her forearm. The sensation barely registered at the time, but now, she recalled the shiver that had run from her occipital bone to her tailbone. From that night on, she'd had an amorphous, primordial sense of inevitability that something was happening beyond her control. She tried to deny her inexplicable desire for one more kiss—just one more. *Don't let this happen,* she scolded herself.

"Please, I'm not ready, I can't—" Britt grasped for words to politely stop where this was headed. Her search dissolved as again Rebekah's lips brushed hers. The Colonel's power and mystique were just too, too... Britt could not describe her own melting pot of swirling emotions, even to herself.

"All you have to do is push me away." Rebekah slid her hand up the length of Britt's spine to the back of her neck, guiding her head toward another kiss.

Their lips parted. "All you have to do is push." Between each word, she nibbled feather-light caresses over BJ's ear and neck.

Rebekah leaned back to see BJ's eyes and read the signals she was sure were there. "Just push. I will step back and, when we're safely out of this place, step out of your life completely. That's all you have to do, one little push."

Britt moved her hands to Rebekah's shoulders, she slid one foot back slightly, bracing to make a solid, unmistakable shove, but hesitated.

For whatever reason—was it the lure of Rebekah's charm and power, mixed with her soft vulnerability? Maybe the unfathomable eroticism that danger can bring? Was it the wine and Ouzo? Or was it simple physical and emotional exhaustion? Whatever the reason, Britt wavered. Her move to push-off had created the opening Rebekah was looking for. She deftly eased her thigh into the space between Britt's legs and pressed her powerful quadricep against Britt's pubic bone, eliciting a sigh. BJ could feel the rippling striations of Rebekah's leg muscles

Why don't I stop her? Britt chided herself as she slowly rocked against Rebekah's leg. Rebekah grasped the hem of Britt's t-shirt and began to lift. BJ raised her arms over her head. As the shirt hid her face, she closed her eyes. *I could still stop her,* she told herself. *I'm still in control; just one little push.*

Rebekah lifted the t-shirt free and dropped it on the carpet. Britt lowered her hands and thrust one into Rebekah's wet hair. She pulled their lips together; igniting an eroticism and intimacy that transcended any kiss she'd ever had.

Their breasts touched and BJ gasped as her nipple brushed over Rebekah's scar. Never before had another woman touched her like this. *So different,* she thought, *from being scoured raw by some hairy chest.*

A shudder undulated through her body, following the path of incandescent warmth radiating up and out from her groin. *Could Rebekah feel what I just felt?* Her breasts tingled as if bathed in champagne, with every effervescent bubble lighting it's own miniscule spark. Her nipples became pebbles, standing out from her crinkling areolas. She felt the first tiny contractions begin to ripple "down there."

Why have I never felt this before? she wondered, consumed by a dreamy intimacy, softer, more tender, yet far more arousing than anything she had ever known. She knew she was getting wet. *Did Rebekah feel my knees just wobble?*

Rebekah awoke in the middle of the night, her arm draped across Britt's naked body, holding one breast and pulling her protectively into the spoon position. She nuzzled her nose into Britt's hair, captivated by the fragrance of her shampoo *Coconut with something sweet and tropical. Hibiscus? Maybe orchid?* With the soft glow coming from a living room lamp, she could see the honey blonde highlights streaked through the deep brunette, so silky and natural, and shining like a lifeguard's hair at the end of summer. Rebekah loved the smell and feel of BJ's hair; loved everything about this woman.

"I just made love with an assassin, didn't I?" murmured Britt, mostly to herself and barely loud enough to be heard.

"Technically," whispered Rebekah, surprised that BJ was awake, "the assassin made love to you. Are you sorry about that?"

"Which part, the love or the assassin?"

"One little push was all it took," reminded Rebekah, "and it would have ended right there."

Britt lifted Rebekah's hand from her breast and kissed each fingertip. "I knew that."

As they cuddled together, Rebekah's breasts pressed against Britt's shoulder blades. Each woman thought about tomorrow. Each wondered how many tomorrows they had left? "I want to stay with you like this," said the Colonel, "always."

"It's not that simple," said Britt, placing the Colonel's hand back on her breast and pressing it tightly with her own. "But we'll always have tonight. Nothing can take that away. Thank you."

Rebekah nuzzled closer and kissed BJ's neck as a new plan formed in her head. She pulled BJ's body even tighter to her own and kissed her hair—kissed it goodbye.

CHAPTER 38

New York City
2 November

The chill of fall was in the early morning air when the Sutton Place doorman opened the double glass doors for Mackenzie Collingwood. As she said good morning to her driver, Charles, a figure approached, from under the canopy awning two buildings away. Neither Mackenzie nor the doorman took notice, but Charles's trained eye immediately sensed the suspicious movement.

The man's all black outfit was stylish but menacing, with his face obscured by an upturned collar, a pulled-down hat and dark glasses. Charles's hand darted beneath his suit coat for his shoulder-holstered Glock 9, while his other hand pressed the "auto" button lowering the driver's side window. He could see his breath as he held the weapon out of sight, just below the window. He silently inched open his door, just a crack, not enough to turn on the interior lights.

The figure was moving faster now. As he bore down on Mackenzie and the limo, Charles raised his weapon so the muzzle rested just below the window ledge and slid the safety off. Mackenzie walked a few steps behind the doorman. Charles opened his door and stepped out of the limo, his weapon concealed by his thigh, his finger on the trigger. Unconsciously, he calculated the walking speed and direction of all three people. He could visualize what was about to happen as clearly as watching a movie. In less than a second, the stranger would pass between Mackenzie and the doorman, blocking Charles's vision and his shot.

"Jimmy!" he yelled dropping to one knee as the man darted between Mackenzie and the doorman.

That's all it would take, thought the ex-Navy Seal, as the man continued on and never looked back. Charles watched him every step of the way until he disappeared around a corner.

"Charles? Is something wrong?" Mackenzie demanded, momentarily frozen in the no-man's land between the building and the bulletproof limo.

"No, ma'am," he said, smoothly sliding the weapon back behind his leg. "Just saying good morning to my friend, Jimmy." Charles had seen walk-through rehearsals before. He had led several operational walk-throughs. This had all the earmarks of a dress rehearsal.

"What's the matter with your leg?"

"Just a little leg cramp, ma'am," he said, concealing the pistol while sliding back into the driver's seat, as Jimmy opened the passenger door. "Old age setting in, I guess."

"As long as you're sure you're OK," said Mackenzie, as she eased into the rear seat. "I could go back and get you an aspirin or something. What are you, all of forty?"

"Thirty-eight next month, ma'am. I'm good now. Thank you," he said as the doorman closed Mackenzie's door.

He put the car into gear and drove around the corner. If the early-morning stroller maintained his pace, he should be only a few doors from corner. He was not. Either he had disappeared into one of the neighboring buildings, or he had an accomplice waiting to drive him away, just as he would in a live operation.

CHAPTER 39

Athens, Greece
2 November

In her early morning fog, Britt thought nothing was out of the ordinary when she woke up alone. That was the way she awoke every morning. Then she saw the turned down but unused queen bed that was to have been hers.

"Rebekah! Rebekah!" When she heard no answer, she climbed out of bed to check the bathroom. The door was wide open. The shower stall was empty and dry. She went to the living area of the suite; sure she would find Rebekah nursing a cup of coffee. Instead she found Rebekah's suitcase, the one she never let anyone else touch, open on the couch. It appeared to have been hastily rummaged through. "Rebekah! Where are you?" The safety chain was off the door. *I definitely checked that last night when I put the cell phones on charge.*

She checked their cell phones. Both were still on charge. A search of the suite yielded only a single piece of hotel stationery on the dining table. It lay next to the open presentation binder that contained the software success stories that Mackenzie and Rebekah had put together. She pushed that aside to read the note.

BJ, Gone to get some phone cards and call Brad. Be right back. Stay in room. Do not open the door for anyone, not even the maids. Everything will be all right.

I promise. R.C.

Britt wadded up the note. *Isn't that just lovely*, she thought. *Brad is my friend. I'm the one who got him involved. Now she's calling him, while I site here alone, waiting for some terrorist to knock on my door.*

She grabbed the TV remote and surfed around until she found CNN International. The news was all the same. People were still starving in Africa. The Basques still hated the Spaniards. Millions of Pakistanis were still living in tents in the mountains years after floods and earthquakes. They still hated the Indians. Islamic radicals still hated everyone, but they'd had an off night—no major car bombings of mosques or marketplaces were reported.

She punched the off button on the remote. The audio squawk of turning off the TV coincided with the click of the suite door opening. Britt didn't hear the black-clad figure—a bizarre cross between a ninja and a hump-backed bag lady—coming behind her, but caught a hint of movement in her peripheral vision. "Whaa—" Britt leapt to her feet, assuming the Krav Maga position for lethal self-defense.

"It's OK. It's me," reassured Rebekah, unwinding the black shawl covering her head and slumped shoulders.

"My God! You scared me to death." Britt's heart was trying to beat its way through her chest wall. "I would never have recognized you."

"Good," said Rebekah, taking off her nondescript black top to reveal a small blow-up plastic pillow Velcroed to her bra strap, creating an old woman's hump. She walked toward Britt wearing an ill-fitting black skirt that came almost to the ankles, black hose, and plain black sneakers that looked like they came out of a dumpster. She dragged a beat up suitcase that could have come from the same dumpster. Turning her back to Britt, she said, "Yank this thing off me, will you?"

Britt tugged the pillow. It made that unmistakable Velcro ripping sound as she pulled it loose. "What's this?"

"My old lady's hump."

"Do you always travel with..." The words trailed off. In the silence, Britt recalled Brad's voice loud and clear: "computer whiz, a trained killer and a master of disguise." Slowly she sank back down onto the couch.

"Brad was right. We have to get out of here. Their people are covering every door in and out of the hotel."

"Whose people?"

"People who want to capture or kill me."

"Why?"

Rebekah ignored the question. She reached into her black purse, which could have come from the same dumpster as her shoes, and pulled out a paper bag and handed it to Britt. "Here. I brought you some breakfast, Greek pastries. They're very good."

"What people? What the hell is going on?" demanded Britt, tearing open the paper bag.

"They want me, not you," said Rebekah. "So the first thing we have to do is sneak you out of this hotel before they come to pick us up with that limo at ten-thirty. Unfortunately, I don't have another disguise for you."

"Sorry. I didn't get the memo. 'Always carry a Halloween costume when you travel with Rebekah' because somebody will want to kill you."

"It's only eight-fifteen," said the colonel, preoccupied as she checked her watch. "By nine-thirty, I expect us to walk right past them and they'll never recognize us."

"You might walk by them in your handy-dandy little old bag lady outfit, but I didn't bring my costume, remember? How about if I back out with no pants and you tell them I'm a giant Parker House roll?"

Rebekah smiled at Britt's pluck. "I have a better plan," she said, picking up the phone. "The hair salon, please."

The salon receptionist answered first in Greek, probably with the salon name, and something like "May I help you."

"This is Ms. Chayat."

Before she heard anymore, the receptionist apologized and switched to heavily accented English. "I am sorry. Does madam Chayat require an appointment?"

"I need a temporary coloring for a masquerade party. Can you take someone right now?"

"One of our stylists will be here in about fifteen minutes and can service you."

"Fine," said the colonel. "I want a bright, bright red, but one that will wash out fairly quickly, and I need to be finished before nine-thirty." Britt looked at the woman on the phone as though she was out of her mind. "No way," she mouthed, "not *my* hair." The colonel was unfazed. "And matching extensions to make a nice old lady's bun."

She hung up the phone and began cutting up the battered suitcase. "An hour and fifteen minutes from now you will look like every matronly librarian you've ever seen in the movies, with that old lady red hair not found in nature. We have fifteen minutes for you to get dressed and for us to consolidate our stuff into my suitcase and get out of here. We will not be returning to this room."

Rebekah did most of the consolidating and made most of the decisions about what was essential. A few times she asked BJ if a particular cosmetic or some article of clothing was really necessary. Then she taped the tattered panels of the old suitcase to hers. Just as Rebekah started to zip up the bag, Britt yelled, "Wait!" She ran into the kitchen and returned with the cell phones in one hand and the chargers in the other. She tossed them all into their communal suitcase that on the outside looked like it had come from the city dump.

"Good work!" said Rebekah. "You take this with you to the salon. By the time you're done there, I will be back with the rest of your disguise. You can change in the ladies' room. Then, two old ladies will walk out of this place and right past those people, they will never know. Now, stick my hump back on."

The colonel was pleased with how easily she walked by the eleven men covering the main entrance. Four loitered close by the door with three more across the street. Four men, farther away, were backs ups. Turning left at the corner of the building, she walked past the lesser-used side entrance, the door closest to the salon. Only three men were stationed there. A white panel truck was parked in the adjacent loading zone with one rear door open. She could not read the sign on the vehicle, but she could see a couple of rolled carpets through the open door. The watchers paid no attention to the truck or the hunched-over woman shuffling past them. She would definitely route their escape through this side entrance.

Scouting the area, she decided Karaiskaki Square was a convenient place for a hurried departure—whether escaping an abduction or committing one. The Red and Green Metro lines crossed at the station beneath the square. The map outside the station showed the Green going directly to Piraeus, the port for passenger ships and ferries to all the Greek islands. One stop away on the Red line was the international railroad station and the central bus station, Ktel. Under different circumstances, she might enjoy shopping in the fashionable little boutiques on the side streets, but she was looking for a couple of low-end stores that she would ordinarily never set foot in. Then she saw the exact frumpy, floral dress she had in mind on a window mannequin in a quite fashionable store. It was awful looking, which made it just perfect.

She was the only customer in the store at this early hour, but two clerks instantly began manhandling her toward the door and out of the store, insisting they weren't open yet. They spoke Greek but their message was clear in any language. Humpbacked little old bag ladies were not welcome. Rebekah fought off the urge to deck them both with a martial arts move and instead opened her purse, showing a wad of Euro notes. Magically, everything changed. The saleswomen could not have been more welcoming or apologetic.

Rebekah pointed toward the dress in the window, but the now fawning clerks tried to steer her toward racks in the back, holding dozens of more stylish dresses. She pointed again at the dress in the window. "Go!" She gave one clerk an insistent shove in that direction.

With a little padding, like a folded bath towel pinned around her hips, that dress will make BJ look exactly like a rotund, retired librarian. Then she pulled at the baggy black top under her shawl until the clerks got the idea she was looking for bras. They pointed to a rack and there she saw it—The Mother Lode—

a large cotton bra with wide padded shoulder straps and a nearly three-inch wide back strap. She pitied any poor woman who would actually need to wear this, but stuffed with enough tissue it would nicely complete the look she wanted for Britt's disguise.

While the little old lady in black was playing charades in the dress shop, a large, burly well-dressed man walked down the hotel arcade-level corridor toward the hair salon. The floor-to-ceiling windows gave him a clear view of the beauticians' workstations. He focused on Britt and the stylist long enough to recognize the woman with orange goo in her hair. He turned away before making eye contact.

Rebekah paid cash for the clothes and got directions to a nearby shoe store where she found a pair of cheap, sensible lace-ups with a three-quarter-inch heel and wide round toes. She could not completely hide her smile as the clerk handed them to her in a plastic bag. *Truly hideous,* she smiled at the thought, *but with excellent arch support.*

The stylist tipped her client's chair back toward the shampoo bowl. Britt closed her eyes, luxuriating in the feeling of fingers and warm water working through her hair, sending a pool of reddish-orange dye swirling down the drain. Then the fingers stopped kneading her scalp. With her eyes still closed, BJ gave a disappointed moan and waited for the shampoo to begin. Moments passed. No shampoo, no fingers. A sudden spray of water splashed across her face. Her eyes flashed open then bulged in sheer panic-stricken terror. The man from the corridor—yesterday's limo driver—slammed his huge hand down on her bare throat. From her nearly supine position, with her neck suspended in the porcelain U of the salon sink, she was powerless to defend herself. She tried to scream, but no sound came out. She kicked and thrashed wildly, futilely. The last thing she saw or remembered was the cloth in his other hand descending toward her nose and mouth and the sweet-smell of the surgical anesthetic, Sevoflurane.

CHAPTER 40

Athens, Greece
2 November

Rebekah shuffled two blocks to the main entrance of the international railroad station. Once inside she spotted a bank of phones. Using one of the pre-paid phone cards she bought earlier, she punched in the endless stream of numbers necessary to call Brad's cell phone and charge the call to the minutes available on the card. There was no answer. She tried his home number, no answer. She tried the cell again, leaving a message that she would call back in ten minutes. If they didn't talk then, she would try again when they reached the port of Piraeus.

The little old lady shuffled unnoticed past the stakeout deployed at the side entrance of the Athens Imperial, but Rebekah's trained eye immediately saw that the contingent of three now was reduced to one. The white service van, with its rear cargo door ajar was still parked by the side entrance. She looked back over her shoulder, trying to determine the whereabouts of the two missing goons. She shuffled through the door and two laborers slammed her against the wall, smacking her squarely in the side of her head with the large rolled-up carpet. Neither apologized, oblivious to the fact that they had almost trampled over an old woman.

She cursed the clumsy bastards under her breath, *And people say Israelis are rude!* The workmen never noticed the old woman's speed, grace and athleticism in staying on her feet. Quickly back into character, she shuffled down the corridor and around the corner to the hair salon, which was completely empty. "BJ?" she called out, "Britt?" No answer. She must be in the back, she reasoned, where the shampoo sinks were the only part of the salon not visible from the showcase windows in the corridor. As she stepped around the reception desk, she recoiled at the sight of the receptionist's limp body on the floor.

"Britt! BJ!" she yelled as she knelt down to feel for the receptionist's non-existent pulse. "BJ!" she screamed again, running toward the partition that shielded the shampoo sinks from the rest of the salon. The garrote was still around the neck of the hairdresser's lifeless body lying on the floor next to the sink. The sprayer hose swung like a pendulum, back and fourth, drenching the body of the murdered beautician and inundating the floor.

Rebekah raced back toward the side door of the hotel. Britt was gone. The van was gone, so was the lone stakeout she'd passed just moments ago. She knew immediately what had happened. Worse, she knew the old lady could have easily taken down the two goons while they struggled with the carpet that encapsulated her friend. Then she could have easily disabled the third man outside. He would never have known what hit him.

Sick with grief and guilt, she crumpled to her knees, blaming herself, without thinking that she could never have carried her unconscious friend past the men outside the hotel, thus insuring the capture of both women.

She slowly picked herself up, returning to the salon, she found her suitcase in the closet. She shuffled back to the train station, fighting the urge to run—a dead giveaway that she was anything but a little old lady.

At the station, she inserted her calling card and dialed Brad's number.

"Hello," said the answering voice.

"Brad, they have BJ."

"What!"

"They have BJ! They took her from the hotel hair salon wrapped in a carpet."

"The hair salon!" screamed Brad. "Are you fucking crazy? What the hell was she doing in the hair salon? I said to get out of there."

"Brad, Brad," implored Rebekah, needing to assure him, and herself, that she'd done the right things. "They were watching every door. They had eight men on the front entrance alone. I sent her to have her hair dyed and put up in an old lady's bun for a disguise. I'd gone out to get the rest of the disguise so I could sneak her out of there."

"Why the hell would they grab BJ? You're the high-value target." The pointed reference left no doubt that he blamed Rebekah.

"They took her by mistake. They think they have me."

"Yeah. She's so easily mistaken for a fucking commando."

"When I made the appointment for her, the front desk switched my call to the salon and told them it was me, because my name is on the room. But our cell phones may have played a role."

"Cell phone!" He had been angry before. Now he was furious. "Cell phone? We talked about that. I told you not to use them."

"We were *not* using them. We had turned them off, but when we left the room, Britt grabbed both phones off their chargers and tossed them in our suitcase. Some phones turn on by themselves when you disconnect the charger. Maybe hers, maybe mine, I don't know. She may not have heard the beep when she threw them into our suitcase. That could be how they tracked us to the salon."

Rebekah heard a deep breath expelled into the mouthpiece of the distant phone. "Jesus H. Christ! When they figure out what's happened, BJ is excess baggage, as good as dead, and you're still their primary target. Where are you?"

"I shouldn't say. I've been here too long."

"I'll be on the first flight I can get to Athens. One way or another, I'll be there sometime tomorrow. How will I find you?"

"The Greek Islands are lovely this time of year. Pick any one, I'll find you."

"Rebekah! Rebekah! Which fu—" Click.

When she hung up, the colonel knelt to unzip her wheelie just enough that she could slide her hand in to rummage for a phone. The first one she felt was Britt's phone. It was dark. Next she felt her own. She pulled it out of the bag and stared in disbelief at the little screen glowing brightly.

It was her phone. It was her fault, all her fault.

CHAPTER 41

Varese Province, Italy
3 November

The international transit lounge at Milan's Malpensa airport is a lounge in name only. It is a mostly inhospitable, starkly utilitarian concourse. Brad slung his duffel bag over his shoulder and trudged toward the coffee bar, with that somnambulant, zombie-like gait typical of red-eye survivors everywhere. A middle seat in coach was all he could get on the first available flight with a decent connection to Athens. Rich, warming coffee aromas grew stronger with every step, slowly breathing life into the weary traveler as he reached the counter and ordered a double espresso. He paid no attention to the dark-haired, dark-eyed, dark-complexioned man walking away with a steaming cup. Moments later both men were at the news kiosk, each buying the *International Herald Tribune.* Brad O'Malley also bought the *USA Today* international edition. His fellow coffee addict and news junkie looked vaguely familiar. Pinpointing which dark-haired, dark-eyed, mustachioed man he might be thinking of was like narrowing a manhunt in Oslo to blue-eyed blonds. From the newsstand, the man melted into a collage of similar-looking men.

Brad found a seat on one of the hard metal chairs to which international transferees are subjected. He sipped his coffee and made the one call on his list that he had not made while waiting for his flight from JFK to Milan. Rusty Smith, the legal attaché at the U.S. embassy in Athens, was an old friend. The "LegAt"— the FBI agent in charge for the country—was not in the office, but Brad talked the officious, standoffish operator into calling the agent's cell phone for permission to patch him through. Two minutes later, she returned, friendly as could be. "Mr. O'Malley, I'm so sorry to keep you waiting. I found Mr. Smith at home. I didn't realize you were personal friends. I'm patching you through right now. Have a nice day, sir."

He spoke briefly and finished the call just as he heard the boarding announcement for business class passengers on Alitalia Flight 0275 for Athens. *Thank God there was an open business class seat on this flight.* No sooner had he settled into seat 3-C than the flight attendant was by his side asking for his beverage preference and offering to take his empty cup and the rumpled *USA Today*, but he barely saw her. His attention was drawn to seat 2-B—one row forward and across the aisle. The same dark-haired, dark-eyed man with a mustache was sliding into that seat. Brad looked away and turned his attention to the *International Herald Tribune.* As he folded back the first page he let out an audible gasp. Full-column width, side-by-side blow-ups of BJ's and Rebekah's passport photos stared back at him from above the fold. Greek police had declared them persons of interest in connection with a double murder in an Athens hotel hair salon,

Across the aisle, 2-B was giving the same story equal—maybe greater—scrutiny, but 2-B was making notes in the margins, then carefully tearing the article out of the paper. Brad flipped rapidly through the pages of his mental photo album looking for a match for 2-B. He couldn't find one, but, thanks to the *International Herald Tribune,* several intelligence services were already running Rebekah's passport photo through their face-recognition programs, comparing this picture with their old files on known or suspected Israeli agents. Coded messages flew around the world. Computers cranked through their version of Rebekah's original national security software looking for a connection between her and the unknown female, Britt Jaeger.

Brad had two more hours on the plane to Athens to think about where he would find Rebekah and how they would find BJ. He also thought about what he would tell Rusty Smith when they met for that "cold one." Right now he was just glad he had not seen the murder story before calling him—gladder still that Rusty had not brought it up. *Why would he?* He knew Rusty was looking four weeks ahead to his next, and last assignment, Special Agent in Charge, Burlington, Vermont. Brad could picture him hunting, fishing and skiing in the Green Mountains for the next two years before retiring. The new LegAt was already sitting at Rusty's desk. Rusty had briefed his incoming replacement on all the current cases and handed over a set of office keys, the safe combinations and the codes. "It's your shop, Tiger," he told him. "Go get 'em."

Brad was the first passenger out of his seat, as the aircraft door opened at Athens International. Standing in the aisle, he looked down on the passenger in 2-B. *You don't know it, Zorba, or whatever your name is, but you are my new best friend. Wherever you go, I'm with you.*

As 2-B climbed out of his seat, Brad noticed the huge gold ring, the size of a Super Bowl or World Series ring, on his left hand.

As they entered passport control, Zorba walked away from the queues toward three men in suits standing near an unmarked door. The men nodded deferentially. Zorba produced a United Arab Emirates diplomatic passport identifying him as

Mahoud Farshidi, a second-level deputy minister of Physical Education, visiting Athens to see how the 2004 Olympic facilities were being utilized several years after the games. The U.A.E. was awash in oil money. Dubai was a six-star playground for the world's wealthiest, and slimiest, including an arms dealer recently assassinated in his luxury hotel room by a Mossad hit squad.

With its manmade islands and indoor ski run, an Olympic bid was well within its means. Zorba and the other three men disappeared behind the unmarked door. *So much for following him*, thought Brad. *Man plans. God laughs.*

Forty minutes later, as Brad was finally clearing customs and immigration, a Mercedes limousine carrying the four men he'd seen in the airport wheeled through the gates of the embassy—not the Arab Emirates but the Iranian embassy. It stopped at the VIP entrance on the side of the ornate building, invisible from outside the compound. Uniformed guards deferentially stepped forward to open the car door. When the passenger stepped out, the guards saluted—not merely a regulation-fulfilling slap of the hand to the hat—but a very crisp salute for a man they knew was a real VIP.

Two hours, a train and subway ride later, Brad walked though the train arrivals terminal at Piraeus, the port of Athens. He fumbled for a Euro or a dollar bill, hoping that would pacify the annoying old woman begging with an iron-fisted grip on his arm. "The Greek Islands are lovely this time of year." The familiar voice and accent were startlingly out of place.

"Turn around. Go back to Athens—Attiki station," she continued. "I will be one carriage behind you. At Victoria station, come back to my carriage. I will be gone. Get my suitcase from under the seat closest to the rear door on the platform side. Do not forget it. Continue on one stop to Attiki station. Change to the Red line and go back three stops to Omonia, then walk up 28 October Street to Residence Georgio. I called. They have rooms. I reserved one in your name. Don't worry. It's not a bed and breakfast. It's five stars and big enough that we'll just be two more foreign business travelers. Got it?"

"Everything but the last part."

"What part is that?" asked Rebekah.

"The part after 'turn around, go back to Athens.'"

"Very funny. By now they know they have the wrong person, so they're looking for me. If they'd made me, I probably wouldn't be here now, but we can't be too careful. Check in, then follow the same route back to Attiki station and bring an extra room key. One hour from now, I will be begging on the platform. I expect a generous donation and a room key."

* * * *

The plastic key card did not even give the hotel name, and he did not speak to the humpbacked woman on the Attiki subway platform. He handed her two one Euro notes with "956" written on one. Both were wrapped around the plastic key card.

She took the key and disappeared through a detraining crowd and into a public WC. By the time he returned to the room she had already arrived—looking younger and cleaner but obviously fatigued. A cheap straw hat and dark glasses lay on the coffee table.

"Brad, I am so sorry. I never imagined—"

"You should be," he said. "They didn't even want her. You were the target. You are still the target."

"Who are *they*?"

"You should know who wants to kill you."

She flipped her hands open, palms up. "Lots of people for lots of reasons."

"You know they're following you."

"I'm sure they're trying, but still waiting for a little old lady to come out of the WC."

"Then you're probably safe for now. Take a shower and get some rest. You can have the bedroom, if you like. I'll take the foldout in the living room. If you order room service, sign my name. It's the only name on this room. I'm off to see a man about a dog. Double lock the door behind me."

Brad pulled the door closed and waited to hear the inside lock latch. Through the door he faintly heard her voice, "Brad, I will trade places with her, if that's what it takes to get her free."

"She'd have to be alive for that to happen."

CHAPTER 42

Mossad Headquarters
Herzliya 3 November

Jock Ayalon sat on the front of his desk looking down at Dani and Rafi Herzog. "Gentlemen, I'm sorry it took so long to get our calendars coordinated, but I understand Deputy Director Herzog has had a busy travel schedule."

Rafi blanched at the obvious slap but handed Jock a copy of the *International Herald Tribune* opened to the pictures of Rebekah and Britt, hoping to deflect the insinuation. "I think this shows that Colonel Chayat is not the same revered officer we once knew. We must assume she's capable of anything, even espionage against Israel."

Jock studied the paper, then slapped it against his leg. "I agree. She's capable of anything."

"Including a backdoor into our systems," added Rafi. "It's just unclear whether that's for purely commercial reasons or her political loyalties have changed."

"We need to know which," said Jock, punching an extension into his desk phone.

"Ayalon, here, immediate cable to all station chiefs, Priority One alert. Locate retired Kidon operative Colonel Rebekah Chayat by any means possible. For her own personal security and comfort, she is to be detained as a special guest of our nearest embassy, prior to safe transport as directed. Signed, Jock, DDG.

Rafi bit his lip to suppress a smile, while shaking his head. "Sad. Sad. She was a legend."

"She may be a different kind of legend now," said Jock. "Rafi, I need you to go back to your day job and stop worrying about the colonel and these supposed intrusions. I know now what needs to be done.

"I'm bringing in an outside IT security team," said Jock, getting up off his desk. "I've ordered a forensic examination of the entire Colonel Chayat project from the day she was selected until she retired. That was Dani's suggestion. He will interface with them."

Rafi was livid at the prospect of outsiders rummaging around but he talked like a team player. "Ah, ah, an excellent idea, sir. I'm ready to help."

"I know you are," said Jock, extending his hand, signaling the end of the meeting. "Just tell your entire technology unit this is going to be more in depth than a colonoscopy. They should all prepare to bend over."

"Of course, sir," said Herzog.

* * * *

"It seems so long ago," said Dani, "this is the very table where you were sitting the first time I saw you and wondered: What's Hélène doing here?"

"I thought the same thing when I saw you," she said, taking a forkful of her salad. "Now I'm the one wondering what I'm doing here."

"What do you mean?"

She leaned toward him and lowered her voice. "Dani, I need a favor, a personal favor. It's probably against regulations, so if you say no, I'll understand."

He looked panicked. "Hélène, I can't afford to break any more regulations around here. I'll be out on my ass."

She laid down her fork and looked directly at Dani. "I need to know anything you can find out about an email address that contains hiker787878. It's a personal matter, of the heart."

"An online romance?" said Dani, relieved. "I'll do a little snooping from home. Why don't you come by tonight? We'll grab something to eat and take it back to my place." He sucked on the straw in his drink. "That probably won't get me fired again."

Shortly after lunch, Hélène was outside Rafi's door reading a magazine when he stopped in front of her chair. "Shalom, agent Seiderman, a pleasant surprise. Please come in."

As Rafi closed his door she gave him a quick kiss on the cheek. "I'm going to my parents tonight—" She ended on an up note, as if there was more coming, and winked.

Rafi froze.

"Rafi, what's the matter with your face? You look like you have Bell's Palsy or something." She smiled. "I want you to come to my apartment for dinner tomorrow night. I want a normal night. No King David, no filet mignon, no flaming desserts. We both need to see what a normal life might be like."

"I'll bring champagne."

"No. I said normal. I want a simple bottle of white table wine."

"What kind?"

"I don't care. Surprise me. Look," she said, almost pleading, "I want this to work for us." *You better not be playing me for a sucker.* "I'm getting tired of sneaking to mosques listening to Friday diatribes from imams who want to destroy us all. I'm tired of taking eight taxis and four trains, through the rain, to some late night meeting in a deserted bus stop where the contact doesn't show. I want to have a normal life—with you." *Don't screw it up.*

"Are you going to announce to your parents—"

"Not tonight," she cut him off. "Maybe after dinner tomorrow night you can ask my father for permission."

* * * *

Six hours later, she was sitting in front of Dani's laptop in his apartment sharing a pizza. "Hiker787878 is a yahoo account," said Dani, "housed at hk.yahoo.com. Yahoo Hong Kong. It's a very small file, so there's almost no traffic. Its only incoming mail is an occasional spammer selling Viagra or penis enlargement."

He doesn't need either of those, she thought. "There's no ongoing lover's exchange?"

"Hardly, but here's what's interesting." He ran his finger through the headers at the top of the message. "Even incoming spam gets bounced around about four times. First stop, Yahoo Canada; then on to Baidu, China's Google; then to Google Switzerland, finally Yahoo Hong Kong again."

"What's all that mean?"

"It means someone has gone to a lot of trouble to make messages untraceable and they've probably succeeded. If you were trying to cover your tracks, and knew what you're doing, a message could be inserted or retrieved from any point in the chain without ever accessing the home base Hong Kong account. Definitely not for paramours trading 'I love yous.'"

"Well, maybe he's telling the truth," she said.

"Who?" asked Dani.

"A boyfriend. I was worried there was someone else. You've made me feel a lot better, Dani. Thank you."

Dani didn't appear so pleased. "Hélène, you should know this hop-skip-jump pattern is used by several intelligence agencies. They use it to communicate with deep cover agents and assets."

She instantly turned to face him. "Like who?"

"Like the Iranians, the Russians, the Chinese, the North Koreans, the U.S., France, England, Germany and us, of course. Rafi Herzog claims to sort of have invented it."

"Sort of invented it?"

"Like Al Gore sort of invented the Internet."

CHAPTER 43

Athens, Greece
3 November

"Good Afternoon, Excellency," said Abu Ghorbanifar. The title on his office door read, Cultural Attaché. That designation was the diplomatic cover for the Ministry of Intelligence and Security resident agent, assigned to Iran's embassy in Athens.

"May I offer tea?" asked the burly cultural attaché, with huge hands.

"I did not come all this way for tea, brother. You have my goods packaged and ready to ship to Tehran? Take me to her now."

An hour later, the two men climbed the 107 steps up the metal stairway secured to the hull of a super tanker. The ship's captain met the two men as they stepped onto the main deck. Despite four stripes on the epaulets of his white open-collared shirt, he treated both men as his superiors. He led them to a watertight steel door, thick enough for a small bank vault, with a large steering wheel-like locking device in the center. All three went single-file down a passageway lit every ten feet by glass and metal caged bulbs. Finally, the captain pulled a key from his pocket and opened an unmarked door.

"Stand her up," ordered Mahoud Farshidi.

Ghorbanifar yanked the prisoner up off the bunk to a standing position. Slowly and menacingly, Mahmud Farshidi dragged a hand up her arm to her shoulder. The woman tried to jerk away but could not move without falling. "So, my dear Colonel, we shall finally have the pleasure of spending some time together. And let me assure you, we will be spending many pleasant hours with each other. Pleasant for me."

Ali-Albadi slid his hand up over the slope of her shoulder, along her neck, to the top of the hood covering her head. He grabbed the hood, catching a small shock of hair.

"Captain," he asked in Farsi, "is transportation ready to take this piece of garbage to the rendezvous point?"

"It is, Excellency. After dark, when activity slows in the harbor, a small work boat will take you and your cargo to meet the submarine."

Without warning, Ali-Albadi violently yanked off the hood, brutally twisting her neck and bringing with it a small handful of hideously red-orange hair. Britt screamed as the hair was ripped from her scalp. Ordinary room light instantly blinded her. Before her scream ended, her tormentor was yelling just as loudly.

"What have you done?" he roared in Farsi. Still holding the hood, he spun around and grabbed his subordinate by the throat, choking him against the wall. "Do you know who this is?"

"The Z-Z Zi-o-nist spy," he gurgled through the spasms of his constricted windpipe.

"No, you idiot!" growled Ali-Albadi, turning his attention back to the woman blinking her eyes, still trying to focus. "This is not the murderer—the spy. This is an American. She works for the Collingwood woman. She is not even a credible double!" he screamed, dragging his fingers disdainfully through her matted, repulsively-orange hair before roughly pulling the hood back over her head, plunging her once again into darkness,

"Are you working for the Zionists?" he ranted at the subordinate.

"Excellency," babbled the underling, almost as terrified as Britt, "this woman identified herself as Chayat—to me! I picked them up. I drove the car. The appointment book in the salon said 'Chayat 8:30'"

Britt understood only two words in that angry exchange— Chayat and Collingwood. "I don't know who you are," she shouted from under the hood, "but you have to let me go. I am an Ameri—"

Smack! For a second Britt did not comprehend what had happened to her. Then the pain set in. Her ears rang. Stars streaked across the darkness inside the hood. She tasted the salty, metallic ooze dripping from the corner of her mouth and she realized she was on the floor and bleeding. Waves of green and yellow light flowed and ebbed as she teetered on the edge of consciousness. If the vicious roundhouse backhand had landed an inch or two higher on her temple, she could be dead.

"My associate can be premature in the application of his persuasive techniques. Let us begin again. Why were you impersonating Colonel Chayat?" demanded the Chairman of Department 36 in very passable English.

"I was not—" *Thwump!* The underling lashed out again, with a vicious kick to her midsection, hoping to restore his image with his superior by inflicting maximum violence.

Still on the floor, her body knotted involuntarily into a ball. The pain came simultaneously with her attempt to breathe, but she was suffocating. Try as she might, she could not inhale, could not exhale, could not scream. The shoe had slammed into her gut so hard that it literally kicked the gastric acid upward into the esophagus. Stomach acid is less than one percent hydrochloric acid, but that was enough to make her throat burn with liquid fire.

She stopped gasping for breath only when she lapsed into unconsciousness. That allowed her diaphragm to relax enough for a small breath, then another. Through her semiconscious haze of pain, she heard the fierce yelling continuing.

"We know the answer!" Ali-Albadi screamed in Farsi. "Collingwood betrayed us. She tipped you off. We poured in money to save her company, in exchange for delivering Chayat, and she betrayed us." Britt understood the same two words: Collingwood and Chayat. After more yelling and screaming, she felt herself being lifted back onto her feet. She cringed as she tried to steady herself and get her bearings, sure that more blows would soon send her crashing helplessly back to the floor. Yet she surprised herself when she realized she was not crying. She was furious. *Who the hell were these bullies?*

"My dear," said the slightly familiar voice in English, "what is your name?"

"None of your business. Just let me go."

"As the Prophet is my witness, my associate will have you screaming your name within fifteen seconds—and screaming everything we want to know and more. So why do you insist on making this unpleasant?"

Britt assumed she was about to die, just as she had assumed she would die on that bus ride nearly a year ago, but this time she was ready to fight—if she only got the chance. The self-defense lessons seemed so theoretical and so far away. Those nights with Rebekah had been rough and tumble, tomboyish fun, kneeing "Mr. Predator" in his rubber groin, grabbing each other by the lapels of their *doji* and throwing one another other across the padded mats. Learning from a teacher as interesting and mysterious as Rebekah made those one-on-one classes even more exciting, but she was never taught how to fight blindfolded with her hands behind her back. Of course, that was all practice, a make-believe game. Now the game was real. From somewhere in the back of her throbbing head, she felt Rebekah's presence, heard her voice from their first dinner with Brad: "Come in second, you die or go to the hospital, if you're lucky." She could almost feel Rebekah's hand on her shoulder; see her *doji* with the black sash. "First and foremost, stay alive. Do nothing that will get you killed. Live to fight or escape later, but stay alive."

"Britt Jaeger," she finally whispered.

"Ah, yes, Miss Jaeger. Now I remember. We met in Madam Collingwood's office, I believe, although your hair was quite different then. You were with Colonel Chayat. That was not so difficult, was it? Now, why were you masquerading as her when you landed in Athens?"

She recognized the voice of Prince Abdul. "I was not masquerading as anyone."

"Do not lie to me. Must I remind you of my associate, who is more than capable of extracting the truth? Why did you accept first-class travel from New York and accommodations from a customer ready to pay millions to buy her software, then decide to flee the country in disguise?" He tugged a lock of hair hanging out from under the hood, "In this disgusting color?"

"It was not a disguise. Coloring your hair is a girl thing. You wouldn't understand. Your women aren't even allowed to show their hair."

"Then why did you and Colonel Chayat attempt to flee from the hotel?"

"We learned that the supposed customer was a bogus company. Rebekah was afraid they might try to steal her program and not pay for it." The two women had never discussed that possibility but it sounded plausible to Britt under the circumstances.

"Miss Jaeger, we know that no less than four phone calls from the Collingwood Company were put through to your suite, but only one was answered. That was the only phone call you received. So your information came from Madam Collingwood, did it not?"

"Collingwood is a large company, more than two hundred people work there. It could have been any one of them." *The hotel obviously had Caller ID*, she thought, *but how did Prince Abdul get the call records?*

"Who else, besides Madam Collingwood, knew you were here?"

"You seem to know everything already. Just let me go."

"You've told me all I need to know," he said.

"Good. Now let me go!" implored Britt.

"I am afraid that will not be possible at this time."

Again Ali-Albadi turned on the cultural attaché and fired another vitriolic barrage. This time Britt understood three words—Collingwood, Chayat and New York. He barked more orders in Farsi. She could tell the other voice was agreeing to or accepting instructions, whatever they might be.

Then the third man, who had not said a word and taken no part in Britt's brutal questioning, spoke.

"Excellency," he began in English, nodding toward Britt. "May I suggest, that if it please the Prophet—peace and blessings be upon him—he has sent you honey to bait your trap to ensnare the one you seek."

BJ struggled to make sense of the third voice. *Who is he? Is he in charge?*

"Allah be praised!" exclaimed Ali-Albadi in English. "My compliments, Captain. At last, someone here thinks."

"Thank you, Excellency."

Not in charge, she decided.

"She consorts with the Zionist spy," said Ali-Albadi, still in English and twisting his gold ring. "So she is no better than the infidel whore. Therefore, Captain, you may use her as the whore she is, until I say otherwise, with my compliments." Ali-Albadi walked toward the cabin door.

"Thank you, Excellency. When you are ready, the launch will take you ashore."

Ali-Albadi pulled the hood so Britt's ear was inches from his mouth and hissed, "Miss Jaeger could of course save herself any such discomfort simply by telling us where Colonel Chayat is. If not, Captain, she is yours to enjoy as you see fit."

Britt could feel herself begin to shake as she heard the cabin door opening and closing. Sure that she knew what was coming, she drove one of her thumb nails into the fleshy space between her other thumb and forefinger to quell the shakes. She struggled to keep her wits while recalling the mantras she had learned in Rebekah's self-defense classes. She spoke in the direction of the third voice. "Captain?"

"Madam," he was quick to assure her, "I am sea captain, not rapist or pirate. My only interest is to get you and the others off my ship and never see any of you again. I am not here to harm you."

Britt heard the cabin door open and close again. When she finally stopped shaking, she hobbled and waddled backward to where she thought the bunk had been. Something about bed height bumped solidly against her leg. She half sat, half fell sideways on to the bed, battered, bruised, scared and exhausted—but determined to fight or escape as soon as a chance presented itself.

CHAPTER 44

Berlin
4 November

Hubert Wayne Church, Vancouver diamond dealer, sat in his room in the Kempinski Hotel, overlooking Berlin's world-famous shopping street, the Kurfürstendamm. He shuffled through the array of passports he carried, deciding which one to use should he receive the orders he expected.

The Canadian identity was his favorite. He passed effortlessly through airport after airport, crossed border after border with never a problem. Everyone liked Canada. *When I retire, I'll take the trans-Canada train clear across the country,* although he knew he was unlikely to live long enough to ever collect a pension.

He had hoped his Raptor problem had gone away, but it hadn't. No operation went flawlessly. Two months ago, Mr. Hu had sent Beijing a routine update that his Geneva contact, code-named "Raptor," had sent a message about a shipping clerk causing delivery problems but insisted it was under control.

It was no longer under control. Raptor had left another note demanding an emergency meeting in Geneva. "Last shipment may have been final delivery. Shipping clerk issue requires immediate attention to eliminate the problem, if we are to continue doing business." Then, in a second draft, he asked for extraction and new identities for him and his wife. That set off alarm bells in Hu's mind.

He expected orders to eliminate the shipping clerk. *A relatively simple job*, he thought. *If everything goes well, problem solved.* But Mr. Hu never counted on things going well. Even if Raptor could contain the problem, his request for new identities was a sign of panic. *Shipping clerk is no longer the problem, Raptor, you are.*

His coded message started alarm bells ringing in the Second Bureau of Guóanbù, the foreign intelligence division of China's Ministry of State Security. In many ways, the Guóanbù was the same as government bureaucracies around the world. They didn't like surprises and this would surprise them. He would wait for the bureaucratic cobwebs to be cleared away.

He expected clear concise orders, but that's not what he received.

Protect Raptor. Protect the operation, but above all protect our leadership against embarrassment. Raptor's government is providing valuable technology to convert our old, manned jet fighters into modern pilotless drones.

Repeat: Protect Raptor and his operation, but protect the Mother Country above all else.

Mr. Hu's life just became much more complicated.

CHAPTER 45

Eastern Mediterranean
4 November

The Sea of Crete, due south of Greece, is one of the deepest points in the Mediterranean. It is also one of the busiest commercial shipping lanes in the world. Hundreds of ships and boats ply its waters every day: yachts, cruise ships, fishing boats, freighters, ferries, super-tankers and warships. The trailing wakes of these ships crisscross so closely and in so many directions that a satellite photo makes the water's surface look like a giant irregular spider web.

Far beneath the surface, a volcanic mountain range creates hundreds of peaks and valleys. Halfway between Greece and Crete, in international waters, is an undersea mountain range with valleys nearly 3800 meters—two miles—deep.

Two hundred fifty meters below the surface, the submarine *Yunes* lay silently nestled among the highest peaks in the range, partially hidden beneath an overhanging crag. Rigged for silent operation, the old Russian boat was perhaps the quietest diesel sub ever built. Constant engine noise from shipping traffic above made it practically undetectable.

IS-903 could remain submerged for several days if necessary, but every night it would ease out from under the overhang, and rise to snorkel depth to recharge its batteries and oxygen systems. Every six hours it released a small tethered antenna-receiver that rose to the surface on a diminutive floating platform. In less than a second, it exchanged coded data "bursts" of highly compressed information bundles with Iranian naval headquarters in Bandar-e Abbas. The miniature floating transponder was then reeled back into the sub. The only message received so far ordered the *Yunes* to remain on station and standby for orders to rendezvous with an unidentified surface craft.

* * * *

The bilingual sign on a third-floor door of the Israeli embassy in Athens read *Yuri Goldfarb Agricultural Attaché* in Hebrew and English. Yuri Goldfarb, however, was not even slightly interested in exporting Israeli oranges to Greece.

The agricultural attaché was, in fact, the Mossad Chief of Station in Athens. Today he was consumed by the disappearance of one of the Institute's most legendary Katsas—in his jurisdiction, on his watch!

In the wake of a string of embarrassing intelligence debacles, he knew the Mossad did not need another black eye. His career certainly didn't need one. He was not to blame for underestimating Hezbollah's military strength in the 2006 Lebanon crisis; Mossad's inability to pinpoint the Gaza location of the Hamas leadership in 2009; or the security camera pictures shown around the world of a Mossad assassination team leaving a hit in Dubai in 2010. Still, his career certainly did not need a fabled agent disappearing in "his town."

He had been on the scrambled phone line with Mossad headquarters in Herzliya most of the day—one call from the Director General; two more from the Deputy Director General Jock Ayalon; one each from the Director of Collections, his immediate boss, and the Director of Science and Technology. Two of the three agents in the small Athens station were on the phone. One was on the street. They produced a steady stream of incoming but uninformative updates.

Yuri Goldfarb had never met Maurizio Barese. He "inherited" him when he took over the Athens station, but he regularly received messages from the Alitalia steward whenever a passenger of interest boarded one of his flights. Today's problem was far more urgent. Barese's call went to voice mail.

Scores of coded messages flow constantly into Mossad Headquarters, in tightly compressed microbursts, partially obscured in the white noise spectrum. This evening, one was a low-priority note addressed to the Political Action and Liaison desk from the most recently assigned junior katsa in Athens. He was clearing up routine odds and ends that his boss, Yuri Goldfarb, had put aside during this anything but routine day.

The duty officer looked at the incoming "cable," which showed up on his computer as an encrypted email and entered it into the cable log. Actual "cables" went out with Telex's in the 1980s and had not been used since. Still he handled dozens of similar "cable" messages every night. This was just one more, until he entered the information supplied by Maurizio Barese about a low-level diplomat into another database.

Beep. Beep. Warning messages flashed across his computer screen. This was no ordinary diplomatic passport arrival.

The intelligence software, first implemented six years earlier by Colonel Rebekah Chayat's team, recognized the name Mahmoud Farshidi, U.A.E. Deputy Minister of Physical Education. It was an alias previously used by an Iranian, Muhammad Ali-Albadi, the chairman of Department 36, the action arm of the Islamic Revolutionary Guard Committee for Special Operations. He was wanted in several European countries for orchestrating the murders of numerous Iranian dissidents. The duty officer pressed print, and a new note with bio and arrival details of this international criminal spit out of his private printer. He folded the note; put it into a sealed envelope across which he scrawled "COMTRANS," for communication transmission, plus "important - urgent" in Hebrew, handed it to a clerk and said, "Go. Now!"

In less than five minutes, every western power with whom Israel shared intelligence would know that the man who reported directly to the Supreme Leader himself was in Athens. If those same Western intelligence agencies were paying attention, they would also realize that by entering a country under an alias via a false passport he forfeited any claim to diplomatic immunity. He was fair game. All nations on the "mailing list" would logically expect that Greek intelligence would stake out the Iranian embassy and arrest him the moment he left the sovereign diplomatic enclave.

Mossad headquarters assumed the Greek National Intelligence Service—NIS—was the original source of the information sent to Herzliya, via the Israeli embassy in Athens. Notifying NIS about their own information would be tantamount to an insult. Obviously there was no need for Mossad headquarters to notify its own Athens station by returning the same report that Athens had just filed with the control centre. So, in a classic bureaucratic snafu, the two locations that most urgently needed that information were not notified.

* * * *

After leaving Britt bound and hooded, Muhammad Ali-Albadi returned to the Iranian embassy, unaware that his alias had drawn any official attention. Though furious at Ghorbanifar and wanting revenge, he would grant him one more chance in honor of today, a very special day. On this day in 1979, Ali-Albadi had joined with Mahmoud Ahmadinejad and five hundred other "students" to storm the American Embassy. Of the ninety initial hostages, fifty-two remained in captivity for 444 days. A great day indeed!

As Ali-Albadi returned to the embassy, Captain Jafari carried a tray into the cabin where Britt was held. Even through the hood, she could smell the aroma of roast lamb. He set down the tray and gripped her shoulders, urging her up to a sitting position. She heard a distinctive click and ratcheting sound followed by the unmistakable clanking of a chain. Then hands once again gripped her shoulders and twisted her body so her back was toward her captor. She felt hands sliding slowly down her arms, then even more slowly back up to her shoulders. A montage of movie rape scenes played in her mind. In each scene the attacker gently caressed his captive victim, just like this, before the violent assault.

In the blackness of the hood, she was about to white-out from hyperventilation. The hands resumed their torturously slow journey back down her arms to her wrists, unlocked one handcuff and attached it to a long chain.

"When door close, you remove hood, untie legs. You eat."

"Thank you, Captain. Oh, God! Thank you."

There was no answer. Somewhere between "Oh, God" and the second "thank you," she heard the door being locked once again from the outside. She removed the hood which had kept her in total darkness for more than twenty-four hours, except for the blinding flash of room light that preceded her beating. Once again ordinary room light rendered her sightless, but this time no one hit her. As her eyes adjusted to the light, she scanned the room for any hint of where she was located. The room was clean, small and efficiently designed. The hull served as the headboard of a single bunk. A combination bookcase and desk served as its footboard. Across the cabin, on the other side of the bed, was a tiny bathroom. There was a small table and a steel office chair on wheels that was too heavy for her to wield as a weapon. Everything in the cabin was secured. Nothing could slide off the desk or out of the bookcase. Even the phone was permanently mounted on the desk. On the table was a divided metal dinner tray filled with roasted or baked lamb and couscous. Beside the tray was a pitcher of water, a glass, metal utensils and a clean white napkin.

Final meal for the condemned, she thought, pouring a glass of water and gulping it down, then pouring another. Before drinking the second glass she tried a bite of lamb. It was delicious beyond belief. She could not remember a more delicious meal—and she did not even like couscous. She was in the midst of a satisfied, cat-like stretch, when she heard three sharp knocks on the door, followed by "Put hood on. Lay face down on bed."

"What are you going to do to me?"

"You do as told. Put hood on. Get on bed."

As she moved back toward the bunk, she saw two port holes but both were battened down with steel covers and four formidable wing nuts. *Stay alive,* she told herself. *Do nothing to give them an excuse to kill you.* Then she called out through the hood, "I'm lying down."

The door opened. Once again she heard the voice that she believed belonged to the Captain. "You eat much food. That good. When I leave, you remove hood and take shower. I look for clean clothes for you."

Inside the hood, tears streamed down Britt's face. *Clean clothes*, she thought. *You don't give clean clothes to someone you plan to kill.*

"Can't you please just let me go?"

"If I let go, we both die and my family will also be killed."

Then she tried another tack. "Captain? The chain is not long enough to reach into the shower. If you release me, I won't try to escape, I promise." She could not believe her own ears. She was promising not to escape because she was feeling sorry for her captor and the fate of his family. She had read about the Stockholm syndrome. Now she was living it.

"I remove chain."

"Oh, thank you. Thank you."

"Escape impossible. You jump overboard, you die when you hit water. Main deck is twenty-five meters above waterline. From fifteen meters, water feel like concrete; rip shoulder from socket." He held one shoulder and rotated it for emphasis. "From twenty-five meters, you die of internal injuries. You will not escape."

A little more than three feet to a meter, she calculated, *times twenty-five.* The math was ugly. The main deck was about eighty feet above the surface—almost twice as high as a silo back in Abilene.

CHAPTER 46

Mike's Irish Bar, Athens
4 November

"Saints preserve us, Molly O'Rourke!" Rusty Smith shouted across the room in his best imitation brogue, "would you be bringin' us somethin' to slake the parch before old age sets in?" Shooting a wink to his companion across the table, he said quietly, "Her real name is Melina O-something-or-other. She's as Greek as the Parthenon, but she loves to pretend she's a colleen."

"This one of your regular haunts?" asked Brad.

"After lunch, it's usually deserted like it is now." With a sweep of his hand Rusty gestured across the room. "But tonight they'll be six deep at the bar with the music so loud you can't hear yourself think. It's actually a very good place to meet a source. The Company sweeps the joint for bugs every week."

"Every week?"

"Yeah. Once a week your old employer sweeps the place for bugs—including the creepy, crawly kind. They operate a pest-control company as a front. Gets them into all kinds of places they'd never get into otherwise, and they make a profit with it."

A conspiratorial smile crossed Brad's lips. "Imagine that, the CIA in the exterminating business."

Molly delivered a pair of black & tan pints—a half-and-half mix of Guinness and Harp. She also delivered a panoramic view of her own impressive pair, veritably soaring out of her peasant blouse.

"Sweet Jesus, Molly, you're as pretty as the Lakes of Killarney on a sunny Sunday morn," said Rusty. As she walked away, he grinned and whispered to Brad, "If she wants to pass for a lass from the old sod, she needs to do something about that little Mediterranean patch of black hair between her boobs." Then he took a sip of his beer, licked his lips, and the smile disappeared. "Now let me tell you, our embassy here wants no part of this business. Zip. Zero. None."

"When does our embassy ever want a problem?" Brad pushed his beer to one side. "Come on, an innocent woman has been kidnapped!"

"And you just *might* know where this Israeli agent is that they want? Are you kidding me?"

"Who said she was an Israeli agent?" asked Brad.

"Buddy, we know she's ex-Mossad, if there's any such thing as an ex-Mossad agent, and, no, she's not likely to go around randomly murdering beauticians. But as far as the Greek police are concerned, she's a perp or at least a material witness. The cops, or what's left of them since the layoffs, are not looking for more victims. They've got two of those. So if you know where she is, you are harboring a fugitive, obstructing justice and making yourself an accessory after the fact. Now remind me, one more time. I want to get involved in this, why?"

"Because you're not ready to be put out to pasture, you old warhorse."

"Buddy, I am so far out to pasture, I have to stand on my tiptoes just to see over the horse shit." Rusty Smith took a long thoughtful drink, contemplating his status. "But, what the hell. Since I have nothing but time on my hands, why don't we kick up a little shit for old time's sake?"

Rebekah was sound asleep in the bedroom when Brad returned and crashed on the foldout couch, bone weary. Too restless to sleep, he was relieved when his cell phone rang. He might as well get up anyway. Caller ID read "restricted." He answered, then stepped into the bathroom and shut the door.

"Stockboy?" asked the caller.

When Brad heard the code name, he immediately resumed the persona of his earlier life. "This stock is up a dime in a falling market," was his coded response. A one-word difference and the caller would have hung up immediately.

"We have something," said a voice that Brad recognized. "I got on this as soon as you called, but you never heard this from me. Do you understand? I don't intend to spend the rest of my career in Langley as the overnight duty officer on the East Timor desk for helping you, even if you were one of us."

"Copy that. Now what do we know?"

"It's the Iranians."

"Are you sure?"

"Hell, no. When are we ever sure?"

"How do you know?"

"I'm not going into how we know, but Chayat's software is a commercial rip-off of the military and national intelligence software she developed and interlinked with all the Israeli security agencies."

"I told you that."

"You suspected that, pal, so do the Iranians. I just confirmed it. They want to reverse-engineer her commercial version into their own espionage and intelligence software. We heard they tried to turn a young Mossad computer jockey a while back but that didn't work, so now their move is getting the colonel to talk. That will save time and wear and tear on their Ph.D.s. More important, if they can force her to reveal the source code, they'll have the crown jewels. They can tunnel back into the systems of almost anyone who trades intelligence with the Israelis, including us. Break the colonel and you break into practically all the intelligence systems in the Western world."

Brad was appalled by the idea. "How do you know all this?"

"Sources and methods, pal. You know I can't tell you that. I can tell you, they want your girlfriend as much as they want the colonel."

He felt his blood begin to run cold. "That's ridiculous. Number one; Ms. Jaeger," he emphasized the formal address, "is not my girlfriend. "Number two; she doesn't know shit about software code. She is useless to them."

"No, she's very valuable."

"That makes no sense."

"They think your girlfriend is the key to getting Chayat and making her talk." The voice on the phone coughed, as though he didn't want to say the next part. "They figure the good colonel will talk if they torture your girlfriend right in front of her eyes. They won't give up on this. They sent their number two spymaster to Athens yesterday, a guy named Ali-Albadi traveling under a UAE diplomatic passport. And they have a submarine operating in the Med. It's the first Iranian warship to transit the Suez Canal since Cyrus the Great ran the Persian Empire or something like that."

A submarine would take them back to Tehran. Brad knew the scenario was chillingly credible. "No way I can do this alone. I need help."

"Not from here, pal. Your colonel is an Israeli problem and your girlfriend is strategically useless. You said so yourself."

"She is *not* my girlfriend."

"Well, she better hope you're here boyfriend because no one else is coming to help. You're strictly on your own, pal."

"I'll get back to you."

"No, you won't. I'm done with this, pal. You've used up your chips."

Closing his phone, Brad charged into the bedroom planning to wake the real target of the kidnapping. He bent over the sleeping woman and reached to shake her bare shoulder but stopped short. Instead, he reached for the blanket and sheet and pulled them up over her shoulder, turned off the light she'd left on, closed the door and returned to the foldout couch in the living room. As he sank into the couch, he heard a faint "Thank you." He punched a number into his cell phone and waited.

"Do you have any idea what time it is, buddy?" mumbled Rusty Smith. Brad ignored the question and quickly summarized the phone call he'd just received. "Your guys always overstate the worst possible case scenario," Rusty yawned, "except when they grossly understate it. Let's say your guy is right. As of now, they don't have the colonel, so her friend is worth more to them alive than dead."

"We could put a little heat on them," suggested Brad. "Let them know that we know."

"Not at this hour, buddy. They may be intelligence operatives, but they're civil servants first. They go home at six o'clock. You call their embassy and you'll get an answering machine until nine o'clock in the morning. I'll see you for breakfast—at nine."

Actually, Iran's Cultural Attaché had stayed after six to send a secret message to Tehran, in order to regain some favor with the man who could destroy his career—and his life. The Ministry of Intelligence did not have secure lines connecting every station to every other station. For Athens to make a direct call to another Iranian embassy required a regular long-distance call. Secure lines went only to and from Tehran. Any secret communication had to pass first through Tehran, then be relayed to its ultimate destination—in this case, a call to the VEVAK station chief attached to Iran's Permanent Mission to the United Nations in New York. "Require immediate report on your readiness to execute orders relative to initiative C," said Ghorbanifar.

"Two dry runs complete," was the answer. "Standing by. Ready to implement."

"Proceed to wet, but operation must be untraceable. Confirm wet."

* * * *

Brad, Rebekah and Rusty Smith crowded around the small table drinking coffee and eating pastries from room service. Together they filled in the blanks that were left out of last night's call to "Stockboy." For nearly an hour they discussed options. They had only two kinds—bad and worse. "We could get Rebekah safely out of Athens and back to Tel Aviv or New York and hope the Iranians freed Britt." suggested Rusty.

"Why would they free her?" Rebekah challenged.

"They wouldn't," acknowledged Brad. "They'd dispose of her."

"Unacceptable," insisted Rebekah. "I will not leave her to die."

"What's left?" asked Brad. "We just call the Greek cops, then sit back and do nothing," he said, answering his own question.

"We try to find her through old-fashioned gumshoe detective work." Rusty said.

"Chance of success?" asked Rebekah.

"We might get lucky."

"In other words, zero. I'll offer to trade myself for her," said Rebekah.

"Heroic but stupid," was the predictable FBI answer.

"That will only get you both killed," said Brad. "Do you want to be responsible for BJ's death?"

"I already am," she said, her eyes darting from one man to the other. "We will get her back or I will die trying. You can help or not help. I will do it alone, if I have to."

Brad and Rusty both looked across the table into Rebekah's eyes. Her warrior's gaze left no doubt she was as ready to die as any suicide bomber, but her mission was to save a life.

For the next two hours, they worked on a plan that was amazingly simple. "Too simple, too brazen," said Smith.

"But it's all we've got," said Brad.

Rusty groaned. "Why do I see my fly rod and that Vermont trout stream getting farther and farther away?"

CHAPTER 47

Athens, Greece
5 November

On the phone in Brad's suite, Rebekah Chayat followed the electronic prompt, "For English press three," and the electronic greeting continued. "Embassy of the Islamic Revolutionary Republic of Iran. If you know your party's..." Without waiting for the rest of the announcement she punched zero and, as Rusty Smith had told her, asked for the Cultural Attaché.

"Shalom," she began, knowing the Hebrew greeting would get the undivided attention of whoever answered the attaché's phone. "I want to talk to Muhammad Ali-Albadi. Is he in?"

"I am sorry. No one here named Ali-Albadi."

"You are the Ministry of Intelligence resident agent, your diplomatic cover is Cultural Attaché, is it not? Then you should know him. He is your boss."

"I am senior clerk to Second Deputy Attaché," lied Ghorbanifar. "There are no intelligence agents here."

"Right. And you have no nuclear weapons or homosexuals in Iran," she said sarcastically. "This is Chayat," she said, lapsing into the Israeli last name only form of address, "Colonel Rebekah Chayat, like the hotel. Tell Mr. Ali-Albadi to call me at this number. Do you have a pencil?"

"You may proceed."

She ended the conversation as she began, "Shalom."

"How long you figure?" asked Brad. "A day?"

"Hours," said Rusty, "I need longer. A lot of moving parts."

As Rebekah closed her phone, Abu Ghorbanifar, the Cultural Attaché, was already racing to the VIP guest quarters in the embassy residence. "Excellency," he said, pounding on the bedroom door with one hand and holding Rebekah's number in the other. "Excellency, the Zionist Chayat has called the embassy asking for you by name."

"Which name? Ali-Albadi or Farshidi?"

"Ali-Albadi, Excellency."

"I will meet you in your office in ten minutes. I want a secure line to Tehran when I get there. Oh, you did send the orders I gave you last night, did you not?"

"I did."

"Amazing. You actually did one thing correctly. Remind me to have you executed with minimum pain when I get you back to Tehran."

* * * *

Ghorbanifar paced in the hallway outside his office, from which he had been expelled, while the Chairman of Department 36 talked to Tehran. The pacing continued for nearly thirty minutes. When the door finally opened, Ali-Albadi ordered his underling, "Take notes."

"If the Chayat woman called for me by name, my presence here is known and no doubt the circumstances of my entry. I anticipated this and planned for it, but not this quickly. We shall initiate full execution of the plan immediately. For now, you will go to the ship and take charge of the consort woman. You will receive further orders to dispose of her or bring her to the rendezvous point. If it is Allah's will, the spy Chayat will soon be in our control along with her American consort."

"As you order, Excellency, it shall be done."

"You will have all members of the operation team that took the woman—the wrong woman—here in this office in ninety minutes."

"Yes, Excellency."

As the Cultural Attaché left the room, the Chairman of Department 36 nervously tapped his gold ring on the secure-line phone for several seconds before lifting the receiver. "Relay this to the captain of the *Yunes*.

"Message in three parts:

"One, check for messages every hour until notified otherwise.

"Two, prepare to off-load special operations team now onboard. Details of rendezvous with receiving surface craft to come soon.

"Three, stand by to receive two to four new passengers for transit back to Bandar-e Abbas. Allah Akbar."

He hung up the phone and tap-tap-tapped the gold ring on the desk.

* * * *

A knee-high cylindrical ashtray stood at one end of the couch of the Omonia Grand lobby, where Rebekah sat. Using his body to block the view, Rusty lifted the sand-filled tray nestled in the top of the cylinder. Rebekah turned off her phone's ringer, placed it in the bottom of the cylinder and Rusty replaced the tray full of sand.

Rusty had selected the Omonia Grand because of its vehicular and pedestrian traffic patterns. The five-star hotel's main entrance sat on a one-way traffic circle around Omonia Square with several spoke streets facilitating a rapid departure. Inside, all three lobby entrances could be observed from a corner of the balcony, where Rusty and Brad had pulled together two chairs, a love seat and a table into a conversation group, partially obscured by a pair of potted plants. It was a near perfect surveillance setting.

Still, Brad was nervous that a technical snafu would thwart any possibility of success. "There are too many moving parts in this operation, and it all hinges on them tracking Rebekah's phone. I'm going to test it," he declared, punching in Rebekah's cell phone number.

Moments later Rusty Smith's cell phone rang. "Yep," said Rusty, looking at Brad two feet away, "call forwarding works even in Greece. VEVAK can still track Rebekah's cell phone's location, but the trail stops at that ashtray. The call gets forwarded to a secure line in my office at the embassy, where it's recorded, scrambled and forwarded, but they won't see that. At least we hope they don't."

The FBI agent pressed "end" and handed his phone to Rebekah. "From now on, you answer whenever this rings. If he calls, talk as long as he will talk. Give them plenty of time to track your phone's position.

* * * *

Six men stood or sat chatting idly among themselves in the office Ali-Albadi had taken over from the Cultural Attaché. Despite their apparent nonchalance, each was nervously focused on the man on the phone. When he hung up, he rapped his huge gold ring on the desk, demanding their attention.

"Does everyone completely understand his specific role? Technical officer? Be courteous. We want her to come voluntarily to meet with me. If she refuses, you have the needle and syringe, correct?"

"Yes, Excellency, all is ready."

"Transport?"

"We are ready, Excellency."

Muhammad Ali-Albadi then turned his attention to his whipping boy, the Cultural Attaché. "You will go to the ship now and prepare that package for transport. You will await further instructions. Do what is necessary to ensure she will say exactly what we tell her to say, should we need her to talk on the phone, but she needs to be able to talk convincingly."

"Understood, Excellency," said Ghorbanifar, licking his lips. "She will know her place."

"I presume the captain has guaranteed we will not be sending a martyred virgin to paradise. I'm sure you will also see to that, but I want no visible marks or bruises above her neck or on her arms."

CHAPTER 48

Piraeus, Port of Athens
5 November

Two hours later, the Cultural Attaché, Ghorbanifar, climbed the metal ladder to the deck of the *Iran Abadan.* Senior First Captain Ahmad Jafari met him at the top of the ladder and once again escorted him through the thick watertight steel door and down the passageway, lit by glass and metal caged bulbs, to a locked cabin.

"Key!" he demanded, holding his palm up. "Have you enjoyed her company?" he asked as he opened the cabin door.

The opening door shocked Britt. No one had told her to put the hood on.

"I am sea captain, not criminal." Jafari held out his hand for Ghorbanifar to return the key. "She is here only because your superiors ordered my company headquarters to permit her to be brought aboard."

"I will keep the key," said Ghorbanifar.

"This door locks from outside," said Captain Jafari. "You have only bolt on inside."

"Then lock it and leave. It's too bad you did not enjoy her when you had your chance. She has ruined my career and probably my life. Now I will repay the favor."

Britt could not understand the Farsi conversation, but as soon as she recognized Ghorbanifar she began backing away.

"...beat you to death with a shoe filled with pig fat," the captain murmured under his breath as he stepped out of the cabin into the passageway. To a Muslim there was no more vile an epithet.

"What did you say?"

"I want you both off my ship as soon as possible," he yelled as he locked the door.

"I can assure you, Captain, neither of us will be here when the sun rises."

Britt cowered in the corner as he walked slowly toward her. He stopped midway between the cabin door and the small table.

"I see the captain has made our whore an honored guest— no hood, an excellent meal, and only a chain to keep you from wandering away."

Britt tried to sink deeper into the corner, but she could get no smaller. For long seconds he said nothing, did nothing. Then his lips curled into a cold, lecherous, evil smile, devoid of human feeling.

He took the chain in one hand and Britt's hair in the other and yanked her to her feet, spun her around and wrapped the chain around both wrists behind her back, looping the chain twice around her neck. He sat on the bed and pulled her to him by the chain. Slowly, painfully slowly, he let the links slip like worry beads between his fingers.

"Don't do this," she said. "Please, don't do this."

"Silence, whore! You will do as you are told." He grabbed the front of her blouse with both hands and ripped it open from collar to shirttail. Buttons flew across the room, landing with small popping sounds.

"P-p-p-please don't do—"

A vicious backhand ripped across her face, twisting her neck with such force she thought she had dislocated a vertebra. "Silence!" he screamed, grasping the front of her bra with his giant hand. He jerked with all his force. Instantly, Britt found herself sprawled face down on the cabin deck, bleeding from her lip. Her seemingly indestructible bra, still intact, proved to be a self-destructive lever that catapulted her face first onto the deck.

"Get up! Get up!" he yelled, landing a kick that knocked the wind out of her.

First and foremost, stay alive. Through the pain and the terror she heard Rebekah's voice in the back of her head. *Do nothing that will get you killed. Live to fight or escape later, but stay alive.*

She rolled onto her side, struggling to get up—a nearly impossible task with her hands secured behind her back. Images of Mr. Predator, the practice dummy she had kneed so many times in his rubber groin, flashed through her mind, but she had never practiced fighting with her hands tied behind her back.

As she licked the blood from her lip, she realized her only chance was to take control of the situation. "This does not have to be ugly. Help me up," she grunted, still struggling to get her breath. "Untie me so I can please you. I can't run away. I won't run away. Let me undress for you. I will please you. I promise."

Ghorbanifar looked at her in disbelief. He had never heard a woman so brazen, not even a whore. Nor had a woman ever offered to undress for him. He grabbed her upper arms and pulled her to her feet. His eyes studied her from head to toe, examining every inch. Slowly, he turned her away from him and ran his hands over her flanks sliding up and over the swell of her buttocks in her skintight jeans.

She felt his hands lingering there, rubbing, patting, squeezing places he had never touched on any woman The hands did not move. She waited and waited. *Just untie me*, she thought.

Then the huge hands begin to paw her breasts through the bra that refused to rip.

"Untie me," she whispered. "You will not be sorry. I will please you. I will pleasure you the way you deserve. You do not deserve to be treated the way that other man treats you. You are better than that."

He released one breast and grabbed her crotch with such force she nearly doubled over.

What does he think he's doing? He can't reach through denim?

The hand still mauling her breast, slid down then up under her bra. With the hand still cupping her mound, he pulled her backward, forcing her bottom against his crotch. She could feel his hardness against the seat of her jeans. He stopped squeezing but held her breast firm.

She waited, afraid to move, feeling him grind against her bottom, wondering where he would grab next. Moments that seemed like hours passed. Then he let go of her crotch and she felt a hand grab the chain behind her head.

God, please no! He tugged the chain he'd looped around her neck. *He's going to strangle me.* "Please, don't." A moment later, she felt the chain being unwound from around her neck. Then she felt hands fumbling with hers, slowly at first, then urgently, unwinding the chain around her wrists, freeing her hands. She rubbed her wrists, then turned to him and began to unbutton his shirt. "Thank you. Thank you."

"Humph!" He grunted as he shoved her away. "Whore, undress!"

Britt remembered the striptease she had once done for Jack when they were first married, before he became almost as brutish as this son-of-a-bitch. *That's not fair,* she thought. *I never feared for my life and Jack would kick the shit out of this guy if he were here.* Her hands rose slowly to seductively unbutton her blouse but there were no buttons. The blouse was already wide open. There was little mystery or allure left there. All she could do was take it off.

He motioned for her to continue.

Taking one sleeve in each hand, she flipped the blouse over his head and behind his neck, pulling him to her. She rubbed her breasts against his shirt. His eyes grew wide—his pupils so large that she could see her own reflection. He ripped the blouse out of her hand.

Live to fight later, she chanted silently. Then the corners of her lips curled up in a slight involuntary smile. She prayed he could not read her mind. *If my blouse can go around his neck, so can that chain.*

She slid her hands down over the bra, over her bare abdomen, and slowly down the front of her jeans. One hand found the zipper and began its downward journey one zipper tooth at a time. His hand came forward, encasing her hand and the zipper tab, pulling both down as far as the zipper would go. *You can do this,* she told herself. *Don't stop now.*

Her hands went to her hips and started working the jeans to her ankles. She wiggled and wriggled—the only way these jeans went on or off. She wanted this to be the most blatantly suggestive act he had ever seen. As she bent over to work the jeans past her ankles, she saw the unmistakable bulge in his pants. She tossed the jeans casually across the room.

As slowly and seductively as she could, Britt reached behind her back, then paused and waited. *How would a stripper do this? Tantalize. Titillate. Tension—build the tension,* she told herself. Her hands let go of the bra strap without unsnapping it. Again she stepped forward and rubbed her breasts against him. His eyes widened again. She could feel his bulge pressing against her underpants. Her hands slid up his chest, and she began to unbutton his shirt. This time he did not push her away. She loosened four buttons on his shirt and began caressing his chest. Suddenly her fingers were entwined in the thickest, darkest mass of chest hair she had ever seen or felt. Like some wolf man, hair grew from his neck over his shoulders and down to his chest and stomach. She couldn't even see his nipples. It was horrible. Her stomach twisted into a nauseous knot. *Don't puke,* she thought. *Not now.*

Breathe. Give him more sighs and moans. Make it good. She moved her fingers through the disgusting thicket and up to his face, caressing it. His close-cropped beard was softer than she expected, far softer than the tangled pelt of chest hair. *Don't puke.* She pressed her mons harder against the bulge. She knew exactly what she wanted him to think about. Her fingertips danced over his lips, toyed with his ears, glided over his eyebrows and down each side of his nose, then over his lips again. With the pressure of a butterfly kiss, her thumbs glided up from the corners of his mouth to caress his eyelids.

Then, just as Rebekah had taught her, she plunged her thumbs, nails first, deep into the inside corners of his eyes, sweeping her hands outward with all her might. She heard a nauseating pop. One eyeball dangled near his jaw, hanging by the optic nerve; the other's cornea lacerated by her nail. He screamed—an agonized, incomprehensible shrieking wail. His hands flew to his empty, bleeding eye socket.

Instinctively she followed through with the move she had repeated so many times on Mr. Predator, smashing her knee deep into his groin. The bulge disappeared. As the man doubled over, she grabbed a mop of greasy hair and yanked him to the deck, where he thrashed and screamed, first holding his giant hands over the empty, crimson-oozing socket, then grasping futilely at the air as though he might recover its lost contents.

She grabbed another handful of oily hair and yanked his head backward, arching his neck. Then, just as she had practiced, she dropped straight down on one knee, driving all of her 145 pounds into his Adam's apple, crushing his trachea with a momentary impact force of nearly half a ton. The screaming turned to a sickening gurgle and stopped.

Again Rebekah's words came back to her. "Congratulations!" she said, panting, "on second prize."

CHAPTER 49

Omonia Square
Athens 6 November

Rusty Smith, Brad and Rebekah all looked at the cell phone ringing in her hand. She looked up from the phone at both men. Rusty nodded. She pressed the talk button. "Shalom."

Rusty rose from his seat, silently mouthing the words, "Keep him talking," and pulled out a small walkie-talkie and popped in the ear bud. Brad could only hear Rebekah's side of the conversation. "This is Rebekah Chayat."

Brad's eyes darted between Rebekah and Rusty listening to his walkie-talkie.

"I am president of a publicly traded company. I am not hard to find. You could have picked up a phone at any time and gotten a message to me."

Brad looked over at Rusty, who was urgently fluttering his thumb and fingers together signaling that Rebekah needed to keep Muhammad Ali-Albadi on the phone. The origin of the call had not been traced. Brad mimicked the signal as Rebekah listened to the Farsi-accented, English-speaking voice on the other end of the phone.

"I will only discuss meeting with you after you have released Ms. Jaeger, unharmed," she said.

Nodding in agreement with her negotiating strategy, Brad looked at Rusty, who was walking back to their little cluster of chairs. His disappointment was obvious. Rebekah saw him just as he shook his head. No luck on the trace. The implication of that was obvious. Rebekah was no longer stretching a conversation to simply trace a call. She was now negotiating for Britt's life.

"Don't waste the time of either of us with lies, Mr. Ali-Albadi. I saw her carried out of the hotel wrapped in a carpet."

Accusations and denials continued. Rebekah's lips twitched in frustration and rage. Worse, Brad and Rusty could hear the fury rising in her voice. If Ali-Albadi heard it, he would read weakness. They motioned for her to hang up.

"Check your facts, Mr. Ali-Albadi. Release Ms. Jaeger immediately and I will meet with you anywhere you name."

She had barely pressed the red button ending the transmission before Rusty was grabbing the phone out of her hand and checking the caller ID. "God damn it! It *is* an Iranian number! He has either flown the coop and is back in Tehran, or he routed the call through there."

* * * *

Quaking with anger, fear and exhilaration, Britt looked down at the man she'd just killed. A shiver raced up her spine as she realized that the pig that lay dead on deck had not died alone. An innocent Midwestern farm girl had died with him. She was a different person, changed forever, and she knew it. *In forty-eight hours, I not only slept with a female assassin, I have become one.*

She wriggled back into her jeans, then retrieved her blouse from across the cabin and tied it in a knot just above her navel. She stepped over the motionless figure on the floor to grab a towel from the sink. She began to unroll the toilet paper as fast as she could. When she held the entire roll in a bundle, she piled the tissue on the bloody face and covered it all with the towel—not out of respect but revulsion.

She systematically began rifling his pockets, finding money—Euros and Iranian Rials—and a name. Business cards identified him as Abu Ghorbanifar, Cultural Attaché attached to the Iranian embassy in Athens. She found a photo ID with Arabic writing—probably what he needed for entry to his embassy—and a Swiss Army knife. She looked at the multi-purpose tool's tiny pliers and shuddered as images flashed through her mind of how he might have used those.

"Keys? Where are the damn keys?" she mumbled. "He must have the keys somewhere!" She rummaged through the side pockets of his suit jacket and found an Iranian diplomatic passport, but no keys. She went back to his pants pockets. The keys had to be in there. She turned the pockets inside out. No keys.

As the adrenaline rush slowly evaporated, it was replaced by fear and remorse. She slumped against the bulkhead as the enormity of the situation washed over her. She was a prisoner on an Iranian ship with the body of an Iranian diplomat she had just killed—and no witnesses to prove that it was self-defense. Exhilaration turned to anger. She pounded her fists on her thighs. She struggled to her feet and kicked the corpse. Something seemed strange. She kicked again. The sound of her soft sneaker striking soft tissue did not sound right. She kicked again. Instantly she was back on her knees, her hands diving into the inside breast pocket of the suit coat. She felt something solid.

"BINGO!" she cried, flipping open the phone. The screen glowed with an Arabic message. She dialed 9-1-1. She prayed that was a universal emergency number. She pressed "Send" but nothing happened. She dialed and pressed again. Still nothing. She dialed Brad's number. Nothing. Rebekah's number. Nothing. The same message remained on the screen. The bastard had key-locked his phone. She hurled it across the cabin and watched the battery separate from the phone as it smashed against the bulkhead. Then she slumped against the locked door, completely drained. She had nothing left in the tank, not even enough to cry.

Sean Eagan

CHAPTER 50

Residence Georgio
Athens 7 November

"Well, well. Our guests have arrived," said Rusty Smith, checking his watch as he looked down on the lobby below. Four men with light beards entered the lobby almost simultaneously from three directions. Each wore a suit coat, no tie—in the style prescribed by Iranian president Mahmoud Ahmadinejad. At least two wore easily seen, old-style hearing-aid earpieces with wires into their jackets. To an experienced agent, their entrance was as stealthy as a brass band.

"Well, they were damn quick getting here. Either they have very good tracking and GPS equipment, or a very good friend at the cellular company, or both." It was public knowledge that security at Greece's biggest wireless company, Vodaphone, had long ago been breached. *The Wall Street Journal* broke the story on their front page in June 2006, reporting that before the 2004 Olympics, thousands of cellular calls had been tapped, even of those visiting heads of state. The technician who discovered the breach was found hanged in his apartment immediately after informing management and the authorities of his findings. No one was ever indicted.

As the last of the four men took up position in the lobby, the cell phone in Rebekah's hand vibrated silently. "Ding-dong," she whispered. Rusty turned his attention away from the scene below, smiled, and nodded for her to answer.

"Yes," she answered, deciding now was not the time to deliberately tweak her caller with "Shalom." It was forty-three seconds, by Rusty's watch, before she said another word. As she listened, Brad and Rusty watched the four men eye one another while intently scanning the lobby.

"How many more do you think they have outside?" asked Brad. Rusty held up two fingers, then four fingers, and shrugged his shoulders as if to say "who knows?"

The man who had entered from the main hotel entrance carried a handheld electronic directional pointer. Following its lead, he walked toward the empty couch next to the ashtray. The other three converged on the same location. He scanned the room, obviously disconcerted. He rapped on the pointer as if banging on it would unjam it. As he held it up to his ear, two female travelers with briefcases hustled from the front desk to the couch and sat down right in front of the four men. Neither woman was talking on a cell phone.

Rusty, who was listening to a small walkie-talkie, looked at Rebekah, concerned that she seemed more interested in his conversation than hers. He motioned, by flapping his thumb and fingers, together for Rebekah to keep Ali-Albadi on the line.

Below the balcony, in the main lobby, consternation washed over the four men's faces. They were looking for a woman—the right woman this time—and they knew she was on her phone at this instant and she should be standing right in front of them. The two Western businesswomen complained to each other in English about their rooms not being ready for check-in. They looked at the four Iranians as if to say, "We got here first, find your own damn seat." The men glared at the women. According to the electronic tracker, the women were sitting exactly where their target should be sitting. They pointedly ignored the men.

"Of course, I am interested in helping my country and saving innocent lives," said Rebekah, "and we can discuss that as soon as Ms. Jaeger is released unharmed." Brad and Rusty were now both standing at the balcony rail, motioning for Rebekah to join them. The bearded men were agitated and frustrated as they searched furtively around the lobby before they headed to the door in a group. Rebekah began pointing urgently at one of the men, mouthing "That's him! That's him!"

"I repeat, Mr. Ali-Albadi," she said, turning her attention back to the phone, "I am not an agent of the Israeli government, nor am I an intelligence officer of any kind. I have absolutely no information that would be of any use to you."

It was now Rebekah's turn to listen. The color drained from her face. She gritted her teeth and her free hand knotted into a white-knuckled fist. "Britt Jaeger has nothing to do with your interest in me! If you and I have any business with each other, we will conduct it immediately after she is freed."

Brad and Rusty began motioning for her to hang up. She was on the verge of losing her composure and her bargaining position. "You call me back with a place and a time. If Britt walks free, I *will* meet with you." Both men were incredulous. Rusty looked skyward in dumbfounded exasperation. Brad just shook his head as Rebekah snapped the phone closed.

"I had no choice," she said. "He's threatening to take BJ back to Tehran. And they *will* do that. Obviously her only value is to trap me. Otherwise, they will kill her. I have to meet with him. I have no choice."

Brad put an arm around Rebekah's shoulder and squeezed. "That is not going to happen."

"You can't stop me," she replied, stepping away.

"Whoa!" interrupted Rusty. "What exactly did he say about Tehran?"

"He said he would take her back to Tehran."

"Thank you," said Rusty. "That means she's still here someplace and probably so is he." He pressed the talk button on the walkie-talkie. "Tackle box, this is Fly Rod," he said, plugging an earpiece into one ear. "Commence Landing Net. Four males. Well-trimmed beards. All in suit coats—no ties. Exiting front door."

Outside the hotel, a television crew with camera, reflectors and a big furry-looking boom microphone, shooting a movie scene or commercial, captured the attention of pedestrians and passing cars.

Rusty pulled the ear bud free and put the walkie-talkie back into his coat pocket. "We are now operational. Let's get out of here."

As Rebekah walked out with Brad and Rusty, Operation Landing Net was concluding almost before it started. Eight men—two each—had surrounded the four bearded Iranians and were hustling them into four unmarked black SUVs with darkened windows. There were two American-built GMC Yukons and two Toyota Land Cruisers. Each of the eight men wore sunglasses, close-cropped haircuts and black Members Only-style jackets—a nearly satirical B-movie caricature of special ops agents. Exactly what Rusty wanted.

There was nothing funny about the Heckler & Koch .45-caliber Counter Terrorist semi-automatic pistols they carried. Though not standard issue for any government, many agents bought them personally. So their weaponry, while extremely lethal, did not point to a specific agency. Two agents were already re-holstering their HK 45-CTs as others pushed the Iranians into separate SUVs. Two of the SUVs had already secured their human cargo and were pulling away. The two female travelers who had occupied the couch in the lobby were jumping into the drivers' seats of the remaining pair of SUVs.

A few bystanders watched the whole scene. Most passersby stopped, looked, then went on their way, assuming it had to be a film shoot for a movie or TV show. Three backup agents manned a camera, boom mic and sun reflector, while a fourth completed the illusion by barking commands into a megaphone: "Quiet, please," "Roll camera," "Action," "Cut."

One spectator—illegally parked in a black Mercedes less than a hundred meters away—recognized a disaster unfolding. He honked at the lone cop directing traffic through the Omonia Square traffic circle. The driver pointed urgently at the activity in front of the hotel. The cop looked hard at the driver, whose car clogged traffic through the circle, and motioned for it to get moving. He did glance once or twice toward the hotel, but the line of SUVs blocked any view of what was taking place on the sidewalk, so he started walking toward the Mercedes with his ticket book in hand.

To onlookers standing right next to the unfolding scene, the next bit of action appeared to be just another part of the script. It wasn't. It was an entirely different script than anyone had rehearsed. To Rusty's "cast," the unplanned scene unfolded like a slow motion, multi-car wreck on a slippery highway. As the colonel walked past one of the GMC Yukons, she spun backward on her heels and lunged through the open, passenger-side, rear door. Her body hung in the air, like Michael Jordan levitating to the basket. With a banshee's scream, she sprawled across the lap of the agent nearest the door, as her right hand flew like an arrow to the jugular of the prisoner she recognized as one of men who carried the rolled-up carpet out of the hotel. With frightening speed and power, she dug her nails into his throat, screaming, "Where is she? Where is she?"

Until the scream, Brad and Rusty had not even noticed she had backed out of their group. The two agents in dark glasses, sitting on each side of the Iranian, were too shocked to react. Finally in a delayed reaction, the abductors became defenders as Rebekah locked onto the Iranian's throat with a pit bull's grip shouting, "Where is she? Where is she?"

Brad grabbed her around the waist and tried to pull her off the prisoner by jamming a foot against the running board for leverage and tugging backward. Rusty had no point of leverage as he grabbed an ankle and pulled like the last man in a tug-o-war. The agent nearest the door was pulling Rebekah's hair back toward the street. Oblivious, she continued to shout, "Where is she? Where is she?"

The prisoner was turning from red to blue. The man next to the window was trying to break Rebekah's grip. "Let go! God damn it! Let go!" yelled the agent, trying to push Rebekah off the prisoner. "He can't talk if you strangle him."

If her grip was not broken, Rusty and Brad believed she might well yank out the Iranian's Adam's apple along with any information he might have.

"Let go!" someone shouted. The agent on the far side of the prisoner, fired an open-handed, football-style straight arm smack into Rebekah's forehead. The blow stunned her enough to relax her grip. Its power helped push her out of the truck.

Rusty and Brad fell backward on to the sidewalk. Rebekah was not entirely out of the Yukon. Her elbows and forearms were on the running board, her eyes at ankle level of the men inside.

"Go! Go! Go!" shouted the men in dark glasses as the SUV started to pull away with its side door still open. The man closest to the open door put a foot on Rebekah's head and gave a powerful shove, propelling her backward far enough that she would not be dragged by the truck or hit by the closing door. The "camera crew" packed up and disappeared nearly as quickly as the SUV.

"Fuck this!" yelled Rusty, picking himself up and looking down at Rebekah still sprawled on the curb. "Fifteen people risked their jobs, their careers and their lives to help you in a totally unauthorized operation, and you pull a stunt like that! Fuck this!"

Rebekah scrambled quickly to her feet. "Rusty. Rusty, I'm sorry, don't—" Brad wrapped a restraining arm around her shoulder to keep her from chasing after their angry partner.

"Let him go."

"We need him. He's all we've got!" She struggled to get free and run after the FBI agent.

"He needs to cool off and so do you," Brad replied, extracting his handkerchief and carefully wiping the blood from her chin where she hit the running board and where her cheek hit the pavement.

"He's the kidnapper—the actual kidnapper! We need his information!"

"That's exactly why we need Rusty to cool down. Right now his team has orders. If we chase him down and piss him off even more, he may cancel those orders. We have to chill out. It's our only shot."

He looked down to find a clean spot on his handkerchief and noticed drops of blood falling one by one on the sidewalk. She was bleeding from abrasions on both elbows and forearms. He handed her the handkerchief and hailed the first taxi in the hotel waiting line.

From the Omonia Grand, Brad and Rebekah's hotel, the Georgio, was no more than a Tiger Woods four-iron away, barely far enough to trip the taxi meter past the €1.16 initial fare. The driver was furious after a long wait in the taxi queue only to get a fare that barely covered the gas he'd burned while in line. Without looking, he pulled away from the curb and into eight lanes of kamikaze Greek drivers.

"Stop!" yelled Brad.

The driver slammed on his brakes, narrowly avoiding a collision with the black Mercedes speeding past the hotel to follow the departing SUVs. In swerving to avoid the collision, the Mercedes missed the turn taken by the SUVs, forcing it to circumnavigate the traffic circle one more time, as the black trucks disappeared. The Mercedes driver angrily punched a stored number in his cell phone. "Excellency..."

Oblivious to the Mercedes driver, Brad jumped out of the taxi and ran back into the hotel. He returned a minute later with Rebekah's phone. He turned it off, removed the battery and simm card, and handed all three pieces to her.

She immediately shoved them back into the phone. "I want him to find me. He must find me."

Sean Eagan

CHAPTER 51

Herzliya, Israel
7 November

Dani Abramowitz was strolling up Herzliya Beach, only fifteen minutes from Mossad headquarters, with an hour to kill before he and the forensic security team would resume the painstaking deconstruction of the entire Chayat project. He was passing the Sharon Beach Resort when his cell phone rang. The caller ID read Restricted. *Why even bother?* He couldn't remember the last time he received a call that wasn't restricted, except from his girlfriend. He punched the green button. "The warranty on my car expired before I bought it."

"What?" replied a puzzled-sounding female voice. "Dani, Dani is that you?"

"Oh, Hélène! I'm sorry. Where are you?" He was surprised to hear her voice.

"I'm still in Israel, but not for long. My friend wants me to come to Geneva on my way back to my duty station."

"I never heard back from you after we looked up that stuff you were curious about."

"Dani," she said, "I didn't want to involve you in this, because it's all personal. I told you, it's about a boyfriend that I'm not sure I can trust. That's why I didn't call back."

"Now you're calling."

"I may have been stupid, but I had to find out more about that hiker787878. I set up a bogus Gmail account at an Internet café in the Old Quarter of Jerusalem, and sent an email to hiker. I said, 'We have pictures. We should meet or they will appear in the *Jerusalem Post*, the *London Evening Standard* and the *International Herald Tribune.*'"

"That was you?" asked Dani. He sat down on the sea wall, separating the lawns of the resort from the Mediterranean beach. "I didn't know it was you, but I read it."

"You what?"

"And I read the reply. I know you didn't ask me to do this, but I've done a little extracurricular prowling around. You stirred up a hornets' nest. Hiker is not one person."

"What do you mean?"

"Hiker is a private, call it secret, bulletin board. Whoever uses that account, and it could be several users, writes, saves and erases drafts. They don't send anything. Your note and the reply you got saying your picture threat went to the wrong address are the only two recent emails to or from hiker. That keeps it totally off the radar."

"What else did you find?" she asked.

"Your email made someone panic. Shortly after that a new draft appeared saying there's no proof there are any photos, continue business as usual. There's also some chatter about a shipping clerk that someone wants removed. I have no idea what that's about, but hiker is demanding an extraction from wherever he is, before the photos can be published."

"Extraction? That was the word used?"

"Yeah."

"Dani, this is not good. Hiker is obviously somebody's asset."

"And he's panicked. He wants to go to the U.S., San Diego, Miami, Los Angeles, someplace warm near the water..."

"And how do you know he is a he?" asked Hélène.

"*He* has a wife. *He* wants new identities for both of them."

Rafi's not married. She breathed a sigh of relief.

"The handler insists that he continue working but says the shipping clerk will be removed and hiker given more money. Apparently the handler has a new boss who's trying to make a name for himself. The new guy won't honor some deal made by the previous boss. The new one demands one last major delivery before he'll spend the money for relocation and new identities."

"Classic asset management, Dani. Once you've got your hooks into an asset, you don't let him quit just because he's nervous."

"I'll take your word for that."

The tone of her voice changed. "Dani, how well do you know Rebekah Chayat?

"Not as well as you," he said. "She only talked to me once while I was at her company."

"Why would every Mossad station in the world have been alerted to look for her?"

Shit, Dani said to himself. "They think she may have written a backdoor into our computer systems and is hacking in through it."

"That's impossible, isn't it?" She fired questions faster than they could be answered. "Why would they think that?"

"Because I said so, but I was wrong. She was my first guess but I spoke too soon."

"You told Jock she is spying on us?" demanded Hélène.

"I was wrong. It's not her. We've brought in an outside forensic security team and we now know it's not her. Haven't told Jock because the first thing he'll ask is, 'Who is it?'"

"Well, who is it?"

Dani took a deep breath and exhaled slowly. "I can't say."

"Dani, if I said my boyfriend might be Hiker, would you tell me?"

He looked down at his feet and drew a pair of initials in the soft sand. "We're damn close. I think I know but I guessed wrong before." With the toe of his shoe, he brushed away the initials. "But I can't say now."

CHAPTER 52

Alimou, Greece
7 November

Deep in the bowels of an abandoned airfreight warehouse, near the old Athens airport, four bearded men with black hoods over their heads, sat naked and shivering, handcuffed to chairs in the unheated building. In a room next to them, each of their cell phones was plugged into a separate laptop computer and all of their stored numbers disgorged and downloaded. Then the computers dialed the voicemail number for each phone and began automatically churning through high-probability passwords. People hate remembering passwords, so they frequently select a nasty one, often a profanity, as their personal, secret revolt against modern technology. That little rebellion is repeated so often that Western intelligence services have compiled a database of password profanities, in almost every language, captured from confiscated laptops and cell phones.

The interrogators' laptops regurgitated that list into each Iranian's cell phone. If that didn't work, the laptops went on to birthdays—a simple search of fifty years of Arabic and Roman calendars. The next step was combining combinations of passwords and birthdays. If that didn't work, they went on to random alphanumeric sequences. That time-consuming process was rarely necessary. Sure enough, three of the four cell phones coughed up their passwords within minutes and were soon spewing out their call histories, text messages and saved voice mails into the agents' computers. Those voicemails were converted and saved as MP3's.

The fourth phone took a little longer, but it was worth the wait.

* * * *

"I am so sorry," said Rebekah as she rummaged through her suitcase. "I put my heart before my head. The guy I attacked was an actual kidnapper. I recognized him. He can tell us where she is!"

"What's done is done."

"What does that mean? That you're giving up?"

"It means," Brad said with ice encrusting every word, "you pissed in Rusty's Cap'n Crunch. You recklessly blew up an operation. You risked the lives and careers of people who owe us nothing but stepped up because of Rusty Smith—not for you, not for me, not even for BJ. You've probably created an international incident and put BJ's life in even greater danger. Is that enough or should I go on?"

"We need that information," she countered, "and there is no one better than I am at extracting it. I can coerce or cajole. I can play the heavy or be the honey trap."

"Your reputation precedes you, Colonel," he said sarcastically.

"I am not especially proud of that, but I am especially good at that."

"At 'enhanced interrogation techniques?'"

"At what works."

"Your reputation precedes you, Colonel. You don't have to convince me."

She sat down in an easy chair and emptied a collection of odd-shaped plastic-looking pieces from a blue velvet Crown Royale bag onto an ottoman.

"We absolutely must get Rusty back in the game," she said, as she started to assemble the puzzle pieces before her.

"Let's see what the old Rustometer says," Brad licked his index finger and held it up, as if checking the wind direction. "It says, no fuckin' way, Jose."

"You can both go fu—" She stopped herself mid-word then took a long, slow deep breath before beginning to speak again.

"Ten years ago," she said quietly, "I was only twenty-eight, my daughter and my husband were sitting in an outdoor pizzeria in Tel Aviv. Zach and I had argued over something stupid. I don't even remember what it was. I walked across the street to a department store to cool off. Five minutes later, I headed straight back to the restaurant. As I crossed the street, I saw a clean-cut, pleasant-faced teenager, with a bright smile, walk casually over to their table. He was Palestinian, but he looked like a nice young man, charming even. Zach, my husband, was in uniform. I was in the middle of the street when I saw the boy reach inside his jacket. Before I could scream, that charming kid detonated his explosive vest. Eighteen people died, including Zach and Marni, our four-year old daughter. Thirty more were wounded."

"I am sorry," Brad replied, shocked. He walked around behind her seat and put his hands on the back of her chair. She did not look up.

"I am very sorry," he repeated, almost in a whisper, as he lifted his left hand from the chair and lightly squeezed her shoulder.

"In that moment," she said, ignoring the gesture, "I was blind with rage. I screamed. I wailed. But there was no one to attack. There were only survivors to be helped and the dead to bury. Zach, Marni, sixteen others, all dead. The kid was the nineteenth, but he wasn't counted in the death toll."

Brad lifted his other hand off the chair and rested it on her right shoulder.

"There was no information to be gained at that moment," she said. "There never is, but I vowed that if it took the rest of my life, no one connected with that bombing would escape." She finally looked up at him. "Today is different. BJ is still alive. Rusty or someone has the people who did this. We have to move now."

Rebekah patted his hand, then got up and walked silently to her bedroom. She returned, pulling her suitcase. "I am going to tell you something only one other civilian knows. But right now I want—I need—to tell someone. Should anything happen to me, or her, I want someone to know the whole story."

Thus began the second time within weeks she admitted to her life as an assassin. "After the bombing, I demanded a transfer to the *Kidon.* You know what the Kidon is?"

"The Mossad's assassination division—the unit that tracked down the Black September terrorists who hit the Munich Olympics and took 'em out one by one, right?"

Rebekah nodded. "We identified eleven key players in the attack. I took down eight. One died of natural causes; another blew himself up building another bomb. Only one remains: Muhammad Ali-Albadi provided money, training and travel documents."

"Once you identified them, how did you find them?"

"I did whatever was necessary," she said, focusing on the plastic puzzle in her hands.

"Wasn't there a Mossad chief who said in a speech that he expected his female agents to sleep with the enemy, if that's what it took?"

"Delilah may have pioneered the honey trap," she said. "The Mossad perfected it. Meir Amit."

"Hebrew for honey trap?" asked Brad.

"Meir Amit?" Rebekah looked up from the plastic pieces in her lap and smiled. "That was the chief's name. He died in the summer of 2009."

Brad looked down at the ottoman, mesmerized by her story and by the plastic puzzle she continued to assemble. A dozen or more innocuous-looking puzzle parts had been assembled into three larger ones and lay side by side.

With the push of a button she removed the entire pull handle assembly from her suitcase, metal bars and all. Placing the handle on the floor, with the tubular steel rods pointing upward, like a goal post, she stepped on the handle and proceeded to unscrew the precision-threaded bottom eight inches of each tube. She gently tapped each short tube, releasing eight finely machined springs that she carefully placed into the plastic puzzle. Next, she screwed in one of the threaded steel tubes. Returning to her wheelie, she reached inside and withdrew an expensive Monte Blanc pen. She unscrewed the top from the bottom of the pen to release its push button and spring. Both fit neatly into another part of the plastic puzzle.

With two decisive clicks, she slammed together the three big pieces with all of the included metal parts. She gripped the handle of the now fully-assembled polymer and ceramic nine-millimeter pistol—a nearly exact replica of a Glock 9, specifically designed, when disassembled, to pass undetected through both magnetic and X-ray detection systems.

With a marksman's two-handed grip she took aim across the room toward the entrance to the suite, nodded approvingly, and lowered the weapon. Returning to her dismembered suitcase handle, she turned it upside down and eight 9 mm shells fell out, four from each tube.

Loading the bullets into the weapon, she described her assassin's signature calling card. "Before they died, I ensured that not a single one of them would enter the gates of paradise anatomically equipped to deflower any heavenly virgins."

Brad walked behind her chair once again and began to massage her shoulders; as if he could relieve the unbearable weight they had borne for years. "We knew that was the Mossad sending a message," he said, "but we had no idea it was one operative. That was all you?"

"It was. I will give up my life before I will see another person I love die. I'll trade myself for her."

"How about seeing two people die?" Brad recalled what he'd heard on the phone about torturing BJ in front the colonel's eyes, "Slowly and painfully?"

Rebekah stopped loading the pistol and looked at him, a distant, far-away look. She'd seen lots of people die.

"You're offering a bargain to the devil!" Brad insisted. "They'll accept your offer to trade, alright, but they will never keep their side of the bargain. They'll never release BJ. They'll just have both of you."

CHAPTER 53

New York City
6 November

Five thousand miles away, Jimmy opened the thick glass door for Mackenzie Collingwood. Despite signing an annual thousand-dollar Christmas check to James O'Connell, Mackenzie knew him only as "Jimmy the doorman." She started the twenty-four-foot journey, about ten steps in heels, across the sidewalk to the limousine waiting to take her to another early morning breakfast meeting. Charles bounded out from behind the wheel to open the left rear door for her. Neither one noticed the tweedy, professorial-looking man with a bow tie, cane umbrella, and hounds-tooth hat, briskly pacing down the sidewalk—on a collision course with the financier. With just two steps between Mackenzie and the car, he tipped his hat and smiled. Then his feet became entangled with his own umbrella. He stumbled forward, straight toward the woman and her driver. While trying to steady himself with the umbrella, it struck her just above the ankle. Only Charles's quick reaction kept them both from crashing onto the pavement.

"Terribly sorry, madam. No harm, I trust," said the middle-aged man with a peculiar English accent, quickly recovering his balance and helping steady Mackenzie.

Charles grabbed him tightly by the forearm. The clothes, even the hat, were straight from Burberry's, but his dark complexion, thick mustache and dark eyes absolutely did not fit with the rest of the picture. "Watch where the hell you're going, buddy!" but then he let go and turned his attention to his employer.

"Well done, old boy," said Mr. Tweedy, patting Charles paternalistically on the back, "bloody well saved us both, I would say."

Asshole, thought Charles as he helped Mackenzie into her seat, closed her door, then leapt into his seat, slammed the car into gear and squealed into traffic pursuing the man. *Was this a rehearsal? Another rehearsal?* Several yards ahead, he wheeled the limo around the corner onto York Avenue. Mashing the accelerator to the floor, Charles raced through the yellow light, again squealing the tires as he swung a wide turn to head downtown. He then slowed the limo to a crawl to scrutinize every door on each side of the street.

"Charles," sighed Mackenzie, laying down her *Wall Street Journal.* Even before she bent forward to rub her leg, the South

American nerve agent, *Batrachotoxin*, was racing toward her Medula, that fibrous bundle in the brain stem that controls breathing and heart function. "You need to take me back home. I need a Band-Aid and a new pair of hose, thanks to that clumsy idiot."

"Of course, ma'am. I just wanted to get a good look at that guy. I'm not sure that was just carelessness."

"I'm not feeling very well, Charles," she said, now lying down in the back seat. The miniscule dose of the exotic, paralytic poison on the umbrella tip—equal in size to only two grains of ordinary table salt—was paralyzing her heart, diaphragm and chest muscles. "Charles, would you please pull over for just a—"

Mackenzie Collingwood never finished that sentence or any other.

CHAPTER 54

Piraeus, Greece
7 November

The forty-eight-foot *kaiki*, a combination fishing and work boat, common in Greek waters, chugged slowly through the Piraeus harbor chop on what appeared to be a routine ship chandler's trip resupplying the *MV Iran Abadan*. The huge tanker was anchored well out into the harbor, about a mile out from the pumping facility where it had unloaded its cargo of crude oil destined for the Hellenic Petroleum refinery. The workboat tied up at the waterline-level platform at the base of the metal stairway leading up to the main deck. Muhammad Ali-Albadi scrambled out of the well of the boat onto the platform and charged up the one-hundred-plus steps. The late afternoon sun, striking his large gold ring, reflected a series of gold, white and red flashes on the ship's hull as he climbed.

From the bridge, Senior First Captain Ahmad Jafari recognized the Chairman of Department 36. He hurried down to the main deck to greet the head of the most feared section of the entire Iranian state security apparatus.

"Excellency," he said, "what an unexpected but pleasant—"

The man with the gold ring cut him off. "You have my package wrapped and ready for me to transport?"

"Excuse me, Excellency." Captain Jafari looked confused. "I don't know what you are talking about. I have received no instructions from anyone. I was not even informed that you were coming."

"I sent a text to that idiot Ghorbanifar. Is he not here?"

"He has been in the cabin with the woman for a few hours."

"A few hours? What has he been doing?" demanded Ali-Albadi.

Jafari's voice lowered. "That is not my business, Excellency. The door has been locked."

"Take me there at once."

* * * *

Brad was on his cell phone. "He'll answer, Rebekah," he said, switching on the speakerphone. "I guarantee it."

The ringing stopped. After a moment of silence they heard Rusty's voice:

"I don't know why I'm even speaking to you."

"Rusty, she saw one of the actual kidnappers. If you knew her whole story, you'd know she reacted the same way you or I might. It was a momentary lapse, and she knows it."

"Pearl Harbor was a momentary lapse. September 11th was a momentary lapse. Both had disastrous consequences."

"The Christmas Day underpants bomber was another momentary lapse," observed Brad, "but then some folks on that airplane did the right thing. Rusty, we need you to do the right thing."

"I told you from the get-go, this is a matter for local authorities. It is now in their hands. I am out of it. But we might have, accidentally, happened to scroll through some text messages and voice mails on cell phones we just happened to find. We turned over what we learned to the Hellenic National Police. They should be picking up your friend soon."

"Is she all right?" Rebekah yelled into Brad's phone. "Where is she?"

"I think she's on an Iranian oil tanker in the harbor, but like I said, I'm out of it. The National Police and the Greek Coast Guard are mounting a hostile boarding operation."

"A hostile boarding operation?"

"They don't know what the fuck they'll encounter, and they're still not sure whose side she's on."

"What about the guys who took her? You've got one of the actual kidnappers."

"Rebekah fingered the right guy, alright, but they all have diplomatic passports. We can't hold them and we can't exactly just turn 'em loose. So right now they're all sleeping quietly in the back of a truck on its way to the Albanian border. They'll be deposited in the mountains on the other side, without benefit of diplomatic passports, or shoes, which were unfortunately lost. They'll be quite busy explaining how and why they crossed into Albania, illegally. Albanians don't have much patience for Iranians. In fact, the Albanian Prime Minister called Iran and its leaders 'the new Nazis.' And he's a Muslim!"

* * * *

Captain Jafari led Muhammad Ali-Albadi down the ladder and into the passageway leading to the small cabin. He reached around past the captain and tried the locked cabin door. "Open it."

The captain fumbled through his pockets looking for keys. "I gave them to your assistant," he lied.

"He is not my assistant! He is an incompetent idiot!" responded the Chairman of Department 36, violently slamming the flat of his hand on the cabin door. The underside of his gold ring added a metallic ping to his thudding blows. "Break it down!" he screamed in Farsi.

"It is a water and fire resistant door. That would require a cutting torch," lied the captain again. "And would take much time."

"You only have to cut through the lock portion. That should not take more than five minutes."

The captain was running out of lies. "Excellency, there are rules aboard a tanker. There is great fire and explosion risk. I am required to get permission from company headquarters before a cutting torch can be used. The location where it is to be used and reason must be explained." Another lie. "Then the chief captain and chief engineer of the fleet must grant permission. It will be better for me to go back to the bridge and find other keys."

Without waiting for an answer, the captain headed back up the passageway. Muhammad Ali-Albadi followed. The specter of his reaching paradise, incinerated by a giant ball of flame, was not appealing.

On the bridge, the captain opened and closed the large flat drawers of the nearly chest-high mahogany case holding navigation charts. He slammed one drawer closed and was about to open another when he saw a steady stream of flashing red and blue lights driving onto the dock area. He reached into another drawer and pulled out a pair of binoculars.

"What is it?" asked Ali-Albadi.

"Harbor Police. Coast Guard. National police. They go to harbor police dock."

Ali-Albadi slammed the top of the chart case. "I thought they could keep their mouths shut for a little while. Obviously I was wrong."

"Who, Excellency?"

"Never mind. It is no longer safe for me to remain on your ship," he said. Incarceration was now a more immediate worry than incineration. "The authorities will be coming to your ship looking for the woman."

The captain became alarmed. "What shall I tell them, Excellency?"

"That is your problem, Captain." Ali-Albadi was already climbing down the ladder from the bridge to the main deck, his gold ring clicking against the hand rail. "Deny everything. Blame that idiot Ghorbanifar. It is entirely his fault."

The captain stared at the flashing lights, then walked to the other side of the bridge. He reached into his pocket, grabbed the keys and heaved them over the side into the deep water harbor. Then he waited for the inevitable.

CHAPTER 55

Piraeus, Port of Athens
7 November

A postcard perfect Mediterranean sunset cast a crimson light across the harbor, a classic "Red sky at night, sailor's delight." Lights flickered on around the docks and aboard the vessels in the harbor. From Jafari's padded captain's chair on the bridge, the veteran merchant marine officer had a panoramic view of the entire port. Only a few of the flashing red and blue lights that had poured into the dock area earlier were still evident. That puzzled him.

* * * *

Compared to the chipped and peeling paint on the hull of the work boat, its radio room was hospital clean, equipped with more electronic gear than a Russian fishing trawler—the mainstay of the old Soviet spy fleet. As darkness fell, the ancient-looking kaiki ferried Ali-Albadi slowly fifteen miles out into the Sea of Crete. Only the minimum required navigational lights were illuminated.

At 22:02—two minutes late—a periscope rose out of the water two hundred meters off the ship tender's starboard bow. A strobe light atop the periscope flashed once. The fishing boat flashed its red and green navigation lights twice and chugged toward the light. Less than a minute later, the sea beneath the strobe light roiled with millions of bioluminescent "Sea Sparkles" as thousands of pounds of compressed air expelled the water from the sub's ballast tanks. The sea bubbled over like a freshly popped champagne bottle as the submarine rose to the surface. It displayed no navigation lights. A crewmember signaled the workboat with a single flash of a searchlight.

The work boat doused its navigation lights and pulled slowly alongside the sub. Black-clad submariners stood by to grab the mooring lines thrown from the kaiki. When it was snugged up to the sub, a rope ladder was thrown over the side and the Chairman of Department 36 climbed aboard the sub and up to the "flying bridge" atop the conning tower.

After an exchange of traditional Middle Eastern hugs with the captain, plus an exchange of identification, Muhammad Ali-Albadi climbed down the hatch and into the bowels of the submarine. Immediately thereafter, the first of ten *Al Quds*—Revolutionary Guard Commandoes in civilian clothes—climbed out through the hatch and scrambled down the ladder onto the kaiki. Before the last man was fully aboard, the mooring lines were thrown back onto the work boat.

IS-903 was already two-thirds submerged with water splashing down the conning tower hatchway before the last crewman scrambled down the ladder and battened the hatch behind him.

From that single flash of the strobe until the sub disappeared back into the deep waters of the Sea of Crete, 480 seconds had elapsed—eight minutes—unobserved by any satellite, aircraft or surface ship except the rendezvous vessel.

As the sub disappeared, the kaiki relit its navigation lights and began its lazy voyage back toward Athens. In the Port of Piraeus, Captain Ahamad Jafari decided the stream of flashing red and blue lights he had seen encircling the port in the late afternoon may have been for a visiting VIP—maybe some European royalty heading off to the fabled Greek Islands.

He bid good night and delegated command to the junior officer of the watch. Stepping outside the bridge, the captain inhaled the cool salty air and surveyed the lights coming on aboard the other vessels in the harbor. Beyond the harbor, he could just make out the lights flickering high on the hills of Korydallos overlooking Piraeus.

"This is why we go to sea," he said aloud. *I'd rather be an apprentice seaman, with a good ship under me, than the highest bureaucrat, like—* Before he could finish his thought, two helicopters with searchlights roared overhead, hovering directly above his ship. A small armada of armed, inflatable, Zodiac-style high-speed patrol boats circled the tanker at high speeds. Wailing sirens shattered the serenity of the Athenian night. The sky exploded with flares. A loud speaker squawked first in Greek, then English, then barely intelligible Farsi, "*Iran Abadan,* this is the Hellenic National Coast Guard. Prepare to be boarded. Assemble all crew members on the main deck with their hands up."

Captain Jafari frantically crisscrossed his arms back and forth signaling the patrol boats to stop firing flares. One flare could ignite the fumes continuously venting from the huge, empty oil tanks. The explosion would take down both helicopters, incinerate each of the patrol boats and everyone aboard those vessels and his.

* * * *

Rebekah Chayat paced around the hotel suite, stopping to look out the window every thirty seconds or so. "Why haven't we heard anything?" Nervously she unloaded and reloaded her

ceramic pistol, aiming at various objects around the room—
lamps, vases, an ice bucket. "What the hell is going on?"

Brad switched on the TV. Local news looked like local news
everywhere with perfectly blown-dry male and female anchors
flashing toothy smiles and electronic graphics splashed over
their shoulders. He couldn't understand a word. He clicked his
way to CNN International, then BBC World. There was no
mention of Greece, not even its financial woes.

The last red rays of the sun were disappearing when
Rebekah slapped her forehead in the globally understood
gesture that says "stupid me." "Brad, I've got it. I know where
they're holding her. There's an Iranian tanker in the harbor. I
saw it while I was waiting for you."

Brad threw money at the taxi driver as Rebekah jumped
from the cab and raced toward the police cordon blocking
access to the harbor. When Brad caught up with her, she was
urgently running from cop to cop trying to badger her way
through the barricades. She didn't speak Greek. The cops didn't
speak English. They had no patience for a babbling
troublemaker. Brad arrived just in time to ease her away from
the angriest of the cops who had already made a show of pulling
out his handcuffs.

Then they heard the unmistakable two-toned wail of
emergency sirens. A police escort was leading a hearse through
the barricades and out of the area. Brad wrapped his arms
around her and pulled her close, trying to protect her from the
tragedy signaled by the hearse. Not far behind the hearse, a
television news crew was slowly working its way out of the
barricaded area.

Brad let go of Rebekah and jumped onto the truck's running
board. "English! English! Do you speak English?"

"Little bit," replied the reporter in the passenger seat.

"What happened? Who was in that hearse?" Brad fired the
questions too rapidly for the reporter to translate to himself
back into Greek. "Was there an American woman?"

"Yes, yes. American woman" repeated the reporter. "Police
say American woman kill."

Rebekah jumped on the running board alongside Brad, just
in time to hear the reporter's last line. They both stepped back
off the running board as the van pulled away. Rebekah began to
shake so violently that no matter how tightly Brad held her, he
could not stop her shaking. With both arms enfolding her, Brad
tried unsuccessfully to wipe his own eyes on his sleeve. One by

one tears dripped down his cheek and into Rebekah's hair and onto her shoulder.

After several minutes, he slowly released the hug but kept one arm around her shoulder and began steering her back toward the street where they might find a cab back to the hotel.

* * * *

In the back seat of the taxi, Rebekah sat with her face buried in her hands. Brad sat next to her in silence. Nothing he could say would help. He stared out the window as the city passed slowly before him. His cell phone rang.

The caller ID displayed: RESTRICTED. His thumb moved to the red "end" button. He didn't feel like talking to anyone. On second thought, he pressed the green button. "Yes?"

"Well, buddy, that was more excitement than we needed, wasn't it?"

"Rusty, you bastard! She's dead and you call it 'more excitement than we need'!"

Rebekah's eyes flashed in anger.

"Whoa, buddy! She's OK. She's on her way to the hospital for observation, but she's OK."

Brad fumbled for the speakerphone button. "Where? What hospital? We'll be right there."

"What? What happened? What's going on?" Rebekah was yelling, pulling on his arm, which only delayed his punching on the speaker.

"Sorry, buddy, but you two need to wait until tomorrow. I'm having to exert my official position as the American legal attaché—and the Greeks are not being all that cooperative. Technically, she is still a "person of interest," but she's OK, and we should have it all straightened out in a few hours. So unless the hospital finds some serious internal injuries that the paramedics missed, you should be bringing her home by tomorrow."

"Rusty, Rusty," yelled Rebekah. "Thank you. Thank you."

"Don't thank me. A lot of people you'll never see again risked their lives and careers. You owe your thanks to them. I will let them know."

CHAPTER 56

Sea of Crete
7 November

Despite the sophisticated eavesdropping electronics aboard the decrepit-looking workboat, the Iranian communications specialists rarely monitored local police channels. Those were not the transmissions they were typically interested in. Tonight was different. Tonight they were listening to every word on the police scanners and relaying summaries of the conversations to Iranian naval headquarters in Bandar-e Abbas. Every hour those summaries were retransmitted in compressed bursts to IS-903.

As soon as the bursts were unzipped, they were delivered to Ali-Albadi, who had taken over the captain's quarters. As communiqués were deciphered, the whole picture of what had taken place in the harbor became clear. Before the night was over, Ali-Albadi had more information from more sources about the events in the harbor than anyone on the ground. "My compliments, Ms. Jaeger," he said to no one. "You not only disposed of my idiot Gorbanifar, but you set yourself up to be my guest in Tehran, all perfectly legally. I'll simply have you extradited for murdering an Iranian diplomat on an Iranian flag carrier. This is working better than I ever imagined."

He wrote two notes of his own and went to find the captain to have them encoded, compressed and sent to Bandar-e Abbas for relay to the ten *Quds* on the ground and to the Ministry of Justice in Tehran.

Two hundred meters below the surface of the Sea of Crete, less than a mile outside Greek territorial waters, Muhammad Ali-Albadi paced fitfully in the captain's quarters until the knock on the door.

"Excellency, forgive me, the captain says there is news you need to see," said the voice from outside the captain's cabin.

A junior lieutenant escorted the spy chief to the tiny officers' dining room. From its position fifteen miles offshore, the small floating antenna received local television channels better than many people in Athens apartment buildings. Those signals were fed down the two-hundred-meter cable to TV sets in the sub.

Muhammad Ali-Albadi chuckled when the local news bulletin was translated for him. Greece had issued a warrant. "I just broke into double figures." He smiled at the captain and young officer who sat with him. "I am now wanted in ten countries—eleven if you count the Zionist-occupied territories," he added, refusing to acknowledge the existence of the state of Israel.

Ali-Albadi turned to the young lieutenant, "Bring me some paper. I have a message to send." A few minutes later he folded the paper and handed it to the junior officer. "Have this encrypted and transmitted to Tehran immediately."

CHAPTER 57

Athens
7 November

The nurse unwrapped the blood-pressure cuff from the sleeping American's arm as part of her morning rounds. She flashed the OK sign and smiled toward the two people sitting in chairs on each side of the bed. They both nodded and smiled back at her. Taking a wedge of lemon from the untouched breakfast tray, she gently wiped it over the sleeping woman's lips. Britt's tongue extended as if trying to push away the tart fruit. The nurse quickly withdrew it but then swiped it across her lips again. As the tongue protruded, the nurse squeezed the wedge, drizzling several drops of lemon juice directly onto Britt's tongue and between her lips.

"Bliii-ccckkk!" sputtered Britt, opening her eyes and wiping her lips with the back of one hand.

Rebekah leaned over, put one hand behind her neck, and kissed her hair and forehead. "I am so sorry, BJ, so incredibly sorry. Please forgive me?" She then reached across her body to hug her.

"Careful, I'm a little sore on that side."

Only then did she notice the man on the other side of her bed. "Brad! What are you doing here?"

"I flew in after it happened," he said, taking her hand in his. "No one is going to hurt you ever again. I promise."

"I don't get a kiss from you?"

Brad bent over with his hands behind his back, making sure he would not touch any part of her that might hurt, and kissed her on the lips. The lemon taste and smell were still fresh. A lemon never tasted so sweet.

"You would have been so proud, Rebekah. I stayed alive to fight later, then I used everything you taught me."

Rebekah smiled at the lines she'd preached as a mantra. "We want to hear the whole story, but you're not ready, not right now."

"I *want* to tell you about it."

Brad reached to hold her hand. Only then did he see that her wrist was shackled to the bed rail.

"She's a prisoner?"

"Doctor want keep one more night." The nurse paused to look at all three faces. "Then police decide."

Brad fired a withering glance at the nurse as he bolted into the hallway toward National Police force cop standing guard, demanding to know where Rusty had gone.

"He go away," said the nurse, answering for the young cop with an automatic weapon slung over his shoulder. "Call from Ministry of Justice."

As Rebekah watched the nurse wheel her cart of bedpans, bandages and blood pressure meters out of the room, she reached into her bag and lifted a corner of Britt's sheet.

"I just want to go home." Britt sighed.

"Soon," said the colonel, sliding her hand under the sheet.

Britt jumped when something touched her thigh. "Ouch!" she said, reacting to her own sudden movement. "My ribs are sore."

Beneath the cover, Rebekah patted Britt's leg, then withdrew her hand, but something hard still lay against her thigh. "Keep that with you," said Rebekah. "Not in the bedside table, not in the closet, take it with you when you go to the bathroom."

BJ rattled the handcuff chain and mustered a weak smile "I think they'll be bringing the bathroom to me.

Rebekah bent over and kissed her on the forehead and patted the hard object nestled next to her thigh. "Just rest. You won't be here long. I promise."

Based on the frequent ambulance-chasing television updates, it was apparent even Greek newscasts were imbued with the time-honored American tabloid axiom, "If it bleeds it leads." All of Athens knew which medical center was holding the American suspected of murder.

Ali-Albadi stationed five of his ten Al Qud commandoes around the hospital observing every entrance and exit. At nine-thirty that evening, one of them went into the emergency room complaining of chest pains. After an unremarkable EKG, and saying he now felt fine, he was released. On his way out of the electronic doors, two men in hospital scrubs slipped in and commandeered a gurney. Outside, the group leader called the hospital and asked for Britt's room. He could hear the operator muttering to herself as she ran through the patients starting with P. "446, 211, 518, 645." Then speaking up, she said, "I'm sorry, no calls are permitted. I can give you the sixth floor nursing station." He hung up and punched in a text message: *#645*. And the orderlies began pushing the gurney toward the elevator to the sixth floor. Ali-Albadi's orderlies timed their arrival to coincide with the shift change. Room 645 was around the corner from the nursing station where two teams of nurses and aides clustered to brief each other and read-in. Visiting hours over, the floor was otherwise deserted.

Her lights out, privacy curtains partially drawn, Britt dosed, not sleeping but not awake, secure in the knowledge that an armed guard was outside her door.

The lift doors opened on six and the orderlies pushed out the gurney, silently lifting its wheels over the gap between elevator and the floor. As they turned the corner, they saw the guard sitting outside room 645, his chair tipped back against the wall, a submachine gun across his lap. He was reading a paper a visitor had left. The orderlies stopped when they saw him and whispered to each other. One took out a cell phone to text a message.

Beneath her lightweight blanket, Britt idly slid her hand back and forth over the ceramic pistol Rebekah had slipped into her bed. *What if I roll over on this in the night? Will I shoot myself?* She switched on her light and took out the note Rebekah had wrapped around the barrel with a rubber band. She checked the safety as explained in Rebekah's instructions. Satisfied, she slid it back next to her thigh where Rebekah had said to keep it and turned out her light.

In the hall outside, the orderlies resumed pushing the cart toward her room.

The guard looked up from his paper just as the man in scrubs read his text and slipped the phone back into his pocket and kept his hand there. They stopped in front of 645.

The guard laid down his paper, righted his chair back onto four legs and stood up, holding his weapon casually, and walked toward them. "Where are you going?" asked the guard.

"Patient in 645, down to surgery."

The guard shifted his weapon to a ready position. "This is a surgical recovery floor." He reached for the radio microphone attached to his shirt pocket. He pressed the talk button but before he could say a word, one orderly pushed the gurney hard into the guard's midsection, driving him backward, against the wall. At the same moment, the other pulled a box-cutter from his pocket and lunged, slicing the guard's throat from artery to artery. The policeman dropped to the ground, his weapon landing silently on the gurney.

The rattle of the cart, the guard thudding against the wall his last gurgling yelp startled Britt. She could see only silhouettes moving in the hall beyond her privacy curtains.

Someone was bent over dragging something heavy. She could see the outline of a gurney stop at her door and a figure reaching under the pillow on the gurney before walking into her room.

"You can't come in here. This is a private room," she said but the figure was joined by a second and both advanced toward her bed. "You can't come in here, I said." In the dark, she fumbled for the nurse's call button and yelled, "Guard! Guard!" As the closest figure reached for her curtain, she grabbed Rebekah's pistol and clicked off the safety. "Stop or I'll shoot."

The shadowy figure whipped back the curtain. She saw two men in scrubs and knew intuitively something was wrong, but what?

IDs! They're not wearing IDs! Then she saw the wadded up white cloth in the man's hand. A vision the hair salon and the descending cloth flashed before her eyes in neon, psychedelic colors.

She fired. The sound was deafening, much louder in the small room than the noise her father's guns had made when he took her hunting wild turkey, coyote and wolf. Her hand jerked wildly, the pistol nearly falling to the floor. The first assailant staggered backward. The second ran for the door but was momentarily slowed by his falling accomplice. As he reached the door, Britt aimed with two hands and fired. She barely heard the second shot. Blood spattered on the far side of the hallway. Buzzers were already buzzing. Sirens wailing, people yelling, the PA system squawking loudly with words she could not understand.

Then her room was awash in light, every bulb shining. Nurses and interns surrounded her, ripping back her covers looking for wounds. Security guards and police were assembling outside her room. "Call the American Embassy!" she screamed. "I am an American citizen."

Later, as doctors, nurses, orderlies, hospital security staff and National Police forensics teams scurried in and out of her room, a man, in a business suit, white shirt and tie but no visible ID badge, a man she'd never seen before, walked up to her bed. He pointed to her handcuff and said something in Greek to a detective who seemed to be in charge. He nodded at a uniformed cop who unlocked the manacle.

"Miss Jaeger? I am Rusty Smith. I am with the FBI at the American Embassy. Are you all right?"

"Am I all right? No, I am not all right. Two men just tried to kidnap me, again."

"And you shot them with an illegal gun, I know. They also killed the guard outside your door," said Rusty. "Unfortunately, your Greek hosts suffer from a bit tunnel vision about all this. They way they see it, wherever you go, one or more Greek citizens turn up dead. Now one's a cop."

"Those men were trying to kidnap me, Goddamnit! And that bastard on the boat was about to rape me. What the hell was I supposed to do?"

The voice sounded slightly exasperated, as if another load had just been added to weary shoulders. "The Hellenic National Police will be posting two guards outside your room for the rest of the night. One is to insure that you don't leave the hospital."

"What? What are you saying?

"I'll see you in the morning," said the legal attaché. "I don't suppose either of us will be getting much sleep tonight. I'll be doing all that I can to straighten this out.

CHAPTER 58

Cointrin, France
8 November

Six lanes of traffic on the Route de Pré-Bois separate the tarmac at the south end of the Geneva International airport from the four-star Mövenpick Hotel & Casino. Rafi entered the elevator and pressed the button for the fourth floor and the elevator doors closed. Wanting to reassure himself one more time, he reread the text on his phone, just as he had done nearly every hour since the message arrived three days ago. *Vacation travel package complete. Tickets, transfers and hotel confirmations for entire family ready for pick-up.* He erased the message, exhaled and smiled. Then he walked down the hall and knocked on Suite 415.

"I'm sorry," said Rafi as the door opened. "I must have the wrong room."

"You have the correct room," said the thirty-something-appearing, American-looking backpacker with fashionably long hair and expensive hiking boots, wearing a bicycle team shirt and Manchester United cap.

"Hiker?" Rafi never envisioned an actual hiker. An executive in a suit, sure, a geek with a pocket protector, OK, but someone who probably stayed last night in a youth hostel, never.

"Come in," he replied. "Church, Hubert Wayne Church."

Rafi remained in the open door. "Turn around. Hands on the door. Assume the position, Hubie. I need to frisk you."

Church turned slightly and began to raise his hands, then in the blink of an eye spun back toward Rafi grabbing his arm, forcing it into a hammer lock, while clamping a choke hold around his neck with the other and mashing his face against the wall.

"Never call me Hubie. I am not your friend. You are my asset. You have an agreement with my employer."

After patting down his guest, Church stepped back and raised his arms to be horizontal with the floor. "Your turn."

Rafi patted perfunctorily down the sides of Church's shirt. After patting the trouser legs he stood up and looked at the doors on either side of the eight-foot hall leading to the main part of the hotel room.

"I'd open the closet first," suggested Church, "and don't forget behind the shower curtain." His tone was condescending, sarcastic.

Satisfied it was not an ambush, without checking the bathroom or closet, Rafi walked toward the main room.

Church followed. "We have a business arrangement. I give you money. You give me what we've agreed on. Now, as we've agreed, if you're ready with the final delivery, we are prepared to do our part and you will never have to work again. You *have* the package?"

"Not so fast. Where is the money? Where are the tickets? Where are we going?"

"The money," said Church, "is here." He picked up a big pull-along case airline pilots use for charts and manuals and opened it on a table, between two wingback chairs. "Five million dollars. Feel free to count it." He pointed to an identical case on the floor next to the table. "All in circulated one-hundred-dollar bills."

"I had no idea it required so much space."

"Five million dollars is about twenty-one kilos, forty-five pounds, plus the cases, of course, another seven pounds or so each. Lucky you're not flying economy class, you'd have to leave one behind or pay hundreds of dollars in overweight charges."

Rafi didn't see Church smile at his little joke because he was already opening the bag on the floor and dumping its contents on the bed. He started thumbing through the bricks of banded bills, then stopped, "I suppose, Mr. Church, you'd like the two flash drives."

"Not necessary. Take them with you."

Rafi could not believe his ears. *Jackpot!* He'd just been handed five million dollars for the source code that would allow his American client to develop software even better than Colonel Chayat's. *A bargain, really, and they will never know they could have tunneled back through the Mossad system to the computers of every country sharing intelligence with the Mossad.*

Rafi was feeling much better about himself now. He wasn't really a traitor. A con man, yes, but since when is that a bad thing in the intelligence business? *Once onboard, I can destroy the drives and flush the parts down separate toilets on the plane. I won't even have to explain it to Hélène. We get off the plane at LAX and take the limo to Beverly Hills.*

"When you land, you and your wife will be taken off the plane before everyone else and driven to a military intelligence compound. There you will stay in a government guest house, in complete comfort, while the materials are examined. If all is in order, your driver will take you and your wife to your apartment."

"What do you mean, military intelligence? You said your client was an American data base company that was getting its ass kicked by Rebekah Chayat's company. And it needs these to stay in business." He showed two flash drives dangling on a lanyard.

"You are familiar with a false flag operation, are you not?" asked Church. "Allow me to reintroduce myself, Raptor. I am Senior Lieutenant Hu Wang-Chen, People's Liberation Army, Second Bureau, the *Guóanbù*. You are my asset. You are an agent of China's foreign intelligence, a spy. Obviously we knew you would never agree to work for China, but an American consulting deal? You were such an easy sell, a pushover really."

"No." Rafi was shaking with anger. "We agreed on a house in Beverly Hills and my fee just went up to ten million dollars or I'll destroy those flash drives right now."

"This is not a negotiation. Your government and your service will consider you a spy and a traitor. And you knew that or you would not have asked for emergency extraction," said Church. "You are being exfiltrated to a luxury apartment overlooking Shanghai's Huangpu River. If you were to buy it, the purchase price would be in excess of three million dollars. So you're actually getting eight million."

Rafi grabbed his chest and steadied himself against the windows as he realized the full meaning of his situation.

"China is the only place you can be safe. Need I remind you of what your own assassination squad did in Dubai in 2010? Your Kidon sent a whole platoon into an Arab county to take out one arms dealer."

Not just to take out an arms dealer, thought Rafi, *it was also to send a message that we can go anywhere.* "I know, I created the fucking passports."

"Your Kidon can't do that in Shanghai. But with all the Jews in your beloved Beverly Hills, once word got out that you sold Chinese intelligence the Mossad source code, Raptor, given our close ties with Syria and Iran, your own agency would sweep you off the streets in a week."

Rafi felt sick when the knock came at the door. When Mr. Hu opened it, Hélène took a surprised step backward. "Who are you?"

"I am Hu," said Hu, smiling at his puzzling non sequitur pun, "indeed. And you must be Mrs. Herzog."

Hélène looked totally baffled.

"Please come in."

Rafi stood frozen at the window, colorless. Money was strewn all over the bed. "Rafi, what's wrong?" asked Hélène. There was no reply.

Hu reached into his pocket and pulled out two airport security IDs. He handed the one with a woman's picture to Hélène. "You've gotten much younger and prettier than the picture your husband gave when he started working for us a couple years ago." Then he looked at the ID with Rafi's picture. "Pity. The same cannot be said for your husband."

"I have no idea who this woman is," said Hélène, obviously angry. "We are not married."

"But—but we're g—going to be." The weak stammer was the only sound Rafi had made since the knock on the door. The flash drives still dangling from the ribbon in his hand, hanging near the floor,

"No, we won't. That is what I came here to tell you, Rafi."

"This is not my concern," said Hu, opening the door. "My work here is done. The extraction team is downstairs. You will find aircraft cleaners' coveralls in the closet. Put them on. Those IDs will get you and the money," he pointed first to the bed then to the flash drives, "and those through a service gate and onto the plane without any exit formalities. Five million dollars in cash leaving the canton would raise even Swiss eyebrows. See that you are ready."

"It's one thing to cheat on your wife, Rafi," said Hélène. "It is quite another to betray your country. Give me those."

"What makes you think? I would never do—"

Her voice was cold, unforgiving. "I know, Rafi. I know everything. Dani Abramowitz hacked hiker787878. I know about one last delivery. It was classic asset management, Rafi. When you get your hooks in, you don't let go. You bit on my email about the photos way too easily. Dani and that forensic IT team figured out you created the backdoor, not Rebekah Chayat." She pointed at the flash drives and held out her hand. "Give those to me."

"These," he held up the lanyard, "they're nothing. Just some database shit, I promised my American client."

"I loved you," she seethed disgust. "You could have every secret we have on those, but for some reason, I still love you. Just give them to me."

He desperately tried the appeal that had worked so well before with her. "You and I can still have the life we wanted, in Shanghai, the next great city of the world. We'll have a three-million dollar apartment on the river and five million dollars in cash, enough to live like royalty for the rest of our lives."

She acted like she hadn't heard a word he said. "I loved you. I guess I always will, a little." She set down the small duffel bag she was still holding and walked across the room, where Rafi stood frozen. "Just give me those and I'll come with you."

"If I don't deliver these," the flash drives were rattling together, "they will kill us both when we land."

She wrapped both arms around his neck and kissed him, her tongue darting quickly toward his. Relieved and excited, his arms encircled her waist. He broke the kiss long enough to breathe a long sigh of relief and say, "You'll come with me after all?" He couldn't believe his ears. "I love you," he said. "I can't live without you."

"I know," she said. With her hands behind his head, she slid her left hand up her right sleeve to extract a syringe, filled with concentrated *Clostridium Botulinum Type E 88-nt*. She eased the glass cylinder down into her left hand. "And you won't have to." She kissed him again, a hard, wet, noisy kiss as she pulled the protective cap off the needle. With their lips still locked together, she drove the needle into the right side of his neck, pressed the plunger—injecting one of the most powerful neurotoxins on the planet—then stepped back.

Rafi's eyes bulged in surprise and terror. Halfway up the neck, between his shoulder and his ear, the syringe bobbed with every pulse of his carotid artery, like one end of a teeter-totter. "What have you done?" he said, grabbing the syringe and yanking it out of his neck.

"What you and I took an oath to do."

As Rafi slumped to the floor, one hand grasping the syringe, she ripped the flash drives from the other. From her duffel bag, she extracted a common wall plug with two alligator clips. Clipping both to one of the drives, she plugged into a wall socket near the desk. There was a brief, bright flash and the desk light went out and the flash drive fried. She could smell the silicon melting.

The lights in the bathroom remained on. There, she repeated the procedure on the second drive, plugging it into the hair dryer socket. The bathroom went dark but not too dark to flush the melted drives down the toilet.

She hurried to the bed and grabbed four bricks of cash. *Shit! I'd just have to turn it in anyway.* She took one last look at Rafi. He actually looked peaceful, relieved. *You do look younger,* she thought. *Maybe you should have tried Botox earlier.*

"I kept my word, Rafi, you won't have to live without me." She dropped the money on his chest and walked out. She smiled and nodded at the three Asian men and one woman in

China Air technicians' coveralls as they stepped off the elevator and she got on.

CHAPTER 59

Athens
7 November

Britt, Rebekah, Brad and Rusty were spotted leaving the hospital in a motorcycle-escorted motorcade of police and embassy SUVs. Three of Ali-Albadi's remaining Al Quds commandoes, posing as taxi drivers, followed the motorcade back to the Grand Bretagne hotel, where Brad, Rebekah and BJ shared the three-bedroom presidential suite because Britt refused to stay alone, even with armed guards stationed in the corridor.

The driver of the closest tailing taxi saw Brad and Britt get out of the SUV and walk through the hotel's main entrance. A National Police SWAT team was standing by to escort them to the suite that was paid for by the Ministry of Justice and the U.S. Embassy. Then, the SUV pulled out of the hotel driveway with Rusty and Rebekah still inside. The man in the taxi immediately began punching a text message into his phone.

Two SWAT agents, with flak jackets, automatic weapons and helmets, escorted Brad and BJ to the elevator and down the hall to the suite door, where two other second cops were stationed. Despite the guards, Britt insisted on the bedroom with no access from the hallway. Actually, it was the suite's master bedroom with a panoramic view and a luxurious bathroom.

Soon rotating shifts of the special Iranian commando agents were monitoring all the hotel doors. Two were sent to the ferry dock in Piraeus awaiting word that the women had left the hotel. Others were assigned to watch the charter and island-hopper terminals at the airport. The weak link for the commandos was the main international terminal.

As they entered the suite, Britt asked, "How long will they be gone?"

"Who knows?" said Brad. "Technically you're both still persons of interest to the authorities but I'm sure Rusty can straighten that out. He is an old-school FBI agent, a lawyer, and he's been here long enough to know where all the bodies are buried."

"That's a horrible expression," said Britt as she welled up, then burst into tears, flinging her arms around Brad's neck and holding on for dear life. "Hold me. Just hold me, please."

He pulled her head onto his shoulder. She smelled clean, antiseptically hospital clean.

Britt burrowed into the crease between his neck and shoulder, swaying slightly from side to side. "What's wrong with me? Thirty seconds ago, I was happy. I was strong. Now I'm a basket case."

"Nothing. Nothing is wrong with you," he assured. "It's post traumatic stress. I've seen it too many times."

"But..." Britt wiped her tears on the shoulder of Brad's blazer, then stood up straight. "I'm sorry. I need a tissue or a hanky."

"Shhh," Brad said. "I won't shrink." He pulled her head gently back onto his shoulder. "It just takes awhile," he said. He held her a long time.

For the first time she realized that, even in flats, she was a smidgeon taller than Brad, but with her head cradled on his shoulder and his arms tightly around her she felt small and protected.

"You know, he said finally, "I love you. I will never let anyone hurt you again. Promise."

She lifted her head to search his face for meaning and took a half step to her right, so she stood directly in front of him and looked squarely into his eyes. "Promise I love you? Or promise to never let anyone hurt me again or promise you won't shrink?"

"All the above." He pressed gently on her shoulder blades, drawing her back to his embrace. She could see he was going to kiss her. She closed her eyes and parted her lips, expecting power and passion.

He kissed her forehead, her eyelids and the tip of her nose. She inhaled sharply and trembled slightly as his lips finally brushed hers in tiny nibbles, soft as an angel's prayer.

"All the above," he whispered between nibbles, pulling her tighter.

She shuddered at the tenderness of his kisses and opened her mouth farther, inviting entry but he did not enter. He traced the edge of her lower lip with his tongue. She leaned into him, her arms around his neck. His lips danced lightly around hers. She flicked her tongue against his lower lip and moaned as his glided over the ridge of her upper lip, avoiding her offer. No man had ever kissed her like this.

She could feel the beginning of his erection, so different than thirty-six hours ago when she nearly vomited over the same sensation.

She grabbed the back of his head and pulled his lips on top of hers. This time he did not disappoint; her entire being consumed by the most incredible tingling as he plunged his tongue between her lips. She shivered, goose bumps paraded up and down her arms. *You blew up a man in Beirut,* she thought, *and an innocent kid died. You're just another government assassin, but right now all I care about is how much I want you in me.*

Brad's hand slid from her back around toward the front. He released her lips and planted a kiss in the hollow of her neck, a kiss so arousing she felt that first tiny flutter between her legs. The heel of his hand pressed on the side of her breast, his fingers on her rib cage.

She stepped back slightly giving him room to continue the journey. *Don't stop.* She wasn't sure if she'd said that aloud or just thought it. She nodded her head slightly, signaling her assent. *Why didn't this happen earlier.* She sighed, "Um-hum." She wanted that to be heard.

Brad nibbled his way upward. As his tongue touched her earlobe she gasped and the tiny flutter was no longer tiny.

I can't take this any longer. She pulled away. "Thank you," she said, wondering if she sounded as breathless as she felt. She grabbed the hand on her side and pulled it on top of her breast. "I need a shower and to wash my hair. I smell like a hospital." She turned, keeping his hand pressed to her breast and pulled him with her. "Come on. Let's see if you're really shrink-proof."

They luxuriated under dueling showerheads, one, an overhead "rain shower," complemented by a handheld shower-massager. He lathered the hotel's expensive shampoo though her hair. Scooping a giant snowball of white foam into his hand, he carefully massaged her breasts. Her nipples sprung to life, instantly rock hard, and tingling.

She liked the thin line of soft dark blond hair that ran straight down the middle of his chest to his navel. She arched her back, sliding her slickened breasts against his smooth chest. He rinsed one hand and wiped the shampoo away from her eyes and tilted her face up toward his. He kept one hand in the snowy froth encasing her hair and guided her lips toward another kiss. He slid the hand in her hair down her spine and cupped her bottom with it, pulling their bodies tightly together.

Definitely not shrinking, she thought.

Their lips separated and Brad whispered, "I know the meaning of no."

Once again, she felt that tingling down there. She knew the soft cycle of gently rippling muscle contractions were close behind. "Did you hear someone say no?"

For the next twenty minutes, they reveled together in the hotel's endless supply of hot water and expensive bath and body potions, alternating between sensuously pampering each other and fits of feverish passion.

When they had scrubbed and rinsed and anointed every available body part, Brad turned off the water and grabbed a massive bath sheet. He dried her from head to toe and towel dried her hair. Then he wrapped her in a second dry towel and carried her, bride like, to the king-sized bed.

He laid her on the bed and unwrapped her like a jeweler revealing a one-of-a-kind velvet-swathed diamond. She felt precious, revered. He kissed her lips. Once again she parted her lips and offered her tongue but he was already kissing his way down her neck toward her breasts. She forced herself to open her eyes. Moments like this don't happen often and they never last, she knew that, but she wanted to capture the memory of this forever. His lips nipped teasingly at her nipples. She grabbed his head and pulled it down hard on her breast. Her nipples pebbled beneath his tongue. Sizzling sensations seared their way down to her vulva.

"Stop!" she screamed. "No more!"

Brad stopped but did not move. Slowly he raised his head, his face frozen in a mask of shock and bewilderment. His eyes puzzled, already watering, showed hurt.

She smiled. The smile turned to a snicker. She grabbed his face and forced his eyes to meet hers, laughing. "I mean no more foreplay, silly. I can't take anymore. I want you now!"

The setting sun cast a golden glow over the city when Brad was awakened by Britt's quiet sobs. She was naked, still lying on top of him, running a fingertip over his lips. He'd insisted she be on top, afraid that he might hurt her. His fingertips traced the length of her spine. Finally he whispered, "Should I say I'm sorry?" He could see tears in her eyes.

"You better not be!"

"Then why are you crying?"

"Because I wanted this to last forever and I know it won't. It can't."

"Unless you want Rusty and Rebekah to find us in here, it probably shouldn't." It was Brad's turn to smile. He nuzzled his nose into her hair. She smelled like vanilla and almonds.

Britt gave a long sigh and slid higher up his body, kissing his eyelids, nose and lips. "I'm safe. I'm warm. I'm clean," she said, cracking a wry smile, "very clean. You made sure of that."

BJ looked into his eyes, happy that she'd touched his funny bone. He loved her sense of humor.

"Bra-ad," she drawled his name out to two syllables, "what does the J stand for?"

"Jeremiah."

"Jeremiah, I like that." She gave him a mischievous smile. "Jeremiah Bradford O'Malley Junior. That will just barely fit on a birth certificate."

Brad's eyes flew open. His Nordic ice blues paled like he'd seen a ghost.

"Relax." She propped herself up on one elbow and patted his chest. "We're OK. My period ended on the flight to London, but never again without a condom, understood? Never again."

He turned his head and looked away. This was the wrong time to avoid eye contact. He turned back, looking straight into her eyes. "I'm sorry. Never again."

She smiled and pecked him on the lips as she threw back the covers. She pulled the sheet with her and headed toward the bathroom. Then she turned around and smiled.

"I obviously have to work on my communication skills. I didn't mean 'no more' and I'm certainly not saying 'never again.'"

CHAPTER 60

Athens
8 November

At 0945 the next morning, what was left of the Iranian stake-out team watched two National Police SWAT SUVs pull into the hotel driveway, with a Mercedes limousine in between. Fifteen minutes later, the Iranian stakeout team saw two women—one with medium-length curly hair, the second with orange-ish auburn hair—get into the limo. It was an unseasonably warm summer-like day. Each woman wore a sundress, sunglasses and sandals; one resolutely dragged a wheeled suitcase. An unidentified American-looking male, wearing a sport coat and open-collared polo shirt, was the last to get in.

The three-car parade pulled away from the hotel and turned toward the airport highway. Another text message was sent from IS-903. The rest of the Al Quds commando team, those not at the port of Piraeus, were directed to the airport. Another of the Al Quds would join the man in the island hopper terminal. To Ali-Albadi, following them aboard an island ferry or seeing them get on an island-bound puddle-jumper was exactly what he wanted. Once they knew which island, the operation would be much easier than at the airport. The sub would station off the island. The women could be grabbed right off the beach and into a fast boat onto the sub. Next port of call, Iran Naval Headquarters, Bandar e-Abbas.

Less inviting, but still workable, was the corporate-charter terminal. A rent-a-jet could take off without a fight plan or change destinations midflight. So he would have to make his move before they took off. Since the financial crisis layoffs, this part of the airport was not patrolled by flak-jacketed police armed with automatic weapons. The rest of his men would converge there for Plan B.

* * * *

Muhammad Ali-Albadi sat in the officers' mess of the submarine *Yunes,* drinking coffee and reading the incoming messages as they were decoded. He had a plan for everything but the worst possible case scenario—an ordinary commercial flight from the main international terminal. That offered so little chance of a successful capture that only one man was stationed there to report which commercial flight they boarded.

Ali-Albadi nodded approvingly at the two messages that had come through the Iranian mission to the United Nations. A third was from the Chairman of the Supreme National Security Council—the only man even nominally between him and the Supreme Leader himself. He crumpled that message and threw it across the room at the bulkhead.

He vowed he would not let the outrageous incompetence of the late Athens VEVAK station chief deter him from capturing the Zionist colonel who had emasculated his nephew. Whatever public and diplomatic embarrassment Greece had inflicted on the Islamic republic, it would be soon forgotten—once his team succeeded in its mission.

He then retrieved the crumpled message, reread it, and shoved it into the shredder. As the shards of confetti dropped beneath the whirling blades, a fourth message arrived. He read it and smiled, then dashed off his seven-word reply and handed it to the young officer. *Execute plan—except in commercial passenger terminal.*

"Send this immediately."

* * * *

The Athens International Airport sewage plant lies at the far northeast end of the sprawling airport—about as far from the airport police station and main road entrance as possible. It is serviced from a perimeter road so far outside the airport proper that an old farmhouse marks the cutoff leading to the security gate at this remote section. Next to the sewage plant is the general aviation terminal, which services private and corporate jets. Aside from an occasional police Jeep patrolling the airport perimeter, an unarmed gatehouse guard provided the only daytime security. His primary responsibility: giving directions to drivers who somehow reached this gate in error.

The motorcade traveled north on the perimeter road approaching the bend where the road turned to the east. Rounding the blind curve, the NPF driver slammed on his brakes, stopping only ten feet short of a traffic accident in the middle of the road. An SUV exiting the private terminal had T-boned a taxi, spinning it crossways in the road, effectively blocking travel from either direction. Two men were exchanging information. It appeared to be a routine accident with no obvious injuries but the SWAT driver in the lead SUV smelled danger. He leaned forward to grab a Heckler and Koch machine-pistol from the floor. His thumb slid the trigger selector to full automatic.

From the limo, Brad saw one of the men in the accident reach inside his coat. Instinct took over. "Get down! Get down!" he yelled, trying to shove Britt to the floor. Rebekah jerked away from his attempt to get her down also. She jammed her hand into her purse, grabbing the ceramic and polymer pistol.

The two men who had been exchanging information pulled weapons from under their coats as four more armed men—two from the taxi and two from the SUV—leapt from the other vehicles and began firing.

The limo driver saw the windshield explode out of the lead SUV and slammed on his breaks. "Down!" he yelled, spinning the steering wheel and stamping on the accelerator to power the car into a 180-degree turn. "Down!" Midway through the fishtail maneuver, the second SWAT SUV slammed into the limo, wedging it helplessly between the two trucks.

Rebekah screamed and dropped the pistol. A red stain appeared on the side of her sundress and bloomed into a large irregular circle, soaking the top of her dress and flowing out onto her chest.

The driver of the lead SUV fired his machine pistol out of his window. Both of the men exchanging information went down.

Within seconds, windows and windshields in all three cars were blown into hundreds of pieces as shots seem to come from all directions. Her hands shaking, Britt picked up Rebekah's pistol and bolted from the car. Using her open door as a shield, she instinctively fired toward the taxi through her shattered passenger-side window. Then she steadied the weapon, gripping it with two hands and she remembered her father's advice. "Don't just shoot in the direction of the coyote, aim for a specific spot." She looked back inside the car.

She could see Brad on top of Rebekah, pushing on her chest to staunch the bleeding from the gaping exit wound in her chest. The shot, through her back, had severed the main blood supply to the pectoral muscles.

He knew at once, she'd been hit by friendly fire from the SUV behind their limo. His was face close to hers, yelling at the top of his lungs. "Stay with me, Rebekah!" Blood was everywhere. "Don't close your eyes! Stay awake!" He yanked the front of her dress down looking for the wound but he could barely see it for all the blood but he could feel it.

Automatic weapon fire, interspersed with single shots, wailed through the air just above them. He looked up, "We need a medic! Get me a helicopter, NOW!"

Britt was vaguely aware of the lead SWAT driver's door opening and the National Police Force corporal on the ground firing from underneath the door. She focused on making each shot count. As she took aim at one of the men firing from inside the taxi, they made eye contact and she realized he was aiming at her.

Again, she heard her father's voice. "Don't jerk, just squee-eeze the trigger" She wanted to block out Brad's shouts, "Don't leave us, Rebekah! You'll be all right, just open your eyes! Don't give up on us!"

She aimed for a spot dead center in the middle of taxi guy's forehead. He aimed back at her. She saw his muzzle flash. Though it seemed she was squeezing for minutes, it was a split second before her weapon fired. She felt the pistol recoil and realized she was still alive. She glanced over her shoulder into the limo, then looked back toward taxi man. The inside of the car and the back window was awash with spattered blood. He had disappeared.

Brad was still yelling—one hand pressed hard into Rebekah's wound, feeling for the bleeder, the other doing chest compressions. Rebekah's eyes were glazed, blinking slowly, closing for longer periods than they were open.

For a moment the firing stopped and Britt heard the ominous swish sound of a sucking wound, hissing with each gasp. Blood sprayed with every exhaled breath and crimson bubbles frothed through her dress near the wound. "Come on, Rebekah, keep your eyes open!" Brad's hands and shirt were covered with blood. "Don't quit on me! Do you hear me? You can do this, Rebekah, just keep your eyes open and don't quit!"

Her eyes opened slowly, unfocused. Her chest, face and hair were bathed with blood. "Rebekah, stay with us! You're going to make it!" yelled Brad, as saw Britt in his peripheral aiming through the shattered door window.

The driver of the trailing SUV had exited from the passenger side and was lying on the ground beneath that door firing.

"They're running," said the limo driver as the taxi doors slammed shut. "Stop them!" he said just before he slumped over the steering wheel.

"Let 'em go! Get me a fucking med-evac!" screamed Brad.

The cab raced past the limo, careening on and off the gravel shoulder. Britt squeezed off two more shots. The back window shattered and the taxi veered sharply across the road, wobbling erratically with two wheels in the ditch. She was sure she'd hit one guy in the backseat, maybe wounded another. Then she turned 180-degrees, now aiming back up the road from where they just came and fired her eighth and final shot at a man staggering in the street but still trying to aim his machine pistol in her direction. He appeared to be jerked off his feet and yanked backwards, then flopped limply to the ground, like a puppet without strings.

The cab swerved back, onto the road, tires squealing, and disappeared. Then there was silence. The whole exchange had lasted no more than thirty seconds. It felt like thirty minutes.

Brad raised his head. "I think I've found it." He didn't know he had clamped the *Thoracoacromial* artery against bone collar bone but blood was no longer spurting.

The corporal was screaming into his walkie-talkie as he slid from under the door. He walked to the SUV in the accident, his weapon in one hand but ready to fire. Four men sprawled on the ground, one groaning in pain. Without looking back at the limo, he waved with his walkie-talkie that it was OK to come forward. Sirens could be heard in the distance.

The corporal looked back toward the carnage of his own motorcade. A look of horror swept over his face. He lowered his weapon and rushed back toward the limo's front passenger door. BJ was standing next to the driver, her fingers on his neck searching for a pulse. The bullet through the right side of his chest left a gaping exit wound in his back and blood bubbling from his lips. Sirens were already wailing. She pulled him out of the car onto the ground and began chest compressions. She stopped when blood squirted from his chest and mouth with each press. The corporal barked into his walkie-talkie. Once again she felt for a pulse in the neck, then shook her head no. She could hear the thump of helicopters.

Minutes later, paramedics had an oxygen mask on Rebekah. One had his fingers in her wound pinching the artery while another started an IV. Three minutes later, the med-evac helicopter lifted off with her on a stretcher. The paramedics loaded the wounded Iranian commando into a police ambulance. Other police choppers were sweeping the airport perimeter looking for a single taxi, identical to two-hundred other taxis leaving the airport every hour, except for a dented passenger door and a missing rear window, neither visible from the air.

CHAPTER 61

Sea of Crete
9 November

Muhammad Ali-Albadi had no need for a translator. Video from the news chopper, hovering over the far end of the airport, told the story, as its camera zoomed into the body bags being tossed like chord wood into an ambulance. Even in broad daylight, the flashing red and blue beacons cast inhuman highlights across the faces of the man in civilian clothes and the woman he recognized as Britt Jaeger.

Ali-Albadi assessed the situation: the woman in the med-evac helicopter had to be Colonel Chayat. Three kidnap attempts had failed miserably. Seven men were dead, five killed by the colonel's "innocent friend," Britt Jaeger, including the Cultural Attaché, which did not bother Ali-Albadi in the least, but it would bother Tehran. Four others were missing and one man wounded and captured. That was a real problem. Ali-Albadi decided there would not be a fourth attempt here, but "with Allah's blessing, those deaths will be avenged."

* * * *

The crime scene investigation was still going on when Brad and BJ were taken to airport police headquarters. After more than four hours of separate questioning and re-questioning by the NPF, National Intelligence Service, Justice and Foreign Ministry investigators, officials were satisfied they had an exact reconstruction of the attack.

The Foreign Ministry representative had them both brought to one room. "The Hellenic Republic regrets that your continued presence in our country is no longer in the best interest of you or our citizens. You are hereby officially invited to leave our country immediately."

"What does that mean?" snapped Britt.

"It means," said Brad, "we've been PNGed. We're persona non grata."

"That is correct," said the bureaucrat. "A national police armored personnel carrier will return you to the general aviation terminal and standby until your plane has left the ground."

Brad stood up. "We have no objections to leaving but not until we're sure Rebekah Chayat is OK."

"Take us to the hospital where she is right now," demanded BJ. "We're not leaving without her."

"I'm afraid that is not possible," replied the official, looking at his Blackberry. "I do have an preliminary medical report. Her condition is listed as critical but stable. Despite major blood loss, no vital organs were severely damaged. Your American Legal Attaché has arranged for Colonel Chayat's transport to Landshuhl Trauma Center, Ramstein Air Force base, Frankfurt, as soon as she can travel safely."

* * * *

"All ahead full," repeated the officer of the watch, echoing the captain's order, as the *Yunes* got underway for the first time in more than a week. Cruising at fifteen knots, just under full speed, two hundred meters below the surface, the submarine was slowed slightly by dragging its tethered antenna. That small loss of speed was the tradeoff that allowed Muhammad Ali-Albadi to maintain real-time communication, by encrypted instant message microbursts, with the Committee for Special Operations HQ in Tehran via Naval HQ in Bandar e-Abbas.

The veins in Ali-Albadi's neck bulged in rage as a highest priority, coded message was handed to him.

The Americans and Israelis had struck again with another cyber-attack called *Flame*. This was worse than the Stuxnet virus. This newly discovered malware was so insidious that an infected machine could record every keystroke of any machine connected to it. Its Bluetooth capability could eavesdrop on cell phone conversations and capture phonebooks and text messages. It could turn cameras and microphones on and off in a room and send those little movies back to the intelligence agency that planted the virus. It could even sense when the host's security software was about to discover its presence and self-destruct. This explained how assassins on motorcycles could take out targeted scientists despite carefully guarded itineraries and randomly varied schedules. It also explained how previously undetected nuclear research sites had been compromised.

The Supreme Leader would be displeased, very displeased. The reputation of his own once-feared Department 36 would be severely tarnished both domestically and internationally. Other Iranian intelligence services might even move to have Department 36 placed under their control. Public disclosure of the money laundering and oil price manipulation through Collingwood and Company could seal his fate.

Ali-Albadi's bulging veins relaxed as the message disappeared into the shredder He would not wait for the Supreme Leader to address the rumors of his dismissal swirling throughout the Revolutionary Guard and the Ministry of Intelligence and Security.

A slightly satisfied look crossed his face as he envisioned his next move. He would walk confidently into the office of the Supreme Leader, and after a show of respect, and a short exchange of pleasantries, he would launch into the reasons why it was unthinkable to abandon the effort to capture Colonel Chayat. *If* there were to be a preemptive strike on our country's nuclear program, it would be orchestrated by the Americans and their NATO partners, but executed by their Israeli surrogates. Rebekah Chayat was and still is the best, and maybe only, route to crack the American and Israeli cyber warfare that threatens us.

If that scenario was not convincing enough, now the discovery of this *Flame* virus played right into his hands. He knew his uncle had no choice but to agree that the nuclear dream to wipe Israel off the face of the earth was at stake. Indeed, the Islamic revolution itself was at risk.

The Supreme Leader had to give his blessing. The fate of the nation and the family honor depended on it.

Muhammad Ali-Albadi knew he would survive an eventual purge, and get yet another chance for his revenge. He smiled.

* * * *

The Foreign Ministry officer accompanied Brad and BJ in the armored personnel carrier to the charter terminal. "The plane will take you to Frankfurt-am-Mein airport where you can wait for Colonel Chayat or continue on commercially to your destination of choice."

Then he handed Brad an *International Herald Tribune.* Brad's eye went immediately to the headline topping the far right column of page one.

INVESTMENT BANKER
MURDER NOW FEDERAL
INVESTIGATION

"Mackenzie is dead." There was a detached finality in his voice.

"Oh! My God!" screamed BJ, "Noooo! No! That can't be!" Sobbing, she turned to Brad as if he could change things. He wrapped his arms around her, pulled her close and said, "I am sorry. I really am."

Brad began to read aloud, but Britt never heard the lead paragraph. He was into the second paragraph, where they started naming names, when she became aware of what he was saying.

"The medical examiner said Mackenzie Collingwood, 51, CEO of Collingwood & Company, died from a lethal injection of

Bahotoxintracin R when she was stabbed with an umbrella tip coated with the venom of the South American golden poison dart frog.

"There are antidotes to the deadly neurotoxin," Brad continued quoting from the article, "produced by the *Dentrobatibae* species native to Colombia. It is so rare, in North America, none of the paramedics or emergency room personnel recognized it. 'In fact,' said an unnamed doctor quoted in the article, 'you could inject a victim right in the middle of the toxicology lab and unless you had an intern from South America who knew to look for that specific neurotoxin, your victim would die right in front of the whole lab staff. A orderly in an upriver first-aid station in the Amazon would have guessed at that immediately.'"

"*The New York Times* had previously learned," Brad went on, "but was withholding publication of reports that certain Collingwood & Company records had been seized as part of separate SEC and Homeland Security probes into market manipulation and money laundering. It was not known if Ms. Collingwood was a specific target of the investigations."

Britt backed away from Brad. She wiped her tears and glared at him. "You tipped off the SEC. That's why you quit. This is your fault."

Brad was shocked by her accusation. "I had a hunch, but I didn't tell anyone, not even you. Those new London subsidiaries and hedge funds we set up overnight didn't pass Manny Klein's sniff test. He asked me to set up a meeting. I did. Then it mushroomed beyond the SEC, into the FBI, Homeland Security and even my old employer, but I never gave anyone any records. Hell, you had more access to records like that when you worked for Manny than I ever did."

"The first time I met Mackenzie, she told me, 'Never underestimate the importance of the Manny Kleins of this world. Manny knows absolutely everything that goes on in this place and has a record of it.'"

"I guess she underestimated Manny," said Brad. "I guess we all underestimated Manny."

Britt took a seat in the small jet as far away from Brad as she could get.

CHAPTER 62

New York City
13 January

The cab fishtailed through the snow-slickened intersection onto Forty-sixth street as the yellow light turned to red. The driver slammed on his brakes and slid sideways, "kissing" the car illegally parked in the commercial loading zone. "I'll get out here," said Britt pushing a handful of bills at the driver through the bulletproof divider and opening her traffic-side door. She hop scotched over the snow-filled potholes and between the cars, also parked illegally, on the downtown side of the street known as Restaurant Row. She hurried through the falling snow toward the shelter of the black and white canopy that marked the entrance to *Joe Allen.*

Beneath the canopy, she stopped and gave a brief shiver to shake the snow from her hair and shoulders. After a quick look, she decided that the two wet, slippery-looking brick steps down to the entrance were safely navigable even in expensive high-heeled boots.

The venerable Westside eatery was crowded with pre-theater diners. After-work imbibers stood two deep around the curve of the long bar on her right. Opposite the bar, on her left, a row seven tables stretched along a brick wall toward the mini-garden at the rear of the restaurant.

She was about to ask the hostess if her dining partners had arrived when she saw a hand waving near the grated portal opening to the mini-garden. "Never mind. I see who I'm looking for," she said as Brad stood up and waved again.

She made her way past the length of the bar to the last table. Brad was the sole occupant but place settings for four shined on the white table cloth. She was walking toward Brad, about exchange kisses, when Rebekah, returning from her inspection of the three lady's rooms, stepped between them.

"All clear," she said to Brad, as she pecked Britt's cheek. Rebekah's arm was still in a sling from the bullet wound. Brad worked his way around the table to kiss Britt and pull out a chair for her. "Are we celebrating or crying?" he asked.

"More like breathing a sigh of relief," said Britt, sliding into the chair Brad held for her. "The judge said I get to stay in the apartment for at least a year. And!" she almost shouted the word and, "Mackenzie left me some money, but the judge said I may never see any it because the investigations will drag on for a long time."

"Four sighs of relief, Innkeeper," boomed a voice over her shoulder. BJ spun in her chair. "Sounds to me like a reason to celebrate," said Rusty Smith, extending a hand as the waiter appeared. "Sorry I'm late. I needed to take a little look around."

"Mr. Smith, I never expected to see you again."

Drinks were ordered.

"Only two months and you've forgotten me already?" asked Rusty, sliding into the open chair where he could see nearly the entire restaurant.

"Closer to three," said Britt. "Aren't you supposed to be fly fishing in Vermont?"

"Can't fish much in January and it turns out catch and release is not in my immediate future. Someday." Rusty Smith leaned to one side when the waiter blocked his view of the restaurant. His eyes darted around the room as drinks were set on the table.

"To fly fishing in Vermont and catch and release," said Britt, raising her glass.

Glasses clinked in the middle of the table. "Now it's my turn to ask you a question," said Rusty. "What are you going to do with your life?"

"Hopefully find another job, doing what I did at Collingwood."

"I hear the boys at the grain elevator would gladly take you back in a heartbeat."

"The boys at the grain elevator? What do you know about the boys at the grain elevator?" demanded Britt.

Rusty strummed his fingers on his glass and cleared his throat. "You were amazing in Athens, on the ship, in the hospital and at the airport. Without training, you had a minimum of five confirmed kills. And you still have your amateur standing. Then there was your performance on the island and what you did down in Alphabet City. So, how do I put this?"

"Put what? I want to know what you know about the grain elevator, and why you know it?" insisted Britt.

"We told you she had a knack for this," said Brad.

"She knows the right questions to ask," added Rebekah.

"It was part of the background check," said Rusty after a sip of his vodka on the rocks.

"What background check?"

"You've already proven yourself under fire," said Rebekah.

"Is this somebody's idea of a joke?" demanded Britt. "Because I'm not laughing."

"It's not a joke," said Brad. "Rusty will be heading a new CIA-FBI joint task force."

"In the past, we never played well together," said Rusty. "Actually we still don't. My job is to change that. The CIA can't spy on a citizen in this country, but with an FBI badge you can follow someone around the world and back, interfacing with the CIA all the way."

"What's that got to do with this little Midwestern farm girl?" Britt pointed to herself with both index fingers. "I'm just a little old Kansas Jay Hawk, remember?"

"Besides getting my ass royally kicked in the Oval Office when the president is not happy," said Rusty, "my only other perk in building this thing from scratch is I can hire anyone I want and I want you. Jay Hawk will make an excellent code name."

"You're not applying," said Brad, you're being recruited."

"To do what?"

"To serve your country," he said, "as an intelligence officer."

"Do you remember my telling you," said Rebekah, "when the time was right, someone would step forward and steer you in the right direction? This is the right direction. You have everything it takes," she added. "You've proven what I always knew. You're a warrior and a leader and this is your time to do something important for the world, not just for women, for everyone."

"This is not what I thought you meant. Not at all. Are the Sisters behind this?"

"No. No one knows about this except the four of us at this table."

"And it needs to stay that way," cautioned Brad."

Britt was conscious of both Brad and Rusty scanning the room.

"Someday," continued Rebekah, pausing to take a sip of wine, "if you decide to do something in the public eye, the Sisters will be behind you. Right now, this is more important than anything you might ever do in public. But I know this is your moment. Don't let it slip away."

Britt eyes darted from one face to the other, once, twice, the third time she kept her focus on Rusty. "Do Brad and Rebekah both work for you now?" asked BJ.

"Not exactly." Rusty swirled the ice cubes in his glass.

"What does that mean?

"It means not until Rebekah's a citizen, but we're working on that."

"So I'd be paired with Brad?" BJ's eyes darted from Rusty to Brad.

"He says you fit together well," said Rusty, almost grinning. "And he'd trust you with his life. Pretty good recommendation, if you ask me."

Brad looked away but not before BJ saw that impish grin.

"If I say yes, what next?"

"I'll be in touch in a few days," said Rusty. "Things might move pretty quickly after that."

Beneath the table, Britt curled the black kid-leather toe of her Jimmy Choo's over-the-knee boot behind Brad's leg and slid it slowly up his calf. "And if I say no?"

"If you say no," Rusty paused and swirled his ice cubes once again, "I swear you to secrecy about this conversation. It never happened. Then we will all have a very nice dinner on Uncle Sam's credit card."

Britt chewed on her bottom lip, just enough to hide her smile. "Then I think we better look at menus."

Rusty gave a disgusted look at his nearly empty glass and hoisted it up for the waiter to see. "You know the FBI always gets their man—or woman. You're a catch, my catch, and as I said, I'm not in the business of catch and release."

"We'll need a wine list," Britt told the waiter. "This could get expensive."

If you are a member of a book group and would like a
list of discussion questions for
Jay Hawk: The Assassin's Lover
email: sean @ seaneaganthrillers . com
SPOILER ALERT:
Don't read the questions before reading the book.
That will ruin the suspense.

While BJ, Rebekah, Brad and Rusty are pondering
the wine list and BJ's future, Sean invites you to
pour a glass of your own favorite vintage and enjoy
this preview of Sean's next *Jay Hawk* thriller.

(working title)
Hu's China White
by
Sean Eagan

If you fail, millions of our people will die.
If you succeed thousand will die.

CHAPTER 1

12 Weiyong Road,
Tiantanghe, Beijing,
China 1971

Prisoner 526292 clutched her swollen belly, screamed and slumped to the ground next to her assembly-line stool. No one moved to help her. Guards in Beijing women's Prison Factory 5 would have beaten any prisoner who left her forced-labor workstation.

Two male guards poked at her with riot batons. She screamed again and begged for help. A guard kicked at her distended belly. She passed out.

Margeaux Raymonde LaVoie had been in China just eight months—nearly seven of them working 12 to 16 hour days, seven days a week in Factory 5. She entered China on a temporary journalist visa to do a freelance investigative story for *Paris Match* magazine on the atrocities of the Cultural Revolution. Of course, her visa application mentioned only "recent cultural advances," not anything about "atrocities."

Ten days after arriving in the capitol, rampaging Red Guards "purging Beijing University of the evils of western influence" arrested her. Charged with Counter-Revolutionary activities, she was found guilty in a twelve-minute trial and sentenced to ten years hard labor.

Inconvenient political niceties, such as access to defense counsel or contact with the French Embassy were of no concern to Mao's marauding zealots. Twenty-four hours after her "trial," she was Prisoner 526292 of Tiantanghe Re-education Through-Labor Center.

She had been a slave laborer for four weeks when she missed her second period and realized she was pregnant. She knew the exact moment of conception. She could picture the room in the four-century-old *Hotel Saint Paul Rive Gauche*. Her boyfriend had begged her not to go to China, but this was the assignment that would firmly establish her as a respected foreign correspondent. She would not be deterred. On their final night together, in a romantic suite in the XVIIth century inn, he proposed. She accepted. They promised to spend their first night in that same suite when she returned.

Ten million people died during Chairman Mao's catastrophic destruction of Chinese social structure. Margeaux Ramonde LaVoie was one of them. In the years following, authorities systematically destroyed almost all official records of that time, including the record of Prisoner 526292's death during childbirth. No record was kept of the freezing cells, maggot infested food, malnutrition and beatings that preceded her death. Though the birth was never officially recorded, it would impact the world far beyond any story Margeaux Raymonde LaVoie could ever have filed.

CHAPTER 2

Great Hall of the People
Beijing 1993

The happiest day of my life was when I destroyed the American Economy. I remember the moment as if it was yesterday. I was twenty-two. My father, Lieutenant Colonel Hu Ning, was never more proud. Sometimes I think I even saw a tear in his eye. Probably not. Chinese Intelligence officers don't cry. Ever.

On that day, high-ranking officers of the People's Liberation Army, the Ministry of State Security, even members of the Communist Party Central Committee, were on the dais in the Great Hall of the People, looking out over a sea of brilliant young men and women from universities across the country. We were all regional winners in the PLA's national cyber warfare competition. I was attending the PLA Military and Political University in Beijing. My father, considered one of the best of the new breed of intelligence officers, had just been named Second Deputy Commander of the PLA Foreign Intelligence Bureau, the Guóanbù, after years in London, Washington, Tehran and Paris as Military Attaché.

The commander-in-chief of the Beijing Region, frequently the next in line for Chief of Staff, General Fang Fenghui, stepped to the podium microphone high above the main floor. He scanned the room below and bowed slightly to the dignitaries to his right, then to his left.

"Comrades, our first great general, Sun Tzu, u-u-u," the public address speakers echoed his voice throughout the Great Hall, "taught us that the greatest victory is defeating the enemy without a battle. The winner of this year's People's Liberation Army prize has shown us that is entirely possible. He has exploited the soft underbelly of the American super power and demonstrated how China can triumph over decadent capitalism without firing a shot. From the Graduate Academy of the People's Liberation Army Military University, I present to you Second Lieutenant Hu Wang Chien."

The Great Hall erupted into applause. I rose from my seat and walked toward the podium. Then the applause turned to gasps followed by silence. The crowd reaction did not surprise me. I had come to expect it. I was an outsider. Assassins always are, but I had been an outsider long before I acquired that special talent.

General Fang, stunned by the sudden silence, looked for guidance at the officials flanking him on each side of the dais—including Hu Jintau, my father's second cousin, who was destined to become general secretary of the Party. To me, he was "Uncle Hu." In return, the General received only blank stares except from my father who tugged at his nose, literally, trying to wipe the smile off his face. Uncle Hu smiled back at him, if only momentarily. It was a long walk to the front of the Great Hall, but nowhere near as long as my journey to get there or the one that lay before me.

My triumph was, of course, all smoke and mirrors, more precisely ones and zeros. It was a virtual economic collapse of the American economy—a computer simulation I had written for the PLA cyber-warfare competition.

As I strode through the silence that day, I was well aware that I had no business winning, though I had fully expected to. In this competition, like everything else in my country—and every other country I know of—politics ruled. I knew our leadership could not resist the vision of the American financial system collapsing and dragging down the other Western economies under a multi-trillion dollar global pyramid scheme of bad debts.

I had devised a computer game that predicted the Western governments would make a show of supporting the markets but their national treasuries were already in our hands and banks of the Gulf-State oil-producing nations. The *coupe de grace* would come when China demanded repayment of America's multi-trillion-dollar debt and refused to rescue the Euro. Once I had decided how I wanted my computer game to end, thanks to my father, it was easy to recruit a team of undergraduate code writers to program a scenario that ended the same way, with America's collapse, no matter what was imputed.

My father taught me this was a scenario so irresistible to our political leaders that they would almost certainly award his son China's greatest technological award, even though I am a G*weilo*—a foreign devil—born in Beijing Women's Prison.

From the day my father brought me home, my "mother" loved me with all her heart. I was the child she could not have and she was the only mother I ever knew.

Like a fairy tale that a child craves hearing again and again, she told me over and over of how I had a life expectancy of less than forty-eight hours when the handsome, fast-rising, young intelligence officer, Hu Ning, went to the Tiantanghe Re-education Through-Labor Center to order the release of Prisoner 526292, the French woman and several other Westerners. The releases were merely window dressing preceding the historic secret meeting between the American president, Richard Nixon, and Chairman Mao in February 1972

As my father walked through the prison gates, I was already an orphan, dying of starvation and dehydration. Even if my birth mother had lived, I would have died. Half starved to death, she could not have produced enough milk to nurse me and gruel made from maggot-riddled rice is bad for a baby's digestive systems. Guards assumed he would pull out his pistol and execute me on the spot. Instead, in my mother's fairytale version, he said, "this child belongs to the state. I will take him now."

Before I could walk, he was climbing the Guóanbù ladder. It's not that he didn't love me, he did. He really did, just not in the way you in the West think of love. He saw me as the son that was destined to bring great honor to our family. As the personal assistant to the deputy director of foreign intelligence, he was determined to groom his once-starving, pureblooded Caucasian "son" as the perfect Chinese spy.

And that is exactly what he did.

CHAPTER 3

Presidio de Monterey
California 2011

Britt Jaeger walked across the lush, green lawns of *The Presidio,* between the buildings leading to the visitors' center. The Pacific breeze carried in the rich smell of the ocean. For a Kansas farm girl, this was one of the things she most loved about this picturesque setting of Spanish-style stucco buildings with red tile roofs.

The beauty of the sprawling campus of the Defense Language Institute was also one of her greatest frustrations. In fifty-three weeks, she'd never had a chance to really enjoy it. In fact, she'd not had one full day off. Her instructors had warned her about that on her first day of class and they were right.

Deb Beauson, as classmates and instructors alike knew Britt, was one of the few non-military students at the best and toughest foreign language school in the world. Her fellow uniformed students all knew that their street-clothes colleagues were anything but "civilians." They weren't even enrolled under their real names. Deb Beauson purported to be a fledging diplomat from the Foreign Service. Everyone knew that was not the case.

Classes went six hours a day, five days a week. She spent at least three hours a night on homework. Weekends were spent catching up on homework, lost sleep and laundry. Some of the more gifted students managed an occasional weekend trip, but never BJ, as she was known before she came here. Of course, they were taking easier languages, like Spanish, or they grew up hearing the language of their parents' homeland.

Pressure to succeed and excel had caused Deb Beauson to lose weight, lose hair and countless hours of sleep. Not all the sleep loss could be blamed on the grueling schedule. Nightmares about her kidnapping played a major role. What she thought were hives turned out to be stress-induced shingles. Still, she was lucky. She never missed a day of class.

Compared to The Presidio, eighteen of her first twenty-two months as an intelligence officer had been a cakewalk. In some desk jobs at Langley, Intelligence could still be a forty-hour a week job, but she was headed to the Clandestine Service and those days were gone forever.

It was going on three years since that fateful dinner in New York. Since then, she'd spent six months on the Far Eastern Desk, a stint at The Farm, and a year on the Middle East desk.

Then someone decided she needed to spend another year learning Mandarin.

Mandarin? she'd thought. *Like I'm going to fool anyone into thinking I'm Chinese?*

As she walked into the visitors' center, her face lit up and she ran across the room to hug the two people waiting for her. "Rebekah! Brad! What are you doing here?"

"We were in town on business and thought we might take you for a graduation lunch," said Brad O'Malley, once a rising star at the investment-banking boutique where she'd first met his companion, Colonel Rebekah Chayat, then one of America's newest billionaires.

"You look terrific," said Rebekah, kissing her on both cheeks, European style.

"And *you* need glasses," replied Barbara Jean, stepping back and gesturing toward herself with both hands as though highlighting the flaws of a bad dress. "Look at me. I'm actually underweight, for the first time in my life. I'm not even thirty-five, my hair is falling out. My collarbones stick up so far they form dents so deep that they'd qualify as protected watershed reservoirs. And if it weren't for long sleeves, you'd see the last of a shingles rash that would make psoriasis look attractive. Yeah, I'm absolutely ravishing. But what about you?" she asked, thinking back to time she'd seen Brad stick his fingers into a spurting bullet wound to stop her from bleeding to death.

"Compared to the knife wound, the scar is nearly invisible." said Rebekah.

Britt blanched; picturing the ugly, raised, purple keloid scar she'd seen on Rebekah's breast the night before the kidnapping.

"Rebekah! Your accent! It's gone!" she shouted. "You sound like you're from Kansas."

"How utterly charming," said the former Israeli Mossad agent, switching effortlessly to the Queen's English, with an upper crust accent worthy of a graduate of Lady Eden's School. "Whilst you were learning Mandarin, I had a speech coach ten hours a week. My accent alone could have given me away even here in America. Then I decided if one accent was bad, three could be quite useful."

"She's also an American citizen now," said Brad. "Some nice folks in Washington got that fast-tracked. Justice Sonja Sotomayor administered the oath."

"Wow! Does that make you a super citizen or something?" asked BJ, idly tugging a few stands of hair that came right out, then slapping her own hand as a reminder to stop pulling her hair out.

"You can't see how much hair I've lost because I haven't had it cut in a year. I still get the heebie-jeebies going into a hair salon without an armed guard."

"Perhaps Rebekah will ride shotgun for you tomorrow," said Brad. "For this afternoon, we have something much more fun: a graduation lunch cruise, guaranteed to put some weight back on. An old friend has a very nice boat down at Monterey harbor."

"His name isn't Gilligan, is it?" asked BJ. The colonel's expression was blank she looked back and forth at Brad and BJ.

"It was an old TV series," explained Brad.

"...Five passengers set sail that day," sang Britt, "for a three hour tour." Brad laughed again chiming in with, "If not for the courage of the fearless crew, the Minnow would be lost." He was almost in tune.

Thirty minutes later a deckhand walked the length of the boat slip holding the bow line of the seventy-foot Bertram cruiser as it backed away from the dock. As the deckhand reached the end of the pier, the captain stopped both engines. The deckhand leaped onto the bow of the *Tax Trix*, as the captain shifted one engine ahead, the other in reverse, to turn the boat away from the dock, into the channel leading to open water. The two women sat on the aft deck as Brad emerged from inside the cabin carrying a tray with three Mai Tais.

In the engine well, five feet beneath the trio, the pulsating growl of twin 2200 horsepower engines made it impossible for anyone to overhear any of their conversation, even with sophisticated eavesdropping equipment. Blond and fit, Brad wore cargo shorts, a jaunty straw hat with mirrored sunglasses hiding his eyes. His Helly Hansen topsiders had never been worn before today. His skin, lightly bronzed from a bottle, was hermetically sealed beneath a coat of SPF 50. The investment banker was very comfortable in the role of a gentleman yachtsman used to delegating the seamanship to a professional crew.

As the *Tax Trix* cleared the breakwater and entered the light chop of Monterey Bay, Brad reticently brought up the subject of the kidnapping, the airport attack and the shootout on the island.

As they discussed their most terrifying and most exhilarating moments, Rebekah studied BJ, searching for telltale signs of post-traumatic stress. She contemplated the metamorphoses she'd seen in the younger woman. When they'd first met, the thirtyish farm girl was a gawky, slightly overweight victim of an abusive marriage—a bumpkin whose only observable attribute was a plucky determination to hang on to her job in Manhattan and not go to back to where she'd been. Less than a year later, she was trim, tanned and toned, with a new coif, clothes and the beginnings of confidence. Then it all fell apart. Rebekah still blamed herself for what had happened.

The boat cruised westward, parallel to the Monterey peninsula, toward Point Cabrillo and Pacific Grove. Brad appeared to survey the coastline, but from behind his dark glasses, he focused on the two women, wondering if this team had even the slightest chance to work. Even at forty-something, Rebekah's looks left no doubt why she had been one of the most successful honey trap operatives in the history of the Kidon— the Mossad's assassination squad—personally tracking down and executing eight terrorists.

"Beej, we have a little surprise for lunch," he said, "let's go inside." He stood and gave an exaggerated sweeping motion of mock gallantry, to usher the two women into the luxury yacht's plush salon. Britt was about to step through the door first when she stopped cold. "I should have seen this coming. Like they taught at the Farm, 'nothing is what it seems.'" A red and blue flame flashed in the galley and she braced herself with both hands on the doorjamb to keep from being forced inside, "Oh, no."

CHAPTER 4

Forbidden City,
Beijing 2011

I had been a foreign intelligence operative in the Guóanbù, Ministry of State Security, for thirteen years, originally as a courier, more recently an assassin, when I was unexpectedly recalled to the Zhongnanhai annex of the Forbidden City. Behind its walls, our Communist Party leaders live in a lakeside enclave of unparalleled luxury. It was my first trip back to Beijing in six years. I really don't like it there. Beijing is crowded, noisy and polluted. Much of my life had been spent abroad, either on assignment or moving with my father to postings in Paris, London, Tehran and Washington. Beijing stinks, literally, especially in the summer.

As always, I took several flights under several names, finally landing in Shanghai via Mumbai on a counterfeit Cayman Island passport. I took a train to Beijing under yet another name. Late that night I slipped into Zhongnanhai through a remote side gate—not the formal New China Gate, the *Xinhua Men*, the one you see in the all the pictures with the big Mao portrait. I was taken to a guest residence.

The next morning I was "smuggled" into the lakeside residence of the President of the People's Republic of China, my father's cousin, "uncle" Hu Jintao. In China, we don't really count degrees of family, either you are or you aren't. Except in my case, I was but I wasn't and never really would be, not with my brown wavy hair, blue eyes and Gallic nose.

My father was now the chief of Military Intelligence, due in no small part to his esteemed cousin. Though technically an army officer, he preferred western suits and ties except for certain ceremonial occasions. Today he wore his full-dress uniform with all his decorations.

A uniformed guard escorted me to the president's office. My father jumped up to hug me. The many medals on his chest jingled like tinny wind chimes in the breeze.

"You remember my son, Mr. President, Hu Wang Chien."

The Paramount Leader of one-point-three billion Chinese citizens extended his hand to me. "You have served China well. At great personal peril, you preserved the secrecy of an important operation and saved China from losing face in the international community. For that reason, I hereby award you our nation's highest tribute, the *Special Class Honor*. As you know, no one outside this room will ever know about your service or this award but I wanted to present it in front of my esteemed cousin." I bowed slightly to make it easier to hang the red ribbon and medal around my neck. Then the head of the world's most populous state stunned me by reaching out and pinching my cheek, like a child's.

"It is hard to imagine I used to do this when I visited your family and you were still in short pants." I had no idea what to say.

"Sit. We will have tea and savor this moment before I ask you to serve your country once again."

He talked for fifteen minutes about his vision for a greater China. It was an upbeat speech. He must have given it hundreds of times. Then his voice changed. His face tightened. He talked about the specter of mass civil unrest if our economy faltered again, if only briefly, and it might. Our competitive advantages are rapidly disappearing. He ticked off a list of economic danger signals:

"Cheap labor threatened by workers demanding and receiving higher wages. Cheap land gone. Real estate needed for factories is skyrocketing. Commodities and raw materials rising.

"Without double-digit growth tens of millions of new workers will be unemployed and forced to return to rural farms that cannot support them. Private forecasts, the optimistic ones, predict our growth dropping to seven percent." He seemed almost terrified that massive uprisings would threaten the very existence of the state if that happened.

"Of course, our Army can contain the uprisings but it would be messy. Tiananmen Square would look like a food fight in a bourgeois American comedy film."

I looked at my father straight-faced and stern but I knew both of us were suppressing smiles. When we lived in Washington, he brought home a video of the movie, *Animal House.* I only got to watch it if I'd excelled in all my American school homework plus all the homework from the Embassy School for children of Chinese diplomats. Watching it was the highlight of my week.

"We could eliminate all the agitators in the provinces," the president continued, "but when the word got out, that could be the ruination of the state. This unrest cannot be contained if it starts. Therefore it cannot be allowed to start. Young Hu, I have chosen you to protect China in these uncertain times."

His vision of a solution went from disturbing to horrifying. When he finished, he shook my hand, then my father's and said, "your son must see that these things do not happen." He then turned back to me and extended his hand, palm up, "The medal." An aide appeared to lift the ribbon from my neck.

My father hugged me once again and as he bid me farewell, whispered a chilling message in my ear. He remained at the president's side as I was escorted out of the official residence to a waiting limousine with darkened windows. Alone in the back, I shuddered at my presidents orders.

"Brazil," he had said, sounding more professorial than dictatorial, "will host the 2016 summer Olympics. The country boasts 35 billion barrels of oil reserves, ranking it just behind Russia. Eighty percent of its power comes from hydroelectric plants. Its cars run on sugarcane ethanol. On paper it is energy independent, but paper is easily combustible. Your job is to light that fire."

Look for the next *Jay Hawk* thriller
Coming in 2013

(Working Title)

Hu's China White
By
Sean Eagan

Jay Hawk: The Assassin's Lover
is available in eBook at
Amazon.com and Smashwords.com.

Search *Jay Hawk* or *Sean Eagan*

Author's Note

Jay Hawk: The Assassin's Lover is pure fiction. The characters drew their only breaths in the toxic atmosphere of the author's imagination. However, well-documented national security and espionage issues, including the facts below, inspired this story.

The *Wall Street Journal* reported in April 2009, Chinese cyber spies have hacked into the computers for the Defense Department's new generation of multinational force fighter planes—the costliest aircraft weapons program ever. Cyber intruders successfully copied several terabytes of data that would make it easier for hostile forces to defend against and even disable the new Joint Strike fighter.

In the wake of September 11th, the National Security Agency outsourced a major part of its intelligence gathering to four Israeli information technology companies. The companies, like Verint Systems, that do this work for the NSA, were founded by, and/or currently run by, Israeli intelligence veterans, especially those from the hyper-secret Unit 8200, the Israel Defense Force's elite technology intelligence division, but also the Mossad and Israel's domestic intelligence service, Shin Bet.

Verint, short for Verified Intelligence, a unit of Tel Aviv's Comverse Technologies, proudly proclaims itself "The Global Leader in Actionable Intelligence Solutions."

Every hour of every day, the companies conduct surveillance and recording of millions of cell phone, landline and Internet phone conversations. Their systems sit in secret, locked rooms in telephone company switching hubs on both American coasts. Based on certain criteria, of who says what to whom, those calls are captured and forwarded to the NSA for further study.

Nice Systems, another Israeli tech firm, singles out calls for NSA special attention based on emotion, and eight other elements of speech. If you're talking to someone in Pakistan and he sounds angry enough, you both could become a target of NSA surveillance.

Narus Inc, based in Herzliya, not far from Mossad Headquarters, offers "real time (network) traffic intelligence, in other words, eavesdropping."

PerSay Biometric Systems provides voice recognition technology that could quickly recognize Osama Bin Laden's voice out of the millions of calls taking place at any given moment and trace the calls. That is why he relied on messengers and never used a telephone, especially a satellite phone. Ironically, it was Bin Laden's most-trusted messenger who was followed to his hiding place and led to his death.

In the arcane world of Internet traffic, millions of messages fly through thousands of undersea fiber optic cables that connect the continents at the speed of light. An ordinary email, from Paris to Dublin or Tokyo to Singapore will likely touch American shores for a millisecond or two before being bounced toward its ultimate destination. During that millisecond, those same companies capture, record, analyze and, if certain criteria are met, send a copy of that email to the National Security Agency. In the blink of an eye, both sender and receiver can become NSA surveillance targets.

As part of their contracts, those IT companies routinely upload software updates from their home offices to the systems housed in those secret rooms in the U.S. That remote access also gives them the power to download the intelligence information they captured on behalf of the NSA—a fact they don't deny. If one of those companies can download the intelligence gathered for its client, the NSA, a hostile power might also pilfer that intelligence by hacking into the computers at the companies' Israeli headquarters. In other words, crack into the right computer, 7,000 miles away from America, and you can tunnel backwards into the national security information systems that guard this country.

To repeat, this story is fiction, but there is no guarantee it will remain so.

Acknowledgements

So many people helped with this story, it borders on hubris to claim sole authorship. I can't say when I passed the one-hundred mark on sources but it was surprisingly early in the process. Among them:

Siobhan Gorman's reporting for *The Wall Street Journal* formed the technical underpinning of the story, along with August Cole and Yochi Dreazen reporting on U.S. spy software and Chinese computer spying. Simon Elegant reporting from Beijing for *Time Magazine* completed the picture.

Calvin Arneson, the only person I know with an IQ in four figures, tried his best to educate me about data mining and computer and spectrum white noise. I'm about 900 IQ points behind Calvin in understanding those, but if he says they could work as described, trust me, they do. In 2006, the *Journal's* Cassell Bryan-Low broke the Greek cell phone tapping story and the murder of the technician who discovered it.

David Ignatius' national defense and security reporting in the *Washington Post* and his novels, *Body of Lies* and *Agents of Innocence* were invaluable; likewise his *New York Times* colleague, Alex Berenson for his reporting and novels *The Faithful Spy* and *The Silent Man*.

Former Deputy Secretary of State for Intelligence, Richard A. Clark's *Against All Enemies* and *Scorpion's Gate* provide insight to the bureaucratic labyrinth that is our intelligence system.

Chinese intelligence maybe described as an impenetrable, indecipherable Gordian knot. To unwind that knot, I went to Nicholas Eftimiades' *Chinese Intelligence Operations*; David Wise's *Tiger Trap*; and *The Chinese Secret Service* by French journalists Roger Galigot and Remi Kauffer.

I learned much from twenty-one year CIA veteran Robert Baer, considered perhaps the best on-the-ground field officer in the Middle East, from meeting him at the International Spy Museum in Washington, his reporting for *Time, Vanity Fair, The Wall Street Journal and the Washington Post*. Lindsay Moran's *Blowing My Cover* was a candid glimpse of the human side of a female CIA case officer's lonely life in a decidedly unglamorous distant land.

James Bamford's books on the inner workings of the National Security Agency, *Puzzle Palace* and *Shadow Factory,* take you deep inside an the most secret organization in America's intelligence apparatus.

Thomas Gordon's *Secret Wars* is a rare peak inside British Intelligence MI-5 and MI-6.

Daniel Silva's insights into the Mossad, told through his incredibly exciting Gabriel Allon series, served a serious research purpose. But it was also hedonistic self-indulgence.

Special thanks to Paige Eagan who read and copy proofed uncountable iterations, versions and entire manuscript revisions. Shannon Eagan, a great teacher and coach, found time in an impossible schedule to bear an important part of that same burden. Along with Holly McConnaughy, they wore out enough red pencils to fell a small forest.

The steady hand of editor, John Payne, universally acknowledged as one of the best book doctors in publishing, led me to and through those wholesale revisions, each time making the story tighter, brighter, tenser and more suspenseful. The intercession of agent Katie Kotchman persuaded John to take me as a client and for that I will always be grateful. My agent, Bill Contari, believed in me and the story when others did not.

ThrillerFest is the Rolls-Royce of conferences for thriller writers, readers and agents. Held each July at the Grand Hyatt in New York, Thrillerfest draws the best mystery and suspense writers in the world. In fifty-minute classes, they generously offer their best insights, plus one-on-one time face time after class or over cocktails, even email follow-ups.

I met CIA disguise genius Tony Mendez at a 2009 function in the Old Headquarters Building in Langley. Tony helped smuggle our diplomats out of the Canadian embassy, past Iranian security, and out of the country during the 1979 hostage crisis. He guidance and silent nods of "approval" led me to tricks like Rebekah's inflatable "dowagers hump" and those flash drives concealed as shampoo and conditioner bottles.

Retired CIA Station Chief, Haviland Smith, served in East and West Europe, the Middle East, as Chief of the Counterterrorism Staff and later as Executive Assistant in the Director's office. Without his insight "Mr. Hu" would not exist nor would he become a major figure in the next Jay Hawk thriller—a preview of which follows this story.

Jeff Marston introduced me to Bill Jenkins, another veteran CIA station chief. His input was most helpful.

Yani Stephano is my official Oracle for all things Greek. A frequent traveler to the Hellenic Republic, he reads the Athens daily papers every morning on the Internet, and knows the highways, byways and back alleys better than a Greek taxi driver.

Early readers, advisors and supporters include, Mary Kay Mock, Bill and Marylou Ball, Rosemary Dunn Dalton, Lea Darley, Maureen Tracy, Joe and Kathy Eagan, Dr. Gretchen Anderson, Greg and Cay Woodson, Patty Beadle, Sue McKeough, Joanne Moody, Bob Runtz, Mike Blandford and Pricilla Shepherd.

Evelyn Cusack-Landesman is a brilliant cardiologist in Stamford, Connecticut. She regularly saves lives with her skill then makes them immensely more enjoyable with her fantastic sense of humor. As a favor to me, she "crossed over to the dark side" to help me kill off some characters you'll meet who needed killin.' But in the end, she just couldn't leave bad enough alone. She couldn't resist teaching Brad how to stick his fingers into a gaping, sucking wound to squeeze a gushing artery against a bone and save a life. I knew all along she was too good a person to be a first-rate assassin, but I thank you for trying, Ellie.

Megan Bagnulo, my BFF for twenty years, introduced me to Evelyn and threw down her own tough love gauntlet by refusing to read anything that was not ready for primetime. After working side by side for two decades, she knows me as well as anyone on the planet and she knew I could never let such a challenge go unanswered. I had to finish this.

I have certainly left out some important contributors, some because they preferred to remain anonymous. To the others, unintentionally omitted, I sincerely apologize and thank you for all your help and support. Without you all, this story would be nothing more than doodlings on a yellow pad and an incomplete file in my laptop.

Sean Eagan
Lake Tahoe 2012

About the Author

Sean Eagan is a three-time Emmy winning producer and director at CBS News and Sports. The late Tony Hillerman was his writing teacher and launched his career at the Associated Press. Sean was a national radio editor for UPI and has written and produced shows and features for Dan Rather, Bill Kurtis, John Madden and Sue Herrera. He is a member of the Directors Guild of America and the Association of Former Intelligence Officers.

Sean insists he was never a paid agent of the United States, or any other country, but his passport stamps show him appearing in the strangest places at the strangest times. He was one of the first American journalists into embargoed Cuba. Other travels found him in Poland as martial law was declared to end the Solidarity reformation; in Egypt ten days before Anwar Sadat's assassination; then on the Thai-Burma border on the eve of the "8888 Democracy Uprising" and Aung San Suu Kyi's rise to prominence.

He splits his time between the Connecticut shoreline and the shores of Lake Tahoe.

Contact Sean at sean @ seaneaganthrillers . com

Look for the next *Jay Hawk* thriller
Coming in 2013
(working title)
Hu's China White
By
Sean Eagan

Jay Hawk: The Assassin's Lover
is available as an eBook at Amazon.com, Smashwords.com,
iBooks, Barnesandnoble.com, and other eBook sellers.

Search *Jay Hawk* or *Sean Eagan*